NETTLE KING

NETTLE KING

A Night and Nothing Novel

KATHERINE HARBOUR

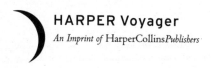

HARPER Voyager

An Imprint of HarperCollinsPublishers

Harper Voyager and design is a trademark of HCP LLC.

NETTLE KING. Copyright © 2016 by Katherine Harbour. All rights reserved. Printed in the United States of America. No part of this book may be used or reproduced in any manner whatsoever without written permission except in the case of brief quotations embodied in critical articles and reviews. For information address HarperCollins Publishers, 195 Broadway, New York, NY 10007.

HarperCollins books may be purchased for educational, business, or sales promotional use. For information please write: Special Markets Department, HarperCollins Publishers, 195 Broadway, New York, NY 10007.

FIRST EDITION

Library of Congress Cataloging-in-Publication Data has been applied for.

ISBN 978-0-06-228678-9

16 17 18 19 20   OV/RRD   10 9 8 7 6 5 4 3 2 1

This book is dedicated to all those who helped me along the way.

NETTLE KING

CHAPTER 1

When Inanna ascended from the netherworld, verily the dead hastened before her.

—A MESOPOTAMIAN MYTH

What if you loved someone and they loved you and you had to walk into nothing and night to find each other?

—FROM THE JOURNAL OF FINN SULLIVAN

Finn staggered down the road, the branches of the trees that loomed on either side twisting together far above. The poisonous flowers blooming inside of her with viral ferocity stung nerves and synapses. Despite the rain, blood clung to her skin and the blue gingham of her dress.

As she collapsed, curling into a fetal shape in the mud, a black butterfly as big as her hand, its wings veined with blue, braved the rain to hover above her.

Then Jack was crouched beside her. "Wake up."

"Finn . . . *Finn* . . . wake the hell up . . . Avaline just spotted you."

The nudge and the frantic whisper jarred Finn awake. She straightened, blinking in the fluorescent lighting of the lecture hall as the nightmare faded, leaving a bittersweet taste on her tongue. Quickly, she glanced at Sylvie in thanks.

It had been nearly three months since Finn had brought her sister, Lily, out of the Ghostlands. Three months since Jack had walked into the underworld in Lily's place. Finn and her friends rarely spoke of the Fatas now—Lily had scarcely mentioned them since returning to the sunlit world. But whenever Finn glimpsed a flash of silver eyes on a dark street, or felt a chill grazing her skin on a warm night, she'd known *they* were nearby.

She didn't want her friends to suspect what she'd been planning for months. According to the books she'd found in Jack's apartment, the boundaries between the true world and the underworld became fragile from the new moon in April through May Eve.

And, tonight, the underworld was where she planned to go.

AS FINN AND SYLVIE STEPPED from Armitrage Hall, Sylvie snapped her umbrella open over their heads to shelter them from the rain. She was celebrating the first warm day of spring in a sleeveless black-and-white-checked minidress.

"Where's Christie today?" Finn had skipped her usual lunch break with Sylvie and Christie to catch up on a research a paper for her Symbolism in Silent Film course.

"Haven't seen him. Have you noticed how secretive he's been lately? I mean, it must be a new girlfriend."

"Probably." Finn hoped Sylvie hadn't noticed how secretive *she* had been lately. She hoped Christie's new girlfriend was human.

A car horn beeped. A sapphire-blue Nissan was parked at the curb in front of Armitrage. When Finn saw it, her world centered with a pang. The driver's window rolled down and Lily Rose Sullivan stuck her head out of the car, her dark hair streaming in rain-swept glory around her head. "Sylvie! That dress is *smashing*."

"Thanks." Sylvie pressed Finn's hand. "Call me later?"

"Sure." Finn strode to the Nissan. As she slid into the seat beside her sister, she poked the tiny doll painted like a skeleton hanging from the rearview mirror.

Lily, swerving out of the parking lot toward the main street, asked, "So what's with all the black?"

Finn became painfully aware of the inky kohl around her eyes, the jet glossed onto her short fingernails, her unintentional proclivity for dark clothes. She shifted the small leather backpack—containing her Leica camera, which she was never without—from her shoulder, onto her lap. "I like it."

"You're dreaming about him, aren't you?" Lily asked quietly.

Finn couldn't tell Lily the truth. *Every night.* "Sometimes."

"What are we going to do?" Dressed in a Guns N' Roses T-shirt, cutoffs, and Keds, Lily still looked like a queen. "It's been nearly four months, but we can't keep avoiding them. I think Phouka Banríon is giving you time to grieve. But they're eventually going to make themselves known again."

Finn absolutely didn't want to deal with the new ruler of the Fata "family." "Maybe we should ask the immortal dean and his secret society of professors."

"A lot of good *they* are." Lily snorted. "In ancient Italy, there were shamans called Benandanti who trafficked with spirits to keep their villages safe. I thought your professors were like that. But have they kept anyone safe? Hells no."

"Well, at least they know about the Fatas and haven't forgotten them like the rest of the world."

"I know more than they do," Lily said darkly.

Finn's heart began to sync with the squeaking thump of the windshield wipers. Lily never talked about her time with Seth Lot, when she'd been imprisoned in the House of the Snake and the Wolf.

Lily pulled into the driveway of their house. The car made a grinding sound as she parked—it was a used car, and already complaining. Lily sighed. "If this car dies, I'm screwed. Unless I get that job at Coldstone."

As Finn ducked out the door, she thought it a little depressing that her sister, once the queen of wolf Fatas, was applying for a job at an ice cream parlor. But, then, dark fairie practices probably weren't skills needed in the true world.

And Lily . . . Lily was happy.

BY SIX, THE RAIN HAD EVAPORATED. Finn took her laptop onto the back veranda to enjoy the sunshine—and to keep an eye on Lily, who sat on the old swing set with Kevin Gilchriste. *That* had been an unexpected development. The actor, movie-star gorgeous with his ruffled brown hair and bee-stung lips, seemed okay, but Finn could never forget he'd once warned her about Jack. He knew something.

He looked up and met Finn's gaze. She squinted at him. He returned his attention to Lily.

Later, Finn wandered into the kitchen and set her laptop on the laminate counter. Her father was frowning into the oven window. There was flour in his blond hair. "Da," she said. "I thought we agreed to let Lily make dinner because she's the only one who knows how."

"It's just a pizza."

Finn watched him with affectionate exasperation as he yanked open the oven door and smoke drifted out. She hurried over to help him get the burned pizza out of the oven.

As they were attempting a pizza resuscitation, Lily came in a few minutes later. She tsked and tossed the charred pie into the trash.

"We'll try again." Determined, their dad turned to open the refrigerator.

At that moment, a book floated into the kitchen.

Finn's eyes widened. Lily snatched the book from the air before their dad could see it. He turned back to them, a bag of dough in one hand. He ushered his daughters out. "I promise I won't leave the kitchen this time, or get easily distracted."

As Finn and Lily stepped from the kitchen, Lily covertly showed Finn the book that had ghosted through the air—a picture book about Orpheus, a musician who had gone into the underworld seeking his beloved. Finn glared at it.

"Gran Rose is getting kind of aggressive. Is there something you want to tell me, Finn?" Lily tilted her head, tapping the book against her chin. "Because we both know what this story's about."

"Gran Rose is cryptic." Finn shrugged, realizing she'd have to sneak out of the house tonight because the ghost of her grandmother knew what she was going to do and Lily was beginning to suspect.

THE GARDEN PLANTED BY SEAN SULLIVAN was now thriving. Pale roses and clematis clung to the house's walls and a trellis at the yard's border, camouflaging the hooded shadow that stood there, gazing in the window at Lily and Finn. The flowers he'd brushed against had blackened, crumbled, and now drifted like ashes around him.

Another shadow, girl shaped, was slinking toward the house, her golden hair braided with charms shaped into little stags. He laughed softly and she whirled.

"Giselle," he said with a seductive smile. "Are you here to avenge the *Damh Ridire*? I can help."

She glided toward him, wary and skittish. "So you're the bad one." She cocked her head to one side. "I heard David Ryder was once your friend. Before you betrayed him and got him cast out."

His smile was a slice of white in the shadows of his face. "I betray everyone."

She smiled archly back. "I'll keep that in mind."

FINN HURRIED TO JACK'S SEDAN, parked around the corner near the wooded lot that separated her street from Christie Hart's. She'd finally obtained her license, but she didn't tell anyone she used Jack's car.

When she'd driven to her destination, she got out of the sedan and hauled her small backpack over one shoulder. The nights were still cool, so she wore a suede jacket with a cowl and wide-cuffed sleeves. As she trudged up the drive toward the abandoned house called Sleeping Beauty, she saw a young man sprawled in a decaying chair on the veranda. A wreath of flowers was set rakishly on his auburn curls. Multiple gold hoops pierced his ears. She halted, daunted once again by his resemblance to Christie.

Whenever she saw Sionnach Ri, Finn's first thought was always: *Don't ever trust him.* It was only out of desperation that she did so now. He'd come to her as she'd been closing up BrambleBerry Books one evening, and that encounter had led to a conversation about Annwyn, the land of the dead. He'd told her how one might acquire a guide into the underworld—an elemental who could open the way.

"Don't *you* look all dark and dangerous." The fox knight swung his legs down from the chair arm and stood up.

"I'm tired, Sionnach. Let's get this over with." She hadn't brought any weapons or Fata repellent, no silver or iron, and she'd left Lily's bracelet of silver charms at home. He'd warned her that an elemental wouldn't come near her if she smelled of silver or iron.

"It's just around the corner." Sionnach Ri glided down the stairs. She followed him through tangles of morning glories and raspberry bushes. Fizzy with energy and nerves, her night vision enhanced by a drop of the Ghostlands elixir she hoarded in a tiny bottle, she asked, "This place . . . it was owned by the Tredescant family?"

"The collectors. '*Trad*escant,' in the old country." He flashed a grin over one shoulder. "They hunted down rarities and oddities. Their cabinet of curiosities was quite notorious. Of course, being blessed gave them advantages when it came to treasure hunting. They changed the spelling of their name when they came to this country, to avoid being harassed."

"How do you know all that if you've only been in the true world a few weeks?" Sionnach Ri had arrived by an illegal Way located in an old building that had been a film studio in the 1920s: StarDust Studios.

"I read books." He winked. "True world books are all the rage where I'm from. How is my original doing? Still as gorgeous and kissable as ever?"

"There's something so wrong about what you just said." Finn thought of Star-Dust Studios. It wasn't like Phouka Banríon, the ruler of the Fatas, to forget such an important detail as shutting down a portal to the Ghostlands. Something must be keeping her distracted.

Finn glanced back at the house called Sleeping Beauty. A Gothic Tudor of pointy towers veiled with briar roses, the mansion resembled a residence from the fairy tale after which it was named. But its windows were boarded up, and the garden was sinister with red toadstools, spiny weeds, and stained and crumbling statues. As they pushed through a cavern of woody vines, a stab of terror made Finn falter. She wished she had Christie and Sylvie with her instead of this capricious Fata.

They eventually emerged onto a stretch of lawn before a grove of blackthorn trees. The moon was a round lamp above the tangled darkness.

"You do know that what you're attempting is something few have succeeded in doing?" Sionnach asked, hands in his hoodie's pockets, regarding the black-thorns balefully.

Finn had to know. "How few?"

"Three divinities that I know of. And at a terrible price."

"Is there ever a price with you people that isn't terrible?"

He turned to her, all mischief vanished. "You won't be dealing with Fatas once you cross into Annwyn." The name of the underworld was a chilly breath on his lips. "It is a place where the dead are angry, vengeful, or tortured by guilt. It isn't a land of souls at peace. And the king of Annwyn . . . he isn't like the Fatas either. He's an elemental force with intelligence."

"That *is* what Fatas are."

"Stubborn girl. I am trying to discourage you." Sionnach Ri's silver eyes warmed to a pale brown. "But I've met your Jack. And I've no doubt that if anyone can harrow the underworld to bring him back, it'd be you."

"Do I really have a chance?" She was terrified and trying not to show it. There was no guide map for the place she was attempting to breach.

"I'd say you've a better chance than most, Finn Sullivan."

He led her into the blackthorns, to a colonnade, its pillars broken, its marble floor spongy with toadstools. In the center, a huge stone face framed by writhing stone hair gurgled lichen and water from its lips.

Sionnach took Finn's backpack from her shoulder and dumped its contents onto the marble. He lifted a freeze-dried possum she'd bought at a taxidermist's from a plastic container. "These are the original eyes? The eyes are the most important." When Finn nodded, he continued, "And you've brought the honey and the pin as well. Good girl."

Finn knelt. She began setting red candles in a circle. "This is really the least dangerous elemental we can call on?"

"Hopefully. Now." Sionnach Ri set the possum in the circle of candles. "Light the candles. Prick your finger with the hat pin, and let one drop fall into the honey."

Finn did as she was told. Following directions was much easier than thinking about what she was actually attempting.

"Now stare into one of the possum's eyes and don't look away."

She settled back to gaze into one of the dead possum's black pupils as Sionnach began to whisper in a language that sounded like wind drifting through an abandoned house, secretive and primitive. The candlelight reflecting in the possum's retina was mesmerizing. The night around it seemed to spill forth in inky streams.

"Good luck, Finn Sullivan. I can't stay. I can't let the Black Thorn know I helped you. In the event things go awry, I've left a dagger in the mouth of that stone head."

Finn blinked. She was no longer gazing into the possum's eye, but at a distant, glowing figure in the blackthorns.

Sionnach was gone. The distant figure flickered as if the breeze disturbed its solidity. The air began to hum.

As the hum grew louder, a swarm of black bees descended on the dead possum, which rapidly began to decay. Finn's animal brain shrieked at her to *run, run, RUN*. She closed her eyes.

She and Jack had been two lost souls, dead in their convergent worlds. What had begun as an enchantment flourished into a friendship, and finally into something that had bewildered both of them. He had sacrificed himself to save her sister. And so now Finn would enter the darkness to lead him out. She would be his sun.

Finn opened her eyes and inhaled a scream so quickly, it hurt. The Black Thorn, the Lunantishee, stood before her. It wore the shape of a graceful young man hidden beneath a veil of black gossamer. Beneath the veil, ebony roses seemed to bloom from both eye sockets, and his mouth was a curve of malice. Hair the color of blackberry wine spilled to feet in platform shoes hooked with tiny thorns. From the ram horns curling to either side of his head were bronze hoops strung with . . . *Oh*, Finn thought, *please don't let those be human teeth.*

"Mortal girl." The Lunantishee extended a black-nailed hand. "I would have the rest of my offering."

Finn grabbed the bronze bowl of honey and blood and held it out. The urge to scream was overpowering.

The Black Thorn accepted the bowl and lifted the rim against his veiled mouth. She looked away as he drank.

He dropped the empty bowl and began pacing around Finn. "Queen killer. Wolf slayer. What do you seek?"

"I want to get into Annwyn."

The Lunantishee came close to her, the veil rippling, and Finn tensed as thorn-nailed hands cupped her face. His white flesh was cold. His breath carried the scent of damp soil. "Give me my due and I shall guide you to Death's door."

Finn's head began to hurt. She tasted blood in her mouth. *I've been scared worse than this.* Desperately, she said, "I thought I already gave you what you wanted."

The Black Thorn smiled, revealing hooked teeth. "You are alone and in my power. I'll take whatever I desire."

"I don't think so." Finn crushed the hollowed robin's egg she'd been holding and flung the elixir she'd filled it with into the Lunantishee's face. He recoiled as she recited the words Sionnach had taught her, "Thou dark spirit, I bind thee to this place and all that's near it—"

The Lunantishee tore the veil from his head, his rose-blinded face twisted with rage. Finn reeled back as he stalked toward her, snarling, "Who gave you those words? *A fox knight?*"

Realizing things had gone awry, Finn dove for the stone-head fountain, frantically scrabbling for the dagger Sionnach had said he'd left there. As the Lunantishee glided toward her, Finn's fingers closed around the hilt. She twisted up—

Light swept around her, burning away the Lunantishee . . . and any hope of entering Annwyn tonight.

Finn turned, shielding her eyes with the hand clutching the elder wood dagger. She saw two figures holding electric lanterns. One of them called, "Finn?"

"Sylv?" Dismayed, Finn hid the dagger behind her, tucking it into the waistband of her jeans. Her legs felt wobbly. "What are you doing here?"

Sylvie, dressed in a black hoodie and jogging pants, shrugged. "We were here because—"

"We were following you." Sylvie's companion was Micah Govannon, Finn's coworker from BrambleBerry Books and, it turned out, a distant cousin. His brown hair was pulled back from his face and he, too, wore clothes for slinking around in the dark.

Moving forward to scrutinize the remnants of the failed ritual, Sylvie flipped Finn's question back at her. "So . . . what are *you* doing here?"

"A ritual. A mourning ritual," Finn said, realizing how ridiculous that sounded.

Micah's gaze flicked over the possum remains—the bees were gone—and the extinguished candles. The bronze bowl was still sticky with honey and a smear of blood.

The sound of snapping twigs and murmurs made Finn flinch and Micah lift his electric lantern.

"Hey!" a voice called as bobbing lights in the foliage became another pair of figures shoving through the creepers.

Sylvie snapped, "Christie?"

Christie Hart had leaves in his auburn curls and a scratch on one cheek. Beside him, Aubrey Drake looked like someone in a varsity jacket who'd just wandered into an awkward situation. Pollen dusted his brown skin and black hair.

"Hello." Finn folded her arms across her chest, hoping she could distract Christie from noticing the paraphernalia of the ritual behind her by acting angry. "Out for a stroll?"

Christie set his flashlight beam on Sylvie. "We were following Sylv."

"Because you're with *him*." Aubrey aimed his light at Micah, whose eyes widened. "We didn't know you were tracking Finn, Sylv."

"Hey, Christie." Micah's smile was fragile. "Thanks for trusting me."

"You worked for a Jill who was a monster hunter." Aubrey didn't drop his light from Micah's face. "And now you work for the Black Scissors."

Finn snatched up her backpack. "I'm going home."

"Finn—" Sylvie started after her, but Aubrey said something and Sylvie turned to snap at him.

It was Christie who caught up to Finn. "What were you doing back there? Finn. Talk to me."

"I was saying good-bye to Jack," Finn lied, an ache in her throat.

"Okay." He sounded subdued. Sylvie, Micah, and Aubrey trudged after them. He glanced back at Sylvie. "Sylv, why were you following Finn?"

"I was . . . uh, worried for her. You're making this awkward, Christie."

"Like it isn't already?" Christie retorted.

As Sylvie and Christie began to argue, Aubrey took Christie's place beside Finn. He said with quiet urgency, "Finn. I need to know how she died."

She realized he meant Hester Kierney. "I'm sorry, Aubrey. It . . . was quick."

He was quiet for a moment. Then he asked, "Was the Wolf's death as bad as Hester's?"

Finn focused on Aubrey's pain, vivid and yearning. "Yes."

"Vic and Nic don't want anything to do with the Fatas anymore. Claude's still afraid of them. And Ijio, like the rest of his hookah-smoking, philosophy-bullshit tribe, needs to wake up."

"Aubrey . . . don't think all the Fatas are like Lot. You and your friends have been attached to them for a while. You shouldn't just . . . drop them."

"Yeah. Well. After the Midsummer Masquerade, I think it's time to cut loose. To stand on our own. Listen, I was going through the stuff on my phone and I—"

"Can we talk about this later, Aub?" Finn had a headache and a craving for sleep. There was a tremor in her hands she hoped her friends wouldn't notice.

"Sure. Later. Okay."

FINN STEPPED INTO HER HOUSE and slumped down against the door. She checked her phone and found two messages; her da was at Jane Emory's—big surprise—and Lily was at a party with Kevin Gilchriste. Lily had even sent a selfie; she was posed with an arm around Kevin, who smiled like the pro he was. Finn thought about Kevin warning her about Jack and the Fatas. *Everyone in this damn town has secrets.*

She let the phone fall into her lap and sobbed once, pushing her hands over her face. She'd failed tonight.

CHAPTER 2

Are they black matter? What is their physicality? Are they manifestations of our psyches? I can't believe what I see. I can't. For my daughter's sake...

—FROM THE JOURNAL OF DAISY SULLIVAN

The mural painted onto the massive wall was black and white with a splash of red in the center. The mural depicted Jack in a top hat and a greatcoat. Looming behind him was a hooded figure that bled into a crimson-gowned girl, Reiko Fata's face emerging from beneath the cowl as her hands, in slow motion, clawed out Jack's heart.

Finn shouted as if her own heart had been ripped from her.

Jack said, from within the mural, "I am not a gentleman."

Finn didn't talk to Christie or Sylvie the next morning. Haunted by the dream, she struggled through Intro to Anthropology and Photography Studio. As she was heading down the Arts Center's main corridor, someone called her name. Finn turned; Miss Perangelo was walking toward her. "A word with you, Miss Sullivan."

Finn reluctantly followed the art instructor, who, with her short red hair and feline eyes, reminded Finn of an adult Tinker Bell, into one of the painting studios. When she saw what waited for her in the studio, she halted.

Propped on an easel in the center was a painting of a figure in a sweeping coat and wide hat.

"Do you know who painted this charmer?" As Miss Perangelo draped an arm across the top of the canvas, Finn stared resignedly at the painting of the Black Scissors, the *Dubh Deamhais.*

"Sylvie," she said reluctantly.

"The wayfarer. The faery doctor. A poor boy who met a wicked faery queen who then led him to his doom. Sounds romantic, doesn't it? An appealing story to a naive girl."

Sylvie was not naive. She'd once told Finn, *The Black Scissors was probably just as much an asshole as Reiko and got what he deserved.* Finn shrugged and said, "Sylvie just painted an interesting figure."

"You know they can influence us in dreams. The Black Scissors is haunting your friend, Miss Sullivan, and you can be sure he's doing it with no good intentions. He's not human anymore. He's not Fata. He's not one of the dead. He is a creature whose moral compass has been stomped on, set fire to, and tossed in the trash."

"He helped me, twice, when none of *you* did a thing."

"He'll expect something in return for that. And I hope that something isn't your friend Sylvie Whitethorn."

"She isn't mine to give away."

Miss Perangelo's gaze was cooler than a Fata's. "We'll need to speak to your sister soon, Miss Sullivan. It's been months since—"

"Over my dead body." Finn turned and stalked out of the room. She pushed through the doors, into the sunlight, and found her way to the courtyard where she usually met Sylvie and Christie for lunch. As she sat at the picnic table and brooded over a flyer she'd been given advertising a midsummer masquerade— *another goddamn revel*—she heard a familiar voice.

"Miss Sullivan."

She looked up at Rowan Cruithnear, the dean of HallowHeart. "Hello, True Thomas."

As sartorially sharp as ever, he sat beside her. He was silent for a moment. Then he said, "Did you know HallowHeart was built in Prague, in the 1800s? It was a school of esoteric knowledge."

"Like Hogwarts?"

His mouth quirked. "I do wish people would stop making that comparison."

Since he was being chatty, Finn decided to drill him for info. "How old were you when you met her? The faery queen?"

"I don't like to calculate my age."

"What was she like? Titania?"

He smoothed a hand over his silver hair. "She was as terrifying and enchanting as you'd expect. She became my obsession and my downfall."

"It's not easy living forever, is it?"

"It's not a blessing." He hesitated. "I have watched friends die. I have watched my descendants pass on. Just when I believe I've grown impervious to grief, I learn that I am not. When you told me what happened to Hester Kierney . . . she was like a granddaughter to me, like Jane. I've allowed Reiko to play queen here so that I could keep an eye on her. I was willing to allow the Teind when I believed it was Nathan Clare. I thought one small sacrifice . . ."

". . . for the greater good." Finn's throat closed up when she remembered Hester dying in her arms. "I think Aubrey and the blessed have quit the Fatas. Will their fortune expire?"

"Phouka Banríon won't curse them, no. Their fates are now their own. The Banríon is a creature of honor, and honor for the Fatas is an unbreakable law. Here are your companions, Miss Sullivan, the young man with witch blood and your lissome and virtuous knight."

He rose and walked away.

Christie and Sylvie were striding across the lawn. Sylvie, dressed as though she'd just stepped out of a Gothic wonderland, was checking her phone.

Christie stuffed his iPad into his backpack as he sat on the picnic table and picked up the masquerade flyer. He sighed dramatically. "Another blessed bash. They've got to be kidding."

Sylvie tore her attention away from her phone and fastened her gaze on him. "Last night, you were following me because, what, you thought Micah was turning me into a monster hunter? Please."

"What about that heart widow business?" Christie returned.

"I'm not going all Ninja girl, if that's what you're thinking. Have you seen Phouka lately?"

Without answering the pointed question, Christie told Finn, "We're sorry we interrupted last night."

"It wasn't anything, really." Finn shrugged.

They were quiet then, and Finn realized they, too, had secrets.

FINN BECAME AWARE OF SOMEONE walking behind her as she was crossing the empty stretch of campus between McKinley and the Arts Center. She quickened her steps, hitching her thumbs through the straps of her backpack, but her pursuer caught up to her easily. "You're dealing with the dead, you know."

She turned on Kevin Gilchriste.

"What did you say?" She narrowed her eyes.

"I think you heard me, Finn Sullivan."

"You *know*."

He nodded once.

"How? You're not one of the blessed."

"No." He almost spit the word out. "I would never bargain with *them*."

"Then how do you—did they do something to you?"

"I know what they did to *you*. You were a lonely, devastated girl, and they prey on lonely, devastated girls. And boys."

Finn wanted to snap at him that she was not a lonely, devastated girl, but he ruthlessly continued, "Do you care about your friends? If you did, you wouldn't be messing around with *them*." He began walking backward. "Part ways with them, Finn, or you and your friends will end up like all their victims."

He turned and strode away, leaving her simmering and stunned.

SYLVIE ARRIVED AT CARVER'S AUTOBODY SHOP just as the garage was closing. She leaned against her bike, listening to Patti Smith through her earbuds as she waited.

A young man emerged from the shop. As he strode toward Sylvie, she took a deep breath. It was always a little daunting to see him in the sunlight. The Black Scissors, William Harrow, had shed his Vampire Hunter D ensemble to blend in with the ordinary folk of Fair Hollow and he was about as successful at it as Jack Hawthorn had once been. Her stomach knotted with sorrow when she thought of Jack.

"So you never told me"—as usual, she was jaunty when speaking with the enigmatic immortal—"why a car mechanic? Didn't you used to be a tailor?"

He nodded, indicating that they would walk, and she wheeled her bike as she strolled beside him. "My father was a blacksmith, so I learned a bit of the trade. I've taken on other trades throughout the years."

"Without a Social Security number or a driver's license?"

He winked. "There are ways of convincing people."

She regarded him sidelong. Jeans and a T-shirt only enhanced his looks. The tattoos on his arms were ornate, beautiful patterns of insects. His blond, black-streaked hair was pulled back from a high-boned face. The persona of an amiable young mechanic was a mask.

Some mortals enchanted by the Fatas—or cursed by them—didn't have shadows, but William Harrow's inked the pavement and seemed to almost have a life of its own. Sylvie was very careful not to tread on it.

"You were right," she told him as they turned a corner into the warehouse district. "Finn's trying to get into the underworld." Her heart felt heavy with betrayal even as she spoke.

His jaw tightened. "I was afraid of that."

They reached a brownstone building that looked condemned. The Black Scissors unlocked the door with a key shaped like a wasp and led her into a hall that didn't match the building's exterior. An elegant staircase of green marble curved beneath a crystal chandelier and the apple green walls were hung with antique and primitive weapons.

Sylvie leaned her bike against the stair and followed him into a narrow parlor where a large window revealed an overgrown courtyard with a graffiti-spattered warehouse rising beyond. The parlor's shelves and a rectangular table were scattered with books and objects: a tiny, bat-winged skeleton in a bell jar, a webbed and taloned hand, a monkey's skull with three eye sockets. None of this belonged to William Harrow, but to a mysterious benefactor, who, in the months of Sylvie's apprenticeship to the Black Scissors, she'd never seen.

The Black Scissors turned to her. "What did you find?"

Sylvie sat on a green divan and, grimacing, tugged the dead possum, wrapped in plastic, from her backpack. "I didn't witness the ritual. Micah and I arrived at the tail end of it."

The Black Scissors took the possum from her. His eyebrows slanted in consternation. "The Lunantishee." He sat on his heels and opened a chest of dark wood carved with images of stylized beetles. He dumped the possum in it, then shut the lid and locked the trunk with yet another key. "Serafina failed last night, but she has three more elemental rulers to contact before May Eve."

"How can we stop her?"

"We can't." William Harrow moved to stand before the arched window. "Just let it run its course, Miss Whitethorn."

"I do wish you'd call me *Sylvie*, and I can't do that, *Mr. Harrow*." Sylvie stood up. She slung her backpack over one shoulder. "When are you going to teach me how to use a sword?"

"Daggers are much better. You don't want to get in a swordfight with an Unseelie—they've been around since rocks."

"I don't want to get in *any* kind of a fight with an Unseelie."

"I'm just teaching you the basics, heart widow."

"I get that." Sylvie headed for the door. She wanted to call Finn and yell at her, but she couldn't let Finn know *she* knew. She paused at the door and looked over one shoulder. "I can trust you, can't I?"

"I'm on your side, Sylvie Whitethorn. *Our* side. The mortal side. If you want to keep your family and friends safe, you'll have to start believing in me and stop relying on those demons pretending to be your allies."

Sylvie scowled at him. She yanked open the door.

In the hall, she grabbed her bike and pushed it onto the street. Reluctantly, she glanced back. As the fading sun melted orange across the windows, she imagined she saw, beyond one of them, a writhing darkness.

What kind of curse had the Fatas placed upon the Black Scissors?

HAVE WE MADE FRIENDS WITH DEMONS? Christie thought as he drove up the cracked road toward the sinister, boarded-up Tirnagoth Hotel. But Finn and Sylvie were both messing around with Fata affairs so he really shouldn't feel guilty that he'd been meeting with Phouka Banríon.

He parked in the crescent driveway and spent the next ten minutes forging through tangles of milkweed and ferns, glad he'd worn silver, although he'd had to leave behind the iron keys he used to attach to his belt for protection.

He made out the sounds of crickets and rustling leaves—lately, he was hearing things with the implants in his ears much more clearly than he should. And that frightened him.

A circle of tiny lights swept from a tower window, spiraling across the night sky. Christie nearly jumped out of his skin when a bundle of sticks and leaves stirred near the front doors, then rose up and skittered into the dark, leaving behind the stink of toadstools.

Reminding himself that he was friends with what haunted Tirnagoth, he glanced over one shoulder at the wilderness surrounding the hotel, then back at the building. As dusk descended, the creepers curled away, revealing unblemished stone and marble, the statues of nymphs and gods. The boards across the hotel's windows faded and light poured through stained glass. Music murmured in the air as he strode toward the stairs. The closer he got, the chillier the air became.

The entrance doors opened, light spilled out, and Christie sighed in spooked irritation. "You."

Devon Valentine, dressed in red, looked wounded. "Christopher Hart." He didn't look like someone who'd slit his wrists decades ago, but he still made Christie's skin crawl. "The Banríon already has a guest. Do you have an appointment?"

A tall girl in Victorian velvet, her gold-and-black hair in plaits, appeared beside the dead young man and curled a finger at Christie. "Come along, witch boy. The Banríon will see you."

Devon seemed about to protest, but Christie strode up the stairs and followed Hip Hop—who had once been Emily Tirnagoth—into the lobby. A number of Fatas lounged in the lobby, which was a luxury of art nouveau detail, of twining metal and glass stained with malevolent-looking flowers. The back of Christie's neck prickled as he felt the Fatas' inhuman gazes following him.

"Why did you change sides?" he asked Hip Hop.

"I chose the winning side—and the Wolf put a needle in my little brother's eye." She led him up a stair, its railing strung with bird skulls, lockets, and butterflies made of gauze. At the top of the stair was a large black door gilded with images of tulips. Candle smoke drifted in the air.

The door opened and the world stopped as if it were a broken clock. A tall figure cut from the dark of the universe stood before them, its eyes and smile like the stars, its hair writhing around a pair of ram horns that couldn't possibly fit through the doorway.

Christie's mind stalled. Neither poetry nor protective words could escape him as a voice as deep as thunder above ancient forests spoke.

"Christie."

Christie felt someone grip his shoulders. He blinked and met a gaze as gray as oceans. He sat in a blue-and-ivory parlor illuminated by alabaster lamps. Phouka Banríon crouched before him. Sleek in a blazer and wide-legged trousers of gray tweed, she wore a diamond headband in her auburn hair and her face glimmered as if she'd walked through pollen. "Don't try to identify what you saw, Christie Hart."

"Who . . ." His hair was plastered to his forehead with sweat. His palms were damp. His heart was jittering.

"An old comrade. I think Hip Hop thought *she* wouldn't be frightened. She hasn't spoken for half an hour. Serves her bloody right."

"Is that how long I've been sitting here?"

"Actually." Phouka sat on the sofa beside him. "You fainted."

Christie hunched forward and clawed his hands through his curls. "Was that who I think it was?"

"Oberon. The king of the English Fatas." She patted one of his hands. "And he does that to every mortal he meets."

"Oberon?" Christie sat very still. "That was *Oberon*? Like from *A Midsummer Night's Dream*?"

"It's one of his names. And it wasn't really him . . . more of a . . . simulacrum."

His teeth were beginning to chatter. "Is it cold in here? Is that fire real?" He indicated the roaring flames in the porcelain hearth.

"Would you like me to fetch you a glass of water?" Phouka's face was still. "Then you could try to steal something else of mine."

His heart jumped. He couldn't deny what he'd once done at the Black Scissors's request. "The ivory book—Phouka, I'm so sorry—"

"I'll get it back." Her gaze shimmered. "It won't work for the Black Scissors."

He pushed the heels of his hands against his eyes. "Good. The bastard deserves to be tricked."

"Your Sylvie has become his apprentice."

He'd suspected that, but the statement was like a knife in his guts. "She wouldn't—"

"She is with him for the same reason you are here—to learn how to defend herself from my kind. And to watch over Finn Sullivan, who is trying to find her way into the underworld."

His teeth slammed together. "I knew it."

The lights flickered. For a second, he glimpsed a darkened room of fallen boards, debris, and mildewed wallpaper . . . and a shadow instead of a girl sitting beside him. *Don't forget what they really are,* he told himself. *No matter how beautiful or kind they seem. Don't ever forget.*

The light and opulence returned and a beautiful girl was again sitting beside him. He said, his voice strained, "I thought I'd be glad Jack was gone. But I'm not. I need to accelerate this *fear dorchadas* training."

Christie was a witch and couldn't control it—a fact he'd discovered when he'd been passing the Dead Kings nightclub one evening and a silver-eyed Fata girl had smiled at him and started to work some love-talker voodoo that had scraped like sandpaper against his brain. His skin had broken out in inky sonnets and he'd spoken a word that had slammed her back against a wall. Finn had hurried out of BrambleBerry Books and hustled him away before the Fata could retaliate.

The scariest thing was . . . he couldn't wear iron anymore. Silver was fine. And steel didn't bother him. But real iron caused a nasty rash.

Red blood out. Black blood in. He was afraid of what might be lurking within him, some spiritual infection born of the Fatas long ago and carried through his bloodline.

Phouka said, carefully, "This isn't a lifestyle choice—this is a life *necessity.* If you don't learn to control the blood, it will twist up inside of you. And twisted witches, Christie, are everyone's problem."

"Are twisted witches powerful?"

"You don't want power, Christopher. You want to protect those you love. So let's continue with your lessons."

Christie wondered what kind of twisted witch became a Fata problem and if any were still running around. "Yes. Teach me."

❖ ❖ ❖

LATER, A SLENDER, ORANGE-HAIRED FIGURE watched Christie being escorted to his car by a chatty Aurora Sae, the nymph's gown wafting like lavender mist. "Christopher's certainly taken up the wand with more enthusiasm than I'd expected."

Phouka, sprawled in an armchair, was gazing into a tall, antique mirror set opposite her. "He doesn't have a choice."

Absalom spun to face her. He skirted the mirror, careful not to step in front of it. "You like living on the edge, don't you?"

She didn't take her gaze from the mirror. "This mirror is harmless for now."

"Why didn't you tell him about Harahkte?" Absalom sat, Buddha style, on the sofa. If it weren't for his flame-gold eyes, he could have passed for any teenager in his Black Sabbath T-shirt and jeans.

"Because as long as the Wolf's house is pinned in the void, we don't have to worry about Harahkte. And they don't trust us, Finn and her friends. Even if Moth does return, why would they believe us? And, remember, Absalom, he might *remain* Moth, even with his past as Harahkte restored."

Absalom slithered to his feet. "I suppose that's nothing to worry about, like you said, as long as Sombrus is spinning in the nether. So—why are you collecting the mirrors?"

"As a precaution."

THE GIRL'S SOBBING ALERTED TYSON FOLLOWS to her shape hunched on the park bench. He slowed down on his nightly jog. "Hey. Hi. You okay?"

She slid up, her golden hair gleaming, and smiled. "Want to live forever?"

He shied back, but the darkness got him nonetheless.

THAT NIGHT, FINN DROVE TO MOONGLASS MANSION. The art deco house had been deserted decades ago, but the neglect wasn't visible until the headlights of Jack's car smeared across the riven stairway and the grime on the faces of the goddesses in the stained glass.

As Finn hurried up the stairs, lights flickered beyond those windows and the doors opened. She inhaled courage and stepped in. She followed a thread of ragtime music to a pink-and-emerald salon, where Sylph Dragonfly sprawled in an armchair next to a table on which sat a gilt phonograph. The Dragonfly witch, Sylvie's replica, wearing a sleeveless black gown, her eyes circled with kohl, looked as though she'd stepped out of a silent film.

"Serafina Sullivan." Sylph Dragonfly rose. She carried a staff topped with a reindeer skull that was painted with symbols. "Are you ready?"

Finn pushed back the hood of her jacket. "Yeah."

"Don't be nervous. Sionnach told me what happened with that flaky earth elemental. Tonight, we summon fire, and that's much more understanding of love."

Finn followed Sylph out into MoonGlass's garden of tall hedges and ornamental trees gone to seed. "So . . . this Phantophage . . . you're sure he can get me into Annwyn?"

"The elementals are from the Houses of Earth, Fire, Water, and Air. If we can't get their rulers' help . . . well, no one from those houses will assist you, Serafina."

Finn glanced sidelong at the Dragonfly witch, bothered as much by her resemblance to Sylvie as she was by Sionnach Ri's to Christie. "Doesn't 'Phantophage' translate to something like 'Eater of Ghosts'?"

"That's right."

"Fantastic." Finn drew a breath in and out.

The Dragonfly led Finn to the garden's center, where stone benches circled a giant hearth of granite hewn into the forms of leaping rabbits. The hearth's soot-blackened interior was a cave wreathed with grapevines.

"Here." Sylph knelt. Finn drew from her backpack four crimson candles, a book she'd made herself, with words and drawings and pretty trinkets, and a tiny bottle containing three drops of her blood. *Blood or a kiss*, Sionnach Ri had warned her, *that's what they'll ultimately want*, and Finn wasn't about to kiss any strange elementals.

Sylph used black chalk to mark the granite floor with an arcane symbol. Then she lit each candle by placing her forefinger on the wicks. "You've got something of your lover's?"

Finn nodded, clutching at the ring of bronze lions clasping a heart. Jack had been wearing it as he'd walked into the underworld, but Finn had found it on a branch when she'd returned to the place where she'd last seen him. He must have removed it . . . as if warning her, in his infuriating way: *Let me go.*

Sylph walked to the giant hearth and set the book Finn had made into it. Then she handed Finn one of the crimson candles. Finn crouched and set fire to the book. As the parchment began to smolder, she experienced a creepy-crawling sensation, the slight pressure in her sinuses that meant something powerful, old, and dangerous was nearby. The air began to hum.

"Finn." Sylph Dragonfly's voice was wary. "He's behind me. I cannot stay."

Finn pushed to her feet and reluctantly peered into the night behind the Dragonfly. Sylph stepped aside with a curtsy, before whirling and vanishing into the dark.

The dark fell away from a figure wrapped in bandages of black velvet, his exposed hands, face, and throat almost luminous. His long hair was obsidian sleek. He was draped in copper jewelry and a black bandage was tied around his eyes. Two red fissures glowed beneath. "What do you seek from me, child?" His voice was a pulse of heat and flame.

Finn's tongue knotted. Then Jack's ring became hot in her clenched fist and she remembered the look of Jack in firelight, the feel of him against her. "I want to enter Annwyn, the underworld, the shadowlands, to right a wrong."

The Phantophage was suddenly too close, the heat emanating from his skin making her flush. Her hair became a static halo. "You have given me a book of your heart, but nothing else." He raised a hand and she saw flames flickering across his black nails before those nails grazed the line of her jaw. "What else do you have, mortal girl?"

She lifted the miniature bottle of her blood.

The copper bangles jingled around his wrists as he accepted the blood. She averted her gaze as he drank it. When he set down the empty vial, he said gravely, "Ask again."

"I want you to guide me into Annwyn."

He turned his blind face to her. His teeth were tiny, sharp, and white. "You mortals . . . like insects dancing around flames. Gone in a single one of our thoughts. I regretfully cannot help you." He stepped back.

"Wait!" she called out. "I gave you something!" Her voice cracked with desperation. "You need to give me something in return."

"And, someday, I will." He vanished in a cyclone of darkness streaked with fire.

Finn sagged against the fireplace, Jack's ring biting into her hand. She couldn't believe she'd failed again.

When another figure emerged from the night, Finn flinched. One hand, flashing a single gold ring, drew back a hood from a tousled mane of pewter-gold hair and a sharply boned face with feline green eyes. His British baritone was chiding. "Haven't you learned how to get around their bloody tricks?"

"*Moth?*" Shock made her breathless. The last time she'd seen him, it had been near the House of the Wolf and the Snake, Sombrus, before it had vanished with him and the Wolf's pack.

"Did the Banríon and her Fool, Askew, tell you what I am yet?" Bitterness tainted his voice.

"No, Moth." She slowly approached him. "What would they tell me?"

"When I was in the Wolf's house . . . all that I had done and been came back." He broke off and rubbed a hand across his mouth.

"You were working for Seth Lot, a monster. You had no choice. Are you feeling *guilty*?"

"There's always a choice." He looked at her, eyes flashing. "What are you doing, Finn? Where is Jack?"

"He's gone." She spoke carefully, so that her voice wouldn't break. "The Wild Hunt took him, after."

He said quietly, "You're trying to get him back."

"Yes." She felt a wary relief, telling someone. "The Wolf's house, Sombrus . . . where is it?"

"In the forest."

"And the wolves?"

"I had to kill them." His expression was stark. "Or they would have killed me."

She thought of him trapped in that supernatural house, fighting for survival. "How long have you been back?"

"A few days. Hunting . . . Finn, something escaped Sombrus when I came back. Something got out. I saw it, a few times, out of the corner of my eye, in that house—and I saw it break free when I returned here."

"What kind of something?" Finn whispered, chilled.

"A shadow man. I've been trying to find him. I fear whatever it is might be a malevolent entity. Nothing good would come out of the House of the Wolf and the Snake."

"You have to go to Phouka."

"No!" His reply was quick and rough. "I don't trust Askew. Forget you saw me, Finn."

As he vanished into the night, she cried out, "Moth!"

FINN TRUDGED BACK TOWARD JACK'S SEDAN, thinking of Moth. Of Sombrus. Of a shadow man. When she saw the young man seated cross-legged on the sedan's hood, she halted, dismayed. "You look different."

The Black Scissors, dressed in a gray T-shirt and jeans, shrugged. "The hat and coat would be a little out of season."

"What do you want?" Hostility crept into her voice.

"I know what you're attempting, Miss Sullivan. I know the fox knight and the Dragonfly are helping you. Stop this." When she didn't say anything, he sighed. "Look where love got *me*."

"You're sitting beneath the stars, young and immortal and—"

"Point taken. Let me tell you what Annwyn is, Finn Sullivan. It's the place where the bad people go to pay for what they've done."

"I've been told that."

"The *evil* dead, Miss Sullivan." He slid from the sedan and walked toward her, the shadows sharp across his face. "It says something for Jack Hawthorn that you're willing to go to hell to get him back, but you should respect his choice. He was their plaything for two hundred years. He has to get the poison out of his soul."

"He can do that here, with me."

"There are consequences, Miss Sullivan, for bringing back the dead."

"Jack didn't die. He volunteered."

In a gentle tone, the Black Scissors said, "I'm not talking about Jack. How many times do you think you can cheat death?"

She opened the driver's door. "As many times as it's cheated me."

SYLPH DRAGONFLY MOVED through the cobwebbed chambers of MoonGlass into a conservatory where the plants had long ago withered to dust. As she approached a large mirror, its glass tarnished, she heard a noise that could have been a footfall. But the mirror was the Way in this house and whatever else was haunting it wasn't her concern. As she drew closer, a flurry of papery insects spiraled around her from out of the gloom. She halted, frowning.

A male voice teased from the shadows, "Mirror, mirror on the wall."

Sylph spun around and found herself facing a lean figure in black, the hood of its jacket shadowing its face. She breathed out a name and a smile glittered beneath the hood as the voice continued, "Are you the fairest of them all?"

"Is it true?" she whispered. "It is, isn't it?"

He stepped toward her.

She whipped her staff up and twirled it. "*Tenebros.*"

Ribbons of darkness twisted around him. He laughed and walked through them. He spoke a word and her staff splintered. "Fata hekas don't work on me. I'm nothing."

As she whirled to flee toward the mirror, one of his arms snaked around her. He raised a fisted hand in front of her face, uncurled his fingers, and she saw, with failing courage, the remains of a brass-and-glass dragonfly.

"Look," he said in his beautiful voice, "I've broken your heart."

The misericorde he plunged into her breast was made of silver. As he released her, she sank to the floor, the poison burning through her like frostbite, shadows bleeding from her, becoming tiny dragonflies that flickered out, into nothing.

CHAPTER 3

. . . behind the visible are chains and chains of conscious beings . . . who have no inherent form, but change according to their whim, or the mind that sees them . . . the visible world is merely their skin.

—THE FAIRY-FAITH IN CELTIC COUNTRIES,
W. Y. EVANS-WENTZ

Finn, submerged in warm water and bubbles, her eyes closed, sensed the dark, sultry presence nearby, and the ache inside of her, as if something vital had broken, blossomed. She opened her eyes. "Are you real?"

Jack, dressed in a dark blue T-shirt and jeans, barefoot, sat on the edge of the tub. His eyes were blue and gray, not Fata silver. There were fresh rose petals in his dark hair. "That depends on where we are."

He leaned down and placed something in the bubbles near her knee—a rubber duck, lurid crimson.

Finn reached out to clasp his hand and saw that he wore their ring, two lions holding a heart.

Red began to pool in the water and Finn saw with horror that the rubber duck had become a human heart. Scrambling back from it, she looked up into Jack's eyes. They were black holes. He said, "Don't come find me."

She woke in the tub with early morning light pouring over her. The water around her was ice cold.

SEATED ON LILY'S BED while her sister searched for a dress to wear, Finn noticed a streak of tarnish across the mirror over Lily's bureau. Lily's room was located on the sunniest side of their elegant Victorian, on the second floor. It might have once been a drawing room, with its octagonal shape, bay windows, and chair rails. One of Lily's most beautiful ballet costumes—the black-and-blue corset and tutu from *Giselle*—was draped on the door. The walls were hung with three of their mom's paintings. On the bureau were two photographs—one of their mom, smiling on the porch of the Vermont house; the other of Finn and their dad in Muir Woods after a hike.

Finn dropped her gaze to her laptop, which displayed the local news page and the picture of a young man with short, blue-dyed hair and a model's face. The accompanying article was headlined EIGHTEEN-YEAR-OLD TRACK STAR TYSON FOLLOWS MISSING SINCE FRIDAY. She felt a sick pang when she saw Hester's name mentioned as another missing teen.

"I am so glad you didn't give any of my stuff away. What do you think?" When Finn drew her gaze from the laptop to the royal blue sheath Lily was holding against her T-shirt, she saw a shadow slanting, wrongly, from Lily's arm. The sun gilded her sister, but that ribbon of shadow made Finn queasy.

"How about this?" Lily lifted a crepe purple shift and the shadow vanished.

Finn pointed at the purple dress. "That one."

Lily hooked the dress's hanger over the closet door and dropped down next to Finn on the bed. "Dad's out in the garden with Jane. I think they're planting tomatoes. I told them: *no* briar roses."

Finn lay back on the bed and gazed up at the sun-dappled ceiling with its water stains and cherub moldings. "What do you think of Jane? You never said."

"She's nice. Not in a boring way either." Lily sprawled beside her. "But she's one of the Hogwarts crowd, so I don't trust her."

"I like her." Finn raised one hand to a strand of sunlight. She decided she'd imagined the velvety band of shadow on Lily's arm.

Lily propped herself up on one elbow. "Do you think she'll become our step-mom?"

"She doesn't seem to be stepmom material, according to Sylvie." In this room glowing with sunlight, the malicious Lunantishee and the uncanny Phantophage seemed like dream figures. Contentment nestled within Finn's heart. She would not fail again.

Lily stretched one bare leg. She sat up, gazing out of the window. Her long hair veiled one side of her face as she said, faintly, "I'm a bad sister, Finn."

"You are not." Finn was unnerved by Lily's mood swing.

"I am. I'm selfish. I'm . . . remember when I locked you in the closet after we read *The Lion, the Witch, and the Wardrobe?* And I told you that you could get to Narnia?"

"I was eight." Finn remembered pushing past the coats with her eyes shut and freaking out when she couldn't seem to find the back of the closet. "And you were a jerk."

"You know, I remember how mad I was when Mom told me you were going to be born." Lily's head was down. Finn couldn't see her sister's face past her hair. "Then Mom said, *You'll be her hero.* Although I think it's been the other way around. Are you mad at me?"

"Lily, that closet thing was ten years ago."

"It's my fault." Lily's voice was strained. "It's my fault you lost him."

Finn flung her arms around her. "Don't think that! *Don't you ever think that.* It's because of the Wolf that I lost Jack."

Lily raised her head and met Finn's gaze. "You're not . . . trying to get him back, are you? I mean . . . there isn't a way. Not there. Not where he's gone. Annwyn isn't like the Ghostlands. It's the underworld."

"Tell me," Finn said calmly, distracting her. "Tell me about the Wolf's house. About Sombrus."

"At first"—Lily knelt on the bed, her gaze wistful—"it was all Seth Lot promised. There were parties and feasts, horseback rides and hunting. I saw a unicorn once—you do *not* want to encounter one of those things; they're big, with sharp teeth and crazy libidos. There was romance and what romance leads to. Lot was beautiful. I thought he was kind. But, then, things turned. First, there was the Black Scissors's warning, when I encountered him in Goblin Market. Then Leander told me that Seth Lot was a monster. And he showed me . . ."

Listening, Finn kept very still. She felt as if something were creeping around the corner to get her.

"Leander helped me to see Lot's court with their masks off. White creatures with nothing but mouths where faces should be. Girls in ruined gowns, girls with claws and fangs. Boys with hooved feet and animal eyes. Then there were the Jacks and Jills . . . Leander unlocked a door and took me to the place where the bodies of two boys and one girl lay on stone slabs." Her nails dug into her palms. "They were like awful dolls opened up and stuffed with flowers that *crawled*. Leander tried to get me out that night. But we were separated. Then Lot came to me, drenched in blood, and told me he'd taken Leander apart. *Leander*"—her voice cracked, but she inhaled and steadied herself. "Lot lied. Leander had escaped. I became a queen that night, a queen of savage things. I learned how to use that world against them, to call on the elements and the stray Fatas who wanted a purpose and needed only a hand to guide them. I met others whenever I was allowed out of Sombrus. I met the Black Scissors again and he taught me, in secret, the few times the Wolf let me out of his sight. We communicated through insects, the Black Scissors and I. You want to see what the Black Scissors taught me? I can still do it."

Finn wasn't sure she wanted to see, but she nodded.

Lily sat with her hands palms up and breathed out. Shadows threaded from the unlit corners of the room and collapsed into her palms. The shadows, streaked with red light from the heart of crimson glass hung at a window, became a velvet black butterfly, its wings patterned with red.

"Lily . . ." Finn spoke past the knot in her throat. "Should you be able to do that? Here?"

"No." Lily lifted her gaze to Finn's. "Only Fatas should be able to perform the *faileas'leas*. The shadow trick."

Together, they watched as the black butterfly glided up and away, through the open window.

"Only Fatas?" Finn asked, uneasy and alarmed. "Can the Black Scissors do it?"

"Him, too."

"Moth is back."

Lily slowly raised her eyes. "*How?*"

"I don't know. He fought for his life in the Wolf's house. He says he's remembered things he's done in the past."

"The things Seth Lot made him do."

"He doesn't trust Phouka or Absalom." Finn was very concerned for Moth. "What was Moth like when you discovered him in the Wolf's house?"

"You mean after a moth transformed into a gorgeous, naked man in front of me?" Lily's smile was mischievous. "He was stupid with shock. I really thought he had brain damage. I hid him at first, until Lot came looking for him. Moth only remembered that he'd been an actor in a theater company, in Elizabethan England. He served Lot for a while and did some things that I'm sure he was forced to . . ."

"He said his old memories returned because of the *Tamasgi'po*, that potion I had on my lips when I kissed him."

"I can't imagine what it was like for him, Finn, afterward, alone in that nightmare house with the wolf pack. And if he's remembered what he had to do for Lot, he's not going to be his usual self. I wish I could talk to him."

"He says something escaped Sombrus and he's hunting it."

"What escaped? One of the wolves?"

Finn thought of what she was going to attempt tonight, again. She clenched one hand so hard, her nails dug into her palm. "No. A shadow man."

Lily was quiet for a moment. Then, "That house . . . Sombrus hoards memories, shades of people. Creatures. Anything could have gotten out, Finn. The memory of a monster. Of . . ." Lily's voice trailed off, but Finn knew what she was thinking. Sombrus had stored a memory of Reiko; perhaps it had kept one of the Wolf.

"It won't last," Lily said abruptly. "Whatever got out. It'll fade without the house to give it energy."

"What if it keeps returning to Sombrus?"

"Then Moth will kill it," Lily said with conviction.

"THERE HE IS."

Sylvie, strolling beside Finn across the HallowHeart campus, followed Finn's gaze to a figure jogging down the steps of Armitrage Hall. Sylvie murmured, "You sure he was warning you about Jack and the Fatas?"

"Absolutely." Finn was grim.

"Let's go then." Sylvie went after Kevin Gilchriste with the ferocity of a crow diving for french fries. Finn, a little concerned about the predatory way in which her friend moved, strode quickly after.

When Kevin saw them heading in his direction, his bored expression became one of alarm. He glanced about as if seeking an escape route.

Finn stepped in front of him. "Hi."

Kevin smiled, automatically and gorgeously, as if it were some sort of Pavlovian response to conflict. "Hi. Are you going to the Midsummer Masquerade?"

"I think we need to talk, Kevin." Finn slid an arm through the crook of his, while Sylvie hooked his other arm. "About your intentions toward my sister."

Sylvie grinned. "You ever play croquet, Kevin?"

"THE GAME WILL BE 'TRUTH OR DARE,'" Christie declared, standing on Finn's lawn with Sylvie, Finn, Kevin, Aubrey, and Micah. His hands rested on the top of a croquet mallet. Finn, standing behind him, noticed how his skin had already begun to brown from sun. The tattoo of the Celtic cross on the back of his neck was as vividly green as new ivy.

Kevin, between Micah and Aubrey, looked wary.

Sylvie handed out mallets. "Here are the rules, gentlemen—get as many balls through as many hoops as possible. Enthusiasm is encouraged. Violence is not. Every score earns you the right to ask someone for a truth or a dare."

"There are too many secrets in this town," Aubrey said darkly, swinging his mallet. "And I think the lot of *you*"—he jabbed the mallet at each player in turn—"are keeping most of them. I'm gonna find out some things toni—"

There was a crack as Christie's mallet struck his ball and it shot past Aubrey's Air Jordans and through two wire hoops in succession. Christie smiled evilly at Sylvie. "Truth, Sylvie. Are you seeing the Black Scissors, a.k.a. the BS, a.k.a., the Bullshitter?"

"Oh." Micah sounded worried, as if he hadn't expected it to be *that* kind of truth or dare.

Sylvie snapped, "If you mean am I seeing him in the biblical sense or buying Victoria's Secret to wear for him, no."

Aubrey said, "If anyone thinks that's too much information, raise your hand."

Finn ruefully lifted a hand. So did Aubrey, Micah, and Kevin.

"That's not what I asked." Christie leaned toward Sylvie. "Are you seeing the Black Scissors or not?"

"He's teaching me stuff." Defiant, Sylvie jutted her chin. "Along with Micah. How to stay safe, and a little self-defense."

Finn felt wounded that Sylvie hadn't shared this information with her.

"Like how to kill things?" Christie persisted.

"My turn," Sylvie said instead of answering. She swung her mallet. Her ball shot through six hoops and struck a tree, bouncing off it, missing Kevin's leg by an inch.

"Whoa," he said, stepping back. "Is this croquet or hockey?"

Sylvie turned and surveyed the players. In her plaid shorts and black T-shirt with a rosy-haired boy on it, she looked deceptively innocent. She said merrily, "Who here has slept with a Fata?"

Finn's eyes widened as Micah and Aubrey raised their hands—*that* was interesting. She leveled a look at Christie, who slowly inched one arm into the air. Finn hoped Sylvie would assume Christie had gone to bed with Phouka, the slinky ruler of Tirnagoth. But Finn knew the truth—Christie had tumbled Sylph Dragonfly, Sylvie's winsome, witchy Fata twin. The truth might cause complications.

Then Kevin Gilchriste raised a hand.

"I *knew* it," Sylvie whispered as Aubrey asked, "Who thinks these questions are way too person—"

Sylvie turned on Aubrey. "Which Fata did *you* sleep with?"

"You already asked your question," Aubrey said quickly. "Finn? Your turn."

Finn glanced at Kevin meaningfully before she swung her mallet. And missed.

"Tough luck there," Christie commented and Finn wanted to throw her mallet at him.

Micah made five hoops. He turned to regard all of them as he set his mallet against a tree and tucked his hair back behind his ears. When Christie cleared his throat impatiently, Micah held up a hand. "I'm thinking." He narrowed his eyes. "Who here isn't human?" Finn looked around at everyone. They all looked at one another. Micah shrugged. "Just checking."

Next, Aubrey scored two hoops. He idly asked Sylvie: "You think the Black Scissors is hot?"

Sylvie pointed at Aubrey. "I've already answered a question of that type. Ask something else."

Aubrey's shoulders sagged. Then he straightened regally and said, "How about a dare then? I dare you to kiss me—"

"Gilchriste!" The shout made Finn glance up to see her sister striding across the lawn. When Lily reached them, she stabbed a dagger into a tree.

Finn stared at the dagger. Its mahogany hilt was carved into the form of a man with a bear's head. The blade was silver and engraved with runes. It looked old.

"You left your jacket in my car the other night," Lily continued, glaring at Kevin. "Guess what fell out of it? Why do you have a dagger, Kevin?"

"Lily." Kevin held up a hand. "Why don't *you* tell *me* why you think I have that dagger?"

Finn sighed. Using the reasoning method with Lily never worked when she was in a temper. "The Black Scissors," Finn said. When Kevin's expression remained remote, she knew she'd guessed correctly. "You work for him, Kevin."

"There are a few of us who work for him, in different parts of the country." Kevin leaned against a tree. "Every place has a dangerous element."

"Fatas," Micah said quietly.

"Bad Fatas," Sylvie added.

Kevin nodded. "We watch and warn. We try to keep potential victims safe."

"And you kill," Lily said pointedly.

"Only when absolutely necessary. We're more exorcists and spiritwalkers than soldiers—Jill Scarlet's people were the hunters." He indicated Micah.

"So you're like the HallowHeart professors, only useful." Christie looked thoughtful.

Kevin Gilchriste moved toward Lily and pulled the dagger from the tree. "I've never met the others the Black Scissors has on payroll. We're all solitary."

"Did you know about the Teind?" Christie pointed at him.

"Yes. But only that it was Nathan Clare. And Clare was, to us, already one of them."

"He's dead." Finn hated saying it. "Caliban killed him."

"We were working on that."

"*Working* on it?" Every muscle in Finn's body pulled taut. "Didn't *anyone* care about Nathan?"

Christie turned to Sylvie. "Sylv, are you really going to join his warrior shaman sect?"

Sylvie shrugged. "I made a promise. And the Black Scissors was human once, you're forgetting that."

"Well, you know what?" Christie retorted. "I'm pretty sure some of the *Fatas* were once human too."

"Don't let the demons hear you say that," Kevin warned.

"They're not demons." Finn watched as Kevin tucked the dagger into an inner pocket of his denim jacket. Remembering the missing blue-haired college student, she breathed out. "Is Tyson Follows one of the Black Scissors's people?"

"I don't know," Kevin said grudgingly. "I'll have to ask."

"If he is"—Christie looked around at everyone—"then we have another problem, don't we? Because Tyson Follows is missing."

MICAH GOVANNON WENT TO WORK that night at BrambleBerry Books. His existence in Fair Hollow had begun at the age of thirteen, when Jill Scarlet had rented out an apartment for him near the warehouse district, gotten him into high school, and assigned him a human guardian to pose as his father. She'd wanted Micah to experience a normal life. And he had . . . until his guardian had been murdered by a silver-haired beast called the *crom cu*. Micah had escaped into the Ghostlands, back to Jill Scarlet, to become a soldier. He'd returned, on an assignment, reconnecting with his friend Christie, to keep an eye on Finn Sullivan.

He was shelving books before closing when the bells above the door chimed faintly. He peered down the main aisle.

His blood iced when he glimpsed a shadow slinking across the floor, rising into a lean form. He whispered the heka Jill Scarlet had taught him, to make the unseen, seen. He kept his back against a wall of books and drew the stiletto knife he kept in his left boot.

A fist struck him in the head and he hit the floorboards. The stiletto was kicked from his fingers. Cursing his carelessness and trying to reason past the smashing pain in his skull, Micah spat blood from his mouth.

A voice casually said, "Isn't Finn working tonight, Micah?"

Micah lifted his head, glad he'd worn his contacts, and focused on the shadow figure circling him. He couldn't distinguish any facial features, but the voice . . .

"Micah? Are you listening?"

Micah scrambled up and lunged for the door.

He only registered the stab wound in one shoulder when the pain and shock of it made him collapse against a wall of books. He could feel blood slicking his back.

The figure crouched before him. It was dressed in black and there was only darkness beneath its hood. The figure said, "I wanted to speak with Finn, but I can't get anywhere near her without the Banríon's people catching a look at me. So, Micah, you can give Finn a message from me: *'Thank you for letting me out.'*"

Micah couldn't move as a hand glimmering with rings folded around his throat and a mouth descended over his in a vicious kiss.

CHRISTIE SCOWLED AT THE DEAD KINGS as he swung the door of his Mustang shut. The music emanating from the club made his skin itch. Outside, a small crowd had gathered. A girl in a frosty white party dress and white cat ears looked at him, her eyes reflecting silver.

Christie turned his back on her and strode toward BrambleBerry Books.

A guy in black, the hood of his jacket shadowing his face, slammed a shoulder into him in passing and continued on without an apology.

"Asshole." Christie pushed into the bookshop—

—and stared at the spattering of red on the hardwood floor. His stomach lurched up into his throat. He heard coughing, retching, in the back of the store. Ripping his cell phone from one pocket, he yelled, "Micah!"

He found Micah crouched against the bookshelves, bleeding and choking. Black butterflies flickered all around him, emerging from his mouth, one by one.

FINN DROVE JACK'S CAR back to the deserted cinema that had been Jack's home. She climbed over the sill into his apartment and switched on the lamp near the window. Although coming here was as painful as a punch to the heart, it was also comforting. Most of the time, she just curled up on his bed. Tonight, she drifted to sleep watching a magic lantern slowly spin the silhouettes of storybook figures across the walls.

She woke to the gentle drift of fingers across her jaw.

Jack, wearing jeans and a crown of velvety red roses, sat on the bed. The scars and tattoos that made it seem as if he'd been marked by some vicious, supernatural entity had returned. He said, "You're determined to do this, aren't you?"

She sat up and wound her arms around him. He didn't feel like a dream, all smooth muscles beneath cool skin that sent heat sharp as butterflies of glass and fire through her. His hair was heavy silk against her cheek as she pressed her face between his shoulder and neck. He whispered, "I won't be able to come to you much longer. This isn't really me."

"I know." She kissed him with lush determination.

After the kiss, he whispered, "Let me go, Finn."

She sat back on her heels. "You know I have a problem with that sort of thing."

Darkness tangled in his hair, inked around his eyes and mouth. She reached out as the shadows veiled his face, as his head elongated and darkened and became that of a jackal, its eyes blue and gray and sorrowing.

"No . . ." Her gaze dropped to the dagger in his hand as he said, "I have to return to what I was."

"Jack—don't—"

He pulled back, rose, and slipped out the window into a night forest. Finn lunged toward the window—

—which erupted into a cloud of huge black butterflies with white skull patterns shimmering on their backs.

Finn flinched awake on Jack's bed. A dark figure was crouched on the windowsill. *Jack.* She kept very still as Jack gazed back at her, his face shadowed by the hood of his long coat. His eyes were frosted silver and regarded her as if she was a stranger.

She blinked and he was gone. She thought, *Am I awake?*

DRAKE'S CHAPEL NOW BELONGED to the wilder Fatas, the ones who had been Jack's comrades. One of them, Atheno, had betrayed Jack in the Ghostlands. Finn didn't trust any of them. But, again, desperation didn't leave her with any alternative.

As she approached the chapel supposedly built at the command of Francis Drake, Queen Elizabeth the First's notorious sea commander, she let the light from her electric lantern glide across the fanciful ship engraved in stone over the doors. Inside, a marble head crowned with ivy and tin stars sat atop the altar. Finn's light illuminated occult graffiti, the brooding stone angel in one corner, a tumor of pale toadstools flourishing on a wooden beam.

This third attempt would work. It *had* to. That dream of Jack, . . . it had been so real . . .

She didn't hear them. She just became *aware* of them. Rising, she pushed back the hood of her jacket as three silhouettes appeared on the chapel's threshold.

"Serafina." Aurora Sae, a golden nymph in a filmy black gown, walked in and took Finn's hands in her own. "You look so serious. Don't be afraid."

"She should be afraid." The Fata boy with long black hair and a pretty face rubbed his fingernails across the tentacle-writhing Cthulu image on his T-shirt. He went by the Shakespearean name of Black Apple.

"She's got nothing to fear." The tallest of the trio spoke gallantly, scarlet hair sweeping across his shoulders. His Victorian greatcoat billowed around a dark blue suit. "She's a queen killer and a wolf slayer."

Finn unslung her backpack. "Farouche." When she spoke his name, he inhaled deeply, as if with pain or pleasure. "You said to bring objects not to be found in the sea—"

Headlights blazed an uncanny trail of light through the chapel and Aurora Sae gripped Finn's hand. "Come on then, Serafina. Let's see if the ocean will let you enter Annwyn and fetch back our Jack."

Their faith in her was disturbing, but encouraging. As Finn stepped out of the chapel with the three Fatas, she felt as if she'd wandered back into the Ghost-lands. A black Model T straight out of a gangster film had halted on the dirt road leading to the chapel. The car's interior lights were on, revealing the water and snails that streaked the windows—on the inside. Beyond the glass, in the backseat, Finn could see a woman's profile, her upswept golden hair adorned with starfish and tiny crabs. The woman slowly turned her head. Her ruby lips curved. Her eyes weren't silver, but dark and cold.

A young man in a black chauffeur's uniform stepped out from behind the wheel, his greenish hair dripping water. His eyes were also black. He opened the back door and assisted the golden-haired woman out of the car. Her coral blue dress eddied as if she were under water. "Queen killer." Amphitrite the elemental tilted her head. She was smiling. Finn hated it when they smiled. "I was intrigued. A mortal girl who has slain two Fatas wants to enter the realm of the dead. And what shall you bargain with?"

Finn reached into her backpack and pulled out a shadow box pinned with the butterflies she and Lily had collected over the years—birdwings, white admirals, tiger swallowtails, and owl eyes. The Amphitrite accepted the shadow box, caressing it. She handed the box to her chauffeur. "Very nice. What else?"

Finn drew from her backpack a box of carved teakwood. The Amphitrite accepted this box also, lifting the lid, tenderly touching what was inside of it: a bone-handled knife and an undying morning glory. Her words lost their lilting regality as her hair began to writhe like golden snakes. "This is all that is left of him? My Leander?"

Finn remembered Leander telling her how this sea witch had transformed him into a Jack in San Francisco. "Yes."

Amphitrite closed the box and raised her black gaze to Finn's. "You killed the Wolf who murdered my Leander. In return, I am going to do you a favor. I am not giving you the way into Annwyn, Serafina Sullivan." At Finn's startle, she smiled briefly. "Don't worry. I know your name, but you didn't give it to me, so I've no power over you." She paused, looking at Finn seriously. "If I led you into Annwyn, I would be destroying you. That isn't how I reward those who please me. Forget your Jack. Find a mortal boy who will worship you, and live."

The Amphitrite turned and walked back toward her Model T aquarium.

For a moment, Finn could only stare after her. Then she found her voice, and it was cold and angry. "How is that a *favor?*—And it's your fault Leander is dead, because *you* killed him in the first place."

Farouche swore in Gaelic. Black Apple and Aurora Sae tensed.

The mermaid and her chauffeur slowly turned, the chauffeur baring a mouthful of sharp teeth.

"Apologize," Black Apple whispered frantically. *"Apologize!"*

Amphitrite looked at her chauffeur. He strode toward Finn. Finn cursed. She hadn't dared bring anything of silver or iron, heeding Sionnach Ri's previous warning that such things would keep the elementals away.

Farouche lunged at the shark-eyed Fata chauffeur, who flung him aside and backhanded Aurora Sae. Black Apple got a boot in the stomach.

Then the chauffeur reached Finn. She stumbled back as he raised a hand, the nails black and curved—

The silver dart that burrowed through the chauffeur's palm—Finn saw it briefly, clearly—was cast into the shape of a sleek crow. As the chauffeur yowled and curled over, Finn lifted a disbelieving gaze to the figure silhouetted by the headlights of a Mustang that had appeared on the dirt road.

Sylvie, wearing a silver slip dress, holding a small crossbow in one hand and a wooden knife in the other, said in an absurdly light tone, "I think you better swim away."

Amphitrite fastened her attention on Sylvie, her eyes flaring silver in the headlights. "I see," she said. Then she began to sing.

The mermaid's voice was as poignant and piercing as a surgical scalpel in the brain. The words flowed around Finn like small, biting things. Sylvie collapsed, curled over, and retched up water. Finn felt her own lungs filling with a tide of liquid and she dropped to her knees. *No. I won't die this way. I won't . . .*

"How fitting you should drown in front of a place built by a son of La Mer." Amphitrite turned and walked toward her car.

"Stop!" Aurora Sae held Finn as she clawed at the ground and vomited water. "The Banríon—"

"I am not under the Banríon's rule." Amphitrite paused as her chauffeur grabbed Black Apple by the hair and bent over the Fata boy as if he were a luscious meal.

Sylvie, still retching, flung the elder wood knife to Finn. It landed in the clover before her, but Finn's vision was darkening even as her fingers scrabbled in the dirt for the hilt.

A car door slammed. Finn blurrily focused on another figure standing before the headlights, saw an arm scrawled with black words reach out, heard a voice that cut through the siren song:

> *Are those her ribs through which the sun*
> *Did peer, as through a grate?*
> *And is that woman all her crew?*
> *Is that a Death?*

"Bloody Coleridge," Amphitrite spat.

The spell broke. Finn gasped a lungful of air, saw Farouche grab Sylvie and yank her toward the chapel. The chauffeur had let go of Black Apple and had his hands over his ears against the poetry.

As Aurora Sae pulled Finn to her feet and toward Drake's Chapel, Christie, his skin patterned with heka, faced Amphitrite. Finn, afraid for him, saw Amphitrite's beautiful face become a white mask with two hollows for eyes and one for a mouth.

Finn yanked her hand from Aurora Sae's. "*Christie!*"

Then Amphitrite and the chauffeur turned and walked away. The chauffeur opened the passenger door of the Model T while Amphitrite sought to keep the tatters of her human semblance around her. Then the mermaid was sliding into her mobile aquarium and the chauffeur was behind the wheel. As the Model T drove off, Amphitrite, not much more than a skeleton webbed in mollusks and seaweed, turned her skull-like head to glare at Finn.

Christie collapsed into the clover. Finn and Sylvie dashed to him. He raised his head. His eyes were clear again, and the inky words had faded from his skin. "I'm okay," he mumbled.

They could have died tonight. Anguished and guilty, Finn whispered, "Why did you follow me—"

Sylvie turned on her. "Don't you *dare*! You came here to bargain with that sea hag to get into the land of the dead, didn't you? *Didn't you?*"

"See here," Farouche began.

"*You* shut up." Sylvie pointed at the Fata, who bowed his head. She swung around on Finn again, almost in tears. "You're selfish, Finn. Goddamn selfish."

Finn helped Christie sit up. Her throat and lungs felt raw. She'd missed a third chance, and it had ended in this.

"Are you listening to me?" Sylvie was still in a temper.

"Ladies." Christie sounded as if he'd lost a boxing match. "We survived. And, yes, Finn went looking for trouble, as usual, but something's come looking for *us*. Micah was attacked tonight."

Finn sank back on her heels and listened as Christie told her how he'd found Micah coughing up butterflies, how Micah had told him about the dark figure that had kissed the butterflies into him. "And he never saw a face." Christie paused. Then he squinted at Sylvie and repeated the words she'd spoken to Amphitrite: "*I think you better swim away?*"

Sylvie shrugged, her anger fading. "It sounded epic in my head."

Finn thought about Moth's shadow man. A chill whispered across her skin. Her heart still racing from the confrontation, Finn told them, "We've got to go to Phouka."

"Micah and Aubrey are parked just down the road." Christie let them help him to his feet. "Now just drag me over to my car. My legs don't seem to be working."

Finn told herself she should be grateful they had all survived, and she should not be thinking she had only one more chance to get Jack out of the underworld.

I BEAT A MERMAID TONIGHT. Christie felt triumphant and grim at the same time. As Finn and Sylvie hauled him toward his Mustang, he looked over one shoulder at Drake's Chapel.

And saw Jack standing in front of it.

Christie yelped and stumbled and his two friends looked at him. He glanced back at the chapel again, saw nothing.

So. He was hallucinating now.

CHAPTER 4

But only a host of phantom listeners
That dwelt in the lone house then
Stood listening in the quiet of the moonlight
To that voice from the world of men.

—"THE LISTENERS," WALTER DE LA MARE

Sylvie had been on her way to a party with her acting class at the Marlowe Theater when Christie had called her about Micah's attack. To locate Finn, Christie had used a bit of his newfound witch skills on a map of Fair Hollow he'd bought at the gas station.

So all the secrets are out, Finn thought as Christie drove his Mustang past the creeper-laden gates of Tirnagoth. They were followed by Micah and Aubrey driving Micah's pickup truck. *Sylvie has joined the Black Scissors and Christie has been learning how to use words as literal weapons.* As Tirnagoth appeared through the trees, a dragon of apprehension twisted through Finn's guts. "Why is it dark?" she asked.

Tirnagoth, usually glowing with the ominous art nouveau elegance of a set design from a Dario Argento movie, was boarded up and silent. Finn heard only the eerily remote chirping of crickets.

The two vehicles halted in the driveway. Finn, getting out of Christie's Mustang, glanced at Micah as he jumped down from the pickup. He looked pale, his face bruised. The stab wound in his shoulder, he'd claimed, wasn't deep, just a slice. "Something's wrong," he said, his voice hoarse.

The five of them stood gazing warily at the hotel. Christie whispered, "It was like this last time. Like it's hesitating. Like there's a glitch."

The glamour appeared as if a switch had been flipped; the boards over the windows disintegrated in shadowy flakes from radiant stained glass. Interior light cascaded over an exterior free of age or brutalization by the weather. The landscaping wavered into a garden with classical statues and tea lights and manicured hedges. As music drifted from the courtyard, the doors of Tirnagoth opened and Absalom Askew stepped out. "Power outage," he told them. His dark orange hair was tangled around his face and his eyes were their semiordinary amber hue. As he led them into the lobby, the odor of damp stone and fungus lingered.

"I really don't see why I need to be here," Aubrey muttered mutinously. "I mean, I thought we were taking Mic to the hospital and then we end up parked on the side of the road while Christie and Sylvie play monster slayer, and then we come—"

"Aubrey." Absalom spun around and became something predatory. "Despite your declaration to sever all connections with us, I'm going to have to advise you not to do that at this particular time. *You are not safe alone.*"

Aubrey looked extremely unhappy. "You saying you need to protect us from something?" His jaw set. "You didn't protect Hester."

Absalom turned and continued leading them across the lobby, where a young man in a black suit, his hair spiky with feathers, twirled a dagger. Two crimson-haired girls in matching white gowns perched on a love seat next to him, holding hands. Everywhere, the shadows seemed to cling or drip or stain. The swooping mahogany staircase was furred with moss. Toadstools had sprouted like leprosy over the face of the wooden nymph on the left side of the staircase. The other nymph had lost her face to rot. Gazing down a gloom-and-creeper-infested corridor, Finn saw broken windows and a statue's hand discarded on the cracked marble. She flinched when the hand scuttled away into the dark.

"Don't look too closely at the shadows." Phouka, a silhouette in a black dress and boots, appeared at the top of the stairs. Her eyes glowed as she moved down.

"Phouka." Finn felt as if the shadows were clinging to her skin. "What's happening?"

"Our power is waning."

The sound of something large being dragged across the floor above made Finn's hair stand on end. Absalom looked thoughtfully up at the ceiling. The chandelier swayed. "We used to be able to hold back the haunts in this place."

"Come." Phouka led her guests through the lobby. She shoved open a set of warped wooden doors, revealing an antiquated parlor scattered with moth-eaten furniture, taxidermied animals, heavy drapes, and candles in Tibetan lanterns. There was a different sort of chill in the air, the kind of cold Finn associated with otherworldliness.

A column of darkness appeared in the parlor's center. The air rippled. There was a soft pulse as something began to manifest, first, as pale hands and black hair, then, as a figure in white suede stitched with patterns of red and black birds. Dead Bird stepped into existence.

Phouka said, "Show them."

Dead Bird walked to the pedestal table near Finn and set down a slim knife. It was a pretty antique, its bronze pommel an intricately crafted leopard, the bronze on its blade flaking away to reveal the silver concealed beneath.

There was blood on it.

"I found it"—Dead Bird sounded as genuinely compassionate as any real person—"in what was left of Sylph Dragonfly."

Sylvie cried out and clapped her hands over her mouth. Christie stared at Phouka, then hung his head, his hands clenching.

Finn, dread clogging her throat, whispered, "That's a misericorde. It belonged to Jack."

"*Who did it?*" Christie raised his head. Something black snaked through his eyes. "Who killed the Dragonfly?"

"We don't know." Phouka's statement carried with it a menace that sparked the same apprehension in Finn as the misericorde. Finn sat down. Her friends took seats as well.

"Would anyone like alcohol?" Absalom opened an ebony cabinet filled with liquor bottles.

"Are you sure she's dead?" Christie asked faintly.

"Yes." It was Dead Bird who answered, still with that gentleness an otherworldly being shouldn't have been able to manage. "And she bled for someone."

Finn thought of Moth warning her that something had escaped the Wolf's house. But his distrust of Phouka and Absalom made her reluctant to say anything. She knotted her hands together, digging her nails into her skin.

Absalom handed out glasses of liquor. Aubrey accepted one, narrowed his eyes at Absalom, then drank down most of it.

Christie, his voice taut, said, "Who do you *suspect* would kill the Dragonfly?"

"No suspect." Phouka was solemn. "Micah, you remember nothing of your attacker?"

"He was a shadow." Micah glanced at Finn, his eyes dark. There was a smear of dried blood at one corner of his mouth. "He said to tell Finn, 'Thank you for letting me out.'"

Finn wanted to hit something, to scream. This couldn't be happening, not now.

Dead Bird was watching Micah. His eyes narrowed when the young man coughed and cleared his throat. Gently, Dead Bird pronounced, "You are wounded."

Micah shrugged, winced. "It's nothing."

"I saw Moth last night." Finn reluctantly spoke up. "He told me something escaped Sombrus when he returned."

Phouka and Absalom went very still. Sylvie said, "The wolves—"

"He killed them all. He was trapped in that house with them and had to fight for his life." Finn straightened and met Phouka's silver gaze. "But something got out."

"I wonder what that might be?" Absalom exchanged a long, knowing look with Phouka.

"He doesn't know." Finn glanced at Micah, worried for him.

"Well." There was a gentle threat in Absalom's voice. "We'll have to have a talk with Moth, won't we?"

"Excuse me." Aubrey raised his cell phone. He was glaring at Absalom. "I think now's the perfect time for everyone to hear this. I was stupid wasted when Hester called me that night. I only checked my messages after she disappeared, when I was home. And I've been saving this." He pushed play.

No one moved as a dead girl spoke out of his phone: "Hey, Aub. You guys *have* to come back here. I'm in StarDust and it's all new inside. It's *amazing*. I found this key and it got me in—I'm going to video this—Absalom? What are you doing here—" Hester's voice cut off and Finn thought, *That's when her phone died.*

Aubrey lowered the phone. Shocked silence followed.

Phouka rose and stared at Absalom, fury in every line of her body. "Tell me, Absalom. Tell me you didn't lure one of the blessed into the Ghostlands, just to get the Black Scissors's key to Finn and Jack in the Wolf's house."

"I couldn't go." Absalom had drawn back into the shadows. "And that key saved their lives, as I knew it would. As Anna had oracled, to me, that it would. Christopher and Sylvie botched it by dropping it."

Christie shoved to his feet and Finn saw words inking across his skin like black snakes. "Hester's *dead because of you*—"

"Christie." Sylvie reached for him.

Micah coughed—a violent, liquid sound. Finn glanced at him in concern, then alarm—Micah had spit blood onto the floor. Fluttering within the blood was a black butterfly with a white skull pattern on its back.

Christie and Aubrey scrambled up. Finn rose and took a step toward Micah, but Sylvie yanked her back. Dead Bird, the lantern light gilding his hawk-nosed profile, sprang forward and caught Micah as he collapsed with a cough that seemed to rip the lining from his lungs.

Finn stood frozen as Dead Bird laid Micah on the floor and placed one hand over his face. The lights and the false glamour of the parlor flickered. Micah convulsed as the *Marbh ean* drew his hand back, pulling a sticky web of darkness from the young man's mouth.

A wind slammed open the windowpanes and extinguished the candles. Darkness descended. Finn could see the silhouettes of her friends, but the three Fatas were nothing but black shapes.

Then the lights came back on and the glamour returned and Phouka raised her head, her eyes pure silver, as if she'd made a great effort to reestablish the illusion of luxury.

Dead Bird was gone. Micah was sitting up, pale and bruise-eyed, but breathing normally and clutching his chest. He convulsed with a shudder and accepted the hand Christie held out to him.

Phouka crushed the black butterfly beneath her heel as Finn wondered, with a deep dread, what had come to Fair Hollow.

❖ ❖ ❖

CLAUDETTE TREDESCANT, her blond hair in a ponytail, didn't notice the figure shambling after her and her two friends as they walked away from the movie theater.

"You won't get her." The voice made the shambling figure turn with a snarl, hiding his knife in his dirty coat. His eyes slitted beneath the pale hair veiling his face as a golden girl in formfitting black velvet stepped before him. She continued, "Finn Sullivan's friends travel in packs now."

"Jill," he grated. "I remember you. The *Damh Ridire*'s bitch."

"I'm Giselle." She glided close to him, smiling, unafraid. She wrinkled her nose. "You look terrible. Who made you mortal? Never mind. Do you want to die? Again?"

CHAPTER 5

Nature itself has a memory: There is some indefinable psychic element in the earth's atmosphere upon which all human and physical actions or phenomena are photographed or impressed.
—The Fairy-Faith in Celtic Countries,
W. Y. Evans-Wentz

Finn had developed a fervent appreciation for the comforts of home—just the sight of sunlight striking the hardwood floors was soothing. Drinking tea in the kitchen at night. Climbing onto the house's widow's walk with Lily to talk under the stars.

But she'd begun to notice—and worry about—the shadows that seemed to have increased in the house. The mold that grew too quickly on the bathroom tiles. The way food went bad even in the new fridge. She thought of the Dragonfly being murdered. Of Moth's desperation. The attack on Micah. Finn hadn't dreamed of Jack last night, but of her mother walking toward her in a field of daisies. In the dream, Finn had felt a radiant relief and joy that her mother wasn't dead.

Finn now stood in the front parlor, considering all that she and Lily had been through.

When one of her mother's paintings clattered to the floor, she flinched.

Lily strode past her and picked up the painting, a pretty watercolor of a girl with birds tangled in her hair—it had always been one of Finn's favorites. Then Lily tugged away the splintered frame and began peeling the canvas from its stretchers.

"Lily, what are you doing?" Finn protested.

"Look." Lily separated two canvases stapled together and a piece of yellowed paper fluttered to the floor. Lily carefully set the painting aside. She lifted the paper and held it out to Finn.

Finn took it, read, "' . . . *just a way of comforting ourselves, a simplification of the universe. Science is our mythology. It isn't theirs.'* It's Mom's handwriting . . ."

"Last night, the painting in my room fell and a paper dropped out—also written by Mom, about shadows and black matter."

"Why would she hide these?" Finn whispered.

"She thought she was losing her mind." Lily sank onto the sofa. "But she knew. She knew about *them*."

Finn, clutching the paper, sat beside Lily. Lily said, "Are you really surprised? They've always been with our family. Ever since they took Ambrose Cassandro. Then Bronwyn Rose Govannon. And then there's Micah—the Fatas stalk other families besides the blessed."

A yell from their father had them jumping up and running to the family room, where their dad stood staring at their mother's watercolors of ornate boys and girls gone askew on the walls.

Lily turned in place.

Their dad looked extremely spooked as he approached one of the larger paintings and straightened it.

"It's just the air blowing through the house, Da," Finn said. She exchanged a glance with Lily. *Gran Rose is trying to tell us something.*

Sean Sullivan adjusted the painting of a green-haired girl holding a frog crowned with little red hearts. As he sat down to study the picture, Finn walked to a painting of a boy with a clockwork heart in his chest and straightened it.

"Just the wind," their dad murmured, as if he didn't believe it.

FINN STEPPED INTO HECATE'S ATTIC and found the shop owners' daughter, Anna Weaver, posing before a full-length mirror, adjusting on her head a little gold crown with a red heart in the middle. She wore a summer dress.

"Anna, you look lovely." Hoping Anna wouldn't ask questions, Finn began collecting purchases for her fourth summoning.

"Thanks. Are you coming to the play?" Anna wandered to the counter and leaned against it, watching Finn.

"What play?"

"*The Tale of Cupid and Psyche*. I'm playing Psyche. Mr. Fairchild wrote it for the summer pageant in the park."

"And who's playing Cupid?" Finn placed two sky blue candles into her basket.

"Aubrey's youngest brother." Anna set the wreath on a stone head with shells in its hair. "Are you buying all that?" She peered into Finn's basket, her wheat-bright hair falling forward over her eyes. "Are you summoning something?"

"No." But Anna's grave expression told Finn the girl knew she was lying.

ROSY LIGHT FROM THE SETTING SUN crossed Anna's face as she watched Finn walk away from the shop.

She thought, turning away from the window, *She's going to the land of the dead.*

As the sunlight faded into violet, Anna rearranged the pewter gods and wooden gnomes in the window. She added to the display Tibetan wind chimes, a book on flower folklore, and a print of fairies at tea. Then she went into the stockroom for more candles.

When she stepped from the stockroom and saw the girl standing near the glass case of jewelry and draping a chain with a pendant shaped like a stag's head around her neck, Anna said, "You can take the pendant. I won't tell."

The girl stepped into the dappled light cast by a stained-glass lamp. She wore a silky purple shift and ballet slippers. Her golden hair was twisted up. She looked like a *Seventeen* model and moved like an assassin.

Anna took a step back.

"I'll just take it." The young woman prowled toward Anna. "And maybe I'll take you as well."

"You're a Jill. I'll tell you your fortune," Anna said, hoping her fear wasn't showing.

"I'm not alive. I don't have a fortune." And then the Jill sat on a table, crossing her legs. The scent of daffodils drifted from her skin. "Okay. Tell me my fortune."

Anna moved to the table and opened the box of Tarot cards. "Tell me your name first."

"Names have power. But you're just a kid. Mine's Giselle." She indicated Anna's fancy dress and crown. "What are you doing, running around, dressed like that?"

"This represents you." Anna set down a card. The illustration was of an ebony figure wielding a glass sword. "That's the queen of Swords. This card that crosses you is the Dragon. This, below, is your past."

The Jill leaned forward. Cold breathed from her as she tapped the Dragon. "What does this one mean?"

"The Dragon means guardian. In reversal, it means malice."

The Jill's mercury eyes became slits. "Go on."

Hoping her mom or dad wouldn't come down into the shop, Anna continued setting cards on the table. "This means death—"

"I'm already dead." The Jill frowned down at the Tarot pattern. She produced an ivory-handled dagger from somewhere behind her back and stabbed it into the card illustrated with the hooded figure holding a rose. Anna flinched. The cards were old, and they had personalities—she almost felt the illustrated figure gasp as the blade went through it.

The Jill slid to her feet, pulled the dagger free of the card and the table, and twirled it. From a hidden sheath, she produced another knife, this one resembling a glass needle with a screaming figure as the hilt. "No more games. I'm supposed to tell you 'You know too much'"—she raised the glass dagger teasingly, pointing the tip at Anna, as if it was a wand—"and prick you in both eyes; don't worry, it won't blind you physically. It'll just stop you from seeing things little girls shouldn't."

Anna stepped back, clutching the rest of the cards to her as if they were babies. She said shakily, "How can that not blind me?"

"Why does the red-haired devil guard you?"

"Absalom's not a devil. Stop it."

Giselle smiled. "Why don't you tell me about Sylvie Whitethorn and Christopher Hart?"

The bells above the door chimed faintly, and Kevin Gilchriste entered. The Jill swiveled around, concealing both knives. Brightly, she said, "We're closed."

"Then why are *you* here?" Kevin's eyes narrowed, and he didn't look like a movie star then. Tension crackled in the air.

The Jill cursed beneath her breath, and her now empty hands clenched at her sides. "Fine. I'm leaving." She kept her gaze on Kevin until she strode past him, out the door. The bells didn't chime with her passing.

Anna breathed out. Kevin waited until the night had swallowed the Jill. Then he said, "I saw her slink in. I could smell flowers a block away. You okay?"

Anna nodded once. "Usually, there's someone here."

"Shall I take down the welcome sign?"

"Please."

FINN, WALKING HOME FROM HECATE'S ATTIC, felt something brush against her cheek, and flinched, and stared at the origami moth that fluttered before her in a spiraling dance.

The moth swept across her lips. She remembered how Moth would change when his insect form received a kiss. She stood very still in the dusk as the paper moth did another dance before her, then glided down Main Street. She followed it past the little old church and a tree-snarled lot, to a deserted courtyard between the library and a bank building.

A hand snatched the paper moth from the air and a figure stepped from the shadows.

"Moth . . ." She saw the bruise shadowing half of his face and her stomach turned. She wanted to run to him. "What happened to you?"

He crumpled the origami moth and tossed it away. "The thing from Sombrus. Now it's hunting me. It's more than a shadow . . ."

"Sylph Dragonfly was murdered. Micah Govannon was attacked last night."

Moth cursed and sank down onto a bench. Finn moved toward him. "You should go to Phouka, Moth."

"No." He rose, reeling a little. "How are you going to get Jack out of Annwyn? Don't deny it. I know you're trying."

She lifted her head sharply. "Tonight's my last chance. You're hurt—"

"It's nothing that won't heal." His mouth twisted. "I'm not human, remember? You still have that, I see." He pointed at the bracelet of silver charms around her right wrist. "How is Lily?"

"She's adjusting." Finn touched the bracelet, remembering that he had once worn it.

The expression on his face was stark. "You trust me? Have you told anyone about me?"

She tensed. "Lily. Christie and Sylvie. Phouka. I *had* to."

"Absalom?" He was taut.

She whispered, "Yes."

He moved quickly and caught her hand, his fingers strong and cool around her wrist.

It blindsided her, the vision. She heard shouting and screaming, saw a fire-lit stone hall. There were bodies. There was blood. And there was Moth, in armor splashed with crimson, his hair golden, striding after a fleeing girl in a green gown.

Reality blinked back. She staggered, fought an urge to be sick, and found herself alone with the origami moth on the ground at her feet.

PHOUKA HAD ASKED CHRISTIE TO FETCH A MIRROR, and he'd asked Micah to accompany him. He was having a hard time concentrating on the purchase, worrying instead about Finn. He knew she was going to attempt getting into Annwyn again.

"Why does the Banríon need this mirror?" Micah glanced at him as they wandered through the enormous salvage warehouse on Worthingmore Road.

"She wouldn't tell me. She's being mysterious."

"You're thinking about Finn and what she's attempting."

"What if she's trying to summon another demon to get into the underworld with the help of Bee Vomit and Snake Spit and the rest of Jack's Fata tribe?"

"Christie . . . She wants to save Jack."

"She can't. He's gone."

"Annwyn is a real place."

"You only believe that because those people raised you with that belief."

"Those people." Micah frowned. "The Banríon's one of those people."

Aware of the shadows lurking behind architectural remnants, taxidermied beasts, and furniture that looked as though it had come from haunted houses, Christie grimly said, "Phouka's different."

"No, she's not." Micah strode toward a large mirror in a sunburst frame decorated with tiny golden mice. "The Banríon said a mirror framed in mice and suns, right?" He examined the tag and read, "'Nineteen seventeen. SunStone Mansion.'"

"That's the one. How'd you do that?"

"Intuition and a fine taste in furniture."

Christie, relieved, surveyed the warehouse for a salesperson—

—and inhaled sharply when he saw a figure standing in the mirror, its dark hair drifting. A girl's voice echoed from the silver: *"Red blood out, black blood in."*

"Sylph . . ." He couldn't move, staring into the mirror. "Mic, do you see—"

"Yes," Micah whispered. "The Dragonfly."

The presence in the mirror eddied as if it were submerged in water. Christie reached out, then let his hand fall.

"With these words, I do bid, that the malevolence near is no longer hid." The voice was sepulchral, familiar, and caught at Christie's throat. He cried, "Sylph! Who killed—"

Something popped like static in the air. A music box tune wound discordantly through the warehouse, and a young woman stepped from among the old doors and rescued statues. She looked like a storybook fairy in a small dress of filmy purple. Her golden hair was coiled up with jeweled pins.

"Christie Hart." The girl smiled sweetly as she sauntered toward them, her ballet slippers soundless on the concrete. Cold and the spice of fresh flowers preceded her. "You remember David Ryder, don't you? You and your bitch girls caused his death."

"Jill." Micah pulled a silver blade from his hoodie.

"My name is Giselle."

Micah sighed. "I hate hitting girls."

"I won't tell," Christie said. "Distract her for a sec?"

As the Jill lunged at them, Micah met her, slamming an arm up to keep her dagger from his throat. The two crashed against a dining set and rolled across the table.

Christie glimpsed a bronze stag head set on a cabinet. Something old and primal slithered through him, as seductive as Fata elixir. The words spilled out of him: *"He that has fallen, is now of the dead, proud of spirit, a crown on his head, I call his likeness into bronze and plastic instead."*

Micah smashed Giselle into a mirror. She snarled, recovered, and sliced off a lock of his hair. Christie finished speaking and felt power move through him like a lightning bolt. *What have I done?*

A man's voice echoed through the warehouse. Giselle twisted around. "*David . . .*"

Christie grabbed Micah's arm and dragged him back. A large silhouette was gliding toward Giselle, who whispered, "David . . . ?"

"What did you do?" Micah said through gritted teeth.

"Created a distraction," Christie muttered. "Help me with the mirror."

His gaze fixed on the Jill, Micah heaved the mirror up with Christie and they backed away toward the exit.

Christie saw the Jill sliding her arms around a thing with a statue's legs, the torso and arms of a mannequin, and a bronze stag's head. It was a thing he'd created from the salvage around them, an illusion of David Ryder that would fall apart the second Christie was no longer near.

"Let's get out of here."

"SYLV, ARE YOU EVEN LISTENING TO ME?"

Sylvie was only half listening to Aubrey as they strolled away from the coffeehouse where they'd stopped for caffeine after picking up a weird mirror from the abandoned house called MoonGlass—the mirror, its tarnished surface surrounded by a silver frame of skeletons and naked women, was now lodged in the back of Aubrey's Camry.

Now she halted. A group of people stood on a corner near the former Excelsior Hotel, which was under construction. The strangers seemed to be of an eerie black-and-white luminosity, their skin pale as paper. They wore suits and dresses straight out of the Roaring Twenties. They were . . . wrong. "Aubrey."

"I see them." Aubrey pulled her back. The Marlowe Theater had just let out its early evening crowds, a contrast to the silent group near the closed hotel. One of the men in that ghostly group turned his head, revealing eyes like burned-out hollows. Aubrey breathed out, "Are they gho—"

"Don't say that word."

Aubrey stared at her. "Are you afraid of gh—"

He broke off because two definite Fata creatures were striding toward them. The girl, her red hair in spiky knots, had the image of a butterfly painted across her lips. Her companion's blue-dyed hair was swept from a face Sylvie had recently seen above the word *Missing.*

"Tyson Follows." Sylvie felt the queasiness of another reality warring with her own.

"Hey, Tyson." Aubrey smiled with his usual cluelessness. "They're looking for you, man—"

Tyson tilted his head and silver ghosted his eyes. The red-haired girl, oozing glamour, moved forward, her filmy baby-doll dress clinging to her body as she parted her painted lips and cooed, "Pretty boy. Pretty girl."

Sylvie had been under the spell of a ganconer before and perhaps was now immune because she barked, "Back off!" She grabbed Aubrey's hand, glad the Marlowe's crowd was still dispersing around them. She continued to feel a grave-yard chill from the Excelsior Hotel behind them.

While reaching beneath the back of her tunic shirt for the dagger sheathed there, she said casually, "So, Tyson, unless you've suddenly begun using jasmine body wash from Bath and Body Works, I think that overwhelming smell might be from the flowers stitched up inside of you."

Tyson grinned. "I'm faster. Stronger."

Sylvie closed her fingers around the dagger behind her back. "Who did it to you?"

"You think I'm going to tell?"

Sylvie glanced at the Fata girl. "They lie, Tyson. She's Unseelie, one of the bad ones—"

"To *you*, maybe." Tyson shrugged. He slid an arm through the crook of the girl ganconer's. "Let's go, Ash. Look out, little crow girl—maybe *you'll* be get-ting stitched up next."

Sylvie stood still as the Jack and the Fata girl disappeared around a corner. Aubrey said carefully, "Sylv, you're going to have to tell Phouka about this."

"Who *did* that to him, Aub?" Sylvie's stomach curdled. She reluctantly turned toward the Excelsior Hotel. The ghostly people were gone.

"Something's wrong," she said softly, surveying the night street. "Something's really wrong."

FINN HALTED AT THE DOOR to Lily's room and frowned at the draft that seeped from the crack beneath the door.

She stepped in and switched on a lamp. The curtains drifted around the open windows. The chimes hanging over one window clinked softly. She approached the mirror, reaching out to touch the tarnish streak in the glass. Above the mirror, on the wall, was a small black stain.

Finn found other blots of mold—behind the headboard, on the hardwood floor. When she turned on the bathroom light, she saw another tarnished mirror and black staining the shower tiles.

She walked to one of her mom's paintings, Lily's favorite: an autumn-haired youth with leaves in his hair, cradling a bird's nest with a ruby heart in it. Lily had shown her more journal pages she'd found in the paintings, their mom's secretive writings, but Finn hadn't been able to read them yet. She couldn't face the evidence of her mom, intelligent and artsy, believing she'd lost her mind.

The doorbell rang. Her da called up to her. She ran to her room, grabbed her backpack, and hurried down the stairs. Her da stood at the door, looking wary and worried. "There's a boy wearing an eye patch asking for you."

Finn straightened her shoulders and tried to appear casual. "That's Eammon. He's a friend of Anna's. See you later, alligator."

She stepped onto the porch and closed the door behind her. Bottle the Rook—Eammon Tirnagoth—was seated on the veranda railing, fair hair drifting over his face and the black patch over his left eye. "Em and Victor are waiting in the car." He nodded to a black Corvair at the curb.

Finn experienced a dizzying rush of anticipation and fear. Tonight, she would enter the land of the dead. Tonight, she would see Jack. She could feel it. "'Em and Victor'? What happened to 'Hip Hop' and 'Trip'?"

"We're no longer going by those names." Eammon slid from the railing, his face expressionless. "Are you ready?"

"I am."

"Finn." His voice was scratchy. "This is suicide."

"No. It's not. Because I'm coming back. And I'm bringing Jack with me."

He retreated a step. His one eye widened and, in it, she glimpsed something that disturbed her.

It was fear. Of her.

STARDUST STUDIOS WAS WHERE CALIBAN HAD DIED, where Christie and Sylvie had entered the Ghostlands—and Hester Kierney, too. It was where the spirit of Nathan Clare and the three ghost girls who had loved Jack had made their home. And it had been a gift from Malcolm Tirnagoth, the wealthy fool who had built the Tirnagoth Hotel, to his lovely wife in the 1920s.

The building resembled a giant glass birdcage, the glass now so misted with grime and dead leaves that only silhouettes could be seen of the objects within. The road and parking lot had been devastated by the roots of oaks and pines. Most of the silent films created here could no longer be found. And the actors who had appeared in them—Jack among them—had all met tragic ends.

Victor Tirnagoth, who had once been Trip Rook, unlocked StarDust with a key shaped like a crow and reluctantly nudged open the door. Stale air swept out. The gloom within seemed a solid thing, cobwebby and dank. As they entered, Finn and Eammon lifted their electric lanterns, shedding light on the Egyptian art deco furniture, film equipment that was rusting and caked with dust. The stage, with its pillars topped by lotus-and-papyrus-scrolled capitals, was a cave of shadows. A chandelier of purple and yellow crystal shards hung from the glass ceiling like some fantastical arachnid.

"Why would an air elemental be here?" Finn set down her lantern. "Is it because it's a Way?"

Victor and Emily glanced at each other. Emily shrugged and pushed up her braided black-and-blond hair. "The elemental's name is Nyx. She was attached to our mother."

Their mother had been Nicollette Tirnagoth, the wife of the man who'd built the Tirnagoth Hotel.

Thunder rumbled in the near distance, disturbing the chandelier, which rattled gently. Finn's hands shook as she tugged the required objects from her backpack. Emily impatiently began to help her and they set the black candles in a circle on the floor with its mosaics of scarabs and Eyes of Horus. Eammon produced a small tin box and reverentially removed its contents—three yellowed molars. He placed the teeth in the middle of the circle with the raven feathers Finn had bought from the same taxidermist who'd sold her the freeze-dried possum.

Eammon handed Finn a black parchment fan, its ebony handle etched with authentic-looking hieroglyphics. Finn unfolded it as she began to walk around the circle of candles. The doors remained open, the night hissing with rain. She softly chanted, "Night has fallen, to cloak the air, to bring her forth, the mother of terror." She hadn't liked that last bit, but Victor had insisted it was just part of the ritual.

Eammon, crouched beside the circle of candles, drew another object from his backpack—a human skull—and set it within the candles.

Finn continued circling, waving the fan. Emily turned down the lanterns and only candlelight illuminated the studio.

When the skull began to spin, Finn halted. Darkness like a shimmering swathe of silk gushed in through the open doors, into the circle of candles, and whirled around the skull. An electric charge made the air crackle on Finn's tongue and shiver over her skin.

The candle flames exploded outward. Finn flung her arms up over her face. Victor swore.

Finn lowered her arms and stared at the circle of candles, which was empty. The skull was gone. Victor, Emily, and Eammon were staring beyond her, at the stage.

Her skin prickling, Finn turned.

Seated in a thronelike chair on the stage was a young woman with bobbed, black hair, her flapper's dress the color of a night sky sprinkled with stars. Her eyes, in circles of sooty kohl, had the sheen of crow wings. The pale glow of her skin made her look as if she'd just stepped out of a silent film.

Finn's gaze dropped to the skull in the woman's lap. She steeled herself and moved forward, her breath misting in the chill that accompanied the elemental.

The entity disguised as a starlet spoke: "I forgot what a *kick* it is to be called down." She rose, gazing slyly down at Finn. "What do you want, girl?"

"I want to enter Annwyn." Finn felt as if an alternate personality—older, stronger, cooler—was taking over.

"Call me Nyx." The creature smiled falsely. "Thank you for the gift. It's something I've always wanted." She brought the skull to one cheek and rubbed it against her skin. Her smile faded. She stared into the shadows beyond Finn, where the three Rooks stood. "Who is here with you?"

Finn didn't move. "Just friends."

"Did you fetch this?" The starlet raised the skull. "Or did they?"

Sensing something about to go very, very wrong, Finn desperately said, "Please show me the way to Annwyn. I've given you the skull—"

"This was a man I descended for." The young woman caressed the skull. "He called me from the air, from among my brothers and sisters. He was beautiful. He'd been a soldier. He was worth it. So I took a human shape. I made him rich. I cut three brats out of my belly for him."

Finn's brain processed this. She breathed, "You're their—"

"She was never our mother." Emily moved to Finn's side. "She only wanted our father. She possessed a poor girl named Nicollette. We were an unfortunate side effect."

Victor stepped to Finn's other side. "She's the one who made us sick."

Eammon came forward. "Reiko's the one who took us in, saved us by replacing us with glamoured corpses—to deceive *her*."

"I *died* in that body," Nyx snarled, clutching Malcolm Tirnagoth's skull against her breast.

"You deserved it!" Victor was tense. "You died of the same thing you tried to kill us with."

Finn turned on him. "If you knew what she was, why did you help m—"

"We didn't know for sure," Eammon explained, not looking away from the creature on the stage. "We weren't sure if it *was* something living inside the woman who was our mother."

"Like a parasite," Emily spat, and she drew two silver daggers from her coat as Victor unsheathed a long knife from his.

Finn backed away as the porcelain face of the creature on the stage cracked. The eyes sank into glittering holes.

"Nyx." Eammon's voice was low. "You killed our true mother." He flung a knife at Nyx. She howled and broke apart into a mass of darkness that seemed to condense into a monstrosity with the face and torso of a woman and the body of a giant bird, dark wings folded at its sides. Its eyes burned silver. Obsidian talons dug into the stage floor.

Finn whirled for the circle. She heard a terrible roar from behind her, the sound of the wooden floorboards ripping as the mother of terror launched herself at the three children who had lured her here to destroy her.

Finn rolled into the circle of candles and yanked out the silver dagger—this time, she'd risked bringing silver and elder wood. She traced the sigil she'd memorized onto the mosaic. It was an Egyptian symbol for protection, and it woke the wards in StarDust Studios, the ones Phouka had told her about, the ones Malcolm Tirnagoth had crafted against his wife when he began to realize what she was.

Relief swept through Finn when the candles righted themselves and the wicks burst into flames.

Emily screamed. Finn watched, her heart thundering, as the harpy, now a shifting darkness, sprang over the three figures. Victor was flung against a pillar. Emily fell beneath a swath of reptilian black. Eammon was drowned in darkness.

Finn, clutching the silver knife, reached for the carved blade of elder wood sheathed behind her back, beneath her fitted jacket. She blinked and Nyx was standing before her, in her starlet form, her eyes voids. Finn whispered, "I know how to end you."

The elemental raised one hand, the nails black claws—

Finn pointed at her with the silver dagger as the candle flames burst outward—

Emily, her black-and-blond braids whipping over her face, stabbed a silver blade into the thing that had pretended to be her mother as Eammon yanked Finn back, toward the exit.

Nyx whirled, grabbed Emily by the hair, and slammed her into a pillar. When Victor leaped at her, desperation on his face and a dagger in each hand, Nyx's talons glided across his throat. Blood arced across Emily's horrified face.

"No! *Stop!*" Finn tore away from Eammon, yanked the elder wood dagger from its sheath, and aimed it at the back of Nyx's head. The elemental swiveled and caught Finn's wrist in a grip that seemed to crack bone. Finn stared as Nyx's smile became a darkness spreading across her false face. Two porcelain teeth fell from her mouth, clicking to the floor.

A gleaming blade sliced through Nyx, and Finn was released. As she staggered back, Nyx swirled into a dark mass, a substance that lashed against Finn. She tasted blood in her mouth.

The colossal darkness that was Nyx screamed, swept Victor up, and tore past the doors, into the night.

Shaking, Finn met the cool, green gaze of Moth. He stood facing her, the jackal-handled sword that had sliced through Nyx's neck in one hand. He said, his voice hoarse, "She'll be back. Don't kill her. You need her."

Headlights silhouetted his lean body. Finn heard the glass doors at the back of

StarDust rattle. Tears blurred her vision as she gazed at the blood smearing the floor. Victor's blood.

As car doors slammed outside, Emily and Eammon, supporting each other, moved into the light. Their faces were ashen. Eammon's nose was bleeding.

"Victor . . ." The name faded on Finn's lips.

"He's dead," Emily bitterly told Finn. "She killed him."

"Finn!" Lily, followed by a grim Christie and Sylvie, strode into StarDust Studios. "What were you *thinking*?"

Sylvie gazed severely at the two Rooks, then crouched down and lifted half of the porcelain face Nyx had worn. It was Christie who said, "Moth?"

There was a stirring in the air and Nyx reemerged from the shadows as a young woman, her black flapper's dress sparkling with hundreds of jet beads. Staring at her, Finn couldn't move.

Christie quickly placed himself between his friends and the elemental. The mother of the Rooks extended one blood-sticky hand. Her hair seemed to ooze black tendrils. "Pretty witch boy. Do you think you can protect them from me? You don't even have the four rings yet. You have no power."

Her face sharpened, became less human.

Christie began to whisper. Inky words bled across his skin.

Nyx laughed.

Lily and Sylvie drew elder wood daggers from their clothes. Finn, finding her feet, stepped forward, past Christie, and said, "You're the one who should be afraid, Nyx. What do you think your chances are against *us*?"

Moth suddenly shouted, "No—"

A shadow moved behind Nyx, who vanished in a geometry of shadows and light. As black liquid rained down, Finn instinctively ducked and closed her eyes. When she dared look again, Eammon Rook stood where Nyx had been, an iron dagger in one blistering hand. Sylvie walked to him and gently took the dagger from him. "She's dead."

"Leave this place." Moth backed toward the doors. "It is poisoned and there are others here who would hurt you."

"Moth—" Lily stepped toward him.

But he was already gone.

"So." Christie looked solemnly at Finn. "We think we know what might have escaped the Wolf's house and killed the Dragonfly—David Ryder had a girlfriend named Giselle, who's now a Jill. And Tyson Follows has been Frankensteined."

But Finn sank to a crouch, her head in her hands. She couldn't listen to Christie. She had lost Jack forever.

WHEN FINN AND LILY RETURNED HOME, Finn walked to the backyard and sat on the swing set. The beautiful spring night was a shield against what she'd faced tonight.

What have I done?

Lily sat on the swing beside her. "I knew you were trying to find him. Finn, please stop. Please. I just got you back. I can't lose you. And Dad . . ." Lily's voice was an unraveling thread. She sat with her head bowed, clutching the swing's chains. Her fingers were covered with silver rings: skulls, spiders, hearts, and hamsas.

"Lily." Finn felt a tearing grief swallow her own voice as her heart constricted. "It's over. I promise I won't try anymore. Tonight was the last night that the door to . . . to where he is would open. He's *gone*."

Lily reached over and hugged Finn as if she'd never let go. "I'm sorry. I'm *so sorry* you've lost him."

Finn held her sister in the warm night perfumed with lilacs and wet grass and felt as if her heart had turned to stone.

FINN REMAINED ON THE SWING as Lily returned to the house.

As soon as her sister was gone, Finn bent over with a soft moan of anguish. Wrapping her arms around herself, she sobbed soundlessly, and it felt as if her heart was being ripped from inside of her.

Be happy, Jack had said before walking into the dark.

She closed her eyes and gripped the swing's chains and tilted her head back. *Jack. I love you.*

And she let him go.

She opened her eyes—

—and met a mad gaze veiled by dirty pale hair falling over a face that had once been angel-perfect. She was too stunned to cry out. "You're dead."

"No, darling." Caliban Ariel'Pan smiled as if his teeth were in her throat. "I'm alive. That's the problem."

And he shoved her back.

She fell from the swing and hit the ground, scrabbling for the silver dagger. She inhaled to shout—and breathed in the shimmering pollen he blew into her face.

Coughing, panicking, she fought the paralysis stiffening her vocal cords. She rolled onto her side before the numbness seized her limbs and saw a dead Fata lying in the woods that separated her house from Christie's. She recognized the Fata as one of Phouka's—his silver eyes had already sunk away to hollows, his body becoming part of the earth.

Caliban grabbed Finn's jacket and hauled her up. He put one of her arms around his shoulders and began dragging her toward a rusty Escort. "I know where you want to go, Finn Sullivan, and it just so happens that I want to go to the very same place."

CHAPTER 6

Finn woke in the rain, on the ground, surrounded by crimson toadstools with white spots—*Amanita muscaria*. Fly agaric. She had learned that from Jane Emory. She gazed at a bright green frog clinging to one of the larger toadstools. She was so cold, it was as if her body had lost its ability to produce warmth.

A scarred hand gripped her jacket collar and yanked her to a sitting position. Caliban smiled at her. "So, now we die, briefly, so that we may pass into the land of the dead. I gave you fairy dust, *leannan*, mixed with Destroying Angel mushroom, elixir, and a little of this"—he indicated the crimson toadstools—"for the hallucinogens. All of which creates the perfect cocktail to produce the walking dead. You can move now. I took the potion earlier than you and we don't have much time." He rose, dragging her up. "Let's get walking before the first symptom hits."

She spoke through clenched teeth, "What's . . . the first . . . symptom?"

"Agonizing pain."

"I'll . . . wait until . . . *you* have agonizing pain, then—"

"I've done the pain already. Second symptom, little hero, is hallucinations. So we better be on our way to Annwyn before that hits me or we'll both be maggot food and you'll never see Jack again."

"How . . ." She stumbled along beside him as he pulled her. "How are you alive?"

"You mean, how am I human?" He guided her through a cavern of dripping ferns. "Thanks to that elixir you poisoned me with and the three crazy ghost girls who haunt StarDust, I was made mortal. Jack's bullet ended me as a Jack. The elixir you poisoned me with prevented my body from fading. Then Jack's three Lily Girls kissed mortality into me. I suppose they did it because I killed one of them. Don't recall which one."

Finn repeated this formula in her head. She said, "I suppose it was the perfect revenge on you."

He grinned, but his eyes were cold.

Despite the rain, the day had begun to arrive in a cloudy half-light that reminded Finn of the Ghostlands. "Annwyn . . ." She swallowed nausea. "Why do you want to go to the land of the dead?"

"The being who taught the Fatas stitchery resides in Annwyn, a lieutenant of the Dark Gentleman, Gwynn Ap Nudd—"

"Death." Finn nearly fell, cried out as he yanked her up, nearly dislocating her shoulder. "You want to be a Jack again? You're dragging me into the *land of the dead* to become a *Jack*?"

"No one knows the art of stitchery—no one left alive, that is—except the Black Scissors, and he won't oblige. You know why Death, Gwynn Ap Nudd, taught the Fata kings and queens how to make Jacks and Jills? It was so Death could have them eventually, and fill his court with real beings instead of confused shades."

Caliban Ariel'Pan wasn't crazy—he was, as Christie would say, batshit insane. She said in disbelief, "You and Jack are enemies." That was putting it mildly; there was an old, dark hate between the two of them. "And you're going to let me trot off into the land of the dead to find Jack while you get your extraspecial supernatural surgery?"

"I need a human soul to lead me back out of Annwyn when I'm done. *You* need me to find the right path to get out."

"And Jack?"

"Bring him along. I'm planning on killing both of you at some point, later on. Of course, if you can't find him in Annwyn by a certain time . . ."

She wrenched away from him. "Then what?"

"Then we're dead, for good. All of us. And the realm of Gwynn Ap Nudd is not for nice people."

"Why would Death's lieutenant help you to become a Jack?"

" 'Cause I have a secret he'll want to know." He grinned. "Something *Death* will want to know."

Finn's hands shook as she pushed her wet hair from her face. She thought of running. Then she thought of Jack.

The first spasm of agony doubled her over.

"Not much time left, schoolgirl. We either get into Annwyn, or—"

Fighting a violent urge to be sick, she breathed out, "Let's go."

The *crom cu* led Finn down a forested path, past a skeletal Ferris wheel dripping moss, up to a roller coaster that twisted like the curving vertebrae of some unknown behemoth through the rain-misted forest. She followed Caliban down the roller coaster's rickety tracks, through a tunnel of ropy vines and ivy. When he jumped down, she clambered after him, wincing as something sliced open the knee of her jeans.

She wondered when she'd last gotten a tetanus shot. Then she reeled against a corroding strut and retched.

He glanced at her. "You see why I don't want to be human?"

She coughed and straightened. "Well, you're still a monster, so . . ."

"And you don't think Jack's a monster?"

"Jack's not a monster."

"Oh, he was, sweetheart. He was." He grabbed her arm and shoved her through a curtain of moss. "Keep moving. There are guards here."

They eventually reached a small river, obviously manmade, its water now black and polluted. Floating near the root-snarled bank were three large and grimy swan boats, the paint peeling away from the plastic beneath, green slime jellying the undersides. The river led to a rectangular building surrounded by grotesquely crooked trees. The tunnel entrance had been spray-painted with a giant skull, but a faded sign, TUNNEL OF LOVE, remained tilted above the darkness within.

"What is this place?" Finn wanted to curl up on the ground, but she forced herself to keep standing even as she experienced another upheaval in her stomach.

"The entrance to Annwyn. I'm beginning to hallucinate. Are you?"

Her vision blurred. Caliban shoved her. "Get into the boat."

She stumbled into one of the swan boats and sank down onto the dirty, wet bench. Caliban jumped in beside her and used a splintered oar to shove them away from the bank. She glimpsed something moving on the shore near an atrophied carousel, something that looked like a tall, twisted-up rabbit without hair, Daliesque and sinister.

Finn turned back and saw a figure standing in the prow of their boat, in a hooded jacket and trousers, facing away from her and rowing the swan boat with an ivory staff on which were carved images of gaunt beings, mouths open in howls. She focused on Caliban, who crouched opposite, gazing out over the black river. The tunnel they entered seemed to be made from the roots of mammoth trees. Tiny orbs flickered in the darkness between the roots. Finn's heart began to pound in her chest. "Are we—"

"Almost. We're in the between. The charon appearing means we crossed the border."

"Charon." She stared at the hooded figure. "As in 'the one who ferries the souls of the dead'?"

"*A* charon. Like *a* chauffeur." Caliban leaned toward Finn and, in an exaggerated whisper, told her, "Don't say anything about his face. They're sensitive about that."

The charon turned his hooded head to reveal absolute blackness beneath the hood. Finn steeled herself against a flinch.

Caliban sprawled back. "We'll soon reach Death's door, Finn Sullivan, and there, we part ways. Annwyn appears differently to everyone. As the living, we'll be noticed, and they'll try to trap us."

"They?"

"Death's hounds. His lieutenants. The *Anubi*. The *Buccan*. They'll take whatever form pleases them." He took from his pocket a pretty talisman on a silver chain—a jewel-hued butterfly encased in glass. "This is yours." He pulled back his coat collar, revealing an identical talisman, only his was a scarab. "When your time is up, it'll break and lead you to the beginning of the path."

Finn accepted the talisman, grimacing when she realized her hand was shaking. She thought of the Black Scissors and his penchant for insects. "Who gave these to you?"

"Is that really an issue? You find Jack, I find Death's lieutenant, the Resurrectionist, then we hightail it out of there and try to kill each other again, like normal."

"It can't be that easy."

"Oh, it won't be easy." Caliban grinned. "Your dark boy is damned, which is why he's here. You're here to save a damned soul. I'm here to become one."

"How do I find Jack?"

"You'll go straight to whatever you desire."

"I don't trust y—"

"Darling, it doesn't matter if you trust me. We're here. It's too late."

The swan boat bumped against a boardwalk of knotted wood. Caliban heaved himself onto the boardwalk, then turned and extended a hand to Finn. She ignored it and pulled herself up. The gash in her knee hurt, but she felt as light as air; the sickness from Caliban's poison had vanished.

Before them rose a massive door of ebony wood carved with images of dancing skeletons. Her vision blurred. For an instant, the massive door became a utility door with a sign that read DO NOT ENTER. Then the giant door returned.

Her shoulder blades tensed when she remembered the faceless man standing in the boat behind her. She said fiercely, "Are there rules? There must be rules."

"There's only one rule—don't get caught." Caliban yanked the door open. She glimpsed a flat black landscape and a sky that was no color she'd ever seen. She drew in a breath and stepped over the threshold.

She heard him say, "Watch out for the eaters of the dead."

"What?" But she stood alone in a forest of white trees that towered above her, their bark peeling like pale paper, violet leaves rustling against a sky that was a deeper violet. Everything, each blade of black grass, seemed to have a velvety shadow. The cool air was silent and carried a scent of burning. There was a path of black-and-white tiles beneath her feet.

She glanced over one shoulder to find that the door through which she'd come had vanished. All her optimism—and there hadn't been very much of it—drained from her. She sank down onto her heels, her arms over her head.

Glimpsing a movement out of the corner of one eye, she peered into the dark between the albino trees. Something whispered in her ear, *"How do you know you're not still sleeping?"*

She scrambled up, glaring around her.

"Sleeping Beauty," the voice cooed from behind her.

She whirled. "Stop it!"

A figure stood nearby, its black gown undulating, its head an enormous bird skull, the eyes to either side black and moist and alien. It resembled a creature from a Bosch painting that Finn had been scared of as a child. She stiffened with terror as it stretched out human hands with broken nails and whispered, *"You're still sleeping."*

"No." She glared at it. "I'm not." *Don't run*, some otherworldly instinct warned her. *Whatever you do, don't run. It will catch you.*

The creature flickered and was suddenly much closer, the ivory flanges of its monstrous head sharp. It tilted its head to regard her out of one black eye. *"Still sleeping. Forever."*

Finn stepped away, her teeth clenched against the scream fluttering in her throat. Slowly, she turned her back on the creature and continued down the black-and-white path. She could see more of the bird skull women skulking in the forest, heard their whispers.

"I am not sleeping." She bit down hard on her lip. "I won't listen. I will *not* listen . . ."

The forest ended as the path led her into Main Street in Fair Hollow—now a ghost town surrounded by the alien forest of white trees. She glanced behind her. None of the bird skull women had followed her. A shaky sigh of relief escaped her.

The bird skull women from a Bosch painting. Main Street in Fair Hollow . . . Finn realized with a shiver that *her* mind was currently shaping the stuff of Annwyn.

Fear a sharp knot within her, she walked past the Crooked Tree Café, now with a tree growing through the window; past a version of Hecate's Attic with an image of a bat over the door; past BrambleBerry Books—now a brick tower, the books crowding the windows like prisoners attempting escape. The commonplace mingled with the strangeness made her brain feel fizzy. There were no side streets, just the mountains—like the Blackbirds—looming at the end.

As Main Street led to an avenue of Queen Annes and Victorians, all painted black, she halted. She could see the foaming cascade of a waterfall on one mountain. Above the waterfall was a grand house on a cliff, among the white trees, its windows catching the violet light.

She started walking quickly, then ran until the road ended at a steep stairway curving up through the forest, alongside the waterfall to what she assumed would be the grand house. *That's where I'm supposed to go.* The house's windows glowed sapphire, apple green, crimson, and topaz. Among the house's towers, a glass dome flashed like a fragile planet come to rest.

Finn began to climb the stairs. They were coated with moss and she stepped carefully. As she ascended, the roaring thunder of the waterfall pummeled at her eardrums and the fragrances of damp stone and earth became overwhelming.

The stairway curved out over the waterfall. Mist from the crashing water made things blurry. If she fell . . . she doubted very much she'd be able to leave this place.

She saw something moving in the cascading water and frowned apprehensively, peering into the foaming waves. Big, curving, silvery things. Fish?

A skeletal woman with a serpent tail lunged at her from the waterfall, shrieking, needle teeth bared. Finn fell back on the stairs, clutching at the roots of a pale tree as the skeletal woman vanished in the cascading water. Shaking violently, Finn pulled herself up and cautiously continued up the wet stairs, clinging to the tree roots and vines webbing the stone. She could see the mansion clearly now, the windows shining like slabs of jeweled light.

The stairs led through more trees to the mansion's front, where the wrought-iron gates were wide open. To either side, topping the pillars, were the marble heads of howling wolves. She recognized the mansion. *Of course*, she thought. *It would be this. This is Jack's hell.*

She moved past the gates, through a topiary garden. The balustrades of the stairway leading to the entrance were shaped into women, their bodies those of serpents. Finn drew up the hood of her suede jacket, tucked her hands into its wide cuffs, and stalked up the stairs to the black doors. She laid one hand on a doorknob shaped into a wolf's head, turned it, and opened the door to Sombrus, the House of the Wolf and the Snake.

❖ ❖ ❖

ANNA WEAVER WOKE FROM HER NAP IN THE ATTIC, surrounded by manga, her drawings and poetry. She missed Angyll. Angyll would have helped her with her costume for the play. Angyll would have probably told that evil Jill how much she liked her boots. Angyll would sometimes come up to the attic, where she and Anna would have midnight picnics and skim through fashion magazines.

There were no more midnight picnics.

The attic was draped in shadows, but the fading sun silhouetted the person sitting in the chair near the window. Anna wasn't worried or scared. Bad things couldn't get in unless invited—Absalom had made sure of that after the Jill's visit.

"Do you know who I am?" the person said in a voice that made her throat hurt.

"You look like him. But you're not."

"I came to tell you something important. The girl with the brown hair and caramel eyes, the braveheart—the crooked dog took her to Annwyn."

Anna blinked and the shadow was gone. *I'm dreaming*, she thought. *Aren't I?*

WHEN LILY STEPPED BACK into the yard and saw the empty swing, fear sliced through her. She thought, *We should have had Moth come with us. To guard her.*

Her phone buzzed. She answered it.

"Lily, it's Anna. Where is Finn?"

SYLVIE CRAVED HAMBURGERS AND ONION RINGS, because terror made her hungry. Max's Diner had the best of both, not to mention milkshakes so thick they had to be eaten with a spoon.

"You really think she'll stop?" Christie asked grouchily.

"Someone, even if he was a Rook, died tonight. Yeah. I think she'll stop."

The diner was nearly empty of customers but for a booth of college students and two elderly men seated at the counter. Sylvie stabbed her straw into her milkshake. When she noticed a shadow cast by nothing gliding across the tiled floor, goose bumps broke out over her arms.

Then the shadow was sitting where Christie had been and the diner had become a bizarre black-and-white version of itself, deserted and decaying. Sylvie couldn't move, but her heart was trying to lunge out of her chest and she was icy and sweaty all at once.

In Christie's place, the shadow became a lean young woman clad in black leather, wearing metal claw-rings and arm bracelets engraved with ravens. Little ebony crows were braided into her hair. Her midnight eyes were framed by designs in ink.

"That's a cheap and familiar trick." With a shaking hand, Sylvie reached for the elder wood knife in the scabbard at her back, beneath her shirt.

"Go on. Attack me." The creature pretending to be a young woman smiled and her eyes flooded with crimson. "It's your nature, Sylvie."

Sylvie jumped as—*whuft*—a pair of black wings emerged from the young woman's shoulders. "Morrigan," she whispered.

"That's one of my names." The diner's fluorescents flickered as Janis Joplin sang raucously on the sound system.

"Why are you here . . . ?" Sylvie didn't know how the Morrigan had slipped her into this border place. She glanced out the window, made a small, hurt noise when she saw what appeared to be a battlefield scattered with bodies.

The crimson-eyed young woman smiled, revealing needle teeth. "They think they're warrior shamans, the Black Scissors's disciples, but they are my children. My daughters, the Belatucadros's sons. The moment you kill, Sylvie, you are mine. Did the Black Scissors tell you that?"

"Why are *you* telling me that?"

"Because the time when you will kill is drawing closer—and it's only fair to warn you."

Then Sylvie was alone in a diner painted red with blood.

She was on the verge of screaming when the true world rushed back.

CHRISTIE WAS STARING UNHAPPILY into his fourth cup of coffee and wondering if his next addiction would be cigarettes or alcohol, when the lights went out.

When the fluorescents flared on again, Sylvie was gone and what sat opposite him was a young man, his skin scrawled with words, his auburn curls tangled with leaves. Ram horns strung with strands of jewels and talismans curved from his brow. He wore a black suit that looked as though it had been woven from leaves, spiderwebs, and insect wings. His tie pin was a bronze face spouting ivy.

"Let me guess." Chilled to the marrow, Christie tried to be a smart-ass but the effect was somewhat ruined by the tremor in his voice. "You're the ghost of Halloween future."

As Bryan Ferry crooned from the diner's speakers, the apparition folded its hands on the Formica tabletop. There were dozens of ancient rings on the young man's fingers. The diner had been transformed into an abandoned place crawling with ivy.

When the young man spoke, power ebbed from a voice with a British accent. "I am your future, Christie Hart."

Christie whispered, "Who are you, really?"

"I am power."

"No thanks." Christie set his hands on the table and began to rise. "I'm not in the mood."

The young man softly recited:

> *"O no, O no, Thomas, she said,*
> *That name does not belong to me;*
> *I am but the queen of fair Elfland*
> *That am hither come to visit thee."*

Christie breathed out, "Hold on a sec. I thought you people couldn't use poet—"

The diner's doors crashed open. A wind rushed in, bringing with it a spiral of leaves and water that fell away from the form of Phouka Banríon, her auburn hair swept back with pearls and tiny stars. A gown of green silk rippled around her as she bent toward Christie and kissed him and Christie's visitor said, "I'm different from the others, Christie Hart."

Phouka broke apart into leaves, bits of animal bone, and mud. Christie flinched.

"Human beings are inconstant and fickle," the ram-horned man said. "We are constant and always. Wilt thou be constant to her, mortal boy? She will never give thee her heart."

Christie couldn't seem to stop shivering. "Oberon."

A smile glinted in the shadowy face. "I made her a queen, but she is still a child. Still reckless. I warned her to stay out of this mess. This land is none of our concern. But she had a debt, she told me, to set things right with a young man she once fed to the Wolf and the white snake to keep her own subjects and her blessed mortals safe. Then the Fool warned her that darkness would rise here, against us."

The Fool. Absalom. Christie clenched his hands on the table's edge. "Help us."

"I cannot help thee. I am not truly here, only my seeming. I cannot leave my place of origin without giving up all that I am. I am not like her. Tell her, Christie Hart, that Oberon waits for her."

The king faded in a whirlwind of leaves and insects.

The illusion of ruin dissolved from the diner and Christie met Sylvie's wide-eyed gaze.

Their phones went off at the same time.

SYLVIE SAT IN THE PASSENGER SEAT of Christie's Mustang as he drove through the warehouse district with Lily Rose in the back, tense and silent. Lily had told them what Anna had dreamed of: Jack's visit and his claim that Caliban was alive and had dragged Finn to Annwyn.

Sylvie thought, *If the dream is true . . . if Caliban's alive and Finn is in the land of the dead . . . what are we going to do?*

"I shouldn't have left her . . ." Lily's voice broke.

"You left her in the *backyard.*" Christie's hands on the steering wheel were white-knuckled. "If the Black Scissors can't help us, we go to Cruithnear. Then, we'll go to Phouka." He parked in front of the Black Scissors's run-down building. "Why's he living in a dump?"

"It's effective camouflage. And he's *borrowing* this dump." As Lily got out of the car, silver rings flashed on her fingers. Sylvie glimpsed a dagger sheathed within her denim jacket.

It was Kevin who greeted them at the door, his brown hair untidy, a mug of coffee in one hand. "Harrow's had a bad night."

Lily moved past him. "Finn is missing. I need him."

"What do you mean she's missing?" Kevin demanded as Christie and Sylvie entered behind Lily.

Lily pushed open the door to the parlor. The curtains were drawn. It looked as though every shadow in the house had gathered there. A figure was seated before the window, facing away from them.

"William." Lily strode into the parlor, her buckled boots making the floorboards creak. She halted when he held up one hand.

"Come no farther." Inky tendrils seemed to swirl around the Black Scissors. Sylvie's ears began to buzz. She remembered it was dark magic—the magic from vengeful Fatas—that had cursed him with immortality; it was not a gift.

"William." Lily's profile was pale and regal against the swarming darkness. "Anna dreamed that Jack told her Finn is in the land of the dead. And we can't find Finn . . ." She drew in a shaky breath. "Please help me."

"I cannot help you now, *elvaude*." The Black Scissors sounded blurry. "I'm sorry. It's all I can do to keep myself together."

Lily reached down and clasped his hand. Sylvie, who felt an irrational pang, watched as Lily leaned down and the Black Scissors whispered in her ear.

Lily strode back to them. "He's coming apart. He can't help us—but Anna can."

As the others moved down the hall, speaking in hushed voices, Sylvie lingered. "William," she said, tentatively.

"Go, Miss Whitethorn." Weariness threaded his voice. "You can do nothing for me."

Sylvie spun and ran after her friends.

THEY DROVE TO HECATE'S ATTIC, where Anna let them into the closed shop. She was solemn, her golden hair in braids, her T-shirt and jeans smeared with dust. She indicated the round, white-painted table where she usually read Tarot fortunes.

"Where are your parents?" Christie set down his backpack.

"Upstairs. We were doing inventory."

"At night?"

"Well, yeah. We're open during the day and it's a pain. I said you guys would come over and help put everything back."

Lily moved to a stack of dishes. "Let's do this."

"What exactly are we going to do?" Christie watched Anna collect glasses.

"We're going to find out if Finn really is in the underworld." Lily handed the dishes to Sylvie.

"This is how we do it." Anna shoved silverware into Christie's hands.

"A dumb supper," Lily clarified, setting a candle on the table and lighting it. "To communicate with anyone in the land of the dead. Better than a séance."

Christie's guts wrenched. His last experience with a séance had been horrible.

"Christie got possessed last time we did a séance," Anna explained as Lily glanced at him.

He shrugged. "Phouka taught me the dumb supper. We'll do it."

"Who, uh, possessed you?" Lily wanted to know.

"Caliban," Sylvie told her. "Finn said Jack shot Caliban with a silver bullet. How'd Caliban survive, if Anna's dream is true?"

"Finn and Jack left Caliban in StarDust. It's a border place with power." Lily set the plates in the center of the table. "That's why the Black Scissors uses it as a Way from the Ghostlands. Something must have saved the *crom cu*. So, hey, we need two more people."

CHRISTIE STEPPED OUT OF THE SHOP after calling Aubrey and Micah. He needed some air.

It was his damn witch blood that scared him. He still wasn't comfortable with whatever was crawling around inside of him, whatever the Ghostlands—and Sylph Dragonfly—had woken within him. But he would use it, he thought fiercely. The Fatas had already taken three away from him. Angyll. Hester. Sylph. They wouldn't take Finn.

He pushed his hands over his face.

He heard a truck pull up to the curb and flung back his head as Aubrey and Micah jumped out of Micah's Chevy. Christie said, "Welcome to the magic show."

He led them into Hecate's Attic, where Anna had turned off the lights. Only the glow from a black candle illuminated the shop, sparkling from the reflective surfaces of bottles, mirrors, and crystals. Sylvie and Anna had traced a pentagram onto the wooden floor with lip gloss and glitter dust from Anna's arts-and-crafts kit.

Aubrey grabbed a chair and began to sit.

"No!" Sylvie grabbed the chair from him and he nearly fell. "We have to do everything backward. And no one speaks until after the summoning. We're inviting the dead to the table. They don't like chatter."

"Who told you this?" Aubrey looked nervous.

"Lily. Christie will explain."

"Well, aside from what Sylv said, this is what we do: Everyone sets something on the table, walking backward. We eat dessert, then dinner. Then we invite the dead."

Sylvie began walking in reverse, setting down the plates at each chair. Everyone followed with their own place setting. Anna lifted an ornate pink cake from beneath a glass dome and sliced it while Lily poured cups of tea.

They all sat. Lily placed her iPhone at the table's center and tapped it to a picture of Finn. They ate dessert. Lily served pizza for dinner.

Then Christie motioned that they all clasp hands. Phouka had taught him the dumb supper a month ago, because she didn't want him to attempt any more séances and this was a safer alternative. He pictured Finn as he remembered her, as if she sat there with them. He felt his skin prickle as the power inked into his skin. He thought the words of summoning:

To this table I thee call,
Good or evil, big or small.
If thou walks at Death's command,
Exists as shadows throughout this land,
To this supper I thee invite,
Any ghost or spirit or sprite.

A wind swept through the shop, rattling the wind chimes, causing the candle's flame to dance. Christie felt something rushing toward him from the depths of his brain. Before he could cry out, the thing he now sensed standing behind him, the one that had entered the true world, set its clawed hands on his shoulders and spoke a word in his ear that plummeted his consciousness into the dark.

SYLVIE OPENED HER EYES. Christie's body was jerking like a marionette's. Then he laughed quietly, a deep laugh that was not his own, and Sylvie thought to herself, *Oh no. Not again.*

The temperature dropped by ten degrees, the candle flame became sapphire blue, and Lily broke the silence with a command: "Tell us who you are."

Whatever inhabited Christie raised his head, revealing eyes that were all black. The voice that issued from Christie was not Caliban's, Sylvie realized, partially relieved. "I was invited, Briar Queen. I'm the one you need to get through to speak to anyone in the land of the dead." The antediluvian gaze slid over each of them and came to rest on Sylvie. "I am the Resurrectionist. Usually, there is no one of any consequence I care to speak to. This . . . this is interesting. I see a fallen queen, a heart widow, a boy with the blood of the Witch of Endor, a nascent knight, and an ancestor of the Drake." The spirit thing's attention slithered to Anna. "And you . . . *you* are . . ." It looked at each of them again and smiled, shadows bleeding from the corners of Christie's mouth.

"Tell us your name," Lily ordered as Sylvie dug her fingernails into the wood of the table.

"You know I cannot do that."

"Where is my sister?"

The inky eyes narrowed. Christie's face became all sharp angles. "Your bright girl is a sliver in the skin of my lord's kingdom. She's fortunate he's occupied."

"Finn *is* there!" Sylvie leaned forward and deliberately wound her fingers around Christie's cold ones. "Please tell us how to get her back."

"You cannot, Sylvie Whitethorn." The Resurrectionist met her gaze. "She must find her own way out. As for the one who took her . . . the *crom cu* is deceiving her."

"It *is* Caliban then?" Sylvie's relief faded. "He took her there."

Lily leaned forward. "Why did you bother speaking with us if you're not going to help us?"

"This is the first time in ages I've been out of the dark lands." The Resurrectionist tilted his head back, stretched his arms up as the windows of the shop began to frost with something like black ice. "I haven't walked in the light for so long."

"You're not staying," Lily informed him. "If you try, you'll never be able to leave this table. Look down."

The Resurrectionist narrowed Christie's eyes and looked down, saw the faintly glimmering pentagram. He bared his teeth.

Lily continued, "Now, tell me how to get my sister out of Annwyn."

The Resurrectionist rocked back on two legs of the chair and regarded her with his tar-black gaze. "Children." He pushed back from the table, breaking the pentagram with the chair legs and rising. "Did you really think a pentagram would hold me? I am not some child of night and nothing."

"Now," Lily said to Sylvie.

Sylvie flung herself at the Resurrectionist. His mouth curled in a snarl, but Sylvie had already grabbed Christie's T-shirt, his russet curls, and was dragging his head down. As weird as it was—*this is for Christie*, she told herself—she pressed her lips against her best friend's mouth. "Christie," she commanded. "Christopher Robin Hart."

He shoved her back. Aubrey caught her.

Christie collapsed onto all fours, gagging. Lily pounded on his back. Sylvie winced when he spit out a knot of black gunk, then crouched there, panting, his head down. When he raised his pale face, Sylvie saw *Christie* gazing out of those warm, brown eyes.

"That is the last goddamn time this is happening." He glanced at Sylvie, his brows knit. "Did you—"

"It didn't work." Sylvie sank down into a chair. "We didn't get to talk to Finn."

"Who did we—"

"Death's lieutenant," Lily said, her voice faint. "But she's there. My little sister is with the dead. We'll go to Tirnagoth. We'll go to the Banríon."

TIRNAGOTH GLOWED IN THE NIGHT, an art nouveau artifact, its garden ablaze with fireflies . . . or maybe they weren't fireflies. Probably they weren't fireflies. Christie gazed out the window as Lily steered his Mustang along the broken road. He'd let her take the wheel because he still felt as if he'd been forced out of his body and jammed back into it. "There's a taste in my mouth," he informed them, "like I've just eaten earthworms."

Sylvie scowled. Lily parked the car. As they got out, jazzy music echoed through the honey warm night. Christie felt offended. "Are they at *another* revel? Don't they ever get *bored*? I'd blow my brains out if I had to party every night."

"They don't ever change." Lily regarded Tirnagoth with an almost wistful sorrow.

The doors swept open and Absalom, wearing skater jeans and a Hawaiian shirt, a lotus tucked into his dark orange hair, stepped forward. He shook a finger at them. "Your dumb supper was paramount to setting off fireworks in a void. The Banríon is a bit peeved. You really need to practice what you pry at, children."

Christie bit down on a scathing comment as Lily said with quiet intensity, "Did your Banríon notice when the *crom cu* dragged my sister into the world of the dead?"

Absalom's golden eyes widened. "I thought I felt Death's door open—the *crom cu* lives?"

"*Did you know?*" Lily shouted. "Did you know what would happen? Is it one of your twisted plans, *amadan*?"

Absalom looked hurt. "My plans are never twisted."

"What you did to Hester was." Christie felt the ink bleeding onto his skin as anger uncoiled within him.

"That wasn't twisted." Absalom turned away. "That was necessary. Come along."

"Are you okay?" Sylvie murmured to Christie.

"One of these days," Christie said, not bothering to lower his voice, "I'm going to—"

"I can hear you," Absalom said.

Christie focused on the mahogany nymphs reaching toward the lobby's ceiling, the windows stained with images of evil-looking flowers. Every time he came here, every time the Fata world entered his life, he felt as if he was becoming one of them.

Absalom shoved open a pair of doors carved into a lattice of vines. They stepped into a small courtyard of ornamental trees with Japanese paper lanterns strung in the branches. The Banríon sat on the edge of a pool glowing with golden carp that matched the stars coiled in her upswept hair. Dressed in a Joan Jett T-shirt and a plaid skirt, she played at being mortal. Christie's heart ached as she spoke without looking at them, drifting one hand through the pool. "We found the remains of one of my people, Grey Hare, near your house, Lily Rose. I sent him to watch over you and your sister. Grey Hare doesn't exist anymore."

"How do I get her back?" Lily seemed calm, but Christie could see her breaking.

Phouka's gaze was catlike. "You can't. You have to wait until she finds her way out."

"Finds her way out?" Sylvie stepped to Lily's side. "One of *your* people dragged her there."

Phouka looked at Christie, who said, "Caliban."

Phouka drew back. "The crooked dog lives?"

"How is he even still alive?" Christie hated feeling afraid. "You said you disposed of his body after Jack shot him in StarDust."

"Obviously"—Phouka's gaze on Christie was ruthless—"the *crom cu*'s corpse was staged. That *wasn't* his body we disposed of. I am most interested in finding out who helped him. And why"—her eyebrows drew together—"he took Serafina to Annwyn."

"Please." Lily's shoulders slumped as if the fight had gone from her. "Please tell me, at least, *where* she entered Annwyn."

"Death's door closed at the oak. The only Way left is Funland," Absalom answered. Phouka glared at him and he shrugged. He addressed Christie, "The one you summoned at the dumb supper—was his name Ankou?"

Christie tried not to cringe, remembering the primordial thing that had spoken through him. "He didn't say his name. He called himself the Resurrectionist."

"Ankou." Absalom sat back. "He's the only one of Gwynn Ap Nudd's lieutenants who likes to visit this world when some idiot lets him in. You're fortunate you didn't have to exorcise him."

Lily said, "A Jill named Giselle visited Anna and threatened to blind her—probably because Anna's an oracle. Do you think the *Jill* put Caliban up to this?"

"Why wasn't I told about this Jill threatening Anna?" Absalom spoke softly, his smile merry, his eyes molten.

Phouka snatched up her coat and headed for the gate. "Because I didn't know about David Ryder's Jill. Send Tinker and Shadowfox to watch over Anna. We'll go to Death's door. Christie, do you have GPS?"

"I warned you something like this would happen," Absalom called after her.

THE SHADOW MAN WHO COULD CAUSE BLIGHT with a touch if he chose to, stood outside the glass dome of StarDust Studios and spoke softly, seductively. "I know you are in there, ladies. I'm not who you think. Open the doors for me, please. I've an offer for you: revenge."

Vague shapes moved beyond the glass walls. The doors slowly creaked open.

CHAPTER 7

Finn studied the silent foyer of the House of the Wolf and the Snake. Serpentine banisters curved up to either side of the ebony stair. Bronze wolves circled the black marble pillars spearing from the chessboard floor. She felt as if she was in a dream, invulnerable, but with a nightmare slinking out of sight, ready to attack.

Two girls were draped on the stairs. They wore silk ball gowns, one in viridian, the other in wine red, and they looked like a turn-of-the-century portrait. One of the girls raised an arm over her face and murmured sleepily.

Finn backed away from them, turned, and walked through the strands of light filtering through a jewel-hued window, past a boy in a suit and a girl in white sprawled on a divan draped with a wolfskin. They, too, slept.

Next Finn turned down a black-painted corridor, its walls decorated with human skulls, antlers curving from their brows.

She stepped into a ballroom of white marble. Pillars shaped into male and female figures clawed at the arched ceiling—the figures had hooves, or bat ears, strange eyes, or too many limbs. She passed a large mirror foxed with age and framed by a motif of serpents and flowers. She knew better than to look directly into the mirror, but she glimpsed something moving in its silver pool like a bloody smile.

Instinct drove her down another hallway, where she found more sleepers, all young and attractive and beautifully dressed. She peered into a narrow, high-ceilinged library, its shelves cluttered with books and fossils. The glamour didn't conceal everything—there was mold on the books and the wooden floor was warped and sprouting ghostly toadstools.

Jack is here. Somewhere.

Finn ascended a staircase that led into a hall with black walls and porcelain sculptures of hands holding flower lamps. At one end of the hall was a glass-walled conservatory. At the other end loomed a pair of black doors that made her spine tingle.

A sound nearby had her swinging around, one of her hands accidentally sweeping a lamp from a table. She winced as the glass broke against her skin and the lamp crashed noisily to the floor.

A girl sleeping beneath a table in the corridor raised her flower-crowned head and blinked at Finn. Her saffron gown rustled as she pulled herself into a sitting position and said, "That's some outfit. What are you supposed to be? A huntress? You're bleeding."

Finn glanced down at the cut on her hand. Crimson drops pattered on the floor. She whispered, "I'm bleeding." She was a living thing in the realm of the dead. Terror almost crushed her.

The chandelier above burst into light, its pendants throwing a dappled glow over Finn. All along the corridor, the lamps lit up. And the world outside the windows became black.

The girl looked at Finn. She lifted a finger to her lips.

And Finn felt something rushing past her, tugging gently at her hair, whispering in her ear. The lights dimmed, revealing glowing motes in the shadows.

"Haints." The girl rose. "This is their time. As long as they don't notice you, you're aces."

The black doors behind Finn rattled. Finn slowly turned to face them.

"That's where they stay," the girl told her, casually. "On that side."

"The ghosts?" Finn felt weirdly grateful for the girl's company.

"No—"

The doors slammed open. An icy wind spun past Finn, causing the gas lamps to blink again. The girl sank into a curtsy as three silhouettes appeared on the threshold, long coats undulating in the draft. Wolflike shadows slinked from the darkness behind them. Finn stood very still as the shadows, passing her, rose upright and became the jeweled and fur-coated pack that was Seth Lot's court. She felt their hungry glances graze her skin, but her attention was on what stood in the doorway—the black-haired girl in scarlet and the man holding a wolf-headed walking stick. And the one who stood between them.

She whispered, "Jack . . ."

Dressed in black suede lined with crimson silk like some Victorian devil, his eyes silvery beneath his hat brim, Jack gazed at Finn with the disdain of a stranger.

Reiko Fata moved forward with Seth Lot, whose cold gaze scathed Finn from head to toe as he passed. He wore a collar of rubies around his throat. Reiko's silver eyes had points of red within them, like flames. The sight of the couple made Finn's insides knot and a cold sweat formed on her skin.

As Jack strode past Finn, he said, without looking at her, "One of your shoes is untied."

Finn frowned down at her red Converses. She turned, watching him descend the stairs with Reiko and Lot. "Jack."

He halted. Reiko glanced back at him. "Did you bring her, Jack?"

"No. Perhaps she followed me." He moved back up the stairs, toward Finn. He removed his hat. "How do you know my name, girl?"

The Wolf and the white snake continued down the stairs, and the girl in saffron silk followed them. As Jack watched Finn, his foxed-silver gaze holding hers, she curled her hands at her sides.

"You're hurt," he said in a voice of velvety menace. He came closer, reached out, and gently took hold of her cut hand. The contact sent an electric pulse through her and caught at her heart, and she *knew* . . . she knew he was not an illusion.

"What possessed you to enter this house?" Jack asked tenderly.

"To get *you* out of it, idiot." Relief and wonder shook her.

He dropped her hand. Then he smiled and it was not a nice smile. He bent close and whispered, "*I don't believe in you.*" He turned away. "You're in the House of the Wolf and the Snake. Good luck." He followed Reiko and Seth Lot down the stairs.

Finn sank against the wall and tried to sort out her courage and her thoughts. He was her Jack. He knew, in some fashion, where he was. And he thought she was an illusion.

A draft tainted with the reek of damp stone and burning wood drifted from beyond the open doors leading to the wing of the house from which Jack, Reiko, and Lot had emerged. Finn peered into the darkness, inhaled sharply when she saw the crescent of a pale face emerge.

A figure reeled out of the dark, blood streaming from one corner of its mouth, its coat sweeping open to reveal a bare chest that had a gaping wound filled with writhing flowers. The figure reached out—

Finn couldn't scream as her throat closed up.

The doors slammed shut on the horrifying figure. Finn glanced down and saw a shadow pooling beneath the door. Her nostrils clogged with the iron stench of blood—

The doors burst open again and she was flung back. Her head struck the table and stars burst across her retinas. She curved away from what writhed between the open doors, a black mass glimmering with teeth and fire and bones.

A lean figure stepped between her and it.

"THAT WAS VERY UNWISE OF YOU."

The velvety voice lured Finn out of oblivion. Her eyelashes felt weighted down. She forced them open, her fingers clenching on the arms of the chair in which she sat.

Jack crouched before her. Behind him was a ballroom scattered with pretty young things in gowns and suits, their faces painted to resemble decorative Day-of-the-Dead skulls. They lounged on divans draped with animal skins or ate little cakes and sipped wine from long-stemmed goblets. As a group of musicians in white, their faces concealed by horned, ivory half masks played "Smells Like Teen Spirit" on cellos and violins, couples waltzed.

Finn looked down. Her cut hand was snugly wrapped in white cloth. She wore a gown as soft as gray smoke and the laces of her Converses had been tied. Her heart beat so fast, it hurt. "Who dressed me?"

"I did. Don't worry—I didn't take any liberties. I was a gentleman."

"A gentleman wouldn't have undressed me." She shivered as she imagined his fingers on her skin, and heat blushed through her.

He shrugged, his mouth curved to one side in that familiar way. The pale light glossed his dark hair, his eyelashes, the strong line of his throat. His proximity made her ache. "Better me than Lot. And there's nothing you've got that I haven't seen before—except that heart-shaped birthmark on your—" He stopped talking as she brushed her hands frantically over the gown, searching. He said, "I put your bracelet in the pocket."

And there *was* a pocket in the gown. She wrapped her fingers around Lily's bracelet, inside. "Jack." She leaned toward him. "I know you remember me."

He smiled darkly. "You're something I dreamed. Something Reiko and the Wolf have conjured to make me behave."

"I'm real, Jack." She touched his face, felt a muscle twitch beneath her fingertips.

He shook his head. "That life was just an illusion, to punish me. For not killing when Lot ordered it."

"I am thine and thou art mine, 'til the ending of the world."

His expression became stark. His fingers closed around her wrists. He pulled her hands from him. "What a grand trick you are. And well made, too. I should have taken advantage."

Dismayed, she pushed to her feet. *"Jack."*

"Jack." Reiko, in her liquid silk gown, glided to Jack and laid her head on his shoulder, her heavy ropes of hair draping his chest. Points of flame flickered within the Fata queen's eyes. She arched her white throat and whispered into Jack's ear. His gaze hardened.

Reiko turned her back on Finn and walked away. Jack uncurled his other hand in Finn's direction and said with mocking courtliness, "Shall we dance?"

The look of him, his hair falling in ragged, red-tipped edges around his sharp-boned face, made her hands clench. But she reached out and twined her fingers with his, scowling as he yanked her close and began to whirl her among the other dancers. The ballroom was gore-dark, blood red, bone white, with touches of infected green. It made her head ache.

His lips brushed her ear. "She wants me to ruin you." His mouth was warm and sweet as summer as he crushed her against him, the rings on his fingers spots of cold through the gossamer of her dress. This was not the place for desire, but, as they whirled, it was as if he was becoming mortal and solid in her embrace, his skin warming, the false, glamorous world falling away.

"Come back," she pleaded. "Come back with me."

There was a tremendous, shattering crash, as if two cars had collided at high speed. Finn almost fell as Jack released her.

Reiko, in her fiery gown, stood near a pool of red liquid and broken glass—a punch bowl that had been on one of the tables. "How clumsy of me." Reiko's eyes were rubies as she watched Jack and Finn. "Time for dinner."

Everyone began to file from the ballroom down a black corridor. The Wolf and Reiko moved to either side of Jack and Finn, Reiko's gown swirling against Finn's. Seth Lot's gaze slid slyly to Jack. They entered a hall lit by a chandelier made from flames encased in crystals. The fireplace was shaped into a wolf's head. The walls of dark green marble soaked up the light that glossed a feast of roasted animals and fish, split pomegranates and sliced apples with snow-white flesh. A tiered cake scrolled with ivory frosting, dripping red, rose in the center.

Finn curled a hand against her aching stomach. Her mouth watered when she saw the goblets glistening with pale, chilled wine. But she knew better than to give in to thirst or hunger in the land of the dead.

After the lord and lady had selected their places, the guests seated themselves at the table. Finn sat next to Jack and focused on a skeletal fossil hung above the fireplace, a humanoid torso with the tail of a fish and ram horns branching from the skull. Her fear wouldn't defeat her if she focused on small details. She could bear this.

The doomed boys and girls drank the wine and ate the absurdly lavish food. Occasionally, the chandelier's light would ebb and the glamour would fade and Finn would glimpse a bruised wrist, a bloody eye socket, a torn rib cage beneath a jacket.

Seth Lot, a horror sheathed in a beautiful skin, stood. He raised a goblet, his gaze as gentle as his voice. "We are here to celebrate the end of one of my enemies, thanks to Jack."

Jack said nothing, his mouth a hard line, as a girl in a white wig and a white gown—*oh, God,* Finn thought, *Antoinette,* another dead wolf—set a platter on the table and lifted it, revealing a roasted human heart.

Rising, Jack walked to Seth Lot. He stood very still as Lot dipped fingers into the heart's blood, brushed them across Jack's brow, his mouth. The pretty young things around the table were quiet.

Finn didn't know if this was a memory, or something Jack's psyche had conjured for his own private hell. She needed to stop it.

"As a gift"—Seth Lot indicated the guests—"you may select one of these fair creatures as a toy."

Finn moved to her feet.

"Not you," Reiko said sharply.

Jack used that low and sultry voice that Finn knew meant he was about to do something kamikaze. "May I say something?"

"Go on." With an indulgent smile, Seth Lot leaned against his chair.

Jack smiled a slow, wicked smile. "If you are lured past their door, fed wine, meat, and cake, their kisses are sweet, but you've made a mistake—for they'll feast on your flesh, and your soul they will take, until there's nothing of you left, in the House of the Wolf and the Snake." He bowed with mocking grace, his dark hair swinging.

The silence was arctic. Seth Lot's hand clenched so hard on the back of the chair, his nails gouged into the wood. Then, without warning, he lunged toward Finn. Finn didn't even have time to struggle as he yanked her against him. His clawed hand pricked through the gown, into the skin above her heart. Blood trickled down her rib cage. She shook more with anger than fear as Lot gently said, "She'll bleed for that, Jack."

"Seth." Reiko sounded as if she was enjoying the show. "You're scaring the children."

Jack's face was stark, the skin tight over the bones. He met Finn's gaze, then folded to one knee, his head bowed. "Forgive me, my lord."

"Jack," Finn told him. "He can't kill me. He isn't real."

"Poor mad thing. When I rip you open"—Lot spoke voluptuously against her ear—"it will *feel* real."

It already felt real, her blood trickling, the steely strength of the arm that held her, Lot's scent of winter and cologne that caused bile to burn in her throat.

Terror cut through Finn as memories of Lot's seductive malice made her momentarily incapable of cunning.

"I apologize." There was a taut plea in Jack's voice.

"All right." Seth Lot was at his worst when he smiled. Dragging Finn, he stalked toward Jack. He swung Jack's empty chair around and propped one foot on the seat. "Lick one of my boots clean and I'll spare her."

Jack shuddered, his head still bowed.

Reiko lazily selected a small cake. "Why don't you just bleed out the girl?"

"A good king." Finn snarled at Seth Lot, recovering. "You once told me you used to be a *good king*. Before you became a monster."

Seth Lot straightened. Losing interest in Jack, he turned, regarding her with those gentle blue eyes. "Reiko. Return our guests to the ballroom. Dinner is over."

Reiko sauntered to Finn and Lot. She kissed Lot with passionate abandon, then turned and gripped Finn's jaw. Finn defiantly met her gaze as Reiko said, "You've failed."

Her nails left bleeding scratches on Finn's face as she spun around and swept from the room, shepherding the confused and pretty courtiers out the door.

When she had gone, Lot released Finn. "When did we speak?"

Finn felt a dark satisfaction as she told him, "Before your head was cut off."

"Finn." Jack pushed to his feet, reaching into his coat.

"Really?" Seth Lot laughed like an amused lover, indulgent. "I would have remembered *that*. I would have remembered *you*. But I will give you credit for your imagination." He came close and spoke as if it was just the two of them, "I was a good king, once. Then I was betrayed by something that had once been mortal, a lovely Jack named Harahkte, a winter boy with no heart." His lips touched her cheek as he whispered viciously, "So you see where my fondness for your kind comes from—"

Jack slammed two daggers into Lot's back, then grabbed Finn's hand and they ran.

JACK AND FINN FLED into the foggy night onto a street that resembled a nightmare Victorian city. Shadow people walked the streets and black coaches drawn by horses with crimson eyes trotted by. Finn allowed Jack to lead until, exhausted, she tugged on his hand and sagged against a grimy brick wall. Jack turned, his eyes silvered and determined. "We'll go to my house."

"Your house?" She scowled as he gently pulled her forward. "We need to *leave*."

"And where will we go? They'll find us."

"Do you know where you are?" She wanted to shake him. "Do you want to know how I got here? Caliban dragged me here, to the land of the dead."

"Caliban?" He turned, wary.

"Yes. To the land of the dead. Which is where we are."

He indicated a boarded-up building. Across its wooden door, someone had written *NOT A GENTLEMAN*. "This is where we are. My home."

"Jack. *Listen*. You walked into Annwyn. This is your hell, which, for some reason that escapes me, you think you deserve."

"Let's get inside." He unlocked the door to the derelict building and led her into a musty-smelling hall, where a black cat materialized from the shadows to weave around his ankles. Discarding his hat and coat, Jack bent to stroke the cat's head. A lamp flared to blue life without his touching it, revealing a dingy parlor with old furniture and patterned black wallpaper peeling from mildewed walls. Piles of books cluttered the floor.

As Jack crouched beside the hearth and began a fire, Finn wandered around the parlor. She glanced at Jack and curled one hand into a fist when she saw that the thorny Celtic cross, black as Reiko's heart, had reappeared on the nape of his neck. She quoted softly, *"Thou art mine and I am thine. 'Til the sinking of the world, I am thine and thou art mine, 'Til in ruin death is hurled—"*

He snapped up to face her, the fire blazing behind him. He spoke through clenched teeth, "Stop that."

"Make me."

Crackling with anger, dark with it, he moved closer. He backed her against a wall and bent toward her and her lips parted beneath his ferocious kiss. As she wrapped her arms around his neck, scarcely daring to believe he was real, that he hadn't vanished forever, the kiss became tender, familiar. A flame coursed through her, conquering death's chill. The breath left her as his mouth traced a warm path along her collarbones. They fell onto the black velvet sofa. She closed her eyes, her hands charting the lines of his throat and shoulders and hips, the muscles in his back as he arched over her like a famished man over a feast. His cool skin warmed against hers as his smile curved against her mouth and he said, "I might have known you'd find your way into the land of the dead."

A piece of wood in the fire popped loudly. Finn's eyes flew open in time to see the parlor swallowed by darkness. A mass of shadows glided above them, its large, staring eyes absent of any feeling, yet disturbingly human. *That's Death.* There was a sound like the discordant shrill of a violin, and a string broke inside of her.

Jack reared back and a creature like something out of a Dali painting, a twisted rabbit man, rose behind him.

"Finn!" Jack vanished into the dark.

FINN STUMBLED, DISORIENTED. Had she been dreaming? Awful dreams about a life of loss, with half her family gone and a lover who had been nothing but a scarecrow of shadows and roses.

Sunlight sifted through the windows of the old house as Finn swept open the doors and moved down the hall, her gray gown rustling. She entered the cluttered study and immediately forgot why she'd come.

She forgot a lot of things lately.

She riffled through books on exotic wildlife, poked at a bird's nest with Kewpie doll inhabitants, and stood on tiptoe to take down a magic orb that, when shaken, enigmatically answered a spoken question. She moved to a cabinet beneath a display of insects in jeweled boxes and opened a drawer filled with colorful dead birds.

Then she remembered.

Something lived in one of the unused rooms in the house's west wing. She'd begun collecting dead birds to feed it. It was only one of many unwelcome residents. Occupying the attic was the red-veiled spirit Finn could sometimes hear weeping, late at night. Dwelling in the salon her mother only used when they had guests was an antlered shadow man who appeared after midnight.

Finn glanced up to see her da leaning in the doorway, a silver fob-watch on his waistcoat reflecting the sunlight. He said, "There you are. Your mother is looking for you."

Finn left her da selecting inks for his pens and moved down the glass-windowed gallery, out into the garden of fruit trees and flowers. Lily Rose sat on the swing that hung from a branch of the biggest oak. She looked up from her book and smiled, her ivory gown billowing around bare legs. "Where's Jack?"

"Jack?" Finn didn't like how the name seemed to fracture the honeyed air of the garden.

Lily swung close, leaned forward, and said, "He's tricking you. *Wake up!*"

Finn heard something rustling through the garden. She whirled, peering into the gloom. She turned back to her sister, but the swing was empty.

"Here, Serafina." Her mother stood with her back to Finn, the daisies in her hair as bright as tiny suns. She began to turn her head. "This is a trick."

And Finn was suddenly alone in a garden that had become a knot-work of nettles and weeds and coiling, crooked trees scaled with lichen and soaked in red dusk. She glanced back at her family's house, to see it melt into ember-singed shadows, as if its silhouette was being eaten away by acid.

She sobbed, gathered up her skirts, and ran. She found herself in a forest black with rot, luminous with pale toadstools and fungus.

"Mom?" Finn hurried through the forest. *"Lily?"*

In the distance, she saw the silhouette of something grotesque and humanoid with the ears of a rabbit, and claws. Terror shot through her. She remembered who she was. *Where* she was.

"No." She whirled in place, shocked. "No. *This isn't real.*" Her heart constricted in her chest. She backed up against a tree and took a few deep breaths. She needed to find Jack again.

She could hear voices, whispers, threading through the forest. She saw what appeared to be the silhouettes of people hanging from the trees and she knew that whatever ruled the land of the dead was *playing* with her.

Finn drew Lily's bracelet of silver charms from the pocket of the filmy gray gown and put it on.

The Dali rabbit, malevolent and contorted, appeared on the path, lurching toward her. Turning, Finn ran.

The structure appeared, first, as a mass of foxfire glints among the trees. As she drew closer, it sharpened into a giant glass birdcage, a once-elegant conservatory now grimy and abandoned. She pushed through the doors—

—and reeled, blinking rapidly in the glow from strands of lotus-shaped lights strung around ornamental trees. She was in a garden again. She could hear splashing, people laughing and talking. The air smelled of chlorine and lilacs.

"Finn." Moth was moving toward her. His pale pewter hair was crowned with black hellebore and he wore his jeans. His feet were bare.

"Moth." She rubbed at her temples. "What is this? This isn't . . ."

"You made it out. You just have to concentrate. The trip to Annwyn left scars."

"Scars? No . . . this isn't right." Her brain felt broken.

"Finn," he coaxed. "Our guests are waiting. You're home now."

Confused, she let him lead her through a curtain of morning glories, to a summer-blue pool. They passed girls in sundresses and boys in casual clothes as pretty music with an uncanny dissonance played in the background. A group of young men and women moved around the pool, carrying poles topped with the wooden faces of animals.

Moth smiled and Finn's heart ached at his sharp beauty. He said, "You've been having bad spells lately. Ever since you lost Jack." He moved closer to her. "We're so happy."

She raised a hand to his hair. A bracelet of silver charms sparked light on her wrist, reflected, for an instant, in the black voids of his eyes. She tore away from him. "*Who are you?*"

His face began to run like melting plastic, revealing the skull beneath, as he bowed. "I'm the Dark Gentleman's right-hand man, his lieutenant." His voice changed to a choked growl. "I am Ankou."

The color drained from everything around Finn. All the boys and girls became corpses. Finn closed her eyes, opened them to find that where Moth had stood was only a shadowy column of white limbs and black feathers and inky eyes.

She ran for her life, back into the murky forest of the dead. When she tripped on a skull glowing in the dark soil, she scrambled back against a tree, leaning against it, catching her breath. Ankou didn't follow. He didn't need to—he'd been tricking her all along.

Against her collarbones, the butterfly in glass fluttered a warning. She clutched at the pendant. "Don't break now. I can't leave now."

Something moved in the brambly darkness and the monstrous rabbit silhouette emerged from the mist, one clawed hand tearing across a tree trunk.

Finn lunged to her feet and fled again. Ankou's manipulations had taught her something—Annwyn was fluid, ever changing—

She closed her eyes, pictured a path before her, and where she wanted it to lead.

When she opened her eyes, she saw, through the lattice of trees and mist, a white cottage with a red door, its roof green with ivy. It stood in a sunlit clearing. Just where she wanted it.

She ran to the cottage, shoved the door open, and stumbled inside. On a rough wooden table lay the silver knife with the ebony, cross-shaped hilt, the knife she'd just now imagined into existence, the one Eve Avaline had given her. She walked to it, grabbed it, and sat in a chair facing the door.

"Why a rabbit?" Now, she had the luxury of figuring things out. *Death's border patrol are supposed to be black dogs* . . . "Why is a *rabbit* chasing me?"

The sunlight outside the windows faded into night as something scratched at the door, rattling it. Her grip was sweaty on the dagger's handle as she mentally riffled through what she knew of rabbit mythology. There was an Aztec rabbit god. There was the Easter Rabbit. The White Rabbit from *Alice's Adventures in Wonderland* . . . "A *guide* . . ." As she breathed out a shocked realization, the window shattered and the monster entered in a spray of glass, lunging toward her on all fours. Finn hurled herself toward it and stabbed the knife down. The creature raked claws across her cheek, but it tipped over and Finn fell with it, ripping the dagger relentlessly into its scaled chest. The monster roared, then went still beneath her.

Wiping blood and tears from her face, Finn gazed down at the ravaged flesh, saw a flash of gold. She placed one hand carefully on the monster's chest, felt the steady drumming of a heart.

She began cutting at the fibrous flesh, careful not to touch the pale skin beneath. She sobbed once, stopped. She had to keep her hand steady. She cut delicately at the twisted face, lifted the skin as if removing a rubber mask. As she peeled away the scaly flesh, her hands sticky with ichor, the face of a young man was revealed, bruised, slicked with blood. The golden phoenix pendant on his chest gleamed against his collarbones. "*Jack rabbit*," she whispered. "*Jack*." She pushed aside the slimy, flayed skin of the reptile rabbit as if she was digging someone from a grave.

Jack's eyes flew open, stricken, terrified, as if he didn't dare believe in her existence. Straddling him, she bent down to cover his mouth with hers, breathing life into him. His lips parted as warmth poured from her into his cold body. He arched and gasped.

"Finn." His voice was hoarse, as if he'd been screaming for a long time. "Is it you?"

"Who asks his girlfriend that on a regular basis?" She smiled and wiped at the tears and ichor streaking her cheeks.

He sat up, shedding the rest of the monster skin Ankou had disguised him in.

Finn led Jack to a claw-footed tub and gently washed the gore from his hair and skin. Her fingers paused over a black tattoo over his heart—an ornate, Gothic key. *That* was new.

He didn't look at her as he whispered, "Are you dead?"

The desperation in his eyes made her press his hands, strong and scarred, to her breast so that he could feel her heartbeat. "I'm real. I'm alive. And so are you."

"I don't feel alive." He closed his eyes, water glistening on his eyelashes.

She pushed her hands into his hair and leaned in to kiss him again. He dragged her against him. She felt him smile against her mouth as she twined around him with a mermaid's strength.

In that cottage Finn had imagined into existence, they discovered how alive they were in the land of the dead.

FINN WOKE TO FIND WILD ROSES curling through the latticed windows and sunlight kissing her skin. Jack slept beside her, one arm flung over her, his brows pinched together. She could sense the woozy dreaminess of the underworld pressing at the edges of her mind, but the scent from the roses was visceral and green.

Jack opened his eyes and smiled drowsily. He tugged her against him, proving again just how perfectly their bodies fit together. "My braveheart. Did you make all this?"

The sun was fading as he kissed her again. Thunder rumbled in the land of Annwyn. Rain began to hit the cottage roof, drifting through the open windows to bedazzle their bare skin.

"I did. Do you like it?" She wanted to pretend this was real, but they were still in the land of the dead.

"Not as much as I like this." He bent his head.

Then Finn saw a girl with long white hair sprawled in the armchair opposite the bed. Jack must have sensed her, because he slithered up, reaching for a weapon he didn't have. Finn, who'd left the silver dagger on the floor next to the monstrous rabbit skin, recognized the girl, and didn't relax as Jack said stonily, "Norn."

"Well, now you've done it." The Fata who was leader of the Wild Hunt and one of Death's lieutenants leaned forward, hands clasped. She looked too otherworldly for the denim jacket and jeans she wore. "An act of life in a place of death. Are you two *trying* to end the world?"

"Not yet." Jack seemed to still be looking around for a weapon while keeping his attention on the Fata girl.

"You need to leave," Norn addressed Finn.

"Not without J—"

"Oh, take him." Norn sat back, legs apart, resignation on her perfect face. "You're lucky the Ankou and his boss are busy at the moment and can't find your"—she indicated the cottage—"bit of paradise."

"How did you—"

"I'm head of border patrol here. Which elemental let you in, Finn Sullivan?"

"Um . . . it wasn't an elemental." She couldn't tell Norn it had been Caliban—she didn't want to endanger their only way out.

Norn's face and hands became shadow. "Fine. Don't tell me."

Then Finn and Jack were standing in a black forest.

"Damn." Finn scowled. "I hate that."

"Well." Jack gestured to their T-shirts and jeans. "At least she sent us packing with clothes on."

Finn clutched at the butterfly-in-glass hanging from the leather string around her neck. Amused, he said, "Are you going to do a magic trick?"

"You're going to be upset when you find out what I did." She felt the glass begin to crack, the butterfly to beat its wings. She let go of the pendant. The butterfly burst free, scarlet as new blood.

Jack was puzzled. "You expected me to be upset over a butterfly?"

"Come on." She tugged at his hand. "We follow it."

They forged onward through the forest. Finn found the hanged bodies in the distance no less frightening with Jack beside her. When he paused to peer at a corpse that seemed to have grown between the cracks in a giant tree, she had to tug him away. The cold mist made her feel violated as it crept beneath her clothing.

"Finn, beloved." Jack's velvety voice made her smile. "Who was it that showed you the Way here?"

In the forest gloom before them, a hand snatched the scarlet butterfly from the air and crushed it.

A figure stepped onto the path before them, its stance aggressive, its soft laugh fluid with malice.

"You're dead," Jack said flatly as Caliban prowled forward, unnervingly pearlescent and platinum-haired once again. His fur-lined coat was open to reveal a bare chest spiraled with Celtic tattoos and scars.

"Well, yes, Jacko. I'm dead, again, thanks to your sweetheart, here." Caliban's smile was terrifying. "Your bullet and your girl's elixir, that border place and your three vindictive bitches . . . all of that made me mortal. I was *human*. Now." He stepped back, arms flung wide. "I'm a Jack again, thanks to the Resurrectionist."

Jack leaped at Caliban, who allowed Jack to slam him against a tree. Jack hissed, "You dragged Finn here just to become a Jack again?"

"What? No thanks?" Caliban grinned. Jack curled one hand into a fist. "Jack, we need each other. You need me to show you the Way out and I need a living mortal to get us through Death's door."

Jack released Caliban, stepped back, and cast a reproving look at Finn.

"Come along now." Caliban began strolling deeper into the forest. "This is where things begin to get unpleasant."

"Who told you the Way in?" Jack asked Caliban in a conversational tone as he and Finn followed.

"A secret admirer of yours," Caliban answered in the infuriatingly sly way of all psychotics. "One who noticed your beloved attempting to find a door into Annwyn."

Jack glanced at Finn, who narrowed her eyes at him and said, "You expected me *not* to come for you?"

"I didn't think it was possible, even for you. What have you been stirring up?"

"She gave up on you, boyo." Caliban climbed lithely over a massive fallen tree scalloped with fungi that resembled human hands. "After the fourth try."

Jack's stare on the back of Finn's neck as she clambered over the deadfall unsettled her more than the lifeless surroundings or the brutal killer leading them.

She felt her skin crawl when they stepped into a clearing of crimson plants with white buds like eyes. They *were*, in fact, eyes, and Finn squeamishly realized they wouldn't be able to get across the clearing without stepping on a few of the Dolls Eye plants. In the murk, she could see the looping wreck of the roller coaster.

As they moved forward, cautious, past rusting concession stands fluttering with bleached banners, Finn glimpsed slinking shadows, heard unsettling giggles. She winced and looked away from a carousel that seemed to be made from the glazed carcasses of real horses.

Caliban stopped in front of a funhouse, its entrance a giant face, its mouth a tunnel seeping blackness. Beyond was an arched sign, rusting and broken: FUNLAND. Caliban gestured. "That's our exit ramp—"

He broke off. Finn's heart slammed in dismay when she saw a young woman gliding from the dark of the tunnel, her gown of crimson silk swirling. *No*, Finn thought, and gripped Jack's hand as a ferocious protectiveness rose in her.

Caliban dropped to his knees and whispered, "My queen."

"Jack." Reiko halted a only a few steps away, her eyes an inhuman burning green in her girl's face. "If you leave, you will never see me again."

"You're not real, Reiko," Jack said, a crack in his otherwise calm voice.

"I love you!" It was Reiko who fractured this time. Her eyes became pleading, her hands outstretched. "I grew a *heart* for you."

"And then you cut it out and hid it," Jack gently reminded her. "Along with several of mine."

Finn felt his hand tightening around hers.

She heard Caliban laugh, glanced down at his white, satiny head. He slowly rose, teeth bared. He spat, "False thing."

"Not false," Reiko whispered. Ignoring Finn and Caliban, she placed her hands on either side of Jack's face. Her ruby lips spoke his name with centuries of longing and desire and possessiveness.

Jack walked forward, *through* her. As Finn and Caliban followed him toward the tunnel, Finn heard Jack's name spoken in a fading whisper.

Caliban led them into the tunnel that wasn't completely dark. There were toadstools and strands of fungus that glowed the blue or green of deep sea creatures. There were tiny lights that Jack softly warned her to avoid. And there were figures that sometimes passed them. Finn tried not to look directly at the figures, as they seemed half formed: half ghost, half darkness, trailing tentacles of shadow.

"Why aren't they trying to stop us?" Finn asked, clutching Jack's hand.

"Because we're real," Jack told her, not taking his gaze from the fungi-lit dark before them. "And they're not."

"Could you two shut up?" Caliban glanced back at them, his face a shadowy sculpture. "I'm concentrating on getting you two *colossally* annoying fools out of here."

Casually, Jack said, "Again, I'll ask: Who told you how to do this? Because I know you're not capable of figuring out an escape this complex."

"I wonder why my queen kept cutting your heart out instead of your tongue?" Caliban mused. "And here we are." He halted, indicating an immense tree in the center of a clearing glowing with mist, and moonlight shimmering on the wings of hundreds of scarlet butterflies. As Caliban walked toward the tree, a strange whispering swept through the air. The tree seemed to be hung with large gourds, but, as Finn and Jack drew closer, it became clear to Finn what really hung in those branches. Her courage turned to jelly.

"It's a thing of beauty, isn't it?" Caliban circled the tree, fascination on his face.

The tree was hung with girls' heads—not bloody, dead trophies, but—worse—pretty, living things with blushed lips. Mercifully, all of their eyes were closed. Their lips moved as each murmured softly.

Jack looked furious. In a voice thick with revulsion, he said, "This is *your* doing. This is something *your* vile mind created."

Caliban shrugged modestly. Then he beckoned to Finn. "Come on, sweetheart. Don't be rude. Introduce yourself to one of my girls."

Finn cautiously approached the tree, casting a ferocious look at Caliban. "What do I do, you bastard?"

"Just talk nice to them. Ask the way out."

Jack casually circled round to step between Finn and Caliban as Finn spoke to the closest girl's head, one with auburn hair and a tiny, diamond crown, "How do we get out of Annwyn?"

The head's eyes opened. It spoke in a sweet voice that had nothing of horror in it. "We are the Door."

"How do we get out?"

Another head spoke. "Your blood." Finn, recognizing the voice, thought she would vomit when she turned and saw a blond head with the face of Angyll Weaver, Anna's sister. The head closed its eyes and continued whispering, "Your blood."

Jack turned on Caliban and asked with quiet threat, "*Damn you.* Who showed you the Way into Annwyn, *crom cu?*"

"Ah, does it matter? Tell your beloved to open a vein so we can get out of here."

Jack stepped toward him with a wild smile. "How about if I open your—"

"Jack." Finn didn't look away from Caliban. She drew Eve's silver dagger from the waistband of her jeans and cut the ball of her thumb. She flung her blood at the tree.

The tree's roots twisted aside and the trunk split to reveal a gaping blackness, a root-clogged tunnel dripping beetles and centipedes.

Jack gestured to Caliban. "It's your exit. You first."

Caliban bowed and slid into the insect-laden darkness. His voice echoed back, "Oh, by the way, Finn, sweetheart, don't look back at Jacko until we're out. You know that story, surely?"

Recalling the tale of Orpheus and Eurydice, Finn whispered, "Jack."

"I'll be right behind you." He laid one hand against the nape of her neck.

Finn plunged into the veil of soil and roots with Jack close behind her. Immediately, the world became pitch-black. She muffled a squeal as something dropped onto her shoulder and seemed to slither into her T-shirt.

Light flared before her, and Caliban smiled slyly back at them. He raised something he'd taken from his coat—a bloodless, dismembered hand with flames flickering blue at the fingertips. As he tossed a match away, Finn flinched and Jack said, "*Is that necessary?*"

"Your girl's seen worse, I'm sure." Caliban waved the gruesome torch.

Finn shuddered as she realized that was true.

As they progressed, the network of roots became a wall of earth on either side. When Finn glimpsed, buried in the soil, a curve of pale stone and what looked like an eye socket, she frowned. Caliban raised the corpse hand to reveal that the tunnel had become an ivory knot-work of skulls, femurs, rib cages, and other skeletal remains.

"More of your victims, *crom cu*?" Jack sounded nonchalant, which Finn knew was usually when he was at his most deadly.

"How should I know if they were mine? They don't have skin anymore."

Finn's hand tightened around the silver dagger as, behind her, Jack bent close and said in her ear, "Do we really need him?"

"I heard that," Caliban called back, and Finn glared at the bastard.

"Finn!" Jack's sudden yell almost spun her around—

Someone grabbed her wrist and jerked her forward—she met Caliban's gaze as he said, "Darling, as much as I hate to be of any assistance to this epic and sickening romance between the two of you, I'm to bring you *both* back. *Don't look at him.*"

"Finn." Jack's voice was clear behind her. His hand fell on her shoulder. "That wasn't me yelling your name." He sounded tense. "Something's trying to trick you."

"Jack." Finn spoke with insane calm, without glancing back at him. "How will I know it's you?"

Gently, wryly, Jack replied, "Even if I was being eaten alive, I wouldn't call out to you."

"Well, that's reassuring." Finn began following Caliban again. She wanted to reach back and grab Jack's hand, but that would be the same as looking at him. She didn't care anymore about the disgusting tunnel or Caliban's hideous torch—she could only think about not making the mistake of turning around.

It seemed an eternity passed, of her pushing past roots and sticky cobwebs, gripping human skulls for balance and avoiding insects. Jack was silent now, occasionally touching her or speaking her name. Doubt and anguish slithered through her. *Is it really Jack? Have I been tricked?* . . . The worry became an almost physical pain. "Jack?"

"I'm here."

"At last!" Caliban halted and raised the Hand-of-Glory. "I hope you two can swim."

Finn edged forward. Hope flickered out when she saw the crimson lake before her. In the center of the lake loomed a massive obsidian arch of skeletal remains. As a carrion reek broke over them, she raised a hand to her nose and mouth. The crimson water was blood. Jack said, still behind her, "We need only get through the arch. That has to be the way out. Isn't that what your new master told you, dog?"

Caliban grabbed Finn by the hair. She indignantly tore at his hands as he said, "If I touch her, in a different sort of way, what can you do, jackal, without risking her seeing you and being stuck here forever?"

Finn stopped struggling. She snapped, "I can close my eyes and not see him, moron." And, as she did just that, she felt Jack tackle Caliban with a fullback's violence. She yelled, "Stop! *Stop it!* We don't have time!" She opened her eyes and waded into the blood, which rippled around her calves with the revolting thickness of cream.

Caliban surged past her, swimming toward the arch.

The floor of the lake fell from under her and Finn began to swim also, keeping her head above the liquid. She heard Jack behind her.

As they drew closer to the arch, the blood began to ripple. She thought of monsters living in it, of finned and teethy things, of eels with human faces. A wave of red from beyond the arch washed over her. She gasped, choked as it went down her throat. She sank. Her mouth and nose filled with blood. Blackness began to close over her—

Hands grasped her, dozens of them, gently, and she felt herself being lifted. Her head broke the surface of the lake. A swan boat drifted nearby, and Finn clutched at it. She glimpsed faces beneath the surface of the blood lake, lithe bodies as translucent as jellyfish. Whatever they were, they had helped her.

Jack popped up beside her. They hauled themselves into the boat. The tall figure in the prow, dressed in a hoodie and jeans, didn't turn.

"Charon," Jack greeted it warily.

"Where's Caliban?" Finn pushed sticky hair from her eyes. She peered over the side of the boat.

"We won't be seeing him. His ghastly mind formed the way out. Some of this blood belonged to his victims." Jack turned to her and his smile was white in his blood-streaked face. "We made it."

"We need him!" Finn leaned down toward the bloody surface of the lake and spoke to the creatures. "Don't take the *crom cu*! Not yet! Please! We need him to get out."

"Finn." Jack spoke softly. "Do you really think they'll listen?"

She glanced at him desperately, met his silver gaze beneath dark hair dripping red.

When he jumped back into the blood, she yelled. She watched him vanish. The surface of the sanguine lake became still.

"The living do not escape." Her head snapped up just as the charon swung the oar in a low arc toward her head.

Before Finn could move, a hand glided from the water and seized the oar, and Jack slithered up from the blood, wrenching the oar from the charon.

Another blood-swathed figure—Caliban—clambered into the boat, behind the charon, took hold of the charon's head, and snapped his neck. Finn and Jack watched in astonishment as the boatman fell over the side.

Jack said to Caliban, predatory, "Did you just murder our guide out of the underworld?"

"You can't murder a shadow." Caliban twirled the oar as if it were a baton and held the grip toward Finn. "And your girl is our guide. Only she can steer us to the door to the living."

"Then"—Jack smiled, his eyes black—"what do we need *you* for?"

Caliban grinned, his teeth streaked with red. "My associate will only let us through the door if I'm with you. Ah, Jack, don't look so disappointed that our bromance is fated to end soon, alas."

Finn pushed to the front of the boat and accepted the oar. As she dipped it into the lake of blood, the first horror of a mermaid emerged, followed by others.

CHAPTER 8

Nobody, nobody told me
What nobody, nobody knows;
Hide thy face in a veil of light,
Put on thy silver shoes,
Thou art the stranger I know best,
Thou art the sweetheart, who
Came from the land between wake and dream,
Cold with the morning dew.

—"UNDER THE ROSE," WALTER DE LA MARE

It had become an endless night fraught with anxiety, and Sylvie's heart was a war drum. But she didn't feel fatigued at all. *Do I like this sort of thing? Am I an adrenaline junkie?* she thought. *What's wrong with me?*

She, Lily, and Christie were following Phouka Banríon across a moonlit meadow in the Blackbird Mountains. They had driven through a town of shabby houses, bars, and convenience stores, and parked in a weedy lot near a cemetery even older than Soldiers' Gate. The iron fence around the graveyard was tilting and the gates hung open. Beyond were weed-choked and tree-shattered crypts and headstones. Even in a night simmering with warmth and crickets, it was a cold place. The faltering streetlights cast their shadows sharply onto the road.

Christie glanced at Phouka. "Can you get past those iron gates?"

"As long as we move quickly and I don't touch the iron."

"Let's go then." Lily, who had driven like a demon to get here with Phouka's directions, strode forward.

Sylvie had noticed something that made her inhale sharply. "Wait—" She grabbed at Lily's denim jacket, missed. She heard Christie also suck in a breath.

Lily had no shadow.

As Lily neared the cemetery gates, she was suddenly flung back by an invisible force. Christie caught her before she fell. While Lily straightened with a little snarl, Phouka carefully asked, "Has that happened before?"

"No . . . but I haven't been near a cemetery." Lily shoved her hands into the back pockets of her jeans. She didn't take her gaze from the cemetery gates. "Go on. I'll wait."

Lily bowed her head. Phouka walked to the gates. Christie reluctantly moved after. Sylvie whispered, "Lily—"

"Just get her back." Lily's face was eclipsed in shadow, one cheekbone made white by the streetlamps. As Christie pushed open the gates and he and Phouka began walking down the weed-clotted road, Sylvie promised, "We will."

Sylvie strode after Christie and Phouka. She was armed with a silver glaive, silver jewelry, talismans, and a wickedly pointed elder wood dagger with roses on the hilt. As they walked, the moonlight glowed on the headstones. They passed a pagoda of crimson basalt, a trio of faceless angels, a tiny stone cross with a stone skull on top.

"It's May Eve. We have to wait until midnight to open Death's door. If we fail, we'll have to wait until midsummer." Phouka led them to the rear of the cemetery, where a forest of yews and elderberry bushes crept up a mossy incline. Another pair of gates loomed here, but these were made of elaborate, interlaced iron and led into the forest.

"Then let's hurry." As Christie attempted to shove open the creeper-veiled gates, Sylvie asked Phouka, "Why can't Lily get into the cemetery?"

Phouka was still. "I don't know."

But Sylvie could tell she did know. She just didn't want to tell Sylvie. And that sent Sylvie's stomach plummeting. "Is she . . . is Lily—" Sylvie couldn't finish. Instead, she asked, "If the door to Annwyn is open, are you going to shut it? Even if Finn is still on the other side?"

"Who told you that?" Phouka's eyes slitted. "The Black Scissors?"

"I'm sorry," Sylvie said, meaning it. "I'm *trying* to trust you."

"Well." Phouka shrugged. "Trust is earned, isn't it?"

"Sylv," Christie called, struggling with the gate. "A little help here?"

Sylvie hurried to him and together they pushed until the gate had opened far enough that Phouka could slip through. As she did, she told them, "There are no roads. Only this path. Stay close to me. There'll be sentinels at four points—east, west, north, and south." She began leading them across a bramble-choked lot. The remnants of a sign rose above the trees in the distance. Sylvie presumed the sign was supposed to read FUNLAND, but the "N" was missing.

"FU Land." Christie regarded the sign with weary skepticism. "Irony, thou art my mistress."

Shadows seemed to skitter through the trees as they approached the entrance to the theme park. As they neared the skeletal wreck of the roller coaster, Sylvie checked her daggers. Phouka leaped onto the roller coaster's fern-swathed track. Christie and Sylvie climbed after her. As Phouka led them through a tunnel of greenery, up a curve of the roller coaster's track flaking with rust, Sylvie looked down at the corroded tracks. "Phouka—isn't this iron?"

"It's steel." Phouka glanced back at them, her lips white, her face drawn. "Not as much iron, so it's bearable." She moved onward. "The mortal who created steel was one of our mortals."

"Andrew Carnegie was one of the blessed? That figures. Was Rockefeller?" Christie trudged after her.

Something crumbled beneath Sylvie's feet and she dropped with a scream—

—a grip on her arm almost wrenched her shoulder from its socket, but kept her from a bad fall into a tangle of metal and rotting timber. She grabbed a steel strut as Christie, the muscles bunching in his arm, pulled her up. Phouka, who had lunged back, steadied her.

"Be careful," Phouka warned her. "This is a borderland and the dead are hungry." She gestured with her head.

Slowly, dreading what she'd find, Sylvie looked over one shoulder. Crouched where the tracks gaped with rot was a pale figure with no face and clawed hands that scratched at the tracks. Sylvie carefully turned her back on the monster and began to follow along the track again. She could see fireflies flickering in the ivy around them. She concentrated on those.

Christie glanced at her. "Did you need to bring all those knives?"

"Are you gonna use a poem on that thing behind us, if it decides to eat us?"

"It didn't even have teeth, Sylv—and, yes, I'd use heka. It'll work fantastic here."

Phouka hushed them and Christie immediately shut up. They slid down the roller-coaster tracks, into a tunnel of vines and trees, and stepped into a field scattered with derelict concession stands, a tilted carousel with grotesquely misshapen horses, and a Ferris wheel spiky and sinister against the full moon. Sinewy, scarlet plants grew everywhere, beaded with white berries with black dots in their centers.

Sylvie recollected Jane Emory's botany course. "That's a lot of banesberry."

"Dolls Eyes." Phouka's voice was strained, and that put Sylvie on edge. "It'll be the creeper-on-the-floor then."

"What's the creeper—" Christie suddenly gasped and bent over.

Phouka looked sharply at him. "Christopher . . ."

He raised his head. Sylvie flinched—his pupils were so dilated, his eyes were almost black. A thread of blood ran from one nostril. A scrawl of words had appeared like an inky tattoo on his neck.

Phouka walked to Christie and placed her hands on his shoulders. Her silver eyes glinted. "This borderland is affecting you. Don't fight it."

Christie nodded and shook his head as if to clear it. "I'm good."

Phouka turned and led them through the abandoned theme park, toward a dark river that snaked into a narrow building painted black, a former Tunnel of Love with a giant Day-of-the-Dead skull spray-painted around the entrance. Two dirty fiberglass swan boats bumped against the river's muddy banks.

"What you said"—Sylvie reached for the elder wood dagger the Black Scissors had given her—"about the creeper-on—"

"A spirit. A sentinel."

"So can we get past it?"

"Probably not." Phouka halted and said softly, "There it is."

A wrought-iron sign forming the words WISH AWAY arched above a well of moss-splotched brick. Mist breathed from the well, curling toward them in smoky wraiths.

I've been scared before, Sylvie told herself, unsheathing her elder wood dagger. A tiny Japanese netsuke carving of a crow and two silver bells dangled on leather strings from the dagger's handle. *This is no big deal.*

As the mist fell away from something huddled near the well, Sylvie could make out long dark hair, a plaid dress, and white skin veined with black. A girl's sobbing echoed.

Christie cursed. A line of poetry blossomed on his arm.

"So." Sylvie gripped the elder wood knife in one hand and a silver dagger in the other. She was shivering. "We're all in agreement that's not really a girl, right?"

"I'm *alone*," the thing moaned. "All *alone*."

The mist curled away from a knobby, long-nailed hand clutching a teddy bear with a doll's head.

"How do we get past it?" Christie sounded ill.

Phouka spoke without looking at either of them. "*You* are going to run, Christopher, and get into that building—use the maintenance entrance. When you come to Death's door, you'll know. Sylvie, I'm going to need you—"

The sentinel materialized from the mist and, although it was the size of a young girl, Sylvie recoiled, because its face was nothing but teeth. Sylvie clenched both daggers so she wouldn't scream. How was she ever going to sleep again? "*Go,* Christie."

As Christie began moving past the sentinel, Phouka stepped forward and said to it, "Let us pass."

"Give me something," it whined. "Give me blood!"

It lunged at Christie. Phouka grabbed it by its hair and yelled, "Now!"

Christie raced toward the Tunnel of Love as Phouka wrenched the sentinel around so that it faced Sylvie. Sylvie, who had never deliberately killed anything in her life, hesitated.

The sentinel turned, snarling, and raked a dirty hand across Phouka's chest. She fell back and her eyes went dark.

Sylvie ran at the teethy thing, panicked, ready to shove both daggers into it.

The sentinel crouched, slavering. Then it leaped, colliding with Sylvie, who hit the ground beneath it. Silently, desperately, she lashed out with the daggers. The sentinel's claws ripped at her and its too-large feet gouged the ground beside her. *I'm going to die,* Sylvie thought as hysteria ripped her breath away. *I'm going to*—then she saw a clear strike.

She shoved the silver dagger into the sentinel's throat. As it reared back, kicking up clots of dirt, and screaming, Sylvie, her skin burning with welts and scratches, rolled over and vomited. Fighting waves of chill and dizziness, she heard the creature turn on Phouka, heard them struggling.

A sound like hundreds of wings calmed Sylvie. When she lifted her head, strands of hair sticking to her face, she saw several crows perched on the nearby carousel.

She spun up as Phouka rolled and pinned the sentinel with a long black dagger she pulled from beneath her jacket. The sentinel screeched. It tore free, slamming its feet into Phouka's chest. As Phouka went backward, into the well, Sylvie shouted and dove forward.

The sentinel shoved a hand against Sylvie's chest. Sylvie fell back against the well, hissing as the impact bruised all along her back. Tears smeared her vision.

The sentinel leaped at her—

—and was struck in the face by a swinging board. As the monster fell, Sylvie, astonished, saw a silhouette step between her and it. *"Lily?"*

The sentinel, oozing dark liquid from its smashed face, twitched itself upright, Sylvie's silver dagger glinting in its throat. It lurched, its face full of chattering teeth. "You will not get *past me*—"

Lily said, "Bitch, you're standing between me and my sister."

The monster, which had been making horrid little starts toward them, scuttled back. As Sylvie pushed herself to her feet, the sentinel leaped, knocking Lily aside.

Sylvie heard a storm of wings, the hoarse call of a crow. A voice whispered in her head: Let me in.

The sentinel hit the ground, face-first, and Sylvie blinked away the fury of dark wings and stared down at the dagger sticking out of the back of the sentinel's skull. Swaying on her feet, watching the thing melt into an ooze of teeth and sour-smelling gore, Sylvie was almost sick again. She said to Lily, "You killed it. I can't believe you killed it. How did you get into the cemetery?"

Lily grinned. "I walked around it."

"You are one badass chick."

"Not compared to *you*. Speaking of which." Lily looked around. "Where's Phouka? And Christie?"

✦ ✦ ✦

CHRISTIE HATED THIS. He hated it. He'd left a girl . . . woman . . . Fata . . . he cared about, and his best friend, to fend for themselves against a . . . whatever that had been. But they had ten minutes, according to the fancy watch he'd borrowed from his dad. Ten minutes to open Death's door and hope that Finn made it through.

The metal maintenance door opened as he yanked it. Drawing a flashlight from his backpack, switching it on, he raced along the rickety walk that ran alongside a manufactured river. The water, swampy with weeds and garbage, was black. The mildewed slats were slippery beneath the soles of his boots.

When he ascended the stairs leading up to a stage that was a parody of a ballroom with a black-and-white floor and a red chandelier, he knew he'd come to the right place. In the center was a massive door of black wood carved with a pair of waltzing skeletons in formal clothing. He strode across the tiled floor.

The water beneath the stage glopped, as if something large had broken the surface. There was a loud thump. Something had flung itself onto the wooden slats of the stairs.

No. No. No. Not again. He could hear what sounded very much like claws and scales on the wood. He imagined a large, eel-like corpse with a skull for a head and water weeds for hair and eyes that were nothing but iridescent beetles—

The heka Phouka had taught him stuck in his throat. All he had for defense were an iron ring and the medieval-looking dagger Sylvie had given him. He pulled out the dagger and turned to see exactly what he'd envisioned crawling toward him, its large, serpentine body scraping on the tiles, the green skull of its head rotating as if it were seeking him by scent. The heka spilled from his lips in words that made his bones vibrate:

> *"The mermaid on her rock did untangle*
> *The ocean of her hair,*
> *With a comb of sailor's bones*
> *While others cried 'Beware . . .'"*

The corpse thing shuddered and recoiled. Christie felt the hekas bleeding onto his skin as he continued,

"And seeing this, the sailor's girl,
Fresh, bright, and full of fate,
Mourning, cursed the mermaid,
Into a corpse of hate."

The eel woman hissed. Christie saw her grotesque form blur and darken like a photograph being burned at the edges. Black flakes began to sift from her scales. He felt the old power slither through him, from his spine, to the nape of his neck. He coughed, tasted blood.

The withered monster coiled back and slid into the polluted water.

Fatigue now dragging at him, fear and triumph warring within him, Christie turned.

As darkness swept out and over him, Christie felt all his sunlit days fading, the kisses from all the girls leaving him, the span of his eighteen years as a human being devoured by the dark.

SYLVIE AND LILY DIDN'T NEED TO HELP Phouka out of the well—she climbed out on her own, drenched, furious, and swearing. As she raced toward the Tunnel of Love, they followed.

The maintenance door was still open. Sylvie lifted her smashed flashlight and was relieved when it switched on. Phouka said, "I don't need that," and stepped into the darkness. Sylvie and Lily ran after her, along the boardwalk beside the black river.

"There!" Lily raced toward stairs leading to a stage where an enormous door rose like a Gothic monument amid tacky red, black, and white props meant to symbolize love. Christie stood before the door, his back to them.

Phouka caught hold of Sylvie and Lily. She said, "That's not Christopher."

Sylvie's stomach heaved as Christie turned, revealing that he now wore an elaborate golden mask—a three-faced design, each face resembling that of a snarling canine. Sylvie's hands began to shake, the glow from the flashlight she held flickering across that grotesque visage. *"Christie . . ."*

Phouka told Sylvie, "You need to ask him to open the door. He's become the final sentinel."

"How?" Sylvie only wanted her best friend back.

"Call him back." There was a crack in Phouka's cool voice.

Sylvie set down the flashlight and approached Christie. She took a deep breath. "This isn't you, Christopher Robin Hart."

The masked head tilted. Sylvie saw only darkness in the eye holes of the canine face. She tentatively reached out, cupped the cold metal of the mask in her hands, and whispered, "Finn is going to die if you don't goddamn remember who you are and get that door open."

"Sylvie," Phouka cautioned. "He needs to be both. He needs to be the sentinel and himself."

"Okay, okay. I got it," Sylvie snapped. She looked back into Christie's eyes, or where his eyes used to be. "Just. Remember. Who. You. Are."

The masked head turned slightly. A hollow voice that wasn't Christie's said, "No one is allowed to come through."

Sylvie hit him in the chest. "I'm not kissing you again to bring you back."

The mask turned to her. Sylvie met Christie's startled gaze within it. He pushed off the golden Cerberus mask and demanded in his own voice, "*When did you kiss me?*"

The mask vanished in his hands like a blown-out flame.

The door whispered open, but it wasn't the view of the land of the dead that Sylvie had expected. Christie said, dumbfounded, "Why does the underworld look like the inside of StarDust?"

"Because that's not the underworld." Phouka stepped toward it. "Someone hacked Death's door."

"Then we've lost." Sylvie wanted to cry. "We've lost her."

"Wait." Lily held up a hand, peering into the darkened interior of StarDust. "What is that?"

CHAPTER 9

Now you have asked me questions three,
Parsley, sage, rosemary, and thyme,
I hope you'll answer as many for me,
And you shall be a true lover of mine.

—"The Cambric Shirt," Anonymous

They had beaten away the mermaids in a brief battle of brutal desperation. Her hands shaking, her heart steady, Finn steered the swan boat to a stone stairway rising from the blood. At the top of the stairway was a pair of doors engraved with flowers, eyes, and hands.

The boat bumped against the stairway. Jack and Finn clambered out. Caliban followed. When she reached the doors, Finn shoved at them, was shocked when they fell open. She stared at the interior of StarDust Studios.

Caliban dashed past her.

"Finn." Jack grabbed her hand. They stepped into StarDust together and the doors clanked shut behind them.

At the back of StarDust, where moonlight poured like venom through the French doors, Caliban turned—and he wasn't the Jack he'd appeared to be, but scruffy and—*mortal.*

"Trick," Finn breathed, as Caliban opened the French doors and fled.

She and Jack raced for the rear doors even as they swung shut with a rattle. Darkness slammed down around them. Jack cursed.

Three girls manifested around them and, her heart sinking, Finn recognized them. The Lily Girls—Beatrice, Abigail, and Eve—Jack's former lovers, each killed by Reiko. Jack greeted them amicably. "Bea. Abbie. Eve. Eve, I remember your collection of fossils and ammonites. You wanted to go to college in California and work in a museum. What've you gone and made an alliance with? I know you, Evie. You don't have a hive mentality."

"We haven't allied with anyone, murderer," spoke Beatrice, her red bob glittering with iridescent water beetles.

Finn stepped in front of Jack as Abigail, her gown swirling like sea foam, glided toward them. Jack didn't look away when Abigail's blond hair fell back to reveal that half her face was withered and eyeless. Calmly, he said, "I led each of you astray. I tricked you for my own ends. I am truly sorry. But you can't keep us here. You need to let us go."

"Jack." Eve's voice was the most human. "You won't be able to leave. This place is a trap."

"This place is where you brought the crooked dog and made him human," Finn accused, seething with fury. "And now he'll be a terror again, thanks to you three and your revenge, because whatever is helping him probably promised to make him a Jack again if he brought us here. *Who wanted us here?*"

Eve bowed her head.

The creak of a film reel was followed by a silvered image of Jack's 1920s actor-self projected over his face. He said, "Let Finn go."

"Eve," Finn first addressed the black-haired girl, then looked at the other two. "Abigail. Beatrice. *Don't do this.*"

They gazed at her with black-rimmed eyes, their deadness icing the air. At last, Beatrice moved toward Finn, her dress of green silk glittering with water drops. "Knowing our names doesn't give you power over us. Serafina."

Bitch, Finn thought. Blood threaded from her left nostril.

Ghostly Abigail drifted closer, her gown billowing with the milky translucence of poison in a glass of water. "You're very pretty. I was pretty, once."

Beatrice circled Finn. Finn didn't take her gaze from the redhead whose death had been the worst, drowned and eaten by a kelpie at Reiko's behest. Beatrice halted in front of Finn, and Finn flinched when she saw tadpoles swimming in the ghost girl's green eyes.

Then the world went dark. Finn's courage dropped like a stone.

When the moonlight returned, Jack knelt, cradling Abigail, whose white dress was stained with blood trickling from her nose and mouth. His voice was a hoarse, broken chant. "I can't save her . . ."

As water began pooling around him, Abigail became Beatrice's remains. Finn had to look away as horror rushed vomit into her mouth and the water around her Converses bloomed with red. Jack was voiceless this time, but his grief and shock were palpable. He was reliving their deaths. *"Let him go,"* Finn cried to the Lily Girls. "I didn't drag him out of Annwyn just so you could bash him over the head with guilt."

You can't get out either came the vicious whisper from the dark.

Shadows clotted around Jack. He was as unreachable to Finn as if he was back in Annwyn. He curled into a fetal position on the floor, cradling a human heart in his hands, "Eve," he said, his voice raw.

Finn lay down opposite Jack, facing him. His gaze was dull. "Jack . . . I need you to hear me: This isn't real . . ."

When he didn't respond, she slid one hand toward him, but her fingers struck an invisible barrier. She breathed in dust and leaf rot. "Your father did exorcisms, didn't he? How did he get rid of mortal spirits?"

She ignored the iced feeling along her spine, as if something crouched in the dark behind her was preparing to pounce. She'd faced down much worse than angry dead girls. "You pulled me from the water when I was little. You saved me. You saved my sister. And Christie. And Sylvie. And now I need you to come back. *Come back!*"

Jack's eyes snapped open and they were as tarnished as an old mirror's. "Finn?"

She sat up. Eve's heart was gone from his hands.

As Jack focused on Finn, desperation tightened his voice. "You need an object belonging to each of them. I have things from Beatrice and Abigail . . . you'll find them in my apartment. In a carved wooden box."

"Can't you tell me exactly where—"

"I can't. They're listening."

"What about Eve? I've got the dagger she gave me in October."

"That's yours now. No, you need a personal item of Eve's. Her sister will have something. I've nothing of Eve's."

Finn realized she'd have to go to Sophia Avaline.

His hand lifted and she raised hers, palm to palm but not touching.

Then darkness swallowed him.

Finn reeled back as the lamps in StarDust blinked on and music blared from a phonograph. The Lily Girls became shadows. The front doors burst open.

Finn heard her *sister's* voice. "*Run*, Finn!"

"Lily?" Finn dashed for the exit as a banshee howl ripped the air. As she passed over the threshold, she felt nails raze the back of her neck.

She was caught in Lily's arms. A giant door slammed shut behind her. She stood on a stage in a dank, gloomy place decorated with faded Valentine's Day ornaments. Her friends, stunned, surrounded her. And there was Phouka.

"Where am I?" Finn stepped back from Lily, who clutched her shoulders and gazed searchingly at her. Finn thought, *I'm covered in blood.*

"You're out of the land of the dead," Lily told her. "Are you hurt?"

"The blood isn't mine," Finn explained.

Lily wrapped her in a bear hug.

As Sylvie and Christie also hugged Finn, Finn met Phouka's gaze. Phouka said, "Were you in the underworld just now? Or StarDust Studios?"

"StarDust. Caliban led us out of Annwyn, into StarDust—*where am I?*"

"FU land," Christie solemnly told her. "So Caliban's alive."

"Yes. Jack is in StarDust, trapped by the Lily Girls." Finn would get Jack away from them, no matter what she had to do. "Is this a stage? Is it spinning?"

Christie caught her as she fell. He said softly, "Lead her past all dark things, to the land where the sun sings, out of the land where death is king."

Sylvie said, "Amen."

JACK FELT AS IF THE DARK were a sludge that held his limbs.

A figure appeared, moonlight pearling skin, silvering the hyacinths in auburn curls. The raw wound in the young man's chest, over the heart, dripped more hyacinths.

"Nate." Jack couldn't control the grief that strained his voice. Nathan Clare had been his brother in a centuries-long battle to remain sane. Nathan had been his responsibility. "Who put you up to this?"

Nathan crouched before Jack. "He just wants the key, Jack. But you have to remove it yourself. Reiko hid it within you."

"Key?"

Nathan pointed and Jack glanced down at his chest, then lifted his T-shirt to reveal the black key tattoo. He whispered, "Reiko." He looked up at Nathan. "What is the key for?"

"I don't know." Nathan set a thin steel blade on the floor. "But you need to cut it out and give it to him or he's going to hurt you."

"Again, I'll ask: Who put you up to this?"

Nathan shook his head. "He won't let me say. Just do it, Jack."

Jack closed one hand around the wooden handle of the knife and smiled fiercely. "Go to hell, Nate."

Nathan sighed. "I told him you wouldn't do it." And vanished.

"WHERE THE HELL HAVE YOU BEEN?" Sean Sullivan stepped back as Lily and Christie came through the door of his house with Finn between them, her arms over their shoulders. Sylvie followed and, with a grin, said, "A paintball rave. Finn got ambushed by the red team."

"Hey, Da." Finn, who'd recovered, smiled weakly.

"A paintball . . ." Sean Sullivan looked after them but asked no more questions as they stomped up the stairs.

When they were in Finn's room, Sylvie closed the door. Lily and Christie eased Finn down onto the red velvet chaise. Lily stepped into the bathroom, then returned with a dampened towel.

"Why are you covered in . . . *is* that blood?" Christie sat on the floor.

Finn's voice was faint with exhaustion as she used the dampened towel to clean the blood from her face and arms. "There was a lake of blood in Annwyn. Caliban is working for someone who wanted Jack *out* of Annwyn. Caliban said he could be remade into a Jack, in Annwyn. He wasn't. Whoever put Caliban up to this promised to turn him afterward, I'm guessing."

Lily curled on the chaise beside Finn. "It must be Giselle, the Jill."

Christie nodded. "There's no way Caliban figured out how to get in and out of the land of the dead by himself. Or to use StarDust as a Way back. Only the

Black Scissors—and maybe Phouka—and those ghost girls know it's a Way. And Giselle would know, from David Ryder."

"And she made Tyson Follows a Jack?" Sylvie hugged one of Finn's pillows. "And promised to do it to Caliban?"

Finn asked, "Who told you I was in Annwyn?"

"Anna dreamed of Jack telling her Caliban had dragged you there."

Finn straightened. For some reason, that news set steel in her spine. "Sylvie, I need you to ask the Black Scissors about exorcisms."

Christie looked warily at Finn. "Why?"

"Because"—Finn's voice was hard—"that's how we're going to get Jack away from the Lily Girls."

A SHADOW MOVED THROUGH THE FOREST, causing blight to blacken the leaves of whatever it passed. It whispered to those hiding in the forest, the ones who didn't want to live under the Banríon's rule.

It gathered the outlaws, the Unseelie, with promises.

CHAPTER 10

Are they the dead? Are they some sentient element we haven't yet discovered? Or are they our dreams and nightmares given form?

—From the journal of Daisy Sullivan

This is not what I expected." Lily surveyed Jack's sun-dusted apartment after she and Finn had climbed in early the next day. "Very intriguing."

Finn began scanning the wall of bookshelves. "Jack said he kept a memento each from Abigail and Beatrice. Nothing from Eve. He had Eve's necklace, but sent it in the mail to her sister after Eve was killed."

"Sophia Avaline lost her sister too. I forgot." Lily grabbed a rail-backed chair and stood on it. She began rummaging through the books and objects on the highest shelves.

Finn opened the door to the apartment's only closet. "Look for something old. A wooden box, something organic and beautiful to store the memories." She walked to the nightstand and pulled the drawer open, found a tin box painted with a garish '60s illustration of a woman with green hair. *Not that.* She turned, frowning. She crouched by the railroad trunk at the foot of his bed. "Locked."

Lily jumped down from the chair and walked over. "You got a key?"

"The key I used last time"—Finn sat back on her heels—"turned into Moth."

Lily crouched and examined the lock. Then she plucked the barrette from

Finn's hair. "Hey!" Finn watched as her sister jammed the metal barrette into the lock, twisted. Finn heard a click and Lily, triumphant, popped the lid open. "Where did you—"

"I dated a bad boy or two. Remember Eddie?"

"Eddie? Wasn't he the computer hacker?" Finn began digging through Jack's belongings. She carefully set aside an old-fashioned revolver. She found a small box of pale wood with lotuses and papyrus carved into the lid and she pried it open. Within was an ivory guitar pick shaped like a cat and a faded bandeau decorated with roses of green crystal. Abigail, Jack once told her, had played the guitar. The bandeau was something a teenage girl in the '20s might wear. *Beatrice.* She turned—and jerked back when she saw a silhouette crouched on the windowsill.

She heard a click from where Lily stood, glanced over, and saw that her sister was pointing Jack's old-fashioned revolver at Moth like she knew how to use it.

Moth slowly raised his hands, palms up. He said carefully to Finn, "You're back."

Lily lowered the revolver. "She's back. Where have you been, Moth?"

He raised his head, his mouth twisting. "The Fatas haven't told you? About my past? Before Absalom's curse?"

"What do you remember?" Lily sat on Jack's bed, worry in her eyes.

When he glanced down again, his face was cast into shadow. "Just the worst parts."

Finn stepped toward him. "You were an *actor*, Moth, nothing else."

He rose and his face seemed drawn and starved. "I was a Jack. And, before that, I was a witch in a Saami tribe, centuries ago."

Finn recalled the vision he'd forced on her, of himself, a murdering knight. *Centuries ago.* This revelation was beyond troubling.

"The Fatas only made me worse than what I already was." Moth looked at Finn, then at Lily. "I was following you when you went to Death's door in Funland, but I lost you."

Finn, choosing to leave questions about his past for later, told him, "Caliban is alive. He dragged me into Annwyn, with someone's help, we don't know who. Then Jack and I were led into a trap in StarDust and the ghosts of his three dead lovers now have him. And someone recently turned a local boy into a Jack."

"Do you know a Jill named Giselle?" Lily asked Moth.

"No. You brought Jack out of the land of the dead?" He moved to his feet.

"Yes, she did." Lily was watching him. She looked down at the antique revolver and traced the engravings on the muzzle. "What was your name . . . way back when?"

He shook his head, the light threading his bright hair. "That, I don't remember. But I was a Jack for a very long time. When are you going to try to get Jack away from the Lily Girls?"

"Tonight."

He nodded. "I wanted to tell you that Sombrus isn't where I left it. Someone's taken it. That's what I've been doing, trying to find it. And Finn, Lily . . . neither Giselle nor Caliban is the dark thing I tracked out of Sombrus. Good luck at StarDust." He turned and slipped out the window.

Finn spoke past the catch in her throat. "You knew him, Lily, in the Wolf's house."

"I knew what he was when he was under Absalom's spell." Lily shoved her hands through her hair. "He never talked about being anything other than an actor named Alexander Nightshade." She sighed. "Let's visit Miss Avaline."

Finn dreaded telling Avaline what they were going to do, but there was no way around it. Tonight, Professor Avaline would have to say good-bye to her murdered sister.

SOPHIA AVALINE LIVED in the gentrified neighborhood of Rose Tree Court, where all the houses had been remodeled with their original architectural charm kept intact. Avaline's residence was a sleek town house with a Victorian flair, all gables and peaked roofs. As Finn and Lily hurried up the stairs, the door opened and Sophia Avaline appeared, as put together as ever in a designer T-shirt and sleek skirt. Carefully, she said, "I got your message. *Jack* . . ."

Finn told her, "I brought him back. And you're going to help us convince your sister to let him go."

AVALINE'S APARTMENT WAS SEVERE AND LOVELY, with Gothic Revival furniture and everything in its place. The dark hardwood floors glistened. Classical music soared at a low volume from a Bose stereo on the kitchen's quartz counter.

Avaline watched Lily, her expression cool, as Finn explained Annwyn, Caliban, and how Jack had been trapped by the Lily Girls. After Finn had finished, Avaline looked out the window. "I knew Eve was dead. I could never prove Reiko and her kind had killed her—I didn't even know what the Fata family was until Rowan told me, after Patrick, Charlotte, James, Jane, and Edmund had arrived. I suspected that my sister had been lured away, not by *whom*—I learned about Jack later." She paused, then continued, "I tried to kill Reiko once. I had a silver knife. I took it to one of their revels. Although Rowan trained us to observe and not interfere, I was going to kill her. I lost my nerve. I thought, maybe if the Fatas trusted us, I could find out what had happened to Eve. It's ironic, really, considering I'm the only one of us who *hasn't* killed a Fata."

Finn thought she'd misunderstood. "*Killed* . . . ?"

"The others in Rowan's circle have each killed a Fata—in self-defense, when they were young. They didn't understand at the time what was menacing them. Their first encounters with the children of night and nothing were not benevolent. That's why Rowan contacted them and brought them here."

"Even Jane?" Lily looked admiring.

Finn remembered Jane Emory's story about her adolescent romance with a mysterious, red-haired boy on the beach, a Fata who had been draining the life from her. Jane had claimed she'd gone after him with an iron spoon but had never seen him again. Had she lied?

"Even Jane. Would either of you like something to drink? Coffee?" Avaline rose. "I'll make some."

Lily leaned toward Finn and whispered, "She's not very surprised you brought Jack back from Annwyn."

"No." Feeling light-headed, Finn stood up. "May I use the bathroom?"

"Just down the hall." In the kitchen, Avaline was opening a cabinet.

Finn closed the door in the bathroom and ran the tap, splashing cold water on her face. Looking up, she noticed the stained-glass window over the tub illuminating miniature bottles on shelves. She walked over and carefully lifted a bottle shaped into a little glass dragon, then regarded a tiny mermaid with a curved tail, a vial with a pewter skull for a cap, and a goblin of scarlet glass.

She reached for the last bottle in the row, then sank down onto the edge of the tub—the bottle was shaped into a sphinx, an exact replica of the one Finn had taken from the Blue Lady's house in the Ghostlands. Finn shuddered and pressed her hands over her eyes.

Why did Avaline have bottles from the Blue Lady? Cruithnear had suspected a traitor among the professors, one who had broken the key to the Ghostlands and nearly sent Finn and Jack into the clutches of Seth Lot.

She tugged her cell phone from her backpack and made a quick, quiet call. Then, still clutching the little sphinx in one hand, she returned to her seat beside Lily.

Avaline set down a tray on the leather ottoman and neatly poured coffee from a silver pot. She said, "I need to ask . . . how are things at your house? Jane told me food rots quickly in your fridge. There is mold. There are shadows where there should be none." Avaline sat opposite them.

Finn whispered, "I think you should shut up now." And she set the tiny sphinx-shaped vial on the coffee tray. "It was you." She thought if she moved even slightly, she might break. "You hexed the key Jack and I used to get into the Ghostlands, didn't you? It was *you* who made the deal with the Blue Lady to give Jack to the Wolf, because you blame Jack for Eve. You weren't very surprised to learn Eve is . . . what she is. And those bottles in your bathroom come from the Blue Lady's house in the Ghostlands. This one is a duplicate of the one I took from the Blue Lady."

"The bottles." Avaline momentarily closed her eyes. "You were never in danger, Serafina. The Blue Lady would have kept you safe. You were to return to the true world. *Jack* would have satisfied the Wolf's desire for revenge. It was only Jack the Blue Lady was to give to Lot."

Lily whispered, "You traitorous—"

"Serafina . . ." Avaline began.

Finn set her cell phone beside the sphinx bottle so that Avaline could see whom she'd called.

Rowan Cruithnear.

CHRISTIE HAD FOUND A MESSAGE from Phouka in a rolled-up parchment—*parchment*—on his windowsill. He didn't understand why she couldn't just use a cell phone. The message inked on the stiff paper was: *Please fetch me a mirror from the Sphinx. The mirror is oblong with a frame of ebony lions. The house will manifest at sunset. I trust you to find a way in.*

Why does she need the mirror now? he thought irritably. "And why doesn't she get it herself?"

It made him worry.

SYLVIE AGREED TO HELP CHRISTIE at the Sphinx an hour before they were to join Finn at StarDust. "I called the Black Scissors and asked him to meet us there," she told him, "because he'll know how to perform an exorcism—and he might have a key to the Sphinx."

As they got out of his Mustang, Christie regarded the Sphinx with apprehension. "Last time I was here, a tooth was shot into my leg."

Sylvie stomped up the stone stairs with him. "Ten to one that was Caliban."

The Black Scissors stepped onto the porch before them. Sylvie had a dagger in one hand before she'd registered that it was him. Christie stared at the dagger, then at her. "Do not jump out at people like that," Sylvie scolded.

"I don't recall jumping." The Black Scissors unlocked the doors to the Sphinx with a key shaped like a dragonfly.

The minute the dragonfly key lit up and flew from the Black Scissors's hand, the Sphinx transformed from a neglected shell into a chic home, with abstract paintings on the walls and sleek furniture. Tall art deco lamps illuminated the bewitched interior.

"So Phouka's collecting mirrors from the seven houses," Christie told the Black Scissors as they moved into the living room. "Do you know why?"

"Mirrors can be used to trap spirits." The Black Scissors glanced at Sylvie. "Does the Banríon know about the StarDust exorcism?"

"No." Christie stepped into another room. "Found the mirror!"

"Sylvie." The Black Scissors walked to the bar in a corner and set down two rings. "There are two other souls we need to send on their way with the Lily Girls."

Sylvie walked over and frowned down at the rings. One was made of pewter and ivory. The other seemed woven from black threads.

"Thomas Luneht stole these from Caliban at my request, when the crooked dog was distracted. These are trophies the *crom cu* made from Nathan Clare and Thomas."

Sylvie recoiled. "Oh." That wasn't ivory in the pewter ring, but bone. And the second ring was made of hair.

She carefully gathered up the two rings. "Have you done an exorcism before?"

"I have. So has Crutihnear. I would like to know, Sylvie, how Finn got out of Annwyn."

So she told him.

LILY HADN'T ARGUED when Finn told her she couldn't come to the exorcism at StarDust. Lily had only said in that bravado way of hers: "You'll get him out."

Even at night, the sky was a mottled green gray, and thunder was rumbling when Jane Emory arrived, her VW Bug pulling into the drive of Finn's house. Finn ducked into the passenger seat just as rain began to ripple across the windshield.

"This should have been done a long time ago." Jane's tousled yellow hair was knotted with daisies and she'd brought a wreath of them for Finn, who wore them with the understanding that Jane had meant well. Daisies were not only Finn's mom's favorite flower, they were protection against Fata malice.

A half hour later, as the Bug bumped up the dirt road toward StarDust, Finn saw a few other cars parked near the glass structure. Rowan Cruithnear, Edmund Fairchild, and James Wyatt were waiting for them, along with Charlotte Perangelo and Patrick Hobson. Sophia Avaline stood between them. When Jane parked, Edmund Fairchild and Cruithnear strode to the car. Fairchild handed Jane his umbrella. As thunder rumbled across the sky, he said, "We're waiting for your friends."

Finn checked her phone, found two texts. "They're on their way."

Avaline was gazing at StarDust. Finn refused to feel sorry for her.

Rowan Cruithnear walked with Finn toward the entrance to StarDust. The doors were open. "The Black Scissors is on his way?"

"With Sylvie and Christie." Headlights flared across the glimmering glass hulk of StarDust, and Finn turned to see Christie's Mustang cruise up the road.

Cruithnear said kindly, "You need to tell Jack to bring the Lily Girls back to the time he loved them and they loved him."

"That's all?"

"Oh no. There'll be more."

Christie and Sylvie emerged from the Mustang, as did the Black Scissors. He regarded the professors with wry amusement as he opened an umbrella over his and Sylvie's heads.

"Finn." Christie, tugging up the hood of his jacket, hurried toward her. Sylvie and the Black Scissors followed. Christie said, "Hey, Mr. Cruithnear."

"Mr. Hart. Miss Whitethorn. *Dubh Deamhais.*"

"Rhymer." The Black Scissors nodded to Sylvie and she solemnly handed Rowan Cruithnear a small jewelry box. "Thomas Luneht and Nathan Clare should be freed too."

"*Dubh Deamhais.*" Cruithnear held the box carefully. "We won't be able to keep this incident from the Banríon for very long."

"No. But this is a mortal matter, not a Fata one."

"True. Come along then, and let's set things right."

They walked toward StarDust, the professors trailing behind.

Cruithnear and Finn stepped in and walked to the center of the mosaic floor, where Cruithnear opened the jewelry box to reveal two primitive rings. "All that remains of Nathan Clare and Thomas Luneht," he told her.

The sight of those awful trophies caused Finn's vision to blur and anger to whip through her. *Caliban.*

Rowan Cruithnear was studying the stage. "I remember watching Nicollette Tirnagoth make her lovely films. This was where I first met Jack. And Beatrice Amory and Nathan Clare. So many lives wasted."

The professors had each taken a white candle from the basket Jane Emory had brought. Finn recognized the candles; made with honey and myrrh, they were from Hecate's Attic. Jane handed a blue candle to Sophia Avaline, one to Finn, and another to Sylvie. "You'll be the ones communicating with the dead, sending them on," Jane said to them; she sounded worried.

"We'll instruct you on what to do." The Black Scissors stepped back. "The dead will try to fool you, make you believe their reality."

"I know," Finn said. "You think they can do better than the Grim Reaper on his own turf? They can't be worse than Annwyn."

"Serafina Sullivan"—the Black Scissors smiled—"I don't think they have a chance against you."

Finn knelt with Avaline and Sylvie in the center of StarDust while the professors, the Black Scissors, and Christie ringed them like sentries. Avaline bowed her head as if she was attending her own execution, not her sister's exorcism.

"You begin," Finn told her softly.

Sophia Avaline whispered, "Eve. Eve. I'm here. I'm here to set you free—"

Her voice broke as the electric lanterns were extinguished. The candles everyone held burst into flame, the golden light casting back the shadows. Wherever that glow touched, the decay was replaced by a surreal shard of newness: One side of a pillar became bright lapis lazuli and shining gold; a moth-eaten chair became a rich, red velvet; some of the lamps sparkled without dust or cobwebs.

On the stage, a wall of darkness folded outward, until Finn, Sylvie, and Sophia Avaline were surrounded by a night illuminated only by the candles held by their now-unseen allies. The air was drained of warmth. Finn's breath became white smoke. She kept very still as a firefly spark appeared and spiraled lazily toward them, followed by two others. She said into the crystalline silence, "Let me speak to Jack."

IN THE DARK OF NIGHT AND NOTHING, Jack heard a familiar voice say his name, but he couldn't move. Held by the past, he believed he hadn't made it out of Annwyn at all.

"LET ME SPEAK TO JACK." Finn was now alone in the ruin of StarDust, with only ghost light glowing over the shrouded furniture, whispering across the dust and deadness. The Lily Girls had drawn her into their world. "Please. I love him. I am like you, almost."

"Like us?" Beatrice materialized from the dark, her green gaze vicious. "*Your* heart still beats. You bleed. You are *nothing* like us."

Cold drenched Finn and she gasped as something tore through her—Abigail, a white wraith with a crimson-streaked face. Circling Finn, Abigail sweetly said, "Let's see how *you* like it."

Finn heard Eve Avaline cry out her name as the floor gave way beneath her and she fell—

She couldn't scream as earth cascaded over her, into her mouth. She felt it binding her arms to her sides, filling her lungs. Panic shrieked into disbelief—

Then the earth broke away over her head and she felt hands beneath her arms, dragging her out. Coughing up dirt on the floor of StarDust, Finn wiped her eyes and saw her rescuer, a young man with black hair. His gaze was dragonfly blue. "Thomas Luneht?" she asked.

He nodded. She saw, behind him, a forest of brambles enclosed by StarDust's grimed glass. She caught the malevolent glint of a pool of black water. Tiny plants with red, heart-shaped flowers bloomed from the floor.

"Thank you." She nodded and rose unsteadily, reached into her pocket to touch Beatrice's bandeau.

As Thomas vanished into his dragonfly shape, Finn, crowning herself with Beatrice's bandeau, moved into the forest, toward the black pool—

—where she found Jack, huddled over the torn remains of a girl he had loved. And even though he couldn't see Finn or hear her, she knelt beside him and whispered, "Remember when she loved you."

JACK BLINKED.

"Jack." Beatrice knelt before him, looking as she had when alive, with her wavy red hair and cherry lipstick, the tassels on her dress sparkling like emeralds. His throat closed up as he thought of her laugh, her fierceness, before his selfish desire to escape Reiko had turned her into a creature of gossamer malice. She touched his face and the dark shattered.

He stood with Beatrice in a StarDust Studios new with Egyptian art deco glamour. His suit was woven from the shadows. Her hair and skin glowed in Technicolor. She sighed and laid her head on his shoulder. "I'm being sent away, aren't I?"

"Bea . . . if I could change it, I would. I did love you."

"And I didn't love you enough." She kissed him and cascaded into an emerald stream of lights in his arms.

FINN SAW THE SHIMMER OF LIGHTS as Beatrice's spirit left the world. The pool vanished and became a cradle of nightshade plants, with Jack kneeling beside the bloodless body of Abigail.

Finn gripped the guitar pick she'd found with Beatrice's bandeau in Jack's apartment. "Abigail. You loved him once . . ."

Abigail's eyes flew open.

THE DARK AROUND JACK became Strawberry Hill Park at dusk. He lay on a blanket with Abigail, who was strumming an Elton John tune on her guitar.

"Abigail . . ." He sat up.

She smiled wryly and said, "You need to forgive me."

"Forgive you? For what?"

"Just say it, Jack. Please."

"I'm sorry, Abbie."

"I forgive *you*, you know."

"I forgive you," he whispered and she vanished into a column of fireflies.

"AND NOW YOU, EVE. And—thank you." Finn drew from her coat the necklace of amethysts Avaline had given her.

"Eve!" Finn heard Avaline call from somewhere else.

Eve's voice echoed back. "Let me go, Sophie."

"Eve. I *can't*."

Finn whispered to the professor she couldn't see, "You *have* to . . ."

JACK STOOD ON THE ROOF of his theater apartment, where he'd arranged a dinner beneath Japanese paper lanterns and summer stars. Eve stood before him, delicate in her chunky shoes and minidress of red plaid, her eyes beneath her bangs making his new heart warm. He bent his head, pressing his lips against her dark hair. She lifted her gaze to his. "I knew what you were, Jack. Your queen of shadows came to each of us and offered us immortality if we agreed to leave you. And we did."

"She tricked you." He cupped her face in his hands and anguish ripped through him, fresh and bloody. "But *I* destroyed you."

"No, Jack. I wanted to live forever." Eve kissed him good-bye.

Jack closed his eyes. When he opened them, Finn was standing before him, her face glistening with tears. She said, "We have one more, Jack."

NIGHT FELL OVER FINN AND JACK. They stood, hand in hand, in a forest, eerie light chalking everything around them. The air was tart with winter. A figure was crouched in the snow a little distance from them. A buzzing sound vibrated in Finn's eardrums.

The figure rose and gazed at them, glowworms tangled in the hyacinths wreathing his auburn curls. His jeans were streaked with blood. A raw wound in his chest, over his heart, spilled more hyacinths. Finn instinctively knew this wasn't how he should appear before moving on. She held out a hand. "Nathan . . ."

He shied back, his voice a husk. "Stop the exorcism. It's a *trap*."

"Nate—" Jack stepped forward. "We're not leaving you here."

Finn lunged and wrapped her arms around Nathan Clare, felt him gasp air as if for the first time. His arms slid around her. He felt solid, warm, and she remembered him as the brave, desperate boy who had loved a girl named Booke.

"Finn," Jack whispered and she opened her eyes to find that they stood on a road in a sunlit forest of ancient trees. Papers—the pages of books—drifted through the air. All of Nathan's wounds had gone. The evil hyacinths spun away from him in withered pieces.

The pages fluttering around them swept into a pale figure that became a girl with a dandelion puff of hair. "Booke," Nathan breathed. He walked toward her and together they vanished into a swarm of glowing lights.

SYLVIE SLIPPED THOMAS LUNEHT'S RING onto her finger and stood unafraid in the darkness, watching the dead boy walk toward her. Barefoot in bell-bottom jeans and a T-shirt, the raven hue of his hair matching the little black wings strapped to his shoulders, he smiled shyly. "Sylvie Whitethorn."

They stood in a simulacrum of Sylvie's Main Street neighborhood, in the courtyard behind her parents' shop. The air was warm, like a summer night. "Hey you," Sylvie said. She didn't know why she was crying.

"We just missed each other, didn't we, by a few decades." He held out a hand and she gripped it. Then she stepped forward and kissed him.

When she drew back, she said, "You've got a girl waiting for you, Tom Luneht, on the other side."

The dark folded gently back over them. Thomas Luneht walked away from Sylvie, toward a tree that morphed into a girl with violets in her black hair.

Then Sylvie heard Christie's voice, tense and sharp. "Something's wrong."

FINN AND JACK WERE BACK IN STARDUST STUDIOS, surrounded by candlelight and friends. The candles were lit, but the flames didn't move. Avaline and Sylvie were in the act of standing, alarm on their faces. Christie was also arrested in midlunge. Rowan Cruithnear and the professors were like statues.

A silent pressure erupted within StarDust and Finn looked up. The glass shell of StarDust had splintered into hundreds of cracks.

Jack gripped her hand. "Don't worry. I've dealt with this sort of thing before."

Five orbs spiraled out of the dark, upward, as the glass began to fall, hundreds of shards glinting—

And the souls that had been released spun above them. The falling glass paused in midair, then ascended. As the sheets of jagged glass snicked back into place and the fissures faded, light swept throughout StarDust, lanterns and candles illuminating Finn's friends and allies, all halted naturally now, and staring at her and Jack.

"Did we win this?" Christie asked. "Jack. Nice to have you back among the living."

AS FINN AND JACK STEPPED onto the widow's walk at Finn's house, Finn tilted her head back and gazed up at the universe of stars. *Her* universe. She closed her eyes, breathed in the air scented with lilacs and chlorine and mown grass and decided she never wanted to leave her world again.

But Caliban was loose here. And something else, an unknown enemy. She was about to tell Jack this, when he dragged her against him and gave her a lingering, openmouthed kiss that almost made her forget what she'd wanted to say. She pulled back.

"Jack. Listen. Someone wanted you out of Annwyn and used Caliban to do it.

Someone murdered the Dragonfly with your misericorde. And someone turned a local into a Jack. And Giselle the Jill is prowling around. What happened at StarDust—"

He pushed his hands over his face. He looked exhausted. "That wasn't meant to kill us. That was a warning. Whoever is behind Caliban and the Lily Girls"—cold rage flashed in his eyes—"wants a key Reiko placed inside of me."

Finn nodded, understanding. "The key tattoo that appeared in Annwyn."

"I believe Nate was assigned to coax it from me. That didn't work."

"Moth is back. With the Wolf's house. He told me he was hunting something malevolent that had gotten out of Sombrus. A shadow man. It attacked him and got away, so that's one possibility. There's also David Ryder's Jill."

Jack nodded. "Where is Sombrus now?"

"Moth lost it."

"Lost it?"

"Well, whatever escaped Sombrus probably commandeered it, don't you think?"

"What happened to the rest of the Wolf's court?"

"Moth killed them."

"All of them?" Jack's voice carried a deep note of concern.

"Jack, do you remember when I told you that one of the living memories in Sombrus escaped once? Your past self?"

He looked wary. "A memory, a shade from Sombrus would fade after a while, without being supported by that damned house."

"But what if it kept going back? It would be able to keep existing, right? And what if the shadow man that attacked Micah and Moth has stolen Sombrus?"

"That's a terrifying thought," Jack said, and Finn knew he was thinking of Seth Lot as a possible escaped memory/shade. He asked, "How does Moth seem to you?"

"Moth has remembered his past because I kissed him with the *Tamasgi'po*. He . . . did things for Seth Lot. And he's a lot older than he thought he was."

Jack sat back, rubbing the bridge of his nose. "If he did terrible things in his past, that'll claw at him. And being in Sombrus with the wolf pack . . . and who knows what else . . . I'm surprised he's even functioning."

Leaning against him, Finn murmured, "Did I tell you how glad I am to have you back?"

"No, but you can show me." His grin was wicked.

"At *your* place. Here's your ring back."

He accepted the lions-and-heart ring, sliding it onto one forefinger. Then, he sobered. "I'm a Jack again, Finn. The Halloween sacrifice . . . I was only given an illusion of mortality. Annwyn pretty much remade me as a Fata thing."

"So what? Deal with it. I love you."

CHAPTER 11

Because I'm able to see the creatures, I know what sort of world I'm being offered . . . a world that has no stability and only a mythic rationale, a world of willpower as physics . . . I refuse it. But if I keep them as hallucinations, if I deny them . . . my daughters will never be safe . . .

—From the journal of Daisy Sullivan

Finn lay on her bed with Lily, savoring the sunlight on her face and arms.

"You slept all day." Lily brushed Finn's hair back from her face. "Dad's worried."

Finn stretched, and smiled dreamily when she remembered Jack's mouth on her skin last night. Then she thought about Caliban and Giselle and sobered. "I was stupid. I thought we could just go back to our regular lives. All of us."

"We can't."

"The Fatas will be with us until . . . until when, Lily? Until that weird adult blindness strikes us and we can't see them anymore? Until I can't see Jack and I forget him?" She couldn't let that happen. Her heart twisted at the thought of it.

"We're like Jane Emory and the professors. We'll *always* see them."

"Like Mom."

"Like Mom. Only we can deal with it." Lily closed her eyes, opened them. "You got him back, you freaking lunatic."

THE SUN SET AND JACK *BECAME.*

He manifested in his apartment above the abandoned movie theater, in a chair facing the window. He could still feel the lingering warmth from Finn's skin. He hunched up, hugging himself. The bittersweet pulse of his new heart was a small pain. He could taste blood when he bit his lower lip.

He looked up and drew in a breath, what there was of it. Phouka was seated on the windowsill, her legs crossed. He glared at her. "I've told you not to sneak, haven't I?"

"Welcome back." Her face was in shadow.

He rested his arms on the back of the chair and stretched out his legs. "You don't sound enthusiastic."

She leaned forward. A thread of light from the streetlamps illuminated her face and its cool expression. "So. You're still a Jack?"

"Tell me about Moth. What is he?"

"Born in Iceland. His people believed his father wasn't human. *Fear dorchadas.* No moral compass. Manipulative. Seductive. Tricked *Absalom.* Met the Snow Queen. Became the first Jack."

Jack refused to reveal any concern in front of Phouka's flinty gaze. He leaned forward. "He claims he's hunting something that escaped from the Wolf's house. There's also David Ryder's Jill, Giselle."

"Yes. Have you heard about what escaped from Sombrus?" She was as intent as a predator.

"A shadow man. Phouka, who might want me out of Annwyn? Whoever used Caliban had a great understanding of Death's realm. And of Caliban."

She looked grim. "If something *did* get out of Sombrus . . . perhaps Absalom will know."

Jack smiled darkly. "Absalom's part in Moth's story bothers me. Let me show you my new tattoo." He lifted his shirt, revealing the key tattoo over his heart where once Reiko's ouroboros had stained his skin.

Phouka leaned forward. "That's interesting."

He pulled down his shirt. "Do you know what it is?"

"No idea." She cocked her head as if listening to something. "Finn has just pulled up. I'll go."

"Why did you come here?"

"Can't I welcome back an old comrade?"

"You're up to something."

"Make sure Serafina stays close. Whatever wanted you out of Annwyn—whatever wants that key—it'll use her against you. Moth needs to tell us where Sombrus is. We locate that, we get the shadow that escaped. It might be best if you keep Serafina out of it."

"Did you just tell me to make Finn do something?"

Her mouth curled. "Right." She slipped out the window.

"By the way," he called after her. "Finn told me Moth lost Sombrus, so good luck finding it."

He heard her swear.

AS FINN DROVE LILY'S CAR into the lot of the abandoned movie theater, she thought she saw Phouka's white Mercedes driving away.

Jack ducked out the apartment window and smiled down at Finn as she clambered up the fire escape. When she was close enough, he caught her hand. "How is the sunlit life?"

"Tentative." As she embraced him, he said into her ear, "If we kiss, it'll only lead to bed. And we've got to talk."

She reluctantly and breathlessly stepped away from him. "Okay." She climbed over the sill into his apartment. On the steamer trunk he used as a coffee table were black cartons from Lulu's Emporium. The aroma of food made her instantly forget her fatigue.

"This is *Strega* liqueur, from the Italian town of Benevento." He poured a golden liqueur into her glass. Finn sipped at it. She could taste cinnamon, mint, citrus, juniper, and myrrh. It made her feel lavish and energized.

The ring of lions holding a heart glinted on Jack's right forefinger as he twirled his chopsticks. She knew he couldn't taste anything. He'd once told her Fatas could live on the nutrition from food, but their true sustenance was mortal energy. He said, "Tell me everything you didn't tell me last night."

She told him about trying to make a deal with the four elementals to get into Annwyn. About the shadows and the mold in her house. As Jack gazed out the window, she thought of his scars, the ones she couldn't see, the ones that had grown over his soul.

"It was too easy," Jack said. "It was too easy to get out of Annwyn. It should have been horrifying."

"The Dali rabbit and the tree of girls' heads and the lake of blood weren't?"

"It was the land of the *dead*, Finn. There should have been indescribable horrors to keep us from leaving."

"Now you're being dramatic. Norn helped us and *she's* the leader of the Wild Hunt. We had it easy." Finn had finished her noodles and shrimp. She stood and began to wander around the apartment, paused before a framed poster of Bogart and Bacall in *Casablanca*. She thought about how many people Jack had lost: his friends Ambrose Cassandro and Nathan Clare, his lovers Eve, Beatrice, and Abigail. Even Reiko.

She turned to find him watching her with a troubled expression that vanished as if he hadn't wanted her to see it. She said, "There's this epic book called *The History of the World in 1,000 Objects*. I want you to choose five objects from your past and tell me what they meant to you—kind of the opposite of what we did with your box of, uh, trophies. The History of Jack in a Few Objects."

He smiled. "Life-affirming and suchlike?" The old Irish had returned to his speech.

"That's right." She hauled up her backpack and drew from it the locket he'd given her—it seemed like ages ago. "Starting with this."

He reached out and clicked open the locket, revealing the portrait of Ambrose Cassandro, the Jack who had been Finn's ancestor and Jack's friend. "There were once two portraits in this—Ambrose and his wife. She was only eighteen when she died of plague. Ambrose had two sons. He was eighteen and a widower—and he'd already been noticed by Reiko Fata, who, at the time, was pretending to be a duchess and an adventuress from Egypt."

His fingers closed tight around the locket. "Before Seth Lot had Ambrose taken apart, Caliban made Ambrose eat his wife's portrait from this locket." He gently took her hand and set the antique locket in her palm. "Do you know why I kept this? Despite being a Jack, Ambrose remained kind. This locket helped me to remember how to be good."

He walked to his nightstand and removed an ebony box. He opened it, then lifted out a pewter pocket watch with a yellowed clock face. "This was my mother's. She let me sleep with it when I was an infant, because the sound of it was as comforting as a heartbeat. At least that's what she said."

Finn touched it, turning it over to see the name inscribed upon it. "Moira Hawthorn."

Jack opened another drawer and produced a crimson cigar box. "My last day in the world as a human being . . . I found this." In the cigar box was a much-worn silver coin, an English one. "By then I knew what Reiko and Lot and their kind were. I remember rolling this coin between my fingers in a dreary inn room and looking out the window at the rooftops of Dublin as the sky turned red. It was a summer evening."

He retrieved a pair of old-fashioned glasses from the bookshelves. "These belonged to a young man I tried to keep from Reiko in the fifties. He didn't make it. He was the seventh person I couldn't save from the Fatas. He may have been one of the Black Scissors's *Taltu*."

Jack next took a black rubber ball patterned with skulls from a box and set it next to the glasses. Finn smiled fondly, poked it. "Cat toy. Blackjack Slade?"

"I found him when he was lost and hurt. He was something else that made me feel human." He removed the ring of lions-clasping-a-heart: *her* gift. "And then there's this, given to me by a girl who was, like me, a lost soul. She bound me with it, thinking me a wicked spirit."

"I didn't think you were—"

"But you should have." He smiled. All of the lamps, but for one, went out. He unfolded a hand.

Breath shivered through her as she laced her fingers with his. He pulled her into his arms and kissed her as if they hadn't seen each other in years, with a lush rapture. He lifted her. They sank onto the bed. As he skimmed off his T-shirt, revealing his scarred torso, the ornate key tattooed over his heart, Finn drew him down against her, sighed at the sweet contact of his skin against hers. He might be a Jack, but he wasn't a danger to her now, not with Reiko's poison gone from him. He still smelled faintly of wild roses and forests. His hair brushed her lips as his mouth trailed down her throat, his hands on her body as sure as hers were sliding over his shoulders, his hips above his jeans.

The sudden buzzing in her ears made her wince. Jack drew back from her, his brows slanting. "Finn . . ."

She felt blood trickle from one of her nostrils, tasted it on her lips. "Something's here," she whispered.

The last lamp went out, leaving only the moonlight.

Jack, whipping up, seized a dagger from the nightstand and a pistol from a drawer. He pointed the pistol at a silhouette in a hooded jacket standing outside the window. Finn tugged down her brown silk dress. "My dagger's in my backpack . . ."

"Can you see your way to it?" Jack's voice was taut.

Trying to ignore the buzzing in her ears, Finn reached for her backpack, found the dagger's hilt.

The visitor rapped a fist against the glass. Jack didn't lower the antique pistol as he approached the window, the pistol still raised. "I know who it is." He glanced at her. "I'm going to let him in."

Finn nodded. He pushed open the window.

Moth drew back the hood of his jacket as he climbed in. "Jack."

"I'm being a gentleman," Jack said, his eyes silver, "and giving you a chance. Phouka told me some things. Convince me you're not the first Jack you once were."

Moth's voice was low, his eyes almost black. "The thing from the Wolf's house—I followed it. Here."

"Did you now? You do realize that's not convincing me?" Jack held the pistol steady.

"Finn is bleeding," Moth pointed out. "Maybe you should see to her?"

"It's stopped." Finn said, relieved. "And so has the pressure in my ears. Whatever it was, it's gone."

"Do you know what causes the reactions you were having, Finn?" Jack didn't take his gaze from Moth. "Bad things. Poisonous things. Monsters. Moth, here, was the first Jack ever made."

Finn tried to absorb that news, because it shocked her. The first Jack . . . it meant Moth was as old as some of the Fatas. Watching Moth, she felt very afraid for him.

"I am not a monster, Jack." Moth spoke with quiet conviction. "Not anymore. If I was going to hurt Finn, don't you think I'd have had ample opportunity by now?"

"Do you know how to enter Annwyn, Moth?"

"The land of the dead? No."

"You don't seem surprised to find that Finn got me out."

"Should I be? She's Finn."

The comment got a reluctant, upward curve of the mouth from Jack, who lowered the pistol and said in his velvety voice, "Yes. She is."

Moth sat on the windowsill and clawed his hands through his hair. "I remember what I was. But it's as if it were someone else using my body back then. I am not that person any longer." He looked up. "And what about *your* past, Jack? What if people judged you by what you once were?"

"My past," Jack replied, "almost ate me alive, just recently. Tell me about this shadow from Sombrus you're hunting."

"Its energy was menacing. It attacked me once." The skin seemed stretched taut over the bones of Moth's face. "I know it took Sombrus." He hesitated, then said, "There's a way to find out what's here. The Grey sisters."

"They can't be trusted."

"Well, according to the Banríon, neither can I, but you're speaking with me, aren't you? What's the harm in speaking to the Grey sisters?"

"I see your point." Jack swept up Finn's coat and handed it to her.

"You can't take Finn there," Moth protested.

"You try and stop her. We'll need an offering." Jack began searching through drawers and cabinets.

Finn looked gravely at Moth. "Who are the Grey sisters?"

"Oracles. Fatas. And to get them to talk, we're going to have to steal something from them."

AT A FADED BILLBOARD advertising a flea market, Jack steered his sedan onto a side road and drove past dreary farmhouses and tracts of untouched land until they reached a suburb that looked as though it had gotten stuck in the Depression era. He parked in front of a faded, pink Victorian with dingy curtains and a dull light glowing in one window.

Out of the car, Finn regarded the house warily. Jack said, "Reiko used to send me here with gifts for them."

"You mean offerings," Moth said darkly, and Jack cast an annoyed glance in his direction.

Finn twisted a hand in her skirt. "What kind of offerings—I mean, gifts?"

"Teeth, handcrafted items," Jack said. "Small animals."

As they ascended the steps, Finn ventured, "Why did they need the animals?"

Neither Jack nor Moth answered, which pretty much told her what Jack and Moth didn't want to. She reached into her jacket to check for the silver dagger and narrowed her eyes at the door. *The Grey sisters. Oracles. Offerings. We're going to have to steal from them.* She breathed out, "The *Grey* sisters. They're *not*—"

"They are." Jack pressed the doorbell. The door opened to reveal a shadow with a faint light behind it and the murmur of a television in the background. A sweetish fragrance drifted outward, mingling with the witchy zest of candle smoke.

"Hi." Finn stepped forward and forced a smile, nervous, because it wasn't every day that one met a mythological creature. "We'd like a consultation?"

The shadow spoke with a girl's voice. "Did you bring payment?"

Jack lifted a lunchbox bearing an image of Saint Sebastian pinned by arrows. "In here."

"I know you." The shadow opened the screen door and a pair of pale, girl hands reached out and took the lunchbox. The lid clicked open. The figure peered inside, breathed out. "A Grindylow heart. Come in. I'm Penelope."

They stepped into a dingy hall lit by a pink-tasseled lamp. The walls were hung with antique photographs of strange-looking people. All the eyes in the photographs had been scratched away.

The girl who had answered the door was pretty and white-skinned, and wore a summer dress of gauzy black. Her Raggedy-Ann-red hair was wound in braids. Across her closed eyelids, two elaborate eyes had been painted. She led them into a parlor with shabby floral furniture. A preserved albino alligator curled beneath a table covered with bell jars containing wax dolls dressed like saints. Next to this display was a big wardrobe of dark wood carved with a design of three Grecian women entwined in grapevines. There were old dolls—with mean-baby faces and staring eyes—on the mantelpiece, on shelves, on the love seat.

"Dolls," Jack said, the way Indiana Jones might say "snakes." "I forgot about the damn dolls."

Penelope called out, "Anya! Di! Guests!"

Finn sat nervously between Jack and Moth on the sofa. Jack gingerly lifted a scowling baby doll and set it on the floor as two more girls in black, old-fashioned dresses entered. The tallest girl, hair sleek and scarlet down her back, sat opposite them on a purple velvet settee. She didn't open her eyes either. Her lids were painted with roses. The third Grey sister, her hair short and red, her eyelids painted with a band of crimson, sat beside the tall girl and said, "I know the dark and beautiful one, Reiko's lieutenant. The girl smells like silver and fear. The other . . . the other . . . I see nothing when I look at him."

"The *girl* is asking, Di." The first sister sat with the others on the settee. She held a small ebony box, which she opened. She lifted out an oval crystal set in a frame of twining gold serpents. Veined with red, the crystal resembled an eye. The Grey sister cradled it in her palms as if it were a baby bird.

The tall one with the painted roses on her eyelids addressed Finn. "What do you wish to ask?"

Jack lifted his shirt, revealing the tattoo of the key. "What is this?"

Moth frowned at the tattoo as Finn hunched forward and asked, "And what has come to Fair Hollow, with malice and evil intent?"

The three sisters each set a hand on the crystal eye. The youngest, the short-haired one, spoke in a low voice. "The key was the crux of Reiko Fata's power. And night and nothing, Death's child, walks in Fair Hollow."

From the wardrobe came a loud and terrifying bang. Finn's stomach twisted into a knot. On either side of her, Jack and Moth tensed.

The first Grey sister turned her face toward the wardrobe. "Don't worry. He won't get out unless we let him. We locked him up tight."

"Locked up who?" Finn flinched as whatever was in that wardrobe slammed against the doors again.

The oldest sister said, "Rag-and-Bone. He was a Very Bad Thing."

"We haven't fed him in such a long time," the Grey sister with the braids said and her eyelids popped open to reveal gaping holes. "Give us the key, Jack Hawthorn, and your companions don't become food for our lover."

Finn stood swiftly as the other two sisters also lifted their lids to reveal the same gaping holes. Horror spiked through her.

Held in a spell, Jack and Moth sat still as waxwork versions of themselves. This was the Grey sisters' place of power—and Moth and Jack were fey beings. The sisters had used that against them.

"Stop," Finn whispered. "Release them."

"You think we wouldn't *know* why you came here?" The first sister's voice was deep and shivery with old power. "Why *he* came here? To *steal*."

Finn heard the wardrobe doors crash open behind her. A gangrene reek washed over her and she gagged. She turned to see a pile of laundry tumbling out of the wardrobe. Then the laundry stretched upright, becoming a grotesque manikin of cloth and animal bones with the skull of a crocodile, antlers, and the claw-tipped paws of a bear.

Finn snatched the box containing the crystal eye from the eldest sister and ran down the hall. All panic and adrenaline, she smashed open the screen door and plummeted down the steps. The sisters followed her outside, stumbling, shrieking.

"Where is it?"

"Give it back!"

"Thieving bitch."

"Here." Finn backed away, holding out the box. From within the house came a terrifying snarl. The shadow of the monstrous wardrobe inhabitant was flung upon the curtains over the parlor window. Finn heard Jack shouting fiercely. By luring away the Greys, Finn had broken the sisters' power over Jack and Moth.

The eldest sister reached out, crooning, "Give it back. Give it back. And we will tell you—"

The crocodile skull of Rag-and-Bone crashed through one of the windows and landed between Finn and the eldest Grey. The eldest sister pointed at Finn. "*You* brought him. He followed *you* out of the dark."

Then the sisters converged on Finn.

The screen door slammed open and Jack stepped out with Moth. They both looked savage.

The door to the house shattered. Jack and Moth ducked as a mass of flies erupted from it.

The sisters turned. The flies swept over their heads. The Grey sisters stood, blind and helpless without the eye Finn had stolen as the flies descended upon them. Backing away, Finn watched in horror as the Greys came apart like bits of burning paper among the insects.

Then the flies spiraled away, into the sky.

Dark flakes drifted around Finn. She gasped when the box in her hands shook as if something had exploded within it.

"Hell." Jack turned on Moth. "I thought you'd killed it."

"I thought I had." Moth gazed after the swarm of flies that Finn guessed had been Rag-and-Bone. He looked at Finn. "You have the eye?"

Jack walked to Finn and gently took the box from her. He opened it, revealing the shattered crystal eye and what appeared to be a pearly human molar with a gold filling. "When they were young," he said softly, "they all fell in love with the same man. When he betrayed them, they killed him."

"Rag-and-Bone." Finn's legs were jelly.

Jack closed the box. "Well, that was a waste of time."

Moth turned away. "Now we'll never learn what's come out of Sombrus."

"No." Jack narrowed his eyes. "Not from them."

Finn's mind had begun to race. She said, her voice steady, "Jack, did Reiko ever teach you what she learned from Lot? The stitchery?"

Jack regarded her warily. "Somewhat."

"The Grey sister said he followed *me* out of the dark. Who would Sylph Dragonfly have allowed close enough to stab her? Who would know about Giselle and be able to make Tyson Follows a Jack? Someone who would want you out of the land of the dead because he knows exactly what that key is for. When the shadow man attacked Micah, his message to me was: *Thank you for letting me out.* And I thought it was just a dream or a trick of my mind, but I saw you, Jack, at your apartment, days ago. It wasn't a hallucination, and I'll bet Anna didn't dream the Jack who warned her that Caliban had taken me to Annwyn. The thing that escaped Sombrus, that's causing all this . . . it's *you*, Jack, the Jack I met when we were running from the Wolf's house. The memory or shade of the Jack you would have become if you'd remained with Reiko and Lot. Your past self is our enemy."

CHAPTER 12

They live a mysterious life on the edge of real life, but their world remains fully mingled with ours, and as soon as night falls, as soon as the living . . . give themselves up to the temporary sleep of death, the so-called dead again become the inhabitants of the earth.

—The Fairy-Faith in Celtic Countries, W. Y. Evans-Wentz

The Sleeping Beauty. It was a fitting name for the forlorn house that had once belonged to the Tredescants. Built in the early 1900s, it resembled a Tudor and slept behind a barrier of ivy and briar roses during the warm months.

As Christie parked his car behind a silver Mercedes, the Sleeping Beauty's windows glowed with light. He could hear jazzy music crackling faintly in the air. He'd promised to meet Phouka here to begin his training in what she unsettlingly referred to as the "art of Endor."

He and Sylvie had agreed to keep their encounters with Oberon and the Morrigan under wraps for now—the experience seemed too private to share with anyone else. And Phouka might not appreciate Oberon warning Christie about her.

As Christie was moving up the stairs, Phouka appeared in the doorway of the Sleeping Beauty, her silky summer dress seeming a little sophisticated for magic lessons. Her eyes, lined in kohl, reminded him of a cat's. "Christopher."

"Phouka. If that is indeed your true name." He stepped past her.

"It isn't." She shut the door and led him across the green marble floor, past glass cases displaying fossils, antique medical equipment, primitive statues, pinned scarabs, and Stone Age weapons. He narrowed his eyes at one cabinet filled with wax dolls in costumes. The jazz music tripping faintly down the hall was spectacularly unnerving, reminding him that this was not a *girl* leading him into the illusion of a grand house, but something that had probably been around when jazz was invented.

She's a fairy. Don't forget that.

She looked over one shoulder and arched an eyebrow at him. "The original Tredescants—*Trade*scant, back then—were gardeners for Queen Elizabeth the First. They became collectors of the eccentric and fantastic." Her fingers drifted across a glass case displaying what looked like the remains of a mummified mermaid.

"Does all this"—Christie scanned the salon with its red coral candelabra and crimson velvet love seats—"disappear when the sun rises?"

"Of course. Most of this exists somewhere else."

He peered into a glass case displaying beaded jewelry and realized the beads were made from teeth, animal and human. "So what's with the teeth? Why were they so important in the Ghostlands? And why did that psycho Caliban once shoot one into my leg?"

"Teeth contain human DNA. There's a connection to their former owner's memory or personality." Phouka walked backward as she explained. "In primitive mortal cultures there were strict rules regarding the disposal of teeth. What Caliban did when he shot that tooth into your leg was create an entrance so that he could later possess you."

Christie experienced a flood of nausea. The thought of Caliban's nastiness anywhere near him made him want to bathe in antibacterial soap.

"Perhaps"—Phouka's gray eyes flickered with mischief—"I should have phrased that differently." She paused before a pair of French doors leading out into the wild garden. Beyond was a small forest of black trees. "Do you know why you took a shine to poetry, Christopher?"

"Sylph Dragonfly told me. It's part of being a witch." Grief cut at him as he recalled Sylph. "And it helped me learn how to speak when I was a kid. Trust me when I say this witch stuff is actually easier than years of speech therapy."

"Your witch blood gave you an edge in that. Unfortunately, it also takes. Those with witch blood are sometimes born deaf, blind, or mute, autistic, or with a congenital defect."

"Can I do that electricity thing that you peop—that Fatas do?"

She said wryly, "I don't know. But your auditory assistance"—she tapped one ear—"is now a part of you. That's why it continued working in the Ghost-lands."

"So . . . being a witch is just the poetry then? And the ink breakouts on my skin?"

"Heka, spells, are words of intent. Yours are more potent because you worked so hard for them. Try not to use them near sources of power, because that'll overwhelm you."

"Like when I was at Death's door and ended up becoming Cerberus the dog-headed boy?" He was glad he couldn't remember that. Or Sylvie kissing him.

"Right." She smiled slyly and pushed open the doors to the garden. "Tonight, you're going to meet the first of four rulers of the elements, people whom, as a witch, you need to know. Time to meet the Lunantishee."

A chill crawled from the nape of Christie's neck to the base of his spine as he gazed at the darkness beneath those trees. Blackthorn trees, Phouka had told him. As she walked toward them, he thought of Angyll and Hester and the Dragonfly.

His jaw set, he strode after Phouka, into the dark.

SYLVIE WAS WORRIED ABOUT CHRISTIE.

Well, she was worried about a lot of things. But Finn was with smoking-hot, back-from-the-dead-again Jack, and Sylvie trusted Jack. She didn't trust Phouka.

Aubrey, who was driving the Camry, glanced at her. "I wish you wouldn't play with knives. You might put one of my eyes out."

Sylvie looked down. She was idly twirling one of her Renaissance blades, the one with the hilt shaped into two curved birds. "I'm good at this. Don't worry."

He threw her a hard stare before returning his attention to the road. "What's with you lately? Ever since you've been hanging around with the Black Scissors, you've been strange. You don't believe the *Black Scissors* is capable of making an army of Jacks and Jills like Tyson Follows?"

Micah Govannon, in the backseat, leaned forward, his hair a tangled knot behind his head. He and Sylvie answered simultaneously, "No."

"Does Christie know about you and the Black Scissors?" Aubrey glanced at Sylvie.

"There *is* no me-and-the-Black-Scissors."

Micah and Aubrey exchanged a look in the rearview mirror.

Sylvie said, "I might not be able to kick Micah's ass, but I'm pretty sure I can kick yours, Aub."

"You're such a flirt." Aubrey kept his eyes on the road. "Here we are—that's Christie's car. I don't think he'll be happy we followed him."

They parked in the drive of the house called the Sleeping Beauty and got out of the car. The air was chilly for spring and Sylvie wished she'd worn a jacket with her filmy black shirt. She'd braided silver talismans into her hair along with botanical protection in the form of daisies and clover.

Aubrey frowned at the lit-up house. "Do we just walk up and knock?"

"Well, we're not going to sneak around." Sylvie stomped up the stairs and pressed the doorbell.

CHRISTIE, WALKING AMID THE BLACKTHORN TREES without a light to guide him, pretended he wasn't nervous. Why was the night so thick here? A chill skittered across the back of his neck when a pillar of darkness glided toward him. He felt a prickling on his skin and knew heka were appearing on his arms and throat.

You will not master me, said the darkness before him.

"That wasn't my plan." Christie felt the heka rise on his tongue. "From the earth you came, to the earth you'll go. All I ask is a bit of you, so that our bond may show." *Not exactly Keats*, he thought, *but that just might work.*

The Lunantishee, the Black Thorn, revealed itself, leaning toward him. Its black lips curved. It whispered to him in a language that forced into his brain images of corpses in graves, roots like massive spiders invading the basements of sunken houses, insects burrowing among bones, translucent flowers blossoming from the blood pooling in a battlefield—

Christie flinched back and breathed out, "*Stop.*"

The Lunantishee peeled back and Christie felt shadows drop from his skin like clots of soil. He choked and bits of darkness spilled from his nose, his mouth, turned into beetles as they fell. Sick and shaking, he looked up into the Lunantishee's obsidian eyes and frantically whispered words he didn't even comprehend.

The Black Thorn seized one of his wrists. Nails gouged into his skin and caused blood to bead. Christie tried to wrench free, but the Lunantishee raised his wrist to its lips and Christie almost fainted as it tasted his blood.

Then the earth elemental was gone.

A ring of black wood shaped into nymphs and stag-headed figures now banded Christie's left forefinger.

"Got you," he whispered.

As he trudged back toward Phouka, he heard a familiar voice arguing with her. He stepped out of the shadowy blackthorn grove and found Sylvie facing off with the Banríon while Aubrey and Micah stood nearby looking worried.

"Sylvie." Christie strode toward them.

"Christie, are you okay?" Sylvie turned. "You better be."

"I'm good, Sylv."

Sylvie glanced defiantly at Phouka. "This isn't technically, absolutely, your place, is it? Not *your* stomping grounds. It's a border place."

Phouka's lashes lowered in a dark sweep. "Sylvie." It was a warning.

Sylvie stepped back between Aubrey and Micah. "We, as three, invoke the law of hospitality, which guards our safety and our sanity."

"You're invoking against me?" Phouka's voice was wry. "What brought this on?"

Christie stared at his friends. "Sylvie. Let me." He held up his hand with the Black Thorn's ring. "Phouka. Would you sacrifice me and my friends to save your Fatas?"

There was silence. Then Phouka said, "You've already answered that question in your mind. Why bother asking it?"

He quoted, "*I asked thee, 'Give me immortality.' Thou didst grant mine asking with a smile.*"

"Don't quote Lord Tennyson at me, Christopher Hart."

He continued. "*Like wealthy men who care not how they give. But thy strong heirs indignant worked their wills.*"

"Uh . . . Christie . . . ?" Aubrey sounded as if he very much wanted to be elsewhere.

"Stop it," Phouka ordered. "You're being idiots."

"*And beat me down and marred and wasted me. And though they could not end me, left me maimed to dwell in the presence of immortal youth.*"

Phouka lost her calm. "Trust me or die! Those are your choices!"

Christie took a deep breath and instantly felt like a jerk. "Sorry. I had to know."

"You've hurt my feelings." But she didn't look hurt; she looked coldly furious.

"Pardon me." A shadow came from the night and became Absalom, in jeans and a jacket lined with red fur. A crimson half mask with horns was pushed up into his blood-orange hair. His smile glittered. "I see you've charmed your way into our queen's heart, Christopher. Oh—wait. She doesn't have one."

"*He's* here in case something went wrong, isn't he?" Christie's triumph faded. He wanted to have faith in Phouka so much, it hurt. "*What could have gone wrong?*" The tangled power within him writhed, snaking beneath his skin.

"Well." Absalom smiled. "The Lunantishee might have drained you of blood and I would have had to clean up the mess."

"Son of a *bitch*," Aubrey muttered.

"You think that's funny?" Christie launched himself at Absalom and Absalom's golden eyes flashed.

CHRISTIE OPENED HIS EYES. He lay in the grass with his head in someone's lap. *I'm at the Sleeping Beauty.* He blinked up at a shadowed face. "Sylv?"

Sylvie's hair hung on either side of her face, the thin braids that framed it knotted with silver talismans and daisies. She patted his cheek with a hand that gleamed with three ornate silver rings. "I think the stress is getting to us."

"Christie?" Phouka's face appeared beside Sylvie, looking concerned.

Christie sat up, wincing at the bass thump of a headache. As he struggled to his feet, he reluctantly turned to Absalom, who leaned against a tree. The Fata boy swept Christie a beautiful bow. "Forgive me for defending myself against your overreaction, Christie Hart."

Christie growled. "Go f—"

"Absalom." Phouka's voice cut through the tension. "What *are* you doing here?"

"I've come to tell you—" Absalom straightened and stared into the wilderness of blackthorns. "Oh dear. Too late."

Christie felt a chill claw across the nape of his neck. *By the pricking of my thumbs, something wicked this way comes.*

Giselle the Jill emerged from the night. Her back to the blackthorn trees, she resembled a fairy-tale princess-turned-assassin, her body lithe in black and a corset embroidered with gold crosses.

Phouka and Absalom moved to stand in front of Christie and his friends. More figures appeared behind the Jill, their faces painted like ornate Day-of-the-Dead skulls, eyes gleaming silver. As Christie and his friends drew together and Phouka and Absalom stood like generals, a Jack and a Jill appeared from between the blackthorns, dragging with them a figure in a coat of ebony feathers. His head was covered by a hood. Christie recognized the Jack hauling the hostage. "Tyson Follows."

"Marie?" Sylvie whispered.

The Jill on the other side of the hostage looked up with a grin. "Hey, Sylv."

Sylvie glanced at Christie. "She is—was—in my theater group. Is she dead?"

Christie said softly, "She looks dead."

"Giselle." Phouka's tone was gentle. "Who put you up to this?"

"No one." Giselle ripped the hood from her hostage's head, revealing the regal face of a furious Dead Bird.

IT WAS A STANDOFF.

Sylvie thought that the glow-eyed tribe behind Giselle looked more savage than Lot's wolf pack, but, not for a million dollars would Sylvie ever mess with Dead Bird. That Giselle was doing so made her scary-crazy. And she apparently also knew the gruesome art of stitchery.

"Don't you dare," Christie ordered Sylvie, "reach for a weapon."

Giselle held an iron blade near Dead Bird's throat. The hilt was pewter, but the nearness of the iron made the skin of her arm blister and Dead Bird's neck blacken. She didn't take any notice, but Dead Bird clenched his teeth and narrowed his eyes as Giselle continued, "Your guardian of graveyards and gates has begun finding replacement sentinels for your Ways. I think he's valuable to you."

Phouka was ice. "I have shut the Ways in the seven houses of the blessed after the Dragonfly's murder. Permanently. And the *Marbh ean* isn't mine."

"But he was once your lover."

Phouka stepped forward and Sylvie grudgingly admired the way she did it, as if she was a six-armed goddess with a knife in each hand. "Who put you up to this, little girl? If you take your pathetic spitefulness out on the *Marbh ean*, there'll be consequences."

Absalom began to whisper softly. Sylvie felt her skin crawl.

Phouka continued, "Why are you doing this now, Giselle? What are you up to?"

Giselle slashed the dagger at Dead Bird. Micah tackled her. Dead Bird twisted away. The Jacks and Jills surged forward.

"*Stop.*" Phouka's command actually halted everyone. As Micah and Dead Bird stumbled away, Giselle glided to her feet, teeth bared, and signaled to her tribe. She and her small army descended into shadows and raced away.

Dead Bird said coldly, "This is why I don't serve kings or queens."

"Why did this . . . what just happened?" Christie looked around as if expecting a sneak attack.

Phouka looked severe. "This was a distraction. Call Serafina. *Now.*"

CHAPTER 13

If one assumes that spirits exist, and that they exist in a different realm from
ours . . . then it follows that, when these things are disrupted, someone must
travel into the realm of the spirits to persuade them to behave differently.
—*SHAMANISM*, PIERS VITEBSKY

It had been a week since the Grey sisters and the standoff with Giselle,
since Finn's realization that Jack's dark, past self must be the one wreaking
havoc in Fair Hollow. Phouka, Jack, and Moth had found no sign of Jack's doppelgänger or of Sombrus. Caliban and Giselle hadn't made any more terrorist
moves.

And to complicate matters further, Finn had begun noticing an unsettling
metamorphosis in her two best friends.

When a student with the hood of his jacket drawn up bumped into Finn in the
corridor of the Arts Center, Christie had turned on him, his pupils so dilated his
eyes had seemed black. A word had inked itself across his neck. Fortunately, no
one had noticed, and Finn had dragged Christie away.

Later, in the bathroom, a panicked Sylvie revealed a tattoo of raven wings
across her shoulder blades.

"It's very pretty," Finn said doubtfully.

"It just appeared last night. It's *swimsuit* season, Finn. I can't hide this."

"I think you should ask the Black Scissors what it is."

"He doesn't need to tell me what it is. I *know*." Sylvie tugged down her tank top. "Do you know what the Morrigan is? Of course you do. Well, she's real. I spoke with her in Max's Diner."

Dismay crested over Finn. The Morrigan was a Celtic goddess of war. *"When?"*

"A week or so ago." Sylvie met her gaze in the mirror, her own dark with worry. "She said I'll be hers once I kill someone. When did this become our life?"

When I moved here, Finn thought. She said firmly, "Don't kill anyone."

FINN SPENT MOST OF THE LATE AFTERNOON huddled over her laptop with her phone beside her. It wasn't the otherworld she was worried about at the moment—it was her future at HallowHeart. Just because Dean Cruithnear was acquainted with her night life didn't mean he'd let her slide on poor grades.

When her da left on errands, Finn decided to make sandwiches for dinner. Listening to music from her laptop in the sunlit kitchen, she could hear Lily moving around her room upstairs.

As she was slicing avocados and humming along to Mazzy Star, the house went dark. Finn dropped the knife. She thought of Shadow Jack.

The sunlight had vanished inside the house, but still shone outside the windows. She retrieved the knife and crouched on the kitchen floor, shaking. The sudden cold caused her breath to mist. Not far from her, something rustled like a giant cockroach, and she saw a figure standing in the doorway between the kitchen and the hall, its too-big eyes staring from a misshapen head.

The door to the backyard was right behind her, but Lily was upstairs.

Finn pushed to her feet and ran past the shadow—it didn't move—into the hallway. She stumbled up the stairs, calling to Lily in the unnatural dark. She heard more rustling around her.

On the second floor, she glanced into her father's room and saw another figure silhouetted against the window.

Her heart slamming, Finn reached Lily's bedroom door. "You can't have her," she whispered and shoved the door open.

The darkness fell like a black veil from her eyes. Disoriented, she blinked in the sunlight drenching her sister's room. "Lily?"

Lily stood before the tarnished mirror, her reflection distorted.

"Lily." Finn stepped in. "There's something—"

Lily turned her head. Her eyes were black.

One of their mother's paintings fell to the floor among a great clattering sound throughout the house. Finn peered out into the hall and saw that the paintings in the hall had fallen, too.

Lily blinked and breathed out, "Finn . . . ?"

"The entire house just went dark," Finn said. "And the dark was like something *alive*." She walked to one of the paintings that had fallen in the hall, the image of a swan-winged girl holding a star. Three yellowed papers had spilled from the painting's broken frame.

"I believe you." Lily strode past Finn to pick up the papers that had fluttered from the painting. "I don't know what happened. I . . . zoned out."

"There were people here. Not human."

Lily shook the papers at Finn. "Well, it wasn't the Fatas." She stalked past Finn and dragged a chair to her window. She stood on the chair, reached up, and felt around on the sill above. Then she turned, solemnly holding a rusting key. "It's iron. Gran Rose put iron at every entrance. Nothing Fata can get in without being invited. Whatever you saw, Finn . . . the darkness . . . I think it's from Annwyn." She jumped down and shoved the yellowed papers at Finn. "Have you been reading what Mom wrote?"

Finn sank down on the bed and gazed down at one page. "It's about Gran Rose."

. . . Rose is intimidating. Like one of those frontierswomen in the movies Serafina loves. When she talks to me, when she visits . . . it seems like she's trying to tell me things. I think she knows. I haven't told anyone. I can't.

Mom, Finn thought, gripping the paper. *You weren't crazy.*

Gran Rose and Grandad had moved from Dublin to Fair Hollow with Finn's dad when he'd been thirteen, because Finn's granddad—who had died when Finn was a baby—had been offered a job here. So if Gran Rose had set iron over the windows and doors . . . she'd suspected what the Fatas were.

Lily sat beside Finn, who asked, "What kind of job did our granddad come here for?"

"You don't know? Same as Dad. He was a professor of literature."

Finn breathed out, saying softly, "Granddad worked at HallowHeart."

They gazed soberly at each other. "Ambrose Cassandro," Finn murmured, "who was Mom's ancestor, all the way back in the Renaissance. And Jill Scarlet who was Bronwyn Rose Govannon Sullivan, from the 1700s. *Da*'s ancestor." She glanced down at the papers in her hand and, her heart aching, read more of her mother's words.

> *. . . I looked out the window and saw one of them; white-haired, feral, with rings on her toes. She was speaking to my Lily. I could only stand there and watch the creature charm my baby.*

Finn clutched the third page, crumpled and splotched with coffee stains, covered with sketches of weird figures and scrawled words:

> *. . . not biological. Nucleus. Ectoplasm? Black matter? Electromagnetic energy?*

Finn swallowed hard as she focused on a sentence inked in again and again so that the paper had torn—her mother, trying with her practical mind to explain the unexplainable.

> *WHAT ARE THEY?*

SYLVIE SAT IN THE COURTYARD behind Whiskey and Pearls, her laptop on her knees, music pulsing from her earplugs, the sun warming the back of her neck as she typed furiously. She was going to fail that calculus exam tomorrow, so she figured it might even out if she wrote a kick-ass paper for her Idolatry in Music course.

When the cold swept over her like the descent of winter, she raised her head and saw the courtyard gate creak inward. She'd assumed, because it was daylight, she'd be safe, so she stared uncomprehending at the massive shadow that spilled over the cracked pavement and tangled greenery. When the darkness pooled at her feet, she stood quickly, her laptop crashing to the pavement. The dark rose like a wave and she saw within it a decaying ballroom and crooked figures waltzing. Something tall stood among them, its enormous eyes fixed upon her.

Her body shook as a chasm to some unknown world opened up before her. *Not unknown. That's the land of the dea—*

A flash of light shattered the darkness and sunlight kissed her skin again. Sylvie blinked as what appeared to be ash drifted around her. Walking through it was Kevin Gilchriste, holding a small, mirrored ball.

"Kevin . . ." Sylvie swayed, then quickly sat down on the edge of the court-yard's fountain.

He pocketed the silver orb. He was chalky pale. "The Black Scissors gave me that device. Mirrors can trap spirits."

"What was it?" Sylvie flinched as a flake of darkness drifted past her hand.

"Death's hounds. They're gone. He wants to see you. The Black Scissors, I mean."

Sylvie lifted her laptop, relieved it was undamaged, and shut it. Shivering, she said, "It's because of what we did at Death's door, isn't it? We messed around with something we shouldn't have."

"Knowing you three, probably."

AS KEVIN STEPPED into the Black Scissors's derelict house in the ware-house district, Sylvie, following, asked, "So have *you* killed Fatas?"

"We're not assassins. We're liaisons. Spiritwalkers."

She almost rolled her eyes. "But the Black Scissors hates the Fatas."

"Yeah." Kevin led her toward the living room.

The Black Scissors sat on a sofa, booted feet apart, hands clasped. He was frowning at an array of tiny glass animals on the coffee table before him. "I don't understand. Why amass such a fragile menagerie?" He transferred his attention to Sylvie as Kevin walked to a battered coffeemaker and poured some brew into a mug with Andy Warhol's Marilyn Monroe on it.

The lights flickered, then hummed back on. Kevin, not disturbed in the slightest, brought Sylvie coffee in a mug decaled with the British flag. He kept the Marilyn Monroe mug for himself. "The dark came for her," Kevin said as the Black Scissors watched Sylvie.

"It was overspill from the land of the dead," the Black Scissors told Sylvie. "But I don't know how. Death's door is now closed. The remaining sentinels are in place. This is very bad."

"You're saying"—Sylvie swallowed bitter coffee—"there's a leak somewhere."

"Lily Rose should have remained in the Ghostlands," the Black Scissors said softly. "The dark will be drawn to her."

Sylvie pushed to her feet. "Are you saying *Lily*'s the leak?"

"It doesn't matter." Kevin cut her off, glowering at the Black Scissors. "She's here now. She belongs in the true world."

"StarDust." Sylvie pointed at the Black Scissors. "That was used as a Way out of the underworld! You use it to get to the Ghostlands. What if we shut down StarDust?"

"Ah. Now you're thinking like one of us." The Black Scissors pushed to his feet. "It's time you met the others."

"The other—" Sylvie glanced at Kevin. He nodded.

The Black Scissors led them down a hallway into a rec room furnished with vintage pinball machines and a pool table. Seated on a sectional of red vinyl was a young man with curly hair and an Asian boy dressed in black, a belt of old-fashioned bullets around his hips. Standing near a window were a tall boy with a shaved head and an air of warrior regality, and a girl in a little black dress, her hair a tousled mane, a lollipop between her teeth.

Something inside Sylvie fluttered, recognizing kindred spirits. These were the Black Scissors's spiritwalkers.

The Black Scissors indicated the two near the window. "Zach's encountered a Fata in New Orleans. Lucy was nearly murdered by a Lamia in L.A. Gabriel"—he gestured toward the curly-haired young man on the sectional—"came across the path of an ancient Italian Fata tribe in Austin. Geo"—the Asian youth inclined his head—"saved his younger siblings from a Fata queen in Chicago."

Sylvie glanced at Kevin and arched an eyebrow ever so slightly. Kevin said, "In New York City, I was at a party in an old building with gargoyles on the roof. I walked in on a ganconer sucking the life out of a girl . . ."

"And you put a knife in his face." Lucy, who had a French accent, made a swirling, stabbing motion with her lollipop.

"Why were you carrying a knife?" Sylvie asked. "You were just an actor."

He shrugged. "It was a cake knife. He was killing her near the birthday cake."

Sylvie felt a quiet, creeping horror as she looked around the room. How many bad Fatas were out there?

"They're real," Zach, the tall boy near the window, told her. "All the monsters. All the urban myths. All the things that haunt the shadows and the night. What kids see in closets and under their beds—"

"Yeah, tell me about it. I've pretty much met three of the worst you can imagine." Sylvie shrugged, thinking of Reiko and Seth Lot and Caliban.

The Black Scissors tilted his head down, but Sylvie caught the curve of his grin. He said, "This is the U.S. chapter, Miss Whitethorn. Each has a place in a Fata-haunted city and there aren't enough of us to go around. They'll be returning after tonight, to their posts—"

"Except for those of us stuck here." Sylvie turned as a man with shaggy gray-brown hair strolled in. When he saw her, Murray the arcade owner halted and grimaced. "Ah, you've told her then?"

"*Murray?*" Sylvie stared at him.

The Black Scissors said, "Miss Whitethorn . . . I know what you want to ask. Kevin . . . turn out the lights, please."

Kevin walked to the wall switch and obeyed. As the lights went out, the Black Scissors's form became a solid blackness drifting with tentacles of shadow veined with iridescent blue.

The lights came back on. Sylvie glanced around. No one seemed startled. *She was trying not to freak out.*

"So you see, Sylvie," the Black Scissors continued, "what the Fatas have made me. I wouldn't force anyone to an existence as something half *other*. Now, I am asking you if you want to be one of us. Or not. I'm not holding you to the bargain I forced on you months ago."

Sylvie looked around at the serious faces of his tribe. "What, exactly, *are* you?"

The Black Scissors answered, "Faery doctors. Shamans. Spiritwalkers. Exorcists. We are *Taltu*."

AS THE FADING SUN TINTED everything the color of burnt honey and the air cooled, saturated with the fragrances of lilacs and mown grass, Christie steered his Mustang down a dirt road, past a sign that read LAKE TRUE. When he saw the beautiful, immortal girl reading a newspaper on the steps of a log cabin, he thought she didn't look deadly—until she raised her head and her eyes reflected the light like a cat's.

Christie had faced a kelpie and Ivan Vodyanoi, killed a siren, and stood at Death's door, yet this creature wearing the skin of a young woman casually dressed in jeans and a black T-shirt with a Hindu god on it still disturbed him.

He ducked out of the car, carrying his scuba equipment. As he walked toward Phouka, he saw the haze of the lake beyond the trees. "I've heard that a grand house slid into this lake, a long time ago."

Tossing aside the newspaper, Phouka stood up. "It's an urban myth. And, like all myths, it has a foundation in truth." She led him to a rickety dock spearing out onto the emerald lake. On the opposite shore was a slope of slate and scrub with the bones of a building protruding from it—stone pillars, a cement foundation, and a huge stairway.

Phouka dropped down into a rowboat that was rusty and reeking of fish water. Christie jumped in after her. They each took a paddle and began skimming the boat out toward the lake's middle. It was only then that Christie felt a gut-twisting fear for what he was about to do.

"Here." Phouka stopped paddling and gazed out over the water. "This elemental is safer than Amphitrite, but dangerous in her way."

"Well, it wouldn't be fun if she *wasn't* dangerous." He stripped down to his swim trunks and tugged his wetsuit from the backpack. Before putting on the goggles and mask, he asked, "How far down? I can't dive deep because of the implants in my ears."

"Far enough to get past the door, but not deep. If anything goes wrong, you'll be able to breathe with the heka I gave you."

"And I just ask her for the Mermaid House mirror?"

"She'll give it to you." Phouka's voice held menace. "The mansion's owners stole it and other things from the houses of the blessed."

"Is that why the mansion's now at the bottom of a lake?" Christie politely inquired. He shook his head. "I thought witchcraft would be learning herbs and chanting and dancing naked under the moon. Maybe summoning a few demons . . . not bargaining with crazy elementals."

"You're thinking of Wicca for the first and sorcery for the second. Two completely different things. You are a *fear dorchadas*. You're from a long line of men and women whose blood runs with the power of the Tuatha Dé Danaan and the Witch of Endor. You can do this, Christie. We need these mirrors to trap our enemy. If this shadow man from Sombrus truly is Jack's past, it is the Jack who remained with Seth Lot and Reiko. It is the Jack who has become—"

"Like Caliban?"

"Maybe." She took a string of charms from around her neck and settled them over his head, across his collarbones. "Coral and pearl. For protection."

"And there are no kelpies or a Vodyanoi in this lake?" He was surprised his teeth weren't rattling.

"Only the undine. Her name is Dahut. She came from Ireland. She took this lake in the 1700s."

"Was there someone who had the lake before her? Like, say, a native spirit? A Blackheart?" He grabbed his snorkel and the goggles and adjusted the oxygen tank.

"Maybe." The kiss she gave him was unexpected, as luscious as if she truly did have a soul. He even dared to crush her body against his. Then she stepped back.

He dove into the unknown.

Phouka's heka bled outward across his skin, scrawling across his hands as he submerged and swam through the murk. Even though he'd been told what to expect, his heart still slammed when he glimpsed the silhouette of a drowned mansion's peaked roofs and towers, the statues of gods and goddesses crumbling in a landscape of eddying algae and water weeds. Fish glided past windows crusted with barnacles. He kept his breathing steady. Panic would be death.

He located the front door and pushed through, into a vast hall. A wineglass floated past, followed by a moldering gown, the tatters of a book. He slid through an archway of stone cherubs—and was sucked up toward a golden glow.

He broke the surface of a lavish indoor swimming pool and yanked off his mask and goggles, sucking in air. Titan mermaids and dragon-faced mermen of sea-green marble formed pillars and arches. He clambered onto the mosaic floor and walked barefoot beneath a rococo arch of marble jellyfish, into a ballroom illuminated by a chandelier like frozen, cascading blood. Awe and fear warred within him.

Surrounded by a hoard of salvaged objects was a girl in a short ball gown of pale satin. A miniature ship listed within the coils of white hair piled on her head. Her voice seemed to echo faintly, like sonar. "Christie Hart."

As she glided toward him, he wanted to kneel before her and promise her anything. He wanted to die for her—this was alarming, his reaction. *Enchantment.* Her eyes weren't silver but the ever-changing hue of water. He suspected that beneath those lush lips were the teeth of a barracuda. He held his ground and bowed to her. "I'm here with the Banríon. I'm supposed to introduce myself to you. I'm a *fear dorchadas*."

Dahut extended one hand. There was webbing between her fingers and her nails were sharp. "Do you have something for me?"

The glamour glossing the chamber flickered and dimmed. Christie glimpsed a drowned reality: crumbling walls covered with cysts of pale coral, witch-hair algae cloaking once-splendid furniture, a human rib cage nestled among red and yellow anemones. Quickly he skimmed his gaze away—

And saw the mirror Phouka had described to him—scarred silver in a gold frame of octopi, sea horses, and coral—leaning against what appeared to be a ship's figurehead. He took from around his wrist the leather thong strung with volcanic glass, painted bird skulls, and clock parts that Sylvie had made at his request.

"I don't want charms. A *kiss*." Dahut moved toward him as he continued to hold out the bracelet. His hand shook now. She ignored the offering, circling him. Then she began to sing.

Christie stopped shaking. He grinned—Dahut wasn't an undine. She was a *siren*. "That doesn't work on me. Ma'am."

FIVE MINUTES LATER, he broke the lake's surface wearing a second ring—this one cast from antique pewter into the twining forms of fish-headed women—and carrying the mirror beneath one arm. He looked around for the boat on the dusk-drenched lake, saw it drifting. Without Phouka.

His heart thundered. For an ugly, paranoid second, he wondered if Phouka had meant for him to die in the siren's embrace. Then his common sense kicked in. He pushed swiftly to the boat and set the mirror in it.

A movement near the shore caught his attention. In a patch of deadfall near a forested bank, a hand burst out of the water.

"Phouka!" Christie pulled himself into the boat, grabbed a paddle, and steered the boat toward the mass of slimed branches and debris. The water here was black. He gazed desperately into the island of decomposing vegetation, pallid roots, and bleached driftwood. When a cloudy eye blinked open in the muck, he fell back.

It wasn't a floating island of deadfall—whatever it was, it was *assembling* itself from human bones strung together with red vines and algae. When a large arm of tangled matter slid from the water and clamped a clawed hand on the boat, Christie saw Phouka's rhinestone headband embedded in the arm. He clenched his teeth and hissed, *"Thing of rot and mud and bone, malevolent beast that feeds on death—"*

A massive face emerged from the slime. Christie fell back into the boat, hitting his head hard enough that stars scattered across his vision. The monster spoke, disturbingly, in a young man's voice: "Please, please . . . I don't want to die . . ."

Christie continued to whisper over the shattering pain in his skull and sheer animal terror. *"Come apart, unknot, be undone. Release what you have taken—"*

An electrical charge sizzled through him. His head snapped back. He tasted blood in his mouth.

He heard a girl's scream.

He dragged himself to his knees and saw the monstrosity twisting to pieces. Rust-colored liquid spattered outward. A splinter of bone clattered into the boat.

Christie leaned over, frantically searching for any sign of Phouka, thinking, *She can't die. She's immortal.*

He spotted a pale form in the sludge of dead bodies and saw her face in the murk.

Without thinking, he slung off his equipment, sucked in a lungful of oxygen, and jumped into the lake. As the water closed over his head, he saw Phouka floating in the gruesome debris and arrowed toward her. He grabbed her. As they burst out of the water, both slicked with strands of red algae, Phouka's arms slid around him.

A rotting arm drifted past and Christie recoiled as a voice gurgled behind them. As he and Phouka swam toward the boat, Christie looked over his shoulder and saw the thing reassembling itself, all sinewy roots and decomposing bodies. He felt as if the heka appearing on his skin were being drawn by cut glass. His vision blurred and his muscles went weak and his grip on the boat failed.

A red vine whipped around one of his wrists and yanked him toward the monster.

Phouka reached for him. "Christie! Dahut!"

As he was pulled beneath the water, he spoke Dahut's name. Blackness tunneled around his vision, and the world went silent. When a series of violent, bruising blows struck him, he thought he was going to die.

He opened his eyes—

Shoals of fish, large and small, were swarming past him, tearing pieces of the monster away, severing the roots that had roped around him. The fish's silvery-scaled bodies buffeted Christie as they went by in a frenzy. He broke away, pushing up.

Then Phouka was beside him, her auburn hair as red as coral in the murk. She tugged at him, guiding him toward the surface.

They pulled themselves into the boat. As Christie coughed up water streaked with blood, Phouka said, "That was a Nucklavee. The vengeful, drowned dead. It should only exist in Annwyn. It's *not supposed to be here*."

"Okay." He met her gray gaze. "So why was it?"

"The realm of the dead is seeping into this world through some other Way I don't know about." She hesitated, then said, "You saved me."

He imagined he caught admiration in her gaze. He shrugged. "It was the siren who saved us . . ."

"And *your* charm that won her assistance." She smiled. "I'd kiss you, but we're both coated in grue right now."

"We could have died . . . so . . ."

"Oh all right." And she folded her arms around his shoulders, drawing him into a dewy kiss as the last of the dusk drowned in the lake.

Her skin was as warm as any human girl's.

FINN WAS ON HER BED, riffling through Lily Rose's journal, when Jack appeared at her glass doors like a dangerous slice of night clothed in skin. She thought of a false Jack incubating in the shadow of the Wolf and the white snake and curled a fist against her stomach.

She jumped up and flung open the doors.

"Ready for our second date?" Jack asked.

"I am." She pulled a long, cowl-necked sweater over her blue gingham sundress. She wore blue Keds and the lionheart pendant he'd given her. The silver dagger was tucked in a hidden sheath at her back—the sheath had come from Sylvie, courtesy of the Black Scissors.

Jack took a package from his jacket and handed it to her. "I meant to give you this . . . I remembered it after you told me how you found those pages in your mother's paintings."

Finn unwrapped the package to uncover a book with one of her mother's paintings on the cover and the word *Between* in gilt script beneath it, and *By Daisy Sullivan* beneath that. Her eyes stung as she carefully opened the book. She sank down onto her bed and gazed at gorgeous prints of her mother's paintings, the stories for each written on the opposite page.

"It's the only copy. The publisher went out of business before he could produce it."

Finn shivered. She gazed down at a glossy image of a dark-haired boy surrounded by roses with eyes in their centers. An elaborate frame of ivy bordered the painting and the boy held a bleeding crow in one hand, a silver needle in the other. "My mom could see the Fatas." She traced the painting's outline. "Maybe she went into science to prove they didn't exist. Or that they did. Your dad knew about them. What about your mom?"

"You know how I learned how to fight? Defending myself against street kids who tried to take all the goddamn silver and iron I was always wearing, courtesy of my mother."

Finn pictured him, a fierce boy facing two Artful Dodger types, his knuckles bruised. She carefully closed the book and hugged it to her. "What would your mom have thought of me?"

His gaze caressed her and she felt those butterflies again, wings like glass and fire within her. "She would have called you a headstrong hoyden. Or maybe a stubborn gadabout. Then she would have said you're too skinny. She would have hugged you and given you something of hers, some heirloom. And then she would have fed you her famous goulash."

"Did you have many girlfriends then?" Finn teased.

"Oh, tribes of them." His eyes darkened and she guessed that he was thinking about the Lily Girls. His voice cracked. "Sophia Avaline was holding Eve here, but it was *my* guilt that kept Beatrice and Abigail trapped."

"They're free now. *You* did that. Not the exorcism." She recalled something Avaline had told her. "Jack, when I spoke to Professor Avaline, she said Lily should never have been taken out of the Ghostlands." Terror tightened her throat. "That it was Lily making things in this house go wrong—"

"Things?" Jack's head snapped up, his eyes silvering. "What *things*?"

She took him to Lily's room, where the butterfly-shaped lights around the ceiling emphasized the shadows in the corners. The new mirror over the bureau was tarnished, as if centuries old. Gazing into the mirror, Finn imagined she saw, not a reflection, but a gloomy interior like some rococo palace gone to ruin.

Jack moved into the room, reached out to touch a patch of mold on the wall. Finn flinched as a jewel-green beetle appeared from the mold and hit the wooden floor with a click.

"Scarab beetle." Jack toed it with one booted foot.

Finn reluctantly switched on the light to Lily's bathroom. The mold had gotten worse here. There were seven bottles of spray bleach in one corner and the bathroom reeked of it, as if her sister had been trying to clean up a crime scene.

Jack led her into the hall and shut the door to Lily's room. With a breeze from the open window curling around them, he said, "We'll find out what is causing this. I promise. I don't know why Annwyn is leaking into this world . . ."

"It began before I entered the underworld." Finn shoved her hands through her hair. "Jack. The oak. Isn't *that* a Way to the land of the dead? Has anyone checked on it?"

"That Way closed after All Hallows' Eve, but . . ."

Footsteps pounded up the stairs and Lily appeared. "Hey, you two," she said, grinning. "Am I interrupting?"

Finn knew she looked guilty and was glad they'd moved away from Lily's door. "Hey, Lily . . . could you drive us somewhere?"

"WELL, *SHE DROWSED OFF FAST.*" Lily glanced at Finn in the rearview mirror as she drove her Nissan down the forest road. Finn snored delicately, her head against Jack's shoulder.

Jack met Lily's gaze and smiled. "She needs to relax more."

"That won't happen. What happened to your car?"

"Finn has been driving it and forgot to put gas in it," he said.

"That doesn't sound like her. She's very particular about those sorts of things. When we were kids, she always knew when one of her toys was out of place. She used to alphabetize the books in our shelves once a month. Can I ask you something? Why were your . . . exes called Lily Girls?"

"Because they were dead and lovely. Reiko named them the Lily Girls." Jack was gazing out the window. "Turn here, please."

"Did I ever thank you?" Lily steered the car onto the dirt road he'd indicated. "For what you did?"

"What I did? Introduced Finn to a world that's nearly destroyed her?"

"Hell, Jack—that world got to our family long before you. Don't be so self-centered."

FINN AND JACK HIKED from the road into the woods—Jack didn't want Lily anywhere near what had once been a gateway into the underworld. When Jack raised the electric lantern to illuminate the young oak that had grown when the old oak the Fatas revered had burned, Finn saw that the tree had been severed by an ax. "He's been here," she said softly. "Your shadow."

Jack walked to the fallen tree and set one hand upon the trunk. He sat on the stump and bowed his head. "This is a message. I was supposed to die beneath the old tree. This one gave me false mortality." He looked around. "Nathan was also supposed to die here." He glanced at Finn, then said, "Nate and I lived in LeafStruck with Colleen Olive. Then I met Beatrice. She loved books. Nathan loved her. Colleen loved Nathan. And I loved nothing."

Finn sank down onto the stump beside him and let him speak.

"Beatrice would never have met the kelpie that killed her if he hadn't been one of my comrades. Then there was Summer-of-Love Abigail, who could play a guitar like Hendrix." His head was down, his gaze focused on his past. "She was poisoned by nightshade wine that I drank because I thought it was blackberry. When I kissed her, the nightshade killed her." His mouth twisted. "You would think, by the time I met Eve Avaline I'd have learned my lesson. But by then I didn't think I was capable of feeling anything. I wanted to feel *something*.

I tricked all three of them because I wanted a heart. Do you know what terrifies me about my shadow being loose? I believe what Sombrus stored away was *me* when I was scarcely even aware of what I was doing. If Lot wanted a Fata enemy dead, I'd do it. If Reiko wanted a mortal threatened, I'd do it. I had no power, Finn, but being a Jack, able to charm and hurt . . . *that* made me feel as if I did. And that's what's loose in the world."

She had no comforting words, only the kindness of listening.

When he rose, she stood with him and they gazed at the fallen tree as if it had been a friend. Then, hands clasped, they turned and walked away.

IT WAS TO CRUITHNEAR, the professors, and Phouka that Finn and Jack presented their plan. Avaline was not with the professors. Finn didn't ask where she was.

Sylvie and Christie had come and sat on one of the paint-gobbed wooden tables in HallowHeart's Arts Center. Lily had brought Aubrey and Kevin. Kevin was here on behalf of the Black Scissors. Leaning near a window was Phouka Banríon, in a chic girl-queen ensemble.

"My play." Mr. Fairchild looked resigned. "You want to use my play to catch Jack's shadow."

"Only the dress rehearsal." Finn tried not to fidget on her stool. "Absalom will be there, to guard Anna. The enemy won't be suspicious if some of you are there, and my friends Kevin and Sylvie are already in the play. We think Jack Daw—that's what we call Jack's shadow—wants Jack to give him the key embedded in him by Reiko. So we give him an opportunity to gain leverage. Me."

"I don't like this," Christie muttered. "We're not even sure if it *is* Jack's double."

"What is the key for?" Jane Emory sounded worried.

"We don't know," Finn said.

"I still don't understand Seth Lot's magical house." Professor Wyatt scrubbed a hand through his dreadlocks. "Sombrus keeps memories alive? It sounds dangerous as hell."

"It is, which is why we need to find it," Phouka said. "I've retrieved seven mirrors originally from the houses of the blessed. These are objects of power."

Cruithnear set an elbow on the table before him and rubbed his brow. "You say these mirrors can be used to trap a wayward spirit?"

"We can conceal the mirrors." Jack leaned forward. "On the stage. At the proper time, they can be revealed and act as a conduit to capture Jack Daw when he makes his move. And concealing them will help protect the one Fata who will be in the play—Absalom."

There was a silence. Finn guessed that everyone was wondering if Absalom deserved to be protected. They all now knew what he'd done to Hester.

"Should we vote?" Professor Hobson asked with a sarcastic edge to his tone.

"*No.*" Finn stood up. "We're going to do it."

"One question." Christie lifted a forefinger. "How will we know our Jack is . . . our Jack?"

Everyone looked at Finn. She said, "*I'll* know."

CHAPTER 14

My Lovely Week.

(During which, I was able to finish course assignments and have a life (without the otherworld rearing its ugly head).

Sunday: *Dusk picnic with Da, Jane, Lily, Christie, and Sylvie at the lake. Christie didn't encounter any water monsters when we went swimming. This was a highlight.*

Monday: *Told Da Jack was back. Da drank some scotch. Took me and Jack to dinner at the Antlered Moon. Jack dimmed his Jackishness and answered all Da's questions. Pretty sure Da now believes Jack might be a hit man or a spy.*

Tuesday: *Girls' night. Da and Jane went out. Lily, Sylvie, and I tried on Lily's old ballet costumes, ate cake, and drank. ("Booze and cake," Sylvie told me, wearing cat ears and black tulle while pouring daiquiris. "What more can you ask for?")*

Wednesday: *Pool party at Claudette Tredescant's. Lily was in her element. Black bikini and sunglasses and Kevin Gilchriste bringing her mojitos. No Fatas. Christie flirted with Lily. Sylvie shoved Aubrey into the pool.*

Thursday: *Dinner at Jack's. He played the violin and said he was rusty. Yeah, right. I brought my Epiphone guitar and played the* *only song I know. "Hero." I sang along even though I can't sing. I can't play the guitar either.*

Friday: Felt like the calm before the storm.

—FROM THE JOURNAL OF FINN SULLIVAN

Kevin drove Finn and Lily to Strawberry Hill Park, where the play rehearsal would take place. He led them to the stone circle of seats surrounding the sunken stage that had been transformed into a landscape of trees, pillars, paper insects, and a backdrop reminiscent of a Maxfield Parrish painting. Gauzy curtains hung on the partitions, concealing Phouka's seven mirrors.

Finn tugged the Leica camera from her bag. She raised it and focused it on the stage, saw Professor Fairchild speaking with Aubrey. Kevin left them to get ready for his role as Apollo. Finn had gotten the part of Athena for this dangerous practice session.

Christie was parked nearby with Micah, ready at a moment's call. Jack had become a shadow so that he might not be seen. Absalom, James Wyatt, and Jane were within shouting distance.

When practice began, Anna appeared onstage, wearing a ruffled dress and a short, hooded cape of scarlet velvet. A banner unfurled above her head in an admirable sleight of hand. It read: *The Tale of Cupid and Psyche."*

"Let the unseen be seen," Anna intoned. "Let him not hide from my gaze. Unveil the mystery. From my eyes cast the haze."

Claudette Tredescant was a perfect Aphrodite, cruelly setting Psyche on her quest, after Cupid—played by Aubrey's younger brother—vanished in folds of gauze. As the lights cast onto the stage became a crimson that reminded Finn of nightmares, Kevin appeared as a gallant Apollo, along with Sylvie in black suede as Artemis.

"Almost your turn." Lily regarded the empty coliseum as Finn took a mirror compact from a pocket of the gossamer gray dress she wore and pretended to check her lip gloss. She saw shadows in the seats, but couldn't tell who they were.

Psyche was pursuing another clue, walking beneath the sea as papier-mâché fish, octopi, and sea horses drifted past her, when Absalom appeared as Hermes. As Psyche turned from Hermes, the lights dimmed to a hazy purple and Hades, played by Aubrey, appeared in a black hoodie and jeans, the hood drawn up to shadow his masked face.

Every nerve in Finn's body crackled. *That's not Aubrey.*

The gauzy curtains were swept away in a howling wind scented with blood and dirty ice. The mirrors from the seven houses of the blessed flashed.

"Finn!" The alarm in Lily's voice made Finn's stomach lurch. "Absal—"

On the stage, Absalom burst into dark tendrils that writhed toward the seven mirrors. Anna screamed. Finn saw Fairchild sprinting toward the stage, followed by Jane and Wyatt. Kevin staggered onto the stage, clutching at his midriff. Anna stood with her back to Finn, facing the hooded Hades, her red-booted feet firmly planted.

Finn and Lily ran toward Anna.

Hades whirled, his face nothing more than shadows.

Finn felt something slam into her. She was swept off the stage, onto the grass. She heard Lily shout her name before strong hands grabbed her, dragging her. Finn looked up into Jack's face and felt shock. His eyes were silver and cold.

This wasn't her Jack. She had been right about Jack Daw.

A figure rose up from the night and Jack appeared behind his double, slamming a fist into the other's throat. Finn stumbled back as shadow Jack burst into dozens of large blackbirds that flocked toward the woods.

Jack whispered, "I've never done *that* before." He glanced at her, fierce. "I'm going after him." Before she could protest, he'd descended into his jackal-shadow form and taken off in the direction of the woods.

WHEN SYLVIE HEARD THE SCREAM, she dashed out of the tent dressing room. She saw Giselle, blond and lethal, dragging Anna toward a blue Chevy. People were shouting and running near the stage.

"Oh, *no*, you don't." Sylvie ran at the Jill, an elder wood blade in one hand and an iron dagger in the other.

Ares, the god of war, stepped before her, wearing a metal mask. His hair was platinum. The blade he held glistened with a dark stain.

Caliban. Sylvie forced down her panic, dove past him.

Caliban caught her and shoved her to the ground. Straddling her, he held her by the throat. When she swatted at him with a hand adorned with three iron rings, he laughed. "Nice try, heart widow." He raised the blade.

Sylvie began to struggle for her life, her feet drumming against the grass. As Caliban's grip tightened, she tried to cry out, but her voice box was being crushed. She could only stare into his alien eyes as he pressed the blade's tip against her left breast and delicately, with surgical precision, inserted it.

A lithe figure in jeans and a hoodie tackled Caliban.

Sylvie, as her consciousness slid away, saw Moth rise up and draw a silver blade as Caliban skirled to his feet.

IT WAS LILY who called Christie on his cell phone.

"No. Oh no . . ." When Christie, still holding the phone to his ear, saw the flashing lights of an ambulance and police cars pass his Mustang in the parking lot of Strawberry Hill Park, he and Micah began to run.

Finn and Lily came hurrying toward them. There was blood on the white corset Lily wore beneath her denim jacket.

"What happened?" Christie asked. "Where's Sylv—" He broke off as he saw the paramedics near the stage, Fairchild and Jane Emory with them.

"Christie." Finn gripped his arm. "Caliban stabbed Sylvie and Kevin. Aubrey was hit on the head—they're going to be okay—"

"Okay?" Christie wrenched away from her. "*What happened?*"

"Jack's shadow happened. Caliban and Giselle happened. Moth saved Sylvie, but Caliban got away. And . . . they've got Anna."

Moth was walking toward them. In one hand, he held an origami insect made from some of the glow-in-the-dark paper used to make props for the play. "I can track where they took Anna Weaver." He whispered to the paper insect, then placed something in it. He looked at them. "A strand of Anna's hair."

The insect—a moth—flapped up. "You've *got* to teach me that trick," Christie murmured.

Finn turned to Micah. "Will you go with Sylv and the others to the hospital?"

Micah nodded grimly and strode toward the ambulance.

A car swerved up over the grass. They all stared at Sophia Avaline's cherry-red Fiat as Avaline stuck her head out the window. "Wyatt called me. How can I help?"

"We need to find Anna." Finn moved toward the car. "We need to follow that paper moth."

"Get in."

CHRISTIE WAS GLAD HE WASN'T DRIVING. He was clenching his teeth so hard, every muscle in his head ached. *Caliban.*

Caliban.

Caliban.

"Christie." Finn, who sat in the backseat with him, gripped one of his hands. "Stop thinking about killing Caliban. We need to concentrate on getting Anna back."

Finn's and Christie's cell phones buzzed. They both received the same text from Micah:

Emergen C Room. Kev on warpth. Aub's head hurts. Sylv OK.

Christie glared down at his phone. "I'm going to *kill* the crooked dog."

FINN WAS OUT OF THE CAR as soon as it stopped in front of StarDust. Lily and Christie shouted at her, but she ran after the paper moth, toward the darkened glass dome that glinted in the moonlight despite its coating of deadfall and bird droppings. The metal doors with their Egyptian eye, hand, and ivy engravings seemed even more mystical than usual. She halted and stared at a piece of red velvet caught on the thorn bushes nearby. Anna's cape had been made from the same material.

"I'm going in," Christie said, appearing next to her.

Then words dripped from his mouth like acid-laced ink, sliced through the air, sank into the metal of the door, and disfigured the designs of hands and eyes.

The doors blew open, releasing a backdraft of malicious enchantment entwined with cobwebs and withered leaves. Lights flared on, revealing StarDust's interior of Egyptian Revival glamour, the roots of the red, black, and white lilies snaking over the floor. Decorative scarabs, gilt cobras, and the colors of lapis lazuli and carmine red were as vivid as if painted on glass. The pillars etched with eyes of Horus and ankhs seemed new. The furniture and film equipment gleamed.

StarDust had gussied itself up for them. It was at once enchanting and disturbing.

"Finn." Lily clasped one of Finn's wrists. "Nyx and the Lily Girls are gone. What's doing this?"

"*He's* here." Finn could *sense* the shadow Jack.

The air hummed.

Moth strode past them, into StarDust, a blade in each hand. Finn turned to Avaline, who stood with the wind sweeping her hair over her face, her cell phone in one hand. "Professor, please stay here. Just in case."

"Be careful."

Finn strode into StarDust with Lily and Christie.

Inside the studio, a whisper trailed through the hazy air, followed by a rush of wind. "Moth?" Finn called.

The metal doors slammed shut on Avaline's red-coated figure. The lamps blinked off.

Finn turned in place, her skin crawling. "*Moth!*"

Christie swore. "Here. I tripped over him."

"Moth!" Finn crouched beside Moth's body, sighed when she felt the pulse in one wrist.

"I thought he was invincible," Lily whispered. "We need light."

Christie's voice shook. "I think the light on my phone's working. Got it." He raised the phone.

The flashlight app flickered over the white faces and shining eyes of a dozen Grindylow surrounding them.

Lily swore as she, Finn, and Christie backed up against one another, keeping their gazes fixed on the creatures. Veiled with cobwebs and dust, the dolls looked like they'd stepped straight out of the Roaring Twenties. Finn would never get used to the creeping horror that slicked her skin whenever she was in their presence.

Lily didn't reach for the silver and elder wood blade Finn knew she had sheathed at her back—drawing a blade would trigger the Grindylow's defense mechanisms.

Finn kept her gaze on the nearest Grindylow. It wore a tuxedo and its dark hair was slicked back.

"Head slowly for the back doors," Finn ordered. As Moth stirred, she and Christie hauled him up between them. They all began to move, keeping their backs to one another.

Christie's gaze was fixed on a big-eyed doll in a tasseled dress. "I'll blow the back doors open. Like I did the front ones."

"Christie, this place will protect itself now." Lily sounded fierce. "That won't work."

A Grindylow appeared near Finn, its mouth open to reveal needle teeth. Finn stumbled. Behind that Grindylow stood another in a red, tasseled dress. They all looked like classical movie stars.

"They're the actors from Nicollette Tirnagoth's silent films," Finn whispered with evolving horror. "This was the bad end they came to."

"Just keep moving," Lily urged. "And try not to think about it."

"They were *people*?" Christie stumbled against a tripod. The resulting crash resounded throughout the glass dome.

A Grindylow in a wine-red gown was suddenly too close. Finn fixed her gaze upon it.

When they reached the French doors, with the Grindylow arrayed before them, Finn said, "Lily, Christie, get out of the way when I tell you to. I'm going to pull a blade on the one who looks like Rudolph Valentino. When he comes at me, I'll step aside and he'll crash into the doors. Maybe a Grindylow can break the glass."

"Whoa! *Whoa!*" Christie's hand shook, and the handheld light wavered as he kept Moth from sliding to the floor. "Let *me* try to get the doors open, okay?" He began to chant. "*Let the glass shake, let the glass break . . .*" His voice strained as the Grindylow who weren't in the light, the ones they couldn't hold with their gazes, crept closer.

Panic shot through Finn in a swooning wave. For Christie's witchery to work, he'd need *energy*. "Christie, *wait*—"

The flashlight on his phone blinked out as his heka drained the cell's battery. Darkness fell. The Grindylow surged forward.

Finn felt Moth slide away from her and realized he was moving with purpose—it was as if he'd been playing possum. She saw his sword glint. The head of one of the Grindylow rolled into a pool of moonlight.

The glass doors behind them shattered.

A hand clamped on Finn's hoodie and dragged her back. She caught hold of Lily's wrist and Lily grabbed Christie. Together, they were pulled through the broken doors. As Moth followed in a breathtaking somersault, Finn imagined she saw a reflection of herself vanishing into the sludgy darkness of StarDust.

None of the Grindylow stepped after them through the shards of glass. They stood within StarDust, eyes glistening.

Finn turned to face Jack. *Her* Jack, cuts on his face and his knuckles bloody. She flung her arms around him.

"I lost my shadow," Jack said into her ear. "What are you *doing* here?"

"Anna was taken by Giselle." Finn stepped back. Her voice shook. "Moth used a spell to track her. It led us here."

Jack was grim. "Jack Daw and his allies used this as a Way. To escape us."

It's my fault they took Anna, Finn thought, and the guilt gnawed at her like an abscess in her heart. "So it was Jack Daw?"

"It was." Jack watched her.

Christie was still staring at the Grindylow. "What do we do about *them*?"

"Nothing." Finn turned her back on the things. "There's nothing—"

"Oh yes there is." And Christie began to chant. Lily clasped Christie's hand. As strands of darkness swirled around Lily, from her hair, her fingertips, Finn was buffeted by a wind that seemed full of shadow locusts. She watched leaves and dirt hurtle past her, converging on the Grindylow beyond the broken glass. Moth stepped back. Jack reached for Finn's hand and gripped it tight.

Christie's words made the air crackle. When Lily began to speak, Finn remembered how her sister had created the butterfly from shadow and light.

Black stains appeared on the Grindylow's skin. Cracks opened up. One of the Grindylow teetered as an arm fell off. As the flecks of darkness continued to swarm over the dolls, one by one, the Grindylow disintegrated.

The wind stopped. The silence was almost an ache.

Christie began to fall and Lily caught him.

"He did it," Jack said, astounded.

Lily caressed Christie's curls as he moaned. His lashes fluttered. "Did I break them? Did I break the Fatas' goddamn toys?"

SOPHIA AVALINE REMAINED AT STARDUST when Finn and her friends had gone, waiting for Cruithnear, whom she'd called, to tell him about Anna. His voice had sounded distorted and grainy as he'd asked her to wait for him at StarDust. No doubt he wanted to do some investigating of his own.

As she leaned against her car, gazing at StarDust's front doors and trying not to think about the decimated Grindylow in the back, Avaline heard a muted sound.

Within StarDust, something slammed against the grimy glass. She gasped when she recognized the smear of face.

She took a step forward. "Sera—"

She never saw the white hyena that lunged from the trees and took her down.

AS FINN CLIMBED AFTER JACK into his apartment, Jack moved to switch on the lights. Then he walked to her and drew her against him. As he stepped back, he said, "Let me take you home."

"I want to stay." She hesitated, then asked, "Is what happened to Anna *my* fault? Because I brought Lily and you out of the Ghostlands and Annwyn . . ."

He dropped down onto the sofa and she sat opposite him. He leaned forward and tucked a strand of her hair back behind one of her ears and gently told her, "It's not your fault. My shadow . . . Jack Daw won't hurt Anna—not if he wants that key."

"And Absalom?"

"He's gone. And I don't know if Phouka can get him out of those mirrors."

She frowned down at her fingers. "It was supposed to be *me. Not Anna.*"

"I'm going to make some tea." He stood and walked toward the tiny kitchen.

Finn got up and moved to the window. She lifted a battered edition of *The Adventures of Pinocchio* from a nearby table and leafed through the yellowed pages.

When she looked up from the book, she found a white barn owl perched on the windowsill, gazing at her with dark, too-intelligent eyes. As the stereo clicked to a haunting song, Finn whispered to the owl, "Colleen Olive, is that you?"

A cold, clear voice spoke in her head: *You are not the lionheart.*

Finn dropped the book. Her eyelashes fluttered. A memory crashed through the doors she'd locked against it. She watched herself being dragged away by shadows as something in the dark of StarDust replicated her, *became* her, and was rescued by Jack.

You're not the lionheart. The owl glided away.

Finn-who-was-not turned as Jack appeared in the doorway between the kitchen and the living room. "Finn?"

Before she could voice her dismay, a warning, the doppelgänger broke apart into nothing, the darkness from which she'd been made drifting like ashes across Jack's lips.

THE SHOCK OF ANNA'S KIDNAPPING had put Lily off her game, and helping Christie destroy the Grindylow had exhausted her. She sat in a fan-backed wicker chair on the veranda of her house and longed for a cigarette for the first time in years.

She leaned forward and pushed her hands over her face. *Anna.* She thought of the innocent girl, of the creatures that had taken her.

"Lily." The familiar voice made her lift her head.

Moth stood on the path, his face obscured by strands of moonlight and shadow flung by the overreaching branches of the oak. His appearance always took her back to the dark times in the Wolf's house, when she had made herself a cold and heartless thing.

"Moth," she said, sitting back.

He moved up the steps and sat in the wicker chair beside her, almost formally setting his hands on the curved arms. Like a king. She realized he was mimicking her current posture and scowled and wriggled and drew her legs up beneath her, yoga style. "Finn's with Jack."

"I came to see you." He was quiet for a moment, then: "Do you really think you can simply return to what you were? You're like me. You have no place here either."

She wrapped her arms around her knees. He was brooding. Leander had never brooded, and that's one of the reasons she'd loved him. So much. Her heart, already bitten and raw, stung. "I do have a purpose, Moth." She spoke in the voice she would use in Lot's house, with the wolves and boggarts, Redcaps and harpies. "To protect my family. And my new friends. And I'll kill whatever or whoever tries to hurt them."

He looked up at her, the light glancing across his beautiful, elvish-green eyes. He'd always been a curiosity to her, an injured, wild animal she'd cared for. Because of Leander, there hadn't been anything more between them, but the possibility had been there. She wanted to reach out to him. She didn't. "Why are you here, Moth? I don't need babysitting."

He shrugged, sprawling in the chair and gazing out at the night.

Lily unwound and stood up. "Do you want to come in?"

"No, Lily. I'll remain out here, thank you."

"Suit yourself." She opened the screen door, glanced back at his profile limned by the porch light. She stepped into the kitchen and let the door shut.

As she was rummaging through the fridge, her dad appeared in the doorway to the hall.

"Finn's with *him*?" Disapproval deepened his voice.

"Finn's with Jack, yes, Dad. She's a young woman now. You'll have to get over it."

"What were you up to tonight?"

"We were helping with the play rehearsal." She hoped he hadn't heard what had happened to Anna. Not yet.

"I found these on my desk this morning." He took from his back pocket a familiar sheaf of folded papers tied with a yellow ribbon and set them on the counter. Lily's heart went into overdrive.

She had placed those journal remnants in a locked trunk.

Gran Rose. But Lily couldn't tell her father that Gran Rose had put the papers on his desk, that those pages from her mom's journal were not delusions, but fact. She was afraid to drag her dad into the Fata realm, wanted desperately to keep reality as majestically commonplace as possible. She still woke believing her recovered life was all some cruel illusion of Lot's, and sometimes she pinched herself hard enough to leave a bruise—just to make sure she was alive and not caught in a trick. She remembered whirling in despair toward the old window in the dance studio, the rage and the grief building, after five years of being with-out her mother. It had been a moment of insanity. As she'd struck the window, as the shattering glass had bitten into her skin, she'd almost believed she wouldn't die . . . until she'd begun to fall.

"Lily." Her dad indicated the pages. There were brackets around his mouth and crow's-feet near his eyes that Lily didn't remember him having. "Have you read these?"

It was time for him to know. There *had* to be a way to break the Fata memory block. "Dad, what if Mom *wasn't* losing it? What if those things were real? Could you handle it?"

"Christ, Lil. They're *not* real. *Fairies* . . . ?"

"What about Gran Rose leaving all those iron nails over the windows and doors?"

"Are you having me on? Are you? Because none of this is . . ." He looked down at the papers in his hand. His eyes grew bright and Lily watched as the sealed door cracked open in his mind. "Fairies who steal . . . does this have anything to do with . . ."

"Dad. *Careful.*" Lily reached out.

"*Fatas*," he whispered. He blinked and frowned and rubbed his temples. "What were we talking about?"

"Dad—" Lily's voice broke. He'd forgotten again. Dismayed, she reached out and gently took the papers from his hands. "Why don't you go lie down?'

Then Jack called, and Lily found out what had happened to Finn.

She flung herself onto the porch, only to find Moth gone.

CHAPTER 15

*Tink was not all bad, or, rather, she was all bad just now, but, on the other hand,
sometimes she was all good.*
—*PETER PAN*, J. M. BARRIE

Anna didn't know who the shadow man was.

She stood in the pink room into which she'd been dumped. A princess bed with spiderweb netting stood in the center. Most of the pretty dolls in the room lay in pieces around her: Anna had smashed them. The door was scarred from the chairs she'd flung at it. The window, unfortunately, hadn't broken like the dolls.

Her throat was hoarse from yelling.

She'd cried a little, thinking of what had happened to Absalom. She'd known him since she'd been little, from when he'd first appeared to her as a child her age, sitting with her on the roof that extended beneath her bedroom window.

The door clicked open, revealing a gloomy concrete hall flickering with fluorescent lights. Clenching one hand in her ruffled dress, fighting the fear like a badger in her stomach, Anna waited.

A shadow scuttled in the hall and rose in the doorway, becoming a girl Anna's age, with a cap of white hair and wide eyes. She wore a ballerina costume of faded ivory and ballet slippers of dirty, pale satin. "Who are you?" Anna demanded.

The girl cocked her head to one side. She moved forward, jerkily, like some kind of clockwork figure. "I'm me. Who are you?"

"I'm Anna."

The girl did a little pirouette, then began slinking around the room. "This is prettier than my room. Mine only has a bed in it and a picture of a lady with no head. There are cracks everywhere. And a bug. I named him Harold."

Anna edged toward the door. "Can you help me get out of here?"

The girl spun around. Her eyes were blue and slitted. "You can't get out *that* way."

"I don't want to be here," Anna said in a small voice.

"Tell you what." The girl leaped onto the bed and began jumping up and down on it. "You can have my room and I'll take this one."

Anna peered into the dirty hallway blinking with fluorescent lighting. A window at the far end revealed a moonlit city scattered with headless statues. "No thank you. I'll stay here."

The girl was suddenly too close, her eyes wide, her smile a terrifying blank. She whispered, *"I want to be you."* She shoved Anna through the door. Anna screamed as she fell into pitch-black.

She landed on a floor, then scrambled up to find herself in an empty ballroom with red walls and an immense mirror of inky glass before her. The mirror was framed by golden dragons.

Anna . . .

She recognized that voice and her heart burst with relief. "Absalom!"

A hand reached from the black glass, sticky webs of silver tangling its fingers. Then a figure with disheveled, blood-orange hair emerged and slid to its knees. There were little flames in his hair, on his fingernails.

"That was a bit painful." Absalom coughed up something like soot, then sniffed and wiped his nose. He focused on Anna and grinned. *"There* you are."

"Absalom." She knelt before him. "Where are we?"

"In Sombrus." He rose and held out a hand to her.

She saw a crack in his skin, between his thumb and his forefinger. There was no blood, only darkness.

"You're hurt."

"Oh that. That's nothing. Sometimes I break. It's annoying." Another crack appeared beneath his left eye. He winced.

She stood and clasped his hand, flinching as another fissure appeared in his neck.

"Absalom—"

His gaze drifted to something behind her. "I don't want you to see this. Go to sleep now."

"What—" Anna didn't feel him catch her as she fell.

AS ABSALOM GENTLY LOWERED ANNA TO THE FLOOR, the shadow man Anna hadn't seen enter walked around them, his voice deep and dark. "Devil. Things not going well for you?"

"This is getting old." Absalom didn't move as another crack opened up in his torso.

The shadow circled. "It's all new to me."

"You're getting rather old as well."

The shadow stopped before him, eyes glinting like poison in the darkness beneath the hood of its jacket. "Stand still or I'll bash your girl's brains in."

As the enemy slammed an elder wood blade into Absalom, the carefully constructed shell Absalom had built around himself fell to pieces and the Fool was caught.

CHAPTER 16

The fairies may be heard singing light-heartedly:
"Not the seed of Adam are we,
Nor is Abraham our father;
But of the seed of the Proud Angel,
Driven forth from Heaven."

—*The Fairy-Faith in Celtic Countries,*
W. Y. Evans-Wentz

Finn stood outside the Lakeside Motel, a dingy and ramshackle horseshoe of a building painted a muted green. Despite the name, there was no lake nearby, only a pond like a black hole in the night.

As the sign buzzed and flickered out, Finn began walking toward the motel. She reached the door with the number 13 on it, and found it ajar, a lamp glowing on a nightstand within.

"Moth?" She pushed the door open farther, saw the moths, the blood on the walls, the shadowy, hooded figure standing in the center of the room.

Finn dragged her head up and forced her eyelids open. She was sprawled on a stone surface. There were lit candles all around her and, high up, a stained-glass window depicting a fiery heart. Beneath the window stood a figure, the hood of its jacket shadowing its face.

She scrambled off the catafalque, then winced as her legs gave way and she fell, knees slamming onto the stone floor. "Who are you?" She hauled herself up and caught her balance against an angel statue. She remembered watching a version of herself being dragged out of StarDust by Jack.

The hooded figure extended one hand to reveal that it held a luminous yellow flower with serpentine tendrils and tiny teeth in its center, a nightmare marigold. Finn shook her head. "*Who are you?*"

The doors to the crypt swept open. Giselle and Caliban entered. "Congrats, Finn." Caliban grinned as he and the Jill took hold of her and dragged her back onto the catafalque. "This is a place of old power, where Reiko made her Jacks and Jills."

"No." Finn couldn't believe this was happening. Not *this*.

"I still think this is a bad idea," Caliban addressed the hooded figure. *Jack Daw*, Finn tried to focus through her panic. "Just have her, without this big production."

"No!" Finn shouted. "No—"

Giselle struck her across the face. Finn saw stars. "*Shh!*" The Jill lifted a finger to her own lips. "No one can hear you. After this, Caliban's going after your pretty witch and the lovely knight. Scream when he brings back pieces of them. Oh, and old Thomas Rhymer? I broke his heart."

"No . . ." Finn attempted to twist away.

A blade gleamed in the hooded figure's hand as it moved toward them. Finn began to struggle for her life.

The knife slammed into her breast. She screamed.

CHAPTER 17

I am bigger than I appear to you now. We can make the old young, the big small, the small big.

—THE FAIRY-FAITH IN CELTIC COUNTRIES,
W. Y. EVANS-WENTZ

Sylvie tried not to think about how the blade had felt—cold and merciless—sliding into her while Caliban smiled down at her. As Moth had fought Caliban, she'd lain there, numb and violated and bleeding. And that was when she'd felt *it* arrive. Darkness like a murder of crows had descended upon her, become a smiling, winged, hook-nosed woman with eyes as black as blood deep in the body.

As Sylvie approached the Black Scissors's run-down building with Christie and Lily, she shrugged her backpack onto one shoulder and winced as her stitches stretched. She felt defeated and depressed. Anna had been kidnapped. Finn was missing. And Sylvie was soon to be possessed by a war goddess.

"What did you tell your dad?" she asked Lily as the other girl knocked on the Black Scissors's door.

"That Finn was with Jack." Lily looked paler than usual. "I didn't use to mind lying to him. Now, it makes me sick. He heard what happened to Anna at the play, to you and Kevin. I said it was a fight that got out of hand and Anna ran away."

"Yeah." Sylvie's voice was husky. "That's what I told the police."

The door was answered by Murray, the Scotsman who owned the arcade. "Welcome"—Murray flung open the door—"to my home."

"This is *your* place?" Sylvie was impressed.

"It is, Miss Whitethorn. How are you?" There was a grim concern in his gaze that didn't match his careless smile. "He's sent the other *Taltu* back to their cities. The exorcism took a bit out of him."

When Sylvie stepped into the parlor with Christie and Lily, they found the Black Scissors leaning against the fireplace. Sylvie flinched when she saw a shadow trickle from his left nostril.

"Sylvie." He lifted one arm. Darkness trailed from a fissure in his skin. Sylvie hurried to him and helped him into a chair. "Do you want this?" the Black Scissors murmured in her ear. "This life?"

"I don't know. Did you ask all the others that same question?"

"All of them. Over the course of two centuries. Here." He held out one hand and the shadows bleeding from him braided around his bare arm to knot into a solid shape in his palm.

The shape blanched, became a small book with a cover of pale ivory and a tiny porcelain hand as a clasp. "Give it back to the Banríon."

"Why did you have us take it in the first place?" She had to look away from his face because one of his eyes had sunk in. Blackness filled the socket.

"I wanted it as leverage. But it hasn't done me any good."

Sylvie lifted the ivory book Christie had stolen from Phouka. "I remember when life was simple."

"Lucky you. I don't. Now. Tell me about Jack's shadow."

AS CHRISTIE ACCEPTED THE IVORY BOOK FROM SYLVIE, the tension strung throughout his body like barbed wire lessened. He looked around Murray's parlor, which didn't match the crummy exterior of the house. With its maroon leather sofa and a picture window overlooking a walled courtyard, it was a cozy room cluttered with books and ephemera.

The Black Scissors leaned forward in his chair, booted legs apart. He was dressed for battle in dark clothing that could conceal weapons. He regarded them soberly. "You believe Jack's shadow took Anna and Finn."

"Yes." Christie watched Murray pour liquor into four cups of tea steaming on a table near the hearth. "I tried to find them with . . . what I can do. Nothing happens."

Murray handed Christie a cup of brandy-laced tea. Christie was grateful for it. The rain had made the day cold and his hands were like ice. When he noticed ink scrawls appearing on his fingers, he sighed.

"Christopher." The Black Scissors spoke. "You realize the more you use the shadows snaking through you, the less human you become?"

If it meant saving Finn, if it meant wasting Caliban—becoming less human was a sacrifice Christie was willing to make. He swallowed the knot in his throat.

"And you, Sylvie." The Black Scissors's eyes seemed to change color in the firelight. "I can see what's hovering near you. It's all right to let them in during a fight, but it gets harder and harder to let them go, the battle spirits. That's why the *Taltu* use violence as a last resort." He glanced at Lily. "I don't know how to find Finn or Anna. We need to go to Tirnagoth and the Banríon."

Her eyes rimmed with red, Lily opened her hands. "We tried Christie's map spell, a strand of Finn's hair in a paper butterfly—methods that worked before. Jack was searching for her until the sun rose . . ."

"Jack's double won't hurt them. He wants that key in Jack."

"What is that key *for*?" Christie glared at his teacup.

"Nothing good." The Black Scissors was still watching Lily.

Sylvie abruptly stood up. "Where's the bathroom?"

A FEW MINUTES LATER, kneeling with her head on the porcelain lid of the toilet, Sylvie felt a little better. The nausea had left her weak, though. And she couldn't be weak now.

She wrapped her fingers around the hilt of the iron dagger the Black Scissors had given her. If she killed, the Morrigan—that entity of blood-soaked earth—would *own* her. She wondered how the others in the Black Scissors's circle handled the divinities nesting within *them*. She wondered how she had lost her best friend, and a small sob escaped her.

There was a knock at the bathroom door. "Sylvie?" Christie called softly. She could almost hear him worrying.

"I'm okay. I'll be right out." As his footsteps faded down the hall, she forced herself to stand. She rinsed out her mouth and splashed cold water over her face.

She scowled at her reflection in the mirror. Other than a slight dilation of her pupils, her eyes were still *her* eyes.

Sylvie stepped into the hall, its moss-green walls hung with old-timey photographs in antique frames. She studied them as she headed back toward the parlor.

When she glimpsed a familiar face in one of the black-and-white Victorian pictures, her blood chilled: Phouka Banríon, in a coat and bowler hat, gazed out from among three gentlemen. One of the men, his face a little blurred, looked like Farouche, the red-haired ganconer. Sylvie squinted at the handwritten note beneath the photo:

THE FATAS. EVIDENCE #62.

Moving farther down, she became intrigued by a photograph of several people standing in front of SatyrNight Mansion, which looked newly built. All the people seemed to be of Asian ancestry and wore Victorian clothing, except for one young man in a black kimono, a sword strapped across his back. His hair was tied in a knot. *"Dead Bird,"* Sylvie whispered. She scanned the handwriting beneath the photograph:

THE VALENTINE FAMILY AND SAMURAI.

She came to another daguerreotype and recognized Jack in a greatcoat and top hat. He stood with Reiko, who looked as ethereal and aloof as an Alphonse Mucha goddess in a sweeping gown and an elaborate updo. Sylvie squinted at the names scrawled beneath the photograph . . . and gasped.

"Murray considered these photos evidence." She looked up to see the Black Scissors leaning in a doorway. He continued, "Proof that the Fatas existed. He wasn't exactly a believer when I set him up here—he'd only had one encounter in Edinburgh—and he thought that was just a demon. He used to be a priest."

"Jack *Harrow*." Sylvie turned from the last photograph. "Is that Jack's true last name?"

"It is."

"He's your *descendant*?" Sylvie walked slowly toward him. "William Harrow, that's why you're here. To help him."

"Yes."

Sylvie wrapped her arms around him.

"Sylvie Whitethorn. What are you doing?"

"Is this awkward for you?" She relaxed against him.

"It'll have to be a missed opportunity." He gently drew away from her, his smile crooked. He looked his nineteen original years. "I *am* a few centuries your senior."

She slid her hands through his golden hair and dragged him down for a fierce kiss that made them both forget who they were.

RAIN SLAMMED DOWN onto the Mustang as Sylvie and Christie followed Murray's Land Rover through the deserted warehouse district, where traffic lights glared like Cyclops eyes amid storage buildings and tractor trailer lots. The Black Scissors, Lily, and Kevin—also stitched up like Sylvie—rode with Murray. Sylvie and Christie had offered to pick up Micah where he was playing with a band at a club called the Penny Dreadful.

As Christie was driving past a wooded lot and a block of seedy brownstones, a brick crashed into the windshield.

Sylvie screamed. Christie skidded to a stop in a gravelly parking lot where a blackened church rose in boarded-up, Gothic glory from a nest of weeds and trash. Christie yelled, "Who threw the brick?"

Peering out the passenger-side window, Sylvie saw a pale, monstrous shape slinking toward them across the lamp-lit parking lot. Sharp, cold fear had her pulling her two daggers from their sheaths.

A heartbeat later, the car battery went dead, leaving them only the sulfurous glow of the streetlamps. Sylvie frantically tracked the shadows. She could hear music thumping from someplace. She said, "I saw something . . ."

"Sylv . . ." The fear in Christie's voice made her quickly turn her head to him. He was gazing into the rearview mirror.

Not wanting to, she slowly looked over one shoulder.

A white, grinning thing with a shock of orange hair sat in the back. It had large scissors instead of hands, resting on either side of its body. The scissor blades had lacerated the vinyl seat.

Sylvie and Christie bolted out of the car. As they ran, Sylvie glanced back and saw the thing slowly turn its misshapen head to gaze after them with cartoon-big eyes.

As Christie tugged Sylvie toward the boarded-up church, a hyena, monstrous, with a wickedly shaped head and Caliban's eyes, crept from behind the church. Christie hissed a series of syllables that made the monster recoil.

Then Caliban shed his hyena form in a cascade of smoky shadows. "Well. Hasn't poetry boy turned into quite the woman of darkness?" The *crom cu* stood between them and the church. The street beyond was crowded with cars. Sylvie could see the neon sign of a club—the Penny Dreadful—next to the church.

Caliban breathed on the blade of an ivory knife, rubbed it on his sleeve, and sighted down it as if it were a sword. "This'll be fun."

"Sylv," Christie whispered. *"Run."*

"The hell I will." Sylvie thought of all the people Caliban had murdered. She heard the rustling of wings in her head. The raw stitches in her breast burned.

"When I'm done sticking *you*"—Caliban pointed at Christie with the dagger—"full of holes, I'm going to let Pete have your crow girl. It won't be pretty. He can't quite get the loving right—those scissors he has for hands and all."

"You talk too much," Sylvie said as the wings rushed over her, into her, and the cawing of crows drowned her fear. She heard Christie shout her name as she launched herself at the *crom cu.*

CHRISTIE TRIED TO CATCH SYLVIE, but her eyes had gone ink-black. Her braid-twisted hair flew across her face as she went at Caliban.

The *crom cu* slammed her against the church wall, his hand clenched around her throat. Sylvie snarled. The voice that issued from her lips was not her own: "How many of my daughters have you slaughtered, beast?"

"Not enough." Caliban grinned. "And I'll be sending you one more."

"Where is Finn?" Christie shouted. The demand tore from his insides and out of his mouth. The demand became a heka, an arrow of intent.

Caliban fell back, gasping, a crack opening up along half his face and neck. Christie reeled, staring at the dark tentacles of shadow that seeped from Caliban's skin.

Micah Govannon emerged from the club. He dropped his cello case. His eyes a luminous blue, he sprinted toward Caliban.

Caliban fell apart into shadows and fled.

Micah, his eyes brown again, held out a hand to Sylvie. His tawny hair was knotted at the nape of his neck and strung with talismans. As he hauled her to her feet, Sylvie's hair fell in her face, and Christie feared looking into her eyes and not seeing the girl he'd known since kindergarten. "Sylvie? *Sylvie!*"

SYLVIE HEARD HER NAME being called and the red fell away from her vision as if she were emerging from a bath of blood. She gasped and blinked at Christie while the sounds of the world rushed back. "Did I get him?"

LILY FELT A FIZZ of unease as Murray pulled into the drive of the Tirnagoth Hotel. She couldn't see any evidence of Fata enchantment, and the building looked abandoned and dark.

As she walked toward it with the Black Scissors, Kevin, and Murray, Lily saw a few toads on the stairs, but no other signs of life. When one of the garden statues moved, she reached for the elder wood dagger tucked through her belt. But the statue melted away into the night.

"Harrow, why is it like this?" Kevin asked, his voice hushed.

The Black Scissors surveyed the hotel. "Something's wrong."

He turned his head as another pair of headlights appeared and Christie's Mustang—its windshield cracked—pulled into the drive. As Sylvie and Christie got out with Micah, the Black Scissors demanded, "What happened?"

"Caliban." Christie's lip was split and a bruise was beginning to shadow his jaw. Sylvie had ugly hand marks on her throat and her eyes were flashing.

"Is he dead?" Murray asked hopefully.

"No. And Micah had to scare away something that looked like Bozo the clown and Edward Scissorhands's lovechild—"

The doors to Tirnagoth fell open.

Rowan Cruithnear, holding an electric lantern, appeared on the threshold. Beyond him was a hallway of peeling ruin. His voice resonated as he said, "The Banríon and her folk have come undone."

Lily moved up the stairs. "What can we do?"

Cruithnear's gaze was dark. "You can give them your blood."

❖ ❖ ❖

AS ROWAN CRUITHNEAR LED Christie and his companions deeper into Tirnagoth, the glow from Cruithnear's electric lantern and their flashlights revealed rotting wood, lichen-furred stairs, and creepers like rivers of emerald leaves. Christie didn't like this version of Tirnagoth.

"Don't look into the dark," the Black Scissors warned. "The Fatas held Tirnagoth's dead back. They can't now."

Micah asked carefully, "What can ghosts do to us?"

The Black Scissors looked back at him. "I'd rather not find out."

They ascended three stairways, somehow managing to avoid slinking things Christie glimpsed out of the corner of his eye, shadows as graceful as the art nouveau decor, abstract figures of darkness that skittered up walls and across the ceilings.

"Here." Cruithnear indicated a tall door of polished ebony. The Black Scissors and Kevin shoved it open. Their lights dazzled back at them, reflected in the seven mirrors hung upon the walls of an octagonal chamber. "The Banríon had us move the mirrors from the park," Cruithnear told them as they entered. "Since Fatas should not handle them unless using them as a Way."

"It wasn't just to trap the enemy," Christie realized. "Phouka knew something like this might happen to Tirnagoth. Why did she want the mirrors *here*?"

Cruithnear led them to a pentagram carved into the stone floor. "Malcolm Tirnagoth created this room as a séance chamber, after his wife and his children . . . vanished. The mirrors can be used as a battery that, along with blood, will bring power back to Tirnagoth and the Banríon and her folk back from nothing."

From nothing. Christie remembered Phouka's skin and her kiss.

The Black Scissors took a thin silver blade from beneath his jersey. He sliced his hand. Everyone had their own blades, *which says something about the company I keep*, Christie wryly thought as he borrowed Sylvie's dagger.

Cruithnear remained outside of the circle, his face pale and aged. "I can't participate. I do apologize."

"Mr. Cruithnear . . ." Lily reached for him.

Cruithnear flickered and went out like a lamp. Christie's stomach plummeted. "I've been murdered." Cruithnear's voice drifted into a silence caused by the stunned disbelief of everyone in that mirrored chamber. "Tell Janie, I'm sorry . . ." And he was gone. Around them, the seven mirrors went black. Their blood on the stone began to cyclone upward.

"Hands!" the Black Scissors snapped. Everyone clasped hands.

The blood spiraled into a pattern, a sigil in midair, before lashing outward and splashing against the mirrors. Jeweled light radiated over the walls as Fata glamour glazed the ruin. An enormous stained-glass window depicting a forest of brambles beneath a crimson sky appeared behind the Black Scissors. Decay sloughed from elegant furniture. Christie felt as if his blood was being tugged outward. And just when he thought he couldn't bear it any longer, the doors to the séance chamber flew open and Phouka dragged him out of the circle.

"I TRIED TO LOCATE SERAFINA AND ANNA. I failed." Phouka had led her guests to a parlor that now shimmered with glamour and electric light. Christie glanced at Lily, whose face was desolate. Sylvie put an arm around her.

"Sionnach Ri informed me yesterday"—Phouka, with her court of Fatas around her, wore a façade of calm, but Christie could sense worry—"that someone has been recruiting the Unseelie, the criminals of our kind."

Christie sank into his chair. "Please . . . no more bad news."

"We don't know what is causing our power drain." Phouka looked at the Black Scissors. "It can't be Sombrus. The House of the Wolf and the Snake has never affected Tirnagoth before."

The Black Scissors's mouth became a firm line, as if he didn't want to speak. "I believe the underworld is somehow leaking into this world, making the restless dead and the dark they sometimes carry with them more powerful."

"All the Ways have been shut but for StarDust." Phouka sat back. "And I don't know how to shut that."

"We need to find Sombrus," Lily said impatiently. "That's where Jack Daw is."

Phouka leveled a look on her. "What do you think we've been trying to do?"

Lily stood up. "Not much. And if you can't help me, I know someone who can." She turned on her heel and strode out of the parlor.

Christie jumped up and followed. "Lily! Wait!"

"Take me home, Christie," Lily said.

CHAPTER 18

So, with a ready heart I swore
To seek their altar-stone no more;
Thee, ever-present, phantom thing;
My slave, my comrade, and my king.

—"Plead for Me," Emily Brontë

I'm dead. I'm dead. Finn's brain fought against the horror of what had been done to her as she clutched at the raw stitches beneath her gingham dress. The alchemy of marigolds inside of her seemed to whisper and crawl, winding around her bones, taking the place of her organs, filling up all the hollows. She fell to her knees and retched. Her whole body shuddered when she coughed up a yellow petal.

She struggled to her feet and stumbled toward the crypt door in a nightmare of candlelight and razor-sharp agony, snatching up Lily's silver charm bracelet, which had been torn from her. *Tirnagoth*, she thought. *Phouka.*

She emerged into a cemetery and staggered down the path. A gentle, warm rain began, filtered by the branches knotting overhead. A granite angel turned to regard her with stony eyes. A child-faced gargoyle with bat wings stirred as she passed it. Finn ignored them both.

When pain drove her to the earth again, she curled in the mud, closed her eyes, and wrapped her arms around her knees. She rested while the warm rain washed away the blood that had splashed onto her arms and legs from when they had cut her open.

A humming sound made her look up. A black butterfly glided around her. The air crackled and surged through her limbs. She uncurled and moved slowly to her feet, watching the butterfly flicker away through the willow trees at the back of the cemetery.

"And where do you think *you're* going?" Caliban stepped before her, grinning. "Did I leave the door open? Careless me."

Finn tensed.

"It was fun watching you think you had a chance, *leannan*." He reached out and a thin chain with a tiny vial on it glistened between his fingers. "Go on. Take it. It's elixir. Just in case you decide to end it all."

She snatched the elixir from him, shivering although she didn't feel any cold. Something sharp ripped through her and she slid to her knees, tasting blood in her mouth as red blossomed on the front of her dress. *No, I can't fall now . . .*

A silhouette was walking toward her through the rain. The black butterfly swept past its hooded face. A voice spoke and Caliban said defensively, "I wasn't taunting her."

FINN WAS BEING CARRIED like a child in someone's arms, her head against a chest that didn't have a heartbeat. The rain spitting into her eyes kept her from seeing the face of the one carrying her.

She turned her head. Sombrus was now a stately manor, not the rotting Gothic structure it had been when Lot had ruled it. It didn't look the way its mirror image had in Annwyn either, the way Jack had envisioned it. The basalt stairs leading to the doors were guarded by a pair of stone women holding moon lamps above their three-faced heads. The windows were garnet slabs, the exterior white as ash. Carved above the scarlet doors was the head of a grim-looking hare.

Finn slid away again, into the comforting dark.

FINN OPENED HER EYES and gazed up at a red sky through a domed glass ceiling. The pain was gone. In its place was a cool, hollow strength, an absence of exhaustion. She inhaled, although she didn't need to, and turned her head.

She lay on a divan in a solarium alive with exotic plants and ornamental trees blossoming with overripe fruits and flowers that seemed to have tiny teeth. Seated on the floor nearby was a human-sized doll dressed only in jeans embroidered with dragons. A wreath of vines was set on its copper hair. Shadows bled from the joints of its elbows and fingers. The creature was pensively eating a large moth.

Grindylow. But the creature didn't freeze as she gazed at it. It regarded her with glass eyes the color of flames.

"Don't mind him." A girl in a white dress and red cape stepped in front of the Grindylow, her hair a golden halo. "I had to put him somewhere so he wasn't stuck in the mirrors."

"*Anna!*" Finn wrenched into a sitting position, winced.

"I made tea and I brought you some new clothes." Anna set a pink porcelain teacup on a little table nearby. Her gaze was troubled. "Are you a Jill now?"

"Yes." Finn spoke softly. She reached for the girl, clasping her hands. "Are you okay? Has he hurt you?"

"No."

"Is *he* here?" She forced her expression to remain calm as she felt something twine around her rib cage, inside. "Jack Daw?"

Anna shook her head. "He doesn't like to be here. Because he can't find Absalom and he knows he's somewhere in this house."

Finn wondered if her brain rattling around was a symptom of becoming one of *them*, of losing memories and persona and soul. "Absalom?"

Anna indicated the Grindylow, which rose.

"*That's* Absalom?" Finn stared into the Grindylow's glass eyes, saw a flame in each of them. Relief soared through her.

"I found the Grindylow in the attic. Absalom helped me get himself out of the mirrors and into it. But he can't talk."

"That's . . . okay. But we need to—" A faint whisper of sound made Finn turn.

Jack was leaning in the doorway. No. Not Jack. This Jack was dressed in a coal-black suit. This was the Jack she'd met while escaping the Wolf. This was the Jack who had, his face shadowed by a hood, put a knife into her and carved out her mortality. *Jack Daw.*

Jack Daw raised a finger to his smiling mouth. Then he whirled and strode away.

She ran after him, bare feet hitting the marble floor. She lost him in a crimson hall hung with reindeer skulls. Glimpsing a shadow at the hall's end, she ran toward it. She could hear Anna and the Grindylow following.

She stepped into a parlor with a fireplace of red marble carved into the face of a screaming woman. On the black floor was a wolfskin rug. The chairs and the sofa were made of human bones cushioned with ebony velvet. Jack Daw had vanished.

Finn moved to a window, tapped at the glass. Something coiled through her like a living vine. She bit her lip.

"The glass won't break," Anna said, walking in behind her.

"I'll get you out. I promise."

"He's made you into a Jill." Anna's voice was mournful. "He's killed you."

"No, he hasn't." Finn stared at the fireplace that resembled Reiko Fata's face, glanced at the wolf pelt on the floor.

It seemed Jack Daw had defeated *his* demons, here in Sombrus.

CHAPTER 19

If they are heartless, just spirit things, I wouldn't feel so afraid for my daughters. But if they are more . . . if we infect them with our hates, our desires . . . if these undocumented beings have hearts . . . it would be a terrible thing.

—From the journal of Daisy Sullivan

Jack came into existence as dusk bled across the windows of his apartment. His first thought was *Finn*, until he focused on the figure seated in the chair before him. An automatic self-defense instinct had him reaching for the stiletto he kept in one boot.

"Not an enemy." Moth's voice made Jack release the stiletto's hilt and straighten.

"Are you still a Jack, Moth? You don't vanish in the day?"

"I don't know what I am. And I never vanished in the day, after they made me into a Jack. Where would your darkest self take Finn? What did you want when you were a Jack, and alone?" Moth pulled up his shirt, revealing a lacework of old scars. "I was already a freak when they made me a Jack. I know what *I* wanted."

Jack breathed out, "A companion."

Moth stood up, silhouetted against the dying sun. "We need to find Sombrus before it's too late."

"I have something to do first. And I've got to do it alone."

JACK SHED THE SHADOWS as he strode through a mobile home park in the Blackbird Mountain forest. Pine trees, oaks, and creepers embraced nearly every trailer, most of which were empty. He ignored the occasional appearances of the things that now inhabited the hulks of metal and plastic.

The park was surrounded by a curve of disused railroad tracks and abandoned boxcars scrawled with graffiti. This was a place where the Ghostlands had broken into the true world. Whatever had taken up residence in those railroad cars had come here long ago, before Reiko, who had respectfully ignored their existence. The monsters in these rusting train cars could help him get Finn back. He forged through the night-blooming plants to a car painted with the stylized forms of winged beings with cruel faces. He heard a rushing sound like an immense forest in a windstorm, and the doors to the train car opened. He gazed down a gargantuan hallway, its walls seemingly made of charred black paper. At the end of this hall was a cherry-red glow.

He entered, walking toward that glow, and eventually stepped into a mezzanine of black marble, its cathedral ceiling lost in smoldering gloom. At a round table set with a game of chess were two tall figures with alabaster skin, their hair wound in ebony ropes like that of princes in murals from ancient Crete. Their dark suits were made from tiny, scarlet-edged scales. Their fingers were heavy with rings. Their coats of black feathers rustled and billowed, and Jack thought of prehistoric creatures clothed in flesh.

They were called Rue and Ruin. The tallest one turned his head, revealing tilting eyes of blood red. "Look, brother . . . one of the *other* tribe's toys found its way to our door."

Jack stood there, feeling as if the world was falling away, and told them, "I want to find a girl."

"We only bargain with those who have souls." The second young man didn't even look up from the chess game. "You don't have one. Go away."

Jack walked to the chess table and plucked both queens—grotesque figures with skull faces—from the board.

Rue and Ruin were on their feet without Jack having seen them move. They didn't cast shadows. They didn't speak, but Jack felt something inside of him break as inky words bled onto their skin and they set their ruby gazes on him. He gritted his teeth. "I can give you Sombrus."

"We cannot track that entity, that object." Rue or Ruin leaned forward, his large eyes as black as the universe. "That would be a most marvelous prize."

"Tell me where my enemy took Finn Sullivan."

"Your enemy." The devil looked amused. "You don't even know his face. But we can follow shadows and trails of blood. Rue. Where did the Jack's enemy take his girl?"

Rue bowed his head and lifted one black-nailed hand. Jack braced himself when he realized the creature held a raw heart. Rue turned his head. His eyes were red pools. "The girl is in the crypt at the crossroads in the cemetery."

With blinding horror, Jack realized what Jack Daw was going to do to Finn. He knew that place. He had been there with Reiko—

The two creatures became columns of darkness rising toward the ceiling. A voice like earthquakes, a tornado, spoke: *Tell us. Where is Sombrus?*

"I don't know." And Jack turned and sprinted down the corridor. The black paper walls disintegrated into red-tinged flakes as he ran. Claws gouged across the back of his neck as he slid toward the metal doors that began to close.

"*Sombrus!*" a voice roared. "*Where is it?*"

Jack fell out of the train car and rolled into the weeds. He raised his head, blinking in the glare of headlights from the Nissan that screeched to a halt on the broken road.

A silhouette emerged from the car and held out a hand to him. He grasped it, moving to his feet. Looking back, he saw Rue or Ruin standing in the railroad car's entrance, watching them, mortal guise intact, black running from his eyes. The devil said, voluptuously, "And what is this come to our door? A shade in a girl's shape?"

"Get in the car," Lily told Jack unnecessarily.

Jack scrambled into the Nissan. Lily climbed in, put the car into reverse, and floored it. She hit the corner of a boarded-up trailer and spun the car around.

A cloud of darkness fell over the Nissan, but Lily sped down the crooked road, regardless of branches or slinking, inhuman shapes. The grasping darkness slid away.

Jack shoved his hands through his hair. "How did you know where I'd be?"

"Lot told me about the Fallen. I knew you'd do something insane and this was the most insane thing I could think of."

Hope was a fragile, wounded thing in Jack, but it never ceased struggling to lift its head whenever it was offered a chance to do so. He clenched one hand on the dashboard so hard, the plastic cracked. "I know where Finn is. I know where he took her."

SYLVIE, JAMMED IN THE BACKSEAT of Murray's Land Rover with Micah and Christie, felt relief when she saw Jack and Lily standing outside of Soldiers' Gate Cemetery. When the Land Rover pulled up, and the Black Scissors stepped out with Kevin and Murray, Jack walked to them.

The Black Scissors regarded the landscape of headstones and mausoleums beyond the gates. "Why do you think Serafina is here?"

"Two big birds told me," Jack replied. Something in his demeanor began to worry Sylvie very much.

Lily said, "I can't go in. Something won't let me enter cemeteries. Just . . . just find her. Find her alive."

Sylvie saw the Black Scissors and Jack exchange a grim look, as if they knew why Lily couldn't get into graveyards. This worried Sylvie.

"Micah and I will stay with Lily." Kevin Gilchriste's voice was hard, reminding Sylvie that *he* had once killed a Fata.

Jack turned, pushed the gates open, and strode into the cemetery. The Black Scissors, Christie, and Sylvie followed, the Black Scissors stalking among the crooked trees and ancient headstones like an assassin. Sylvie glimpsed the silver revolver beneath his coat.

Finn will be all right, Sylvie told herself. Suddenly feeling as if she was choking on a stone shard, she stumbled, catching herself against a statue of a girl with a bowed head.

Christie nodded to a stone sphinx gracefully reclining on a mausoleum. "I thought I saw it move."

Sylvie kept a wary eye out for moving statuary after that. She had a silver blade and one of elder wood tucked into the scabbards under her shirt. Fear and adrenaline were zipping through her. She reached out and clutched Christie's hand. He glanced at her. She saw her own fear reflected in his eyes.

They reached a crypt collapsing beneath decades of neglect, its black walls and roof marred by weather and age, the robed and hooded statue at its door a forbidding effigy. Jack moved up the steps, and they followed. The moment had the eerie inevitability of a nightmare.

As Jack flung open the rusting doors, black butterflies burst outward, hundreds of them, their parchment wings brushed with light from the dozens of white candles illuminating the crypt. Sylvie bit down on a scream.

As they entered, Sylvie went cold and still, gazing at the stone slab glistening with red. Too much red—on the walls, the floor, as if some sort of pagan sacrifice had been performed.

Moth, his back to them, stood in the center.

When he turned to them, his face was white. "I went to StarDust and found your beautiful accomplice, Avaline, with her throat torn out. I entered and found a Way that led here. Here." He turned in place, as if bewildered, as if he hadn't believed what he'd seen the first time and expected it to change. "He brought Finn here . . ."

Jack was gazing down at Finn's sneakers, flung beside the slab and splashed with more red.

Sylvie's stomach heaved. The smell of blood, heavy and sickeningly sweet, made her dizzy. *Please. Please don't let this be real.*

"Jack." The Black Scissors stared down at something wrapped in what looked like nettles. Jack approached the catafalque.

"Don't—" Christie couldn't finish as Jack reached for the nettles and unwrapped them, revealing a human heart.

Sylvie went momentarily deaf with shock. She thought she might fall. *Please,* she thought again, *don't let this be happening.*

As Christie sank down, his arms over his head, Moth whispered, "*No.*"

Jack made a low, agonized sound in his throat. The darkness in the crypt folded around him and he morphed into something else, something savage that Sylvie only glimpsed out of the corner of one eye. She heard the sound of wing beats, the calls of crows. Night began to gather in her peripheral vision. Beneath the wing beats were voices: "*Sylvie!*"

She snapped out of it. Jack was himself again, standing with his head bowed. Christie, white as paper, was gripping Sylvie's shoulders. The dark wings of the Morrigan retreated from her brain.

Sylvie tore away from Christie to stalk to the catafalque, watching as Jack lifted the heart and tenderly wrapped it in his coat.

A bright splash of color caught her eye and she bent down to pick up a yellow flower—it had tiny teeth and tentacles. She dropped it. *What is it?*

Jack's eyes—Sylvie had to look away. He said, "He's made Finn into a Jill."

Sylvie stubbornly refused to faint. But she had to lean against the catafalque.

"Jack," the Black Scissors spoke gently. "If she's been turned into a Jill, if she's . . ."

"Don't," Jack said in a voice that sent chills up Sylvie's spine. He strode toward the exit, cradling what might be Finn's heart. "We're going to find Sombrus."

THEY DIDN'T NEED to tell Lily what they'd found. As they walked from the cemetery, Lily saw their faces, and knew.

"WITH HER HEART, you can do this," Jack told Lily as he tenderly set Finn's wrapped heart in the grass near the cemetery. He drew a circle in the soil with a branch as Lily stood, shaking with rage, anguish howling through her. *Finn*, she thought, *my little sister.*

She'd been sick a minute ago.

"All we need is an object of power." Jack gestured to Christie. "Your two rings from the elementals, Christopher. A bit of your blood, Lily. This time, Jack Daw *wants* us to find him."

Moth placed an origami moth made from a page of Phouka's ivory book, the one Christie still carried, on top of the heart. Jack slid the ring Finn had given him from his finger and placed it near the paper moth.

The Black Scissors, Christie, Sylvie, Moth, and Jack clasped hands in a circle. Micah and Kevin kept to the side as Lily drew a slim silver knife and extended a trembling hand over her sister's heart. She sliced the ball of her thumb, let seven drops of blood fall. She began pronouncing a string of antiquated words very carefully, heka taught to her by the Black Scissors.

The Black Scissors lifted his gaze to Lily's and a shadow trickled from one of his nostrils.

AS CHRISTIE'S VOICE JOINED LILY'S and the air surged with power, as the blood spiraled outward, Jack realized that Lily Rose Sullivan was a Very Dangerous Young Woman.

The origami moth converged with his ring and flew around them. The ring was gone, but the moth's wings were patterned with bronze shapes resembling the two lions clasping a heart. Jack rose, his gaze following the insect's flight. "Ready, Moth?"

"Ready."

Lily hugged Jack. "I know you'll find her." She stepped back.

Jack and Moth strode after the origami moth.

CHAPTER 20

Jack and Moth followed the origami moth through a wood of mossy oaks and massive ferns, to the House of the Wolf and the Snake now nested in a cavern of black yews and elder trees, its garden a mess of nettles and black marble statues lost within the weeds. Patches of red-tentacled stinkhorn clustered around pools of dead water. The mansion's doors were mottled with lichen. Corruption had overtaken Sombrus—not the blood-dark corruption the Wolf had set on it, but a parasitic decay that fed on life.

Jack knew getting in wouldn't be an issue. Escaping with Finn, if Finn was really in there, would be the challenge. And the only weapons he had were his *kris* and the misericorde. Moth had the jackal sword.

"How do we kill you?" Moth inquired.

"Quickly." Jack plunged through the evil garden, heading for the ivy-clogged wall around the courtyard. He and Moth kept a wary eye on the wall's child-headed gargoyles as they hauled themselves over. They wove through the garden of nettles, heading for a window shrouded in a canopy of creepers. Jack broke a pane with the hilt of his *kris*, unlatched the window, and pulled the panes open. As sepia and ivory butterflies of all sizes swept past him, he swung himself in. The origami moth with the lions-and-heart pattern glided before him.

He landed on the age-stained floor of a ballroom where cobwebs swayed from basalt pillars. Moth followed. He moved to a pair of scarlet doors, opened one, revealed a high-ceilinged hall that stretched toward an archway.

Jack and Moth stepped into the hall where once-elegant furniture languished beneath colonies of bleeding fungi and ivory wallpaper peeled like birch bark. They followed the origami moth to a luxurious parlor with a fire in the hearth and a wolfskin rug on a floor scattered with mirror shards.

Something stirred in the hallway. Jack spun around, saw a shadow at the hall's end that flickered away beneath his scrutiny.

He glanced back at the hearth shaped into the face of a screaming woman. *Reiko*. And Seth Lot must be the wolfskin rug. The crawling shadows he kept glimpsing in his peripheral vision would be the wolves Moth had slaughtered.

"Moth . . . do you know your way around?"

"It's different from when I was here." Moth's voice was hushed.

The origami moth suddenly disintegrated. Jack's ring clinked to the floor in its place. Jack scooped up the ring and walked through another arch. Moth followed.

"It's Jack Daw who rules this place now." Moth was distinctly on edge. "You'll know his mind better than I."

Jack kept his voice low. "It looks as it did when I lived with the Wolf."

Moth halted, raised his head as if he were sniffing the air. He slid past Jack, into a chamber that resembled another ballroom, paneled all in black, with a chandelier of purple crystal hanging from the faraway ceiling. Three statues of black marble, like the ones in the garden, stood in the center. Jack didn't like those statues, with their curling horns, hooved feet, and devil faces. He said, "Moth—"

When the doors began to shut, Jack yelled a warning. Moth spun, unsheathing the jackal sword, slashing it down. The blade wedged between the doors before they could slam all the way shut.

Jack and Moth, on opposite sides, forced the doors open. As Moth slid back through, one of the black statues turned, its eyes blazing blue.

The doors slammed closed.

"Satyrs." Jack took a step back. "I didn't think they were real."

"Anything can be real, here."

To the right, another door suddenly opened, revealing a room lit by a greenish glow from a window covered with ivy. A lithe figure was huddled beneath the window, arms over its head.

"Finn!" Jack strode into the room, halted as the girl looked up and revealed a face with no features at all, only a blank canvas of skin. He backed out.

Moth reached past him and pulled the door shut.

One of the pillars beside them cracked with a sound like bone snapping. Jack saw blood oozing from the pale stone and a translucent tangle of what looked like nerve endings.

They left the hall quickly and came to a huge staircase of green wood, gnarled and twisted into dragonish shapes. Cathedral windows of scarlet glass cast bloody light upon their faces. The posts to either side of the stair were formed into men with the heads of evil-looking deer.

"We'll never find her." Moth's voice cracked. "Not in this mess—"

"He wouldn't keep her in a place of horror," Jack said intently. He wouldn't leave this place without Finn. He would die here if he had to. "He would keep her somewhere pretty."

Moth slid him a look. "*He* would or *you* would?"

"There's a fine line between me and him, remember?"

"The top floor then. Those were usually the clearest." Moth began ascending the stairs. Jack followed.

The steps upon which Moth stood swiveled toward a wall and a set of white doors opened to swallow him. Before Jack could react, his part of the stairway plunged downward, and he was propelled backward. Grabbing hold of one of the deer-men statues, he swung away from the gaping hole that resembled the mouth of a Venus flytrap, and onto the floor.

Catching his breath, he looked up. Moth was gone. Moth knew how to handle himself in this place.

Jack backed away. He turned and moved into a dining hall where murals of white-wigged courtiers decorated the walls. A feast rotted beneath cocoons of spiderwebs. Ignoring the arachnids skittering in the mold, he strode past the table toward yet another arch.

Would he have to carve out his heart and use it as a guide? Abort the third heart Finn had caused to grow within him? What if he remained an empty husk this time?

He could use his blood. He drew the misericorde from its sheath and cut his arm, then watched the blood spiral from him and wind up a black staircase. He followed the crimson ribbon through a windowed galleria, where gauze draped mysterious, unmoving figures.

When his blood splashed against a white door at the galleria's end, he entered cautiously and found a white room with Finn and Anna, asleep, curled on a rug of ivory bearskin. He wanted to yell his triumph. He thought the entire house must hear his heartbeat.

Finn's eyes opened. Her lashes fluttered. She frowned. Then she slowly uncurled, staring at him. "*Jack?*" She glided to her feet. She wore a white party dress and platform-heeled red shoes. Her skin was white. Her caramel brown eyes ghosted silver.

A startling desire sparked through him and left him breathless. Then horror swept over him.

She was like him now.

IT WAS A SPECTACULAR KISS, because Finn matched Jack in strength. She didn't want to stop kissing him, but finally broke away.

He clasped one hand against the back of her neck and touched his forehead to hers. He was smiling as if every joy in his life had converged in this room. "You're real. Hello, Anna."

"Hey, Jack." Awake also, Anna spoke breathlessly.

Finn turned. "Anna—"

Anna's eyes widened, fastened on something behind Finn, behind *Jack.*

Finn whirled as Jack suddenly lurched against her and fell to his knees. She stared at the silver dagger like an icicle in his back, lifted her shocked gaze to the young man in the hooded coat standing before her. He held another dagger.

"What did you *do?*" She sank down and arced her body over Jack's. He appeared to be unconscious. She looked up at the shadow Jack. "He's *you.*"

"No." Jack Daw sat on his heels. "He is an impostor."

Finn cupped her hands on either side of Jack's head and bent close. His eyelashes fluttered. She pulled the dagger from him, winced as blood seeped from the wound. She whispered, "*You* don't bleed." She turned on the shadow Jack, who caught her wrist and took the weapon from her. He said, "I don't want to be here alone."

She stood to face him. "You don't belong here."

"I don't belong out *there*. Which is why I must return to this damned place every night." His eyes were pure silver. "Finn Sullivan."

"You're only a *memory*." Her voice shook. "You can't do this."

He shrugged. "I'll do what I want, Finn."

"Stop." Anna glared at Jack Daw. "We don't belong here and you're ruining everything."

Finn realized why Jack Daw had only wounded Jack. "You can't kill him. It's not this *house* keeping you here . . . it's *Jack*."

Jack Daw crouched down. He held his knife over one of Jack's closed eyes. "Get out or I take an eye from him—it might not kill him, but it'll inconvenience him for a while."

Finn backed out of the room, pulling Anna with her. The door shut before them.

JACK DAW APPEARED IN THE HALLWAY sometime later, walking from a different direction. He bowed to Finn and Anna. "This way, please."

He led them down a cobwebbed hall, up a winding stair, to an oak door. He unlocked it and gestured them in. As Anna stalked past him, Finn asked, "Where is Jack?"

Jack Daw said, "I put him somewhere."

She stepped into a parlor of comfortable velvet browns and elegant royal blues. Embers glowed red in the hearth. Gas lamps illuminated a landscape of books, eccentric objects, and carelessly strewn weapons. It was the chamber of a gentleman magpie. It was what Finn might expect from Victorian-era Jack.

Jack Daw discarded his coat. Then he set two daggers on a table. Finn recognized them; he had gotten them from Jack. Dismayed, she stared at the *kris* and the misericorde as he rummaged in a cabinet and took down three teacups and a tin of biscuits.

Anna curled on the sofa as he set the things on a table. When he moved to the hearth and lifted a teakettle set upon the logs, Finn saw a black butterfly tattooed on the back of his neck.

She drew the vial filled with elixir, the one Caliban had given her, from one pocket. She exchanged a look with Anna.

Jack Daw poured the tea and set the biscuits on a tray. Anna politely asked, "Do you have cream or milk?"

As Jack Daw returned to the cabinet, Finn dumped the elixir into Jack Daw's teacup. She was willing to bet the effect it would have on him wouldn't be a good one.

Jack Daw returned and sat opposite them. He poured cream and spooned sugar into the three cups. As he reached for his cup, Anna and Finn grabbed theirs. Jack Daw brought the cup to his lips.

Anna sprang forward and knocked it from his hands.

"*Anna* . . ." Finn set down her tea as Jack Daw regarded her with shadows in his silver gaze.

"You don't understand," he said quietly. "There is a whole world here. And this house will be mine." He rose, dangerous and menacing, a twisted version of Jack.

"We'll never stop trying to escape," Finn told him.

"You will, eventually." He grabbed his coat and stalked from the room, slamming the door.

When he was gone, Finn turned to Anna. "Anna, *why*—"

"It might have *killed* him. That's elixir, isn't it? The elixir killed Caliban."

"A silver bullet in the head killed Caliban. And this *isn't* Jack, Anna."

"You said Jack Daw dies if our Jack dies. What if it's the other way around, too?" Anna hugged herself.

"Anna, Jack Daw is a shadow—" Finn jumped as the door to their prison clicked open. She rose.

She and Anna moved cautiously forward. They stepped into a red hallway hung with antlers on the walls. The hallway led into a black parlor where pieces of the human-sized doll that had held Absalom's soul—*spirit*, Finn corrected herself, *they don't have souls*—had been scattered over the floor.

"Absalom." Anna fell to her knees beside the head of the Grindylow.

"Anna." Finn crouched beside her and kept her voice steady. "Where was Absalom, before?"

Anna murmured, "In the mirrors."

"Then that's where he is now." Finn pushed to her feet and frowned at the crocodile skeleton hung over the hearth. "This used to be Absalom's house . . . didn't it? That's what I heard."

Anna lifted her head. "Yes."

Finn turned in a circle, surveying the place. "He didn't know the way out?"

"He couldn't speak. He wrote down that he couldn't remember because it's changed so much." Anna set down the Grindylow's head. Her face was pale, her eyes ringed around with bruises.

The neglected look of her made Finn feel all snarly. She said, "Let's find Jack."

"Finn . . ." Anna whispered. "Will you always be a Jill?"

"It's not so bad," Finn lied reassuringly and clasped Anna's hand. "Come on."

They stepped into a black corridor carved to resemble trees, their leaves frosted silver. At the end of the corridor was a door of gray wood with knots in it—she and Anna hurried toward the door, pushed it open, found a room furnished in black with a fur coat draped over one chair. Beyond an enormous window, Finn could see a tundra of snow.

"Look. Mirrors." Anna tugged on Finn's hand, leading her into a blue hallway, its walls decorated with mirrors both small and large. Finn peered into several of the mirrors as Anna whispered, "Absalom, are you there?"

Flames roared in all the reflective surfaces, sending a crimson glow throughout the hall. Anna, like a tin soldier awaiting orders, stood before the largest looking-glass. "*Absalom.*"

There was a booming noise throughout the house. The blue walls turned black and began to burn like paper.

When a tall shadow appeared at one end of the hall, Finn and Anna turned and ran in the opposite direction, up a flight of stairs that disintegrated after each step. Finn heard glass being smashed behind them and realized Jack Daw was breaking the mirrors.

Finn pulled Anna into a chamber with snow drifting across the glass dome of a ceiling and walls of green marble hewn into vines and long-stemmed flowers.

The marble statue of a young woman wearing a tall crown of icicles was seated on a throne of scarlet porphyry.

Finn approached the statue. It was uncanny in the same way that the Grindylow were—it felt *sentient*.

When the stone gown of snowflake-patterned white rippled, Finn stepped back, alarmed. There was a breath from between the statue's parted lips, followed by a young, arrogant voice: "Where is my Harahkte?"

Finn whispered, "Who are you?"

The statue leaned forward, snowy hair slithering over its shoulders. "I am the white knife. The Snow Queen. You're a Jill. Did I make you like Harahkte?"

Finn thought the statue looked familiar and she found that troubling. "Who is Harahkte?" That name also bothered her. She'd heard it before . . .

The statue didn't answer, settling back on its throne, hands folded on the armrests. Its expression became sly. "Are you the girl?"

"What girl?" Finn reached back to grasp one of Anna's hands.

"The girl he wanted to trick, the girl with the caramel brown eyes. '*Jack Daw's girl*,' he said."

"When was this?" Finn thought of the Dragonfly's murder. Of Micah being attacked. Of Caliban knowing the way into Annwyn. Of stitchery.

The statue's lips parted.

A sword flew past Finn and split the statue's face. The statue stopped moving. A single crimson drop slid along its neck.

Finn turned. She stared at the hooded figure standing in the doorway, and she said with anguish gutting her, "It was you."

JACK WOKE FROM THE SILVER SHOCK caused by the dagger he'd been stabbed with. The roses and thorns within him twisted in warning as he raised his head, his vision adjusting immediately to the gloom of the galleria and its gauze-wrapped denizens.

He carefully sat up, trying to keep his eyes on the veiled figures. His weapons were gone. He slid to his feet, his back against a window. He didn't know what had gotten him, but he had an idea.

A wind tore through the galleria. The gauze wrappings floated away like wraiths, revealing seven human-sized dolls that fastened their glass gazes upon him.

Realizing he would have to fight, Jack skimmed his gaze over his surroundings, searching for any object he could use as a—

A harlequin with a rabbit mask and a shock of rusty hair lurched toward him. Jack grabbed a small table and smashed it against the Grindylow's head. The harlequin fell back, but the other Grindylow were all moving toward him now. And his gaze wasn't halting them as it would in the true world.

Jack shoved a doll in a ruffled red dress against the wall. Its face cracked as it collapsed.

Another Grindylow, a skull-headed man in a tuxedo, clamped its arms around Jack from behind. Using Skullhead as leverage, Jack kicked out with both feet and drove back a Grindylow in a witch's hat, another doll in a ringmaster's costume. He and Skullhead hit the window. The glass didn't crack even as Jack attempted to ram the Grindylow through it.

Jack twisted free and bashed a candlestick against Skullhead's jaw. The Grindylow released him, half its face shattered.

When the doll in the red dress crawled over and bit into Jack's wrist, he recoiled and kicked it back. He whirled away. Skullhead lunged. Jack picked up a chair and slung it hard enough to decapitate the Grindylow.

As Skullhead crumpled, the harlequin Grindylow leaped at Jack. Jack, glimpsing the hilts of knives in Skullhead's coat, bent down.

IT DIDN'T TAKE JACK LONG to dispatch the Grindylow once he had the sharp weapons.

Stepping over the broken dolls, he glanced out the window to see a flock of crows burst from the mansion into the cloudy night sky.

He stepped into the hall, determined to find Finn again in this cursed, ever-changing house. He halted at a spiraling staircase, frowned at the shattered bits of reflective glass on the floor, the empty frames on the walls.

"Mirrors," he whispered and loped up the stairs into a corridor badly lit by grimed lamp sconces. Black butterflies of all sizes fluttered everywhere, casting enormous, shifting shadows on the crimson wallpaper.

He heard a sound and pressed against the wall as a silhouette glided past at the end of the corridor. He heard the sound of breaking glass and wondered what allies Jack Daw had set loose in this place.

The black butterflies suddenly glided upward, swarmed past him . . .

. . . and shed their disguise in a cloud of black dust. He stared at sepia wings and wings of paper-white, pale green bodies, and striped. *Moths.* As the horned devils and gypsy, leopard, and ghost moths swept past him, Jack realized with horror how very wrong they had all been.

CHAPTER 21

If you were the queen of pleasure,
And I were the king of pain,
We'd hunt down love together,
Pluck out his flying feather
And teach his feet a measure,
And find his mouth a rein.

—"Hymn to Proserpine," Algernon Charles Swinburne

As Finn and Anna backed toward the statue of the Snow Queen, the figure who had flung the sword drew down the hood of his jacket, revealing the enemy—the stranger who had recently worn Moth's persona and physicality like a costume, with as much cunning and artifice as any Fata.

"You were never Moth," Finn whispered. "Who are you?"

He strode past them, toward the statue. Gripping the sword by the hilt, he yanked it free. As he turned and approached Finn and Anna, the marigolds inside of Finn fluttered. His black jacket glimmered with bits of mirror. There were small, bloody cuts on his hands.

Finn realized with absolute hopelessness that it was not Moth who had emerged from Sombrus after killing the wolf pack. Moth had died shortly after she'd kissed him with the *Tamasgi'po* on her lips.

"Moth was a fiction. I am Harahkte." Even his smile was different from Moth's, a vicious flash. His silvered green gaze was icy.

Finn kept herself between Harahkte and Anna. "I don't believe Moth just stopped because old memories returned."

"Haven't you learned anything?" His mouth curled in scorn. "Memories are souls. Memories make us what we are."

"And what are you?"

"I thought I was human until I met the Fatas. Stop trying to be clever. And Askew won't help you—I've broken all the mirrors in this house." He led them into an elegant chamber with night-blue walls and carved furniture draped with animal pelts. As he shed his jacket, Anna curled up in a chair and put her arms over her head.

Pain coursed through Finn. She leaned against the wall, folding her arms across her midriff.

"The pain will cease," Harahkte told her. "You're immortal now, Finn. Like your Jack. You won't age or decay. You'll stay like this, perfect, forever."

Finn lifted her head to stare at him even as another arc of breathtaking pain ripped through her. "*You* murdered me."

He walked to a tall window to gaze out at a night roaring with rain. "You're strong now."

"Why did you do it?"

He glanced over his shoulder. His eyes reflected the firelight. "Because I wanted you." He turned and sauntered toward her. When Anna uncurled as if to speak, he gestured at her. She slumped in the chair like a broken doll, eyes closed.

"Ann—"

"She's only sleeping." He moved closer to Finn, who refused to back away.

She hated that she hadn't known Moth well enough to detect the deception. She said, "Do you remember *being* Moth?"

"You won't let that go, will you?" His expression was amused, but his eyes were cold. He reached out to tap her temple. "No. How long do you think it will be before Jack realizes his double isn't the real enemy?"

"What is that key for? The one Reiko hid in him. The one you want."

"As if I'd tell you." He took from around his neck a thin chain with a tiny vial. "Drink this. It will ease the pain."

"No thanks."

He tilted his head to one side. "When you first found me in that empty house, how do you know that it wasn't *me* the entire time?" He stepped close and whispered in her ear, "*Me* that you wanted? That there never was a Moth?"

She drew back. She changed the topic. "Why did you send Caliban to take me to Annwyn?"

He shrugged, watching her. "He was a drastic last resort. I thought you'd succeed with one of the elementals. How disappointing that was." He sauntered to the door and opened it, stepped into the hall. "Jack's a bit slow, isn't he?"

When he remained with his back to her, Finn reached for the jackal sword, her hand shaking. She gripped the hilt and moved toward him as he said, "After Jack gives me that key, Finn, I'm going to kill him."

Moth would never have butchered her as this creature had, and if she waited for Moth to reemerge, everyone she loved would be in danger. *Moth. I'm sorry.*

Grasping the sword hilt with both hands, she swung.

The blade sliced through Moth's—*Harahkte's*—neck with a sickening crunch. Finn stumbled back and dropped the sword, shaking with horror, her stomach heaving as she stared at the line in his neck.

The wound sealed over, a sinister miracle in this impossible house. He slowly turned, his eyes green ice. "I knew you'd do that."

"You cut out my *heart*." Her voice broke as she backed away from him. *What was he?*

He locked the door behind him as he left.

He hadn't taken the sword. Finn folded beside it. She could still feel the impact the fine-edged blade had made against his neck bone. She hunched over and retched, but all that came out was a single marigold petal. Bewildered and very afraid, she curled on the floor, gazing at her reflection in the sword.

When flames blazed in the sword's blade, she scrabbled to her feet.

She felt a sudden heat in the pocket of her hoodie. She reached in, took out the small compact mirror Sylvie had given her. She opened it. A cherry-red flame flickered in the small mirror, the only mirror in Sombrus that hadn't been broken.

"*Absalom*," Finn breathed.

Something slammed against the door. Finn flinched, heard Anna stir behind her. As the door splintered, Finn snatched up the jackal-handled sword.

Vines, ivy, and creepers exploded through the room. Finn saw the monster in the doorway—a thing with a marble face like a mythical green man spewing vines from its grinning mouth—before a silver dagger swept through the stalk of its neck, beheading it, sending it back into the shadows.

Jack Hawthorn, battered and bleeding, stood on the threshold. "So . . . who stabbed me in the back?"

Anna, rising, answered, "Jack Daw."

"Well." His mouth curled wryly. "That figures." His gaze fastened on Finn. "*Finn.*"

She dropped the sword and strode to him and wound her arms around him. "It's not Jack Daw behind all this. It's Moth—Harahkte. That's his real name."

"I know." His voice was low and hard.

"I've got Absalom." She produced the geisha compact and clicked it open, revealing the little mirror filled with fire.

Anna took it from her and said to it, demanding, "Absalom, you've *got* to remember the way out."

Jack accepted the sword Finn handed to him. He said, "No time to hunt down Harahkte?"

"*No.*"

He nodded. "I'm going to end him eventually."

"I tried." Finn gestured to the sword. "That didn't work."

"What do you mean—"

A spark shot from the mirror, formed into a silver fly, and sped down the hallway. Finn, Jack, and Anna hurried after the fly, through a galleria where the remains of several Grindylow lay scattered. Finn glanced at Jack's face and said nothing.

The fly led them down a rotting staircase, through a narrow greenhouse bursting with a forest of thorn-stemmed roses the color of old blood. When they reached the entrance hall, they found that the doors had vanished into a wall. Finn was grimly unsurprised.

"The windows won't break." Jack sank to his haunches as the silver fly buzzed around the chamber.

Finn, becoming aware of a noise from above, lifted her head.

Swirling across the ceiling was a mass of reflective shards. Jack rose. The three of them backed away as the broken pieces from all the mirrors that had been shattered in the house rained down.

A pool of glimmering silver formed before them. Anna walked to it, holding the compact open. The silver fly vanished back inside.

"Our way out?" Finn peered apprehensively into the silver vortex. "How did he do it?"

A low muttering came from a nearby corridor where a swarm of large moths fluttered. Finn took hold of Anna's hand, then Jack's. "Never mind. We don't have a choice."

"Remember," Jack said. "We're trusting Absalom."

They jumped.

IT WAS EXACTLY AS FINN HAD IMAGINED falling through a looking glass would be—a silvery, molasses-like descent, without breathing and a *lot* of panic.

Then she smacked into a solid surface. A floor. She pushed to her feet, Jack beside her. Anna lifted her head woozily from the pentagram-etched floor of a huge chamber with seven mirrors in elaborate frames.

Jack strode to the door and yanked it open. Beyond was a hallway illuminated by lamps on twining bronze stems. The walls were bright with art nouveau nymphs.

"*Tirnagoth?*" Finn couldn't believe they'd made it to the one place that might actually be able to help them.

Then she saw the dark shapes forming in the seven mirrors.

A man in a long coat emerged from one of the larger mirrors. Only his shiny smile could be seen in the shadows beneath the brim of his tricornered hat. He swept a bow as more Fatas slipped with oily grace from the other mirrors—a ruby-eyed girl in a gown of flowers, a redheaded boy with scissor hands, a woman whose skin was tattooed with emerald scales.

"Thank you." The shadow-faced man spoke through his smile. "For creating a portal where there was none. For getting us into Tirnagoth."

Finn, Jack, and Anna backed away, staring at the rogue Fatas they had just led into Tirnagoth.

CHAPTER 22

"O no, O no, Thomas," she said.
"That name does not belong to me;
I am but the Queen of fair Elfland
That am hither come to visit thee."

—"THOMAS THE RHYMER," ANONYMOUS

Christie and the others had left Soldiers' Gate and returned to Tirnagoth with the horrifying news of Finn's disappearance and possible transformation into a Jill. He was now pacing in the lobby and wondering how Sylvie could drink the coffee Devon Valentine the dead ballet dancer had brought for them and speak with the Black Scissors as if they were in her own living room. Christie was quietly freaking out, unable to stop thinking of Finn being torn open, turned into a zombie . . .

The lights flickered.

"Christie." Lily handed him a cup of coffee. "Don't. That's not helping."

Phouka had left the room half an hour ago. Christie watched Micah and Kevin as they sat edgily on a sofa, clearly uncomfortable amid the lethal elegance of Phouka's Fatas.

"Jack and Moth will find Finn and bring her back." Lily's voice shook only a little.

"And dismember Jack Daw."

"That, too."

Christie sipped at the coffee, and regretted it when he thought he might be sick again.

The lobby doors opened. Eammon Tirnagoth stood in the hall, the moonlight shining on his yellow hair. He looked waiflike with the eyepatch. "Christopher. The Banríon wants to see you."

As Eammon strode into the gloom, Christie hurried after, balking as the interior flickered from lamp-lit luxury, back to shadows and decay.

"Eammon . . ."

"Careful, here." Eammon guided him through a room that blinked from darkness into a decadence of red tulip lamps and scarlet furniture. When the glamour blacked out again, Christie tripped on a piece of splintered floorboard. Eammon said, "The Banríon is hurt. She didn't want the others to know and concealed it." He pushed open a door, revealing a pillared hall, its ceiling draped with shadow. "Some of the dead have become aggressive. The Banríon usually manages to keep them at bay . . ."

Christie flinched as moonlight illuminated a white-faced boy in a bloody gown crouched near a wall.

Eammon strode past the creature. "It's just a haunt. Ignore it."

Christie felt inky words bleed onto his skin as they passed a love seat where a girl in a gas mask sat, cradling a little white pig with no face. Eammon led him into a salon, half of which was in darkness, the other half illuminated by lamps shaped like evil-looking flowers. Phouka sat on a sofa surrounded by three Fatas in sleek suits. Aurora Sae was carefully binding Phouka's torso with bandages.

Glancing at the half of the room veiled in darkness, Christie glimpsed a gaunt creature curled on the floor, its mouth gaping, its hair white. *That's Hip Hop. Emily Tirnagoth.*

Eammon said, his voice muted, "Caliban killed my sister."

Christie quickly averted his gaze from what remained of Emily Tirnagoth.

Phouka regarded him coolly. "Christie. Your eyes are black and bad words are staining your skin."

"Because I want to tear Caliban's head off."

"He attacked me when I was out with Emily earlier this evening." Phouka's eyes became silver, and her expression was one of haughty disgust. "I let my guard down and Emily died because of it. We rode the shadow here, as she was dying . . ." Phouka didn't look at the corpse.

As Eammon draped his sister's body with a black quilt, Christie walked to Phouka and sat opposite her. He wanted to ask her why she was *bleeding*. Fatas only bled when they were in love. The thought made him twitchy.

Phouka's eyes were dark. "I need your assistance. Caliban stabbed me with a dagger made from mistletoe. As you can see"—she lifted a hand and Christie wrestled with a primal terror when he saw the crack in her wrist seeping a ribbon of shadow—"I don't have much time."

"What do you need me to do?"

"Please leave us," Phouka said, speaking to her Fatas. As the others moved from the room and the door closed behind them, Phouka looked at Christie. "The poison must be burned out of me. You're going to summon a fire elemental."

No was his first panicked thought. Dread formed an icy lump in his gut. He kept thinking of Emily Tirnagoth's corpse behind them.

A small crack appeared on Phouka's smooth brow. Her eyes were gray as rain, as if her deterioration were making her human.

"You need to give the elemental *that*." Phouka indicated a small golden casket on the table next to Christie.

"What's in it?"

"Nothing I need anymore, something I can't afford to have, and a valuable object to the Red Claw."

"The Red Claw." Christie picked up the casket. He wanted to open it, but it had a tiny lock. He thought he felt something fluttering within it. He didn't want to speak with another crazy elemental. With each step deeper into the Fata world, he felt he was losing himself.

Phouka was dying. He swallowed his fear.

"The fire elemental." Phouka pointed to the cavernous hearth framed by stone gryphons. "You'll have to summon Red Claw there. She's a bit unpredictable." And then, without warning, she keeled over on the sofa. Her eyes seemed to disappear, leaving only dark hollows.

"Phouka!" Christie took a step toward her, then turned to face the hearth. The illusion of warmth and light vanished from the room. Cold gusted around him.

He riffled his memory for the poetry he knew, seeking sonnets about flames, fire, infernos . . .

He found the words of Robert Frost.

"Some say the world will end in fire
Some say in ice.
From what I've tasted of desire
I hold with those who favor fire."

When a flame appeared in one of the charred logs, he wondered if he'd faint, then told himself he'd killed a siren, disintegrated a lake monster, and destroyed a pack of Grindylow. The flames roared up, causing the air to blister. Christie stepped back. He felt as if the words appearing on his skin were burning him.

A sooty figure emerged from the flames, the ashes drifting from a young woman who might have stepped from a war band in ancient Britain. Her long red hair was strung with bits of copper and bronze. Her face was concealed by a horned mask of greenish copper. Serpent tattoos snaked up her arms. As if to contemporize herself, she wore a moss-green corset and suede jeans. A belt of bronze triskelions clinked around her hips.

"Why am I here?" Her eyes behind the mask glowed orange. Christie wasn't certain whether her voice was inside or outside his head.

"I need . . . the Banríon has been poisoned with mistletoe."

Red Claw began to circle him. The air sizzled around her. "Have you brought an offering?"

He held out the golden casket, and she lifted it from his hands and touched the lock, which pooled into molten metal. She opened the lid to reveal something smoldering within. She shut the casket and set it down on a table as Christie wondered what Phouka had just sacrificed to save her life. "I'll have something from you as well, gallant infant." Red Claw walked toward him.

He held his ground, his heart hammering. He should have known this wouldn't be easy.

When she kissed him, he was reminded she was a primordial and dangerous force of nature—fire, wild and eternal and always hungry.

Red Claw released him and he almost collapsed. He watched her walk toward Phouka. He felt something pinch his right index finger and looked down at a new ring of reddish-gold salamanders.

WHEN THE FLAMES HAD BECOME flickering embers, Red Claw returned to them. The lurid glow that had filled the parlor as she'd bent over Phouka, whispering words that had hissed and snapped at the air, had faded. The room remained in its decayed state, illuminated only by firelight. Afraid to approach, Christie tensely watched the shadows writhing on the sofa where Phouka had been.

Then a tide of glamour spilled through the room in a shining wave and Phouka became a young woman again, curled on the sofa like a fairy-tale heroine sleeping off a bad spell.

A green door flew open at one end of the salon. Air scented with clover eddied past him. Christie stared into a green-and-white room, where ivy draped the treelike posts of a bed and a large portrait hung above a porcelain fireplace. He moved into the room. The regal girl in the painting gazed at him, her red hair coiled elaborately beneath a small crown, her face framed by a high, ruffled collar. Her hands were folded in the lap of a jeweled gown. He'd seen similar portraits of this girl as a severe, aged woman.

He heard Phouka's voice behind him, faint and wry. "I was going to tell you eventually."

He dropped onto a divan and stared at the portrait as his mind grappled with the concept of Phouka being . . . of her being . . .

She sat beside him. "I've still got that crown, you know. I kept it as a souvenir. Do you think that was selfish?"

"Queen Elizabeth the First." He spoke with difficulty. "You."

"I was young when they approached me. I'd done something stupid out of pride and the Spanish had decided to retaliate. I was terrified. So I called on the spirits, the Fatas. And they told me, if I'd agree to become their queen—they used the term *Banríon*—they would turn the ocean against the Spanish. I said yes, with a condition—how could I be a queen in their world when I hadn't yet ruled in this one? So they cast the ocean against the Spanish and then collected me, many years later, as I was dying in my bed. A queen."

Christie turned Red Claw's ring of gold salamanders around and around on his finger. "You sold your soul."

"I suppose I did." She continued, "I can't leave Tirnagoth until I'm full strength. It's all I can do at the moment to hold back the shades in this building, to keep my shape."

"Can't you help Finn . . . when they find her?"

"When they find her, Christie, I will try."

SYLVIE RUBBED THE HEELS of her hands against her eyes. She glanced up when Christie returned with Phouka. Christie looked harrowed. Phouka seemed luminous. The combination worried Sylvie.

A banging at the front doors made everyone except Phouka and her Fatas jerk around to stare at the entrance. "I wonder who that could be?" Phouka's voice was delicate and spiky.

Whoever it was began shouting. Sylvie thought she recognized the voice. She whispered, "Oh *no*—"

Lily jumped to her feet.

The Black Scissors rose with Micah and Kevin. He glanced at Phouka, who nodded to two of her black-suited Fatas. The two Fatas accompanied the Black Scissors and Lily to the entrance. The Black Scissors hauled the doors open.

Sean Sullivan stood in the entryway, his hair and clothing soaked from the rain. Jane Emory moved to his side, lifting an umbrella. Her face was pale. "Rowan is dead. I had to tell Sean everything . . . because he's remembered."

Sean Sullivan gritted out, "Where the hell are my daughters?"

CHRISTIE WATCHED as Sean Sullivan gazed around at the exotic gathering, attempting to process the things he'd just learned. He'd told them he'd been at home watching television when Lily's journal, papers his wife had written, and a letter from his own mother had swept around him with poltergeist insistence. After he'd read them, he'd remembered everything. He'd called Jane and together they had found Rowan Cruithnear, dead from an apparent stroke in his apartment. Jane had known to come to Tirnagoth.

Fata power was waning, Christie thought solemnly. How many others would remember the Fatas' existence as the spell that induced amnesia on the adults (so that their children might be seduced by Fata charm) faded?

Lily was talking to her father now, quietly, telling him what had really happened to her.

"What are we going to do?" Christie leaned toward Phouka, watching the Black Scissors watch Lily and her dad.

"I've summoned the Blackheart Queen," Phouka told him.

"Who is the Blackheart Queen?"

"Someone who can help with Finn. She is called SerpentSkirt."

As if on cue, the entrance doors flew open, scattering rain and flower petals, and a female figure in a green camisole and a long skirt of emerald scales moved with predatory grace into the lobby. Her braided black hair was knotted with green and red feathers. Her brown skin shimmered. She looked as if she was eighteen years old. Accompanying her was a figure in jeans and a T-shirt and a hooded jacket.

As the regal and terrifying Fata girl walked toward Phouka, Phouka stood to greet her. "SerpentSkirt."

"I came here as a favor to you, Banríon." The Fata girl cast a disdainful glance around. "To this place of death."

SerpentSkirt's companion drew back his hood, revealing Sionnach Ri the fox knight, who winked at Christie. Christie sat down, unnerved by his double. He wondered how changelings were made and imagined a scene from *Invasion of the Body Snatchers* and seed pods that popped out people.

Phouka turned to Lily, who rose, cradling a pewter casket. Lily handed the casket to the Blackheart Queen.

"This belonged to the braveheart?" SerpentSkirt cupped the casket containing what Christie realized was Finn's heart. He wanted to cry.

"What is that?" Sean Sullivan whispered. "Lily, *where is Finn?*"

An enormous crash resounded throughout the hotel. The lights went out. Darkness rushed over them, accompanied by the stink of decay. Christie jumped up. He couldn't see Phouka, but he heard her. "*Dubh Deamhais*, get them out of here."

"What's happening?" Sean Sullivan demanded as Micah, Kevin, and the

Black Scissors produced flashlights from their hidden stash of implements. As beams of light circled the room, Christie, teeth clenched against panic, could make out the tenuous forms of Phouka and the other Fatas—

—and see the rot like an infection slowly climbing over the walls and furniture. He reached out. *"Phouka—"*

"We've been breached," Phouka declared. "Get out, Christopher."

"The Unseelie." The Blackheart Queen, a figure of dark tendrils, turned. "I feel them."

The Black Scissors strode past the shifting shapes of Phouka, the Blackheart Queen, and the other Fatas. "Follow me." He stalked out of the room. Micah, Kevin, Murray, Lily, Jane, and Sean Sullivan moved after him.

Christie stepped toward Phouka. "You can't stay."

"Christie!" Sylvie flinched as a piece of wall seemed to crumble beside her. *"Come on!"*

"Sionnach." The command in Phouka's voice resulted in the fox knight seizing Christie's wrist and dragging him away. Sylvie hurried after.

As they ran, a swarm of Unseelie malice riding the shadow burst from a hall to their left and pursued them, extinguishing any remaining lamplight, peeling the wallpaper, ripping the furniture. Claws slashed at Christie's hair. When he saw the open doors before them, the rainy night beyond, he shouted.

Sylvie fell. He ducked a silver-clawed hand and hauled her up. Darkness hurtled around them. He felt as if a hurricane of teeth and sinew had descended upon them. He lunged forward, still gripping Sylvie's wrist, dragging her.

Someone caught hold of his other hand and yanked him into the rain. He glimpsed the Black Scissors's grim face, jerked around to see Sylvie slash her elder wood knife at a corpselike man whose jaw gaped to reveal too many teeth. Sionnach Ri was beside her.

Christie shouted as Sylvie was yanked from his grasp, back into the darkness. Someone surged past him, yelling like a maniac, into Tirnagoth. Christie leaped forward, but Lily and Sean Sullivan seized him, hauling him back.

"Oh *no* you don't," Sean Sullivan said as the Black Scissors, Micah, Kevin, Sionnach Ri, and Murray dashed back into the dark. "Leave it to the professionals."

SYLVIE FRANTICALLY STABBED AND SLASHED at the things she couldn't see as they bit, pinched, and clawed. When the corpse Fata lunged out at her, she flung her dagger at it. Sionnach Ri grabbed her and shoved her back. Then someone was pulling her into the rain, out of Tirnagoth. She tasted blood in her mouth, heard Aubrey—*Aubrey*—saying her name over and over. "I got it," she said fiercely. "I got it." Then: "What are *you* doing here?"

"I just *saved* you!" Aubrey looked savage and distressed. He was drenched from the rain. "I came to talk to Phouka and . . . what's happening?"

Someone glided from the darkness of Tirnagoth. Sylvie's heart almost stopped. "*Finn?*"

Finn whirled to face her.

Micah, held up by Sionnach Ri, staggered out, blood sluicing the lower half of his face. "I couldn't get to them—" Micah gasped. There was a booming roar.

Then Anna Weaver and Jack fled out of Tirnagoth, into the rain.

AS JACK AND ANNA TUMBLED OUT OF TIRNAGOTH, Finn watched the doors slam shut on the Unseelie within. She looked around at Sylvie and Christie, Micah and Aubrey, Lily, Jane, and—

"*Da?*"

AS FINN AND HER FATHER STARED AT EACH OTHER, Lily flung her arms around her sister. Jack rose to study the boarded-up, ruinous façade of Tirnagoth. To Christie, he murmured, "Who's still inside?"

"The Black Scissors, Murray, Kevin Gilchriste. Phouka and her Fatas. And the Blackheart Queen." Christie's voice caught. "Phouka locked herself and the others in to keep those things from getting out, didn't she? Is Finn . . ." He didn't dare look at Finn.

"Yes. She's a Jill." Jack walked to the doors, placed his hands on them, and pressed his forehead against the wood in despair. Christie knew the doors would never open from the outside. He sank down onto the steps, the rain pummeling him as he realized what that meant.

They were on their own.

CHAPTER 23

Grendel was the name of this grim demon
Haunting the marches, marauding round the heath
And desolate fens; he had dwelt for a time
In misery among the banished monsters

—*BEOWULF*, TRANSLATED BY SEAMUS HEANEY

Home.

Finn experienced a small breakdown in the shower, a breathless, tearless glitch in her nascent Jill programming. She sank down, the hot water pouring over her cool skin, and thought, *What if I stay this way? A thing kept alive by magic?*

She could *feel* the heart pulsing within her because of Jack, the strange, warm ebb of blood he caused to course through her. As she considered immortality as . . . *this*, terror overwhelmed her. How had Jack borne it, all these years?

Afterward, she hastily dressed in a T-shirt and jeans. She stepped out of the bathroom to find Lily waiting for her. Lily hugged her tightly. "What he *did* to you . . ." They all knew about Harahkte now.

"Don't." Finn stepped back and said with false bravery, "I'm like a superhero now, with undead powers."

FINN DIDN'T RAISE HER HEAD as Jack joined her on the widow's walk. The rain and clouds had gone. The night was beautiful, as if Phouka Banríon and the Black Scissors's sacrifice had cleared the air. *What are we going to do without them?* Finn wondered.

"Micah drove Christopher home," Jack told her. "Sylvie and Aubrey have gone to his place. Anna's asleep in your room. Jane's making dinner with Lily."

Finn heard the worry in his voice. It caught at her like hooks. He knew that, with Tirnagoth closed up and two Fata queens within, there wasn't a chance of her ever being returned to her original state. She gazed at her neighborhood as she listened to the crickets and the distant hush of traffic on Main Street. "I won't be able to stay home, will I?"

"No." He spoke gently. "For three days, you'll be able to endure the sunlight. After that, you'll fade when the sun rises, return as it sets."

She never thought her next words would cause her so much anguish. "I'll have to go with you."

He hung his head. He was still battered and blood streaked, but the cuts and bruises were already healing.

"*Harahkte* did this to me, Jack, not you—I know that's what you're thinking, don't deny it. I chose everything I've done so far and I wouldn't change it. Not anything. You're free of Reiko. Lily is home. I found out my mom wasn't crazy. And now I'm practically indestructible. So we're going to have to find a way to kill Harahkte, aren't we?"

"Did you really slice that sword through his neck?" A small smile tugged at the corners of his mouth.

"He didn't die. I can't believe all this time he was pretending to be Moth." She drew her knees up and rested her forehead on them. She couldn't feel tears, only a pressure behind her eyes. "Why didn't I see it? That he wasn't Moth?"

"None of us saw it, Finn."

"Absalom's the only one who knows Harahkte and he's stuck in a makeup mirror." Her hand slid to the geisha compact in her jeans pocket. "And it wasn't Absalom who showed us the way out of Sombrus. It was *Harahkte.* Absalom, as the fly, was trying to warn us. Harahkte wanted the Unseelie to shut down Tirnagoth."

"And he wants the key I have." Jack looked at her. Half his face was in shadow, his eyes feral silver. "Did he tell you why he did that to you? Made you . . ."

"No. He let us out of Sombrus for a reason, but I don't think it was just to get the Unseelie into Tirnagoth. Why didn't he just threaten me in Sombrus and get you to hand over the key? What is that damn key?"

"He needed Tirnagoth shut down first. He has another plan to get the key." Jack reached out and tentatively brushed the tips of his fingers across her cheek, as if she might shatter. Grief spilled into his eyes.

Being a Jill had no effect on desire—Jack's touch sent those metaphorical butterflies of fiery glass all through Finn, warming the blood that coursed in the network of alchemical flowers blooming beneath her skin. She slid into his lap and kissed him, her mouth opening against his as he wrapped his arms around her.

Dawn swept across the sky and Jack faded. She remained.

THE NEXT DAY, Finn lifted her fingers to the strands of sunlight drifting through the leaves above her. Lily was sprawled beneath the oak beside her. Finn hadn't slept—she didn't need sleep anymore. That morning, she'd gone with Lily and her father to deliver Anna back to her parents.

"I got lost," Anna had told her mother and father, lying with scary, blithe ease. "When the fight broke out at the play, I got scared and ran and got lost in the woods. Finn found me."

A search had been tearing through those woods for a few days, but Anna's parents didn't care about the holes in Anna's story—they held their daughter, thanking Finn and her family.

Lily slid a hand through the grass and twined her fingers around Finn's. "Dad gave you a break last night, Finn, but you're going to have to have that talk with him." The sound of their dad hammering in the house made her pause. "Where did he get all those iron horseshoes he's hanging up over the doors and windows?"

"From an antique shop on a farm. He went out before you and Anna woke up. He also bought a Civil War saber and a scythe that the seller promised him were iron." Finn didn't tell Lily that the iron made her feel queasy and as if she had a slight sunburn.

"I should have known about Moth." Lily plucked at the grass. "I should have known one of Lot's toys would be a time bomb. He was so broken and so confused. There's no chance, is there, that Moth is still . . . ?"

Finn shook her head, curling her hands against her stomach. "There's nothing I've seen—it's like Harahkte's murdered Moth."

Lily's expression became severe. "He cut you open and replaced your organs with . . ." True rage transformed her for a moment, and Finn saw the Briar Queen then.

"Lily." Finn propped herself up on her elbows. Catching the sweet taint of rot, she turned her head, frowning.

It stood in the shadows near the hedgerow, a black-and-white thing that resembled a jittery film image of a girl in a gas mask. The leaves of the hedge behind it had darkened and curled as if diseased.

Lily sat up. Finn didn't take her gaze from the dead thing. "It shouldn't be here," Lily whispered. The alchemical flowers within Finn writhed and stung. She reached out and gripped Lily's hand. They sat in silence and the dead girl finally drifted away, leaving behind a circle of toadstools in the grass where she'd stood.

IT WAS LATE IN THE MORNING. Christie was sprawled in his bed, wondering why the house was so quiet. He could usually hear Liam and Cynan arguing, the dogs barking, and his parents going about their morning routine of hollering and searching for keys and cell phones. He'd had upsetting dreams about his blood becoming serpents. Of Finn cracking into pieces, marigolds with tiny teeth fluttering from her. Of Sylvie transforming into a giant black harpy. He'd dreamed of being trapped in a cocoon of silence.

He threw an arm over his eyes and thought of Phouka. Phouka who was Elizabeth the First, the queen of the English fairies, and who had sealed herself in Tirnagoth to keep the Unseelie from escaping into the true world.

He rolled onto his side, curling into a fetal position.

On his nightstand, near his dog-eared copies of Robert Graves's *The White Goddess* and a book of Keats's poetry, were the rings he'd gotten from the elementals. They were *glowing*.

Someone sat in the chair in the shadowy corner of his room.

Christie floundered out of bed, sucking in a breath to shout any words that might defend him as the creature that had pretended to be Moth leaned forward, hands clasped, and said, in a perfectly reasonable tone, "You'll be attending the

Midsummer Masquerade, Christie Hart. Won't you? You don't want to disappoint your schoolmates."

Christie was incapable of producing any lethal poetry that might get this creature out of his house. He could only say, his mouth parched, "It's daylight. You weren't invited."

"Thanks to Absalom Askew's curse, I'm no longer just a Jack. I'm human. And I'm Other." Harahkte smiled sweetly. "Fata taboos don't apply to me."

As Harahkte rose, Christie took a step back. Harahkte said gently, "Ask me about your family."

Christie realized why it was so still in the house, and his vision went black with rage and despair. Words meant to obliterate hissed from his mouth.

When he came back to himself, Harahkte was gone and he was staring at the window his words had shattered, at the dent the heka had made in the wall. He listened to his family, alive and well, downstairs.

SYLVIE HAD SLEPT FITFULLY. By the time the sky blazed pink, she was already on her third cup of coffee and preparing Whiskey and Pearls for opening.

When Harahkte sauntered in, she dropped the Venetian mask she'd been hanging.

"Your father's name is Samuel Whitethorn," Harahkte said casually. "That doesn't sound very Finnish."

"It's what his last name means, in English." Sylvie hadn't expected an enemy so early in the morning. She didn't have one of her daggers. Out of the corner of one eye, she caught the glint of the scimitar hanging near the office. She began backing toward it. "He changed it when he was young."

"I see." The sunlight made Harahkte solid. His hood was up, shadowing the upper half of his face. "I want you to come to the Midsummer Masquerade tomorrow night, Sylvie."

Moth had been kind, brave, noble. Sylvie *hated* this impostor. "Why?"

"Does it matter why? You'll do it or I'll set Caliban loose on your family. He ate Sophia Avaline. What do you think he'll do to your father?"

Sylvie wanted to throw up, to scream.

Harahkte strode from the shop. "See you later, Sylvie."

$$\diamondsuit \quad \diamondsuit \quad \diamondsuit$$

AFTER LILY WENT INSIDE to make iced tea, Finn, who'd been putting off talking to her father, settled beside him on the steps of the front porch.

"Fairies," her da pronounced. "And your mom knew. And my mother suspected. *What have they done to you?*"

With care, Finn said, "It's just a spell. It can be reversed."

"Just a spell. And can it be reversed only by the terrifying young women and the strange young man now locked away in that abandoned hotel?"

She looked down at her hands. "Yes."

"I read your mother's notes. And Lily's journal. I remembered it all. The Fata family. Your mom's hallucinations. What really happened to Lil is more believable than the story you two trumped up. Who sent the journal and the papers flying at me? Was that fairies?"

"No. That's a ghost. A friendly ghost."

"Please tell me it's not my mum."

"It's your mom."

He sighed and shoved his hands through his hair. "I should never have scattered some of her ashes around the house."

"You did *what*?" Finn felt her eyes widen. She couldn't believe what he'd done. "*Da*."

He shrugged. "It was a request in her will. Now we know why. I suppose I must have encountered the Fatas when I was younger. I've been asleep all this time."

"I don't know why you can suddenly remember them." Finn plucked a twig from between the porch boards and began twisting it. "Usually, adults forget as soon as they find out what the Fatas are. Gran Rose must have been immune to that spell."

"And Jane knows as well." His tone became ominous.

"Don't be angry with her, Da. She's been dealing with this all her life."

"And Jack . . . he was careful about what he said, but I get the sense that the Fatas have done more than a 'spell' on him."

"Yeah. They have."

He gathered her into his arms. "You're so cold," he whispered. "Now tell me about this Harahkte bastard."

HER FATHER WENT BACK INSIDE and Finn remained on the porch, wistfully watching the sunlight filtering through the leaves of the oak. The alchemical marigolds had calmed inside of her, although she occasionally felt as if tiny teeth were clamping on to her bones. The hollowness, the numb inertia of her nervous system, was no longer alien . . . she was resigned to becoming something else.

When she lowered her gaze, she found Harahkte standing before her.

Finn sat very still as he settled on the steps beside her. The sunlight picked out strands of gold in his hair, the green of his eyes. He draped his hands between his knees and surveyed the street. "If your father comes out, he won't see me."

"He won't come out."

Harahkte nodded. "Since Jack will be hunting me, I thought I'd tell you where I'll be tomorrow night."

"Thank you." Finn curled her hands at her sides. "That'll make it easier to end you."

There was pity in his expression. He said with absolute seriousness, "You can't win this. I know what you're capable of. I've been around far longer than the Wolf and Reiko. Your Fata allies are sealed in Tirnagoth. Rowan Cruithnear is dead and his professors—I've taken care of them. And I can't die."

"What did you do to the professors?" Horror moved through Finn.

He looked at her. "What do you think?"

"What do you want?" Finn snarled softly.

"I believe we've already had this conversation. Tomorrow night, on Midsummer's Eve, I'm going to use the key Reiko placed in Jack because Jack is going to give it to me. Are you and Jack thinking of destroying it? You can't."

"You want my friends there as insurance. What is the key for?"

"Haven't you figured that out yet?"

"Lily Rose never hurt you. Neither did Jack or Cruithnear or the Dragonfly. *I* never hurt you."

"It's nothing personal, Finn." He stood up. "Lily Rose is an illegal immigrant in the world of the living and a magnet for the dead. Jack is a problem for me. Cruithnear and the Dragonfly were just tactical maneuvers."

"Lily is not a . . . she's not—"

"Finn." His voice and expression were unnervingly tender. "Lily Rose is Annwyn's Way into the true world. As long as she remains, the dead and what walks in the land of the dead will find its way here."

Finn flung herself forward with a Jill's speed. She stabbed her silver dagger into the place where his heart should be.

Harahkte stood, unmoving, the shadows molding his cheekbones, his mouth. He took hold of the hilt and pulled the dagger from his chest. Blood spattered the pavement, gleamed on the blade. He flung the dagger at her feet.

Then he lunged forward and gripped her hands. "That's the second time you've tried to kill me." He dragged her close. He gently and firmly placed his other hand over her face.

Her vision blacked out and images moved through her brain. She wanted to struggle, to scream, but she couldn't. She saw *Moth* fighting two of Seth Lot's wolves in a baroque corridor. Dead leaves and lichen peeled from the walls around him as he swung a sword. The gaunt desperation on his face—

She saw *Harahkte* stagger out of Sombrus, remembering every betrayal, every loss he'd ever experienced through countless lifetimes. It swept over her in a brutal rush. She saw him rocking on his heels, pushing his hands through his hair, laughing with the despair of someone who had been broken and knew he could never be fixed.

When the visions ended, he was close to her. His eyes were ice green and narrowed and without compassion. He gripped her by the throat and said, "Ask me again what I want."

She whispered, "What do you want?"

"I want to break the world." Then he burst into a cloud of large and small moths and spiraled away. Finn sank down abruptly on the steps. She gazed at the blood drops on the pavement, and shivered.

SEAN SULLIVAN HADN'T been able to contact Jane Emory—and, after what Harahkte had told Finn about the professors, this was cause for alarm.

As the SUV containing Sean Sullivan, Finn, and Lily screeched into Jane's drive, Finn yelled at her da as he got out of the SUV and raced into the house. She and Lily dashed after him.

They found Jane in the kitchen.

She looked as if she'd been attacked by an animal, marred by bites and scratches on her arms, throat, and face. She was still breathing, but she was a horrible shade of gray white.

"Jane . . ." Panic was an urgent thread in Sean's voice as he fell to his knees beside her.

Finn drew the silver knife from her hoodie. She wanted to kill something.

Lily shouted and Finn looked up to meet the glass gaze of the thing that had appeared from the shadows to stand behind their father.

"No . . ." She dropped the dagger to keep the Grindylow from moving in self-defense, but didn't take her gaze from the Grindylow's face, cracked and beautiful and sly with malice. It had one arm stretched toward their father, its dirty veil and gown eddying in the draft. Its lips had parted to reveal carnivore teeth. The nails on its outstretched hand were streaked with red.

Her da turned, recoiled, and jumped up. "What *is* it?"

"Just don't look away from it," Finn ordered.

Sean reached for a gardening hoe propped near the kitchen door. Lily and Finn yelled at the same time: "No!"

The Grindylow's self-defense instincts sent it lurching toward their father, who swung the hoe. The metal struck the doll's head, smashing half of its face. As the Grindylow crumpled to the floor, Finn and Lily watched, wide-eyed, while their father continued to pulverize its head.

"Heart," Lily told him.

Sean Sullivan promptly smashed through the Grindylow's chest, denting the metal heart within the broken porcelain. As knots of slimy roots and unidentifiable vegetation spilled from the mutilated doll, their father turned away and dropped the hoe. His eyes were wide. "I'm taking Jane to the hospital."

FINN LEARNED FROM HER FRIENDS that all the professors had been attacked: Professor Hobson was in the hospital with heart failure; Miss Perangelo, Wyatt, and Fairchild were in okay shape after nocturnal attacks by Fatas. Perangelo and Wyatt had driven off their assailants. Fairchild had locked his in the bathroom of his apartment until the sun rose and destroyed the creature.

In Jack's apartment, seated on Jack's bed in the sunlight, Finn slid a hand into her pocket and touched the geisha compact containing Absalom. "Who's bringing Anna?"

"Micah." Sylvie was watching Lily chalk a circle on the floor. Christie was tugging Jack's old photos and magazine articles from a black bulletin board. He began pinning up red index cards scrawled with black Sharpie. Sylvie said, "How are we going to do this? How are we going to—"

"We'll figure it out." Finn rose and walked to the middle of the apartment, stood there with the sun on the back of her neck. *I have one more day in the sunlight.* She was so afraid. Harahkte was not a Fata like Reiko and Seth Lot. He was another thing entirely.

Anna arrived with Micah. In a blue dress and a red hoodie, she looked angelically fierce. "We have to wait for sunset," Anna said. "When we try to contact Absalom."

"Anna." Finn sat on the sofa. "Maybe we should let Christie do it. He's the witch."

"No. Absalom talks to me."

Finn took the compact mirror from her pocket and flicked it open. She gazed at the flame dancing in the glass. "You shouldn't trust him. That night, Absalom told Seth Lot where you and Lily were."

"I know. He had to. Absalom said the umbrella he gave me would help kill the Wolf. He made it that way."

"He *told* you—"

"I saw it," Anna said softly. "I saw how the Wolf would die, if things went as they should. And they did. And I've seen how Harahkte will die."

Finn rose. "How?"

"Moth will kill him." Anna looked away. "I see Moth dying with your silver dagger in his heart."

No, Finn thought. *It must be Harahkte you see.*

WHEN THE SUN BEGAN TO SET, Jack found himself standing before the Tirnagoth Hotel, which remained a boarded-up hulk against the darkening sky. He could sense the malevolent dead nearby, in the wilderness that surrounded the hotel. But something was keeping them back. He surveyed the shadows and spotted a few figures with antlers or other types of headdresses flashy with totems and talismans. The Blackhearts had come to wait for their queen.

A young man in a coat of dark blue plumage emerged from the gloom. He stood beside Jack and gazed at Tirnagoth.

"*Marbh ean.*" Jack greeted Dead Bird.

"The Blackhearts won't interfere. Nor will they help. Not until their queen is free."

"What does Harahkte want?"

"What any monster wants. Love and acceptance. Or maybe just to destroy the world that wouldn't give him those things."

"I remember. The part of me that felt that way is still walking around as Jack Daw." Jack turned his back on Tirnagoth.

AS SOON AS THE SUN BEGAN TO FADE, Finn stepped onto Jack's fire escape and found Jack there. She wrapped her arms around him and leaned against him. "Harahkte came to visit me. Why does he think Lily is infecting the world?"

"He lies." Jack lay his cheek against the top of her head.

"What's wrong with Lily? Tell me what's wrong with my sister." Her voice was faint and broken.

"Lily is alive. Nothing's wrong with Lily." He stepped back, his hands slipping down to hers, his fingers cool and strong. "Tell me what's happened while I wasn't here."

"Today, Harahkte threatened our friends, had Unseelie attack the professors—Jane was hurt by a Grindylow—and told me he wants to break the world. Let's plot against him." Finn climbed back through the window and Jack followed her. He walked to the bulletin board covered with Christie's index cards and said, "Interesting. Hello, Anna."

Anna stood in the middle of the room. "Finn has only one more day."

Jack turned to Finn. The despair in his eyes was almost unbearable, so Finn stalked to the chalk circle Christie had drawn on the floor and said, "Should we light the candles and get started?"

FINN SET THE GEISHA COMPACT containing Absalom in front of Anna, who sat inside the circle. Christie, Sylvie, Micah, Lily, Jack, and Finn settled around her. The newest arrival—Aubrey Drake—joined them. When Christie indicated that they all hold hands, Finn shifted uncomfortably. "Is this going to be dangerous for her?"

Sylvie glanced at Anna and grinned. "She's a tough kid."

"I'm not a kid," Anna protested.

"This is theurgy," Aubrey said stubbornly. "If that's the Fool in that object, and he possesses her, he might not leave her."

"He won't hurt me." Anna cupped her hands around the compact.

Christie began to speak in a language that didn't sound like any Finn had ever heard and the air hummed as if live wires were above. As Christie bowed his head, inky words scrawled across his skin. When a drop of blood oozed from one of his nostrils, Finn wanted to stop everything.

"Absalom." Anna, her hair rising as if with static electricity, spoke above Christie's low chant. Tendrils of orange light reflected from the compact in her hands, onto her face, her eyes.

Christie's chant ended abruptly.

Anna's eyes became molten gold and Absalom Askew gazed from Anna's body.

"Absalom," Finn coolly addressed the spirit. "Please turn it down a notch."

The charge in the atmosphere vanished, and the humming noise became barely perceptible as Absalom spoke in Anna's voice, "I almost forgot who I was when I opened my eyes. Been a long time since I've been a girl."

Jack leaned forward. "How can Harahkte be killed? You knew him way back when. You turned him into Alexander Nightshade and a moth."

"He can't be burned, decapitated, drawn and quartered, drained of blood, drowned, blown up, melted, poisoned, stabbed, or otherwise relieved of his existence. His body remakes itself. Silver and iron, mistletoe and elder wood . . . these things will slow him down, not kill him."

"Hell." Christie had gone ashen. "Has all that already been *tried*?"

"Stoning, exposure to extreme temperatures . . . have I left anything out?" Absalom turned his head to regard Finn with his flame-gold eyes. "The Grey sisters told you what he was. And Jack, I see, is having a moment of revelation. Harahkte can't die. He knows the Way into Annwyn. Can you guess now who his daddy was?"

"Death's child walks in Fair Hollow." Finn spoke so faintly the others had

to lean forward to hear her. "That's what the Grey sisters said. Harahkte is *Death's son?*"

Jack's eyes were hooded. "Why didn't you tell us this before, Absalom?"

"I had forgotten and none of you had tried to kill him yet." Absalom cocked Anna's head to one side. "The Harahkte I knew liked to play games. He was bored. He messed with the *Fatas*. This Harahkte seems more focused, less psychotic."

"*Less* psychotic?" Christie's voice was pitchy.

Finn met Absalom's golden gaze. "What can we do to stop him? Can you do to him what you did before? Make him forget? Make him . . . something else?"

"Moth is gone, Finn. He wasn't real."

"*You* created Moth."

"*All* of you created him. He was a story."

"What kind of story were *you*, Absalom?" Finn took a stab in the dark and was rewarded by those golden eyes narrowing.

"Not the kind you tell to children. Do you understand what's come to Fair Hollow? It is Harahkte who made Seth Lot what he was, as Lot made Reiko what she was. It was Harahkte who charmed Sombrus away from me. He has corrupted mortals and Fatas. Because he was neither one nor the other, he had no loyalties to either. He was called the Nettle King because he plotted mayhem and assembled a court of like-minded Jacks and Jills whose sole pleasure in life was causing chaos."

"Sombrus was yours." Jack eyed his old friend. "Before Harahkte stole it from you. And now he has it again."

"How do we free you from the mirrors, Absalom?" Finn asked.

"You can't. Harahkte's used an old trick. If you break the mirror in the true world, you will set me loose as I once was. You don't want to do that."

What were *you?* Finn thought, frustrated.

"We're screwed." Micah hunched his shoulders.

"No, we're not." Finn met Jack's gaze and could almost *feel* he knew what she was about to say. She leaned forward. "Aubrey, is the Midsummer Masquerade still being held at SunStone?"

"Yes, all set," Aubrey said warily. "Because the people paying for it—my parents among them—are in complete denial about the Fatas."

Finn looked around at everyone. "I think I know why Harahkte wants all of us at the masquerade. And I think I know how to trap him."

AFTER ABSALOM HAD RETURNED TO THE MIRROR, Anna yawned and fell asleep. Christie carried her to Jack's bed. Another two hours of plotting was followed by Christie opening his laptop and Skyping their plans to the remaining professors gathered at Wyatt's house, and to the blessed—Claudette, Vic and Nic Tudor, and Ijio—whose families had been planning the Midsummer Masquerade for months and who weren't about to cancel it due to Rowan Cruithnear's stroke and Sophia Avaline's disappearance.

When everyone had gone, Finn stood with Jack before the black bulletin board, reading the red index cards scrawled with Christie's handwriting.

> *Absalom Askew: Ally. For now. Secret weapon.*
> *Giselle the Jill: David Ryder's girlfriend. Weakness: Iron, silver, mistletoe, elder wood.*
> *Caliban: Psycho. Weakness: (see above)*
> *Jack's vagabonds: Allies if we're desperate.*
> *The Black Scissor's Taltu: Micah, Murray, Kevin (Shaman warriors). We've only got Micah.*
> *Jacks and Jills: Harahkte's bitches.*
> *Unseelie: Outlaw Fatas who joined Harahkte.*
> *The Professors: Allies. Rowan Cruithnear. Avaline. Murdered.*
> *The blessed: Keep out of line of fire.*
> *Phouka Banrion: Trapped in Tirnagoth.*
> *Jack Daw: Still loose.*
> *Harahkte: Wants to wreck the world. Weakness: None known.*

"Did you know that Phouka was once the Queen of England?" Finn turned from the board and began helping Jack collect the pizza boxes and coffee mugs remaining from their strategy session.

He set the coffee mugs into the sink. "I did not know. But I now realize that, long ago in London, *she* was the one who visited me and my father and asked for our help in exorcising a malicious spirit from one of her blessed. The malicious spirit was Caliban."

Finn inhaled sharply as something burst inside of her where her newborn heart was. She pressed one hand against her breast—that heart . . . that was Jack's doing. Whenever he was near, she felt it growing from a seed of blood into a living thing. She loved her heart. She didn't understand how Fatas or Jacks and Jills who grew them could cut them out as if aborting a living creature. "Did you know the Black Scissors's name was William Harrow?"

He didn't look at her, the muscles moving in his arms as he sponged the mugs in the sink. "I knew."

"You took your mom's maiden name, but . . ." Finn leaned back against the counter and studied his face as he rinsed the mugs, his head down. "Your dad's last name was Harrow."

His lovely mouth curved. His lashes veiled his eyes. "Yes."

"William Harrow's your ancestor."

"Unfortunately. He doesn't seem keen on admitting that. Which is fine with me."

Finn neatly crumpled the pizza boxes into the garbage because it was something to do. She sat in one of the chairs at his tiny kitchen table as the idea of what they were going to attempt hit her like a speeding train. What if her theory was wrong? "How are we going to do this, Jack?"

He dragged the other chair close to her and sat. He leaned forward and clasped her hands. "We've done all the thinking we can do. You need to sleep—"

"I'm not tired." She wanted to cry, but she couldn't. There was no fatigue at all because she was becoming one of them.

Jack leaned farther forward and his mouth touched hers in a careful kiss. The kiss became carnal and heat blossomed through her, causing a chain reaction of pounding heart and quick breath and a desire for skin against skin. Then he was lifting her in his arms as her legs went around him, her fingers digging into the wings of his shoulder blades. He made a small, hoarse sound in his throat as they fell onto his bed and tangled together in a frenzy of trying to remove clothing as quickly as possible. Buttons and zippers had never been so frustrating. Jack's nimble fingers swiftly undid these obstacles. His wicked smile made her feel like fire in a girl's shape.

They burned together in the dark.

I am thine and thou art mine.

Until the ending of the world.

CHAPTER 24

Our revels now are ended. These our actors
As I foretold you, were all spirits, and
Are melted into air, into thin air.

—*The Tempest*, William Shakespeare

The next day, Finn and Lily sat with their father and Jane Emory—who had recovered from the Grindylow attack—in the kitchen and told them what they needed them to do.

Finn hadn't explained the entire plan because that would upset her father. She said a trap had been laid for Harahkte, the bad guy, and all Sean Sullivan and Jane needed to do was bring Anna to SunStone, where the Midsummer Masquerade was being held. Her da inevitably asked, "How are you going to trap this Harahkte and is there some sort of Fata prison he'll be sent to?"

"Of course there's a prison," Lily said brightly. "And we're just trapping him with silver and iron. It works with all Fatas."

Oh, you're such a liar, Lily, Finn thought gratefully.

Jane was quiet, watching Finn and Lily. She had lost Cruithnear, and Sophia Avaline had been her friend. She looked exhausted; she'd already fought her battle, and Finn hadn't wanted her father or Jane anywhere near Ground Zero. If they wanted to help, Finn could at least place them in somewhat controlled circumstances.

"I don't want you doing this." Sean Sullivan's voice was rough. "Going into battle with some unholy thing."

"We've got experts," Finn reassured him. With the exception of Hobson, who was still in the hospital, all the professors would be at the masquerade. The invitation—a crimson apple and a gilt card nestled in a little black box—had arrived that morning and now sat, vaguely threatening, on the dining room table.

"Have you done this sort of thing before?" Suspicion crept into their father's tone.

Finn exchanged a quick look with Lily. Lily grinned. "Yeah. And we're still here."

Their father pushed his hands over his face. "We can't just call the police?"

"They won't see anything out of the ordinary, Sean." Jane nodded to Finn. "We'll bring Anna."

"WE NEED TO DO AS THEY SAY." When they were alone in the kitchen, Jane sank into the chair opposite Sean, who sat at the table with his head in his hands. He had every book about mythology and folklore that he owned piled on the table. He looked up at her with bleary eyes.

"And what am I to do? My girls know how to navigate through this hidden world—*I* don't. And you . . ."

"In my everyday life, Sean, I like to pretend the Fatas are imaginary. Sometimes, it works. Then I remember shoving a sharpened iron spoon into one of them when I was a teenager."

THAT AFTERNOON, Lily, Finn, and Sylvie went shopping at the most expensive boutique in Fair Hollow's downtown. If the world as they knew it was going to end, Lily said they might as well look fabulous during it.

JACK ARRIVED JUST AS THE DAY WAS ENDING. He and Finn watched the sun fade from the sky, its radiance a final, warm kiss upon Finn's skin.

CHAPTER 25

Art thou that traitor angel, art thou he
Who first broke peace in Heaven and faith, till then
Unbroken, and in proud rebellious arms
Drew after him the third part of Heaven's sons,

—*PARADISE LOST*, JOHN MILTON

Nightfall had turned SunStone Mansion into a place of vampiric glamour. Candy-colored spotlights danced over the exterior walls and sun-rayed windows, the pale statues in the wilderness of the garden. The stone mice running up the stairway's railings seemed to move. The beautiful face of the sun god Apollo—god, also, of plagues and vermin—watched from above the doors.

Finn and Jack stood on the path leading to SunStone. Finn's gauzy gray gown drifted in the breeze. She had painted a band of black around her eyes. She wore a crown of tiny stars and her hair was plaited with talismans. Beside her, Jack, in a dark Givenchy suit, was silent, his face supernaturally feral in the cascading lights. He, too, had a black band painted across the upper half of his face. There was no need for them to wear masks—they would be known.

They headed up the walk together. Lily, Aubrey Drake, Sylvie, and Christie followed. At the doors stood James Wyatt, elegantly attired in a tuxedo and black half mask. There was a bruise along his jaw. Finn flinched when she saw the claw marks healing on his throat. He noticed her looking and grinned. "You should see the other guy."

The doors swept open before them. A tsunami of lights and pulsing bass music swept from SunStone's ballroom, which had been transformed from ruin and neglect. The walls were painted with a mural of a storybook forest, while a night sky shining with stars decorated the ceiling. A topaz chandelier sparkled like a rayed sun. The music, as loud as the heartbeat of some giant god birthed by pagan revels, blasted from enormous speakers. The air was pungent with the scents of earth after rain, crushed flowers, and candle smoke. The guests wore half masks, elaborate makeup, metal faces, headdresses, or crowns. Tattoos resembling streaks of fire or ice banded arms ornate with loops of jewels or metal. The masquerade spilled out into the garden, where a pool glowed with electric blue water and butterfly-shaped lights winked in the foliage. A few brave celebrants had already shed their glamorous gear to swim in the pool.

"It's a goddamn bacchanal," Christie observed approvingly.

Finn saw Victoria Tudor speaking with Charlotte Perangelo, both in gowns of pale green and emerald. Ijio Valentine was chatting up a pale-haired boy in a horned mask. Finn had warned the blessed to wear silver and iron and to be careful not to brush up against any of Jack's vagabonds.

Finn saw one of Jack's vagabond friends in the crowd—Dogrose, brown skinned and regal in dusty velvet. He sat on the stairway with a blue-haired girl wearing butterfly wings.

"You know, at this point"—Christie brushed imaginary dust from his dark blazer and straightened his silver tie—"I'm surprised we're not all talking to wallpaper in the psych ward."

Sylvie murmured, "I don't think they have wallpaper in the psych ward."

"Everyone stick to the plan," Lily ordered. "Harahkte has us here thinking to make us distractions. So let's distract."

They wove into the crowd, leaving Finn and Jack as bait.

"This party was supposed to be amazing," Finn said wistfully.

Jack twined a hand around one of hers. "It will be."

They moved forward as a small band of musicians replaced the DJ, and a few couples began to dance. Jack slid an arm around Finn's waist. As they glided in circles, Finn watched the silver ghost his eyes, the shadows threading his hair and bleeding from his fingertips, remnants of the dark that had held him for so long. The cold, old magic within her began to blossom also, but it wasn't that that made her feel like a warrior.

Jack froze in midmotion. Silence fell abruptly. "Jack?" Alarmed, Finn turned in place. Everyone in SunStone—*everything*—had stopped.

With the exception of Dead Bird, who was moving toward her from among the immobilized revelers, dressed in black suede, netsuke charms banding his wrists, scarlet feathers in his hair. Sylvie had told Finn about Dead Bird's photograph from the 1800s, his beginnings as a bodyguard for Ijio Valentine's ancestors. He stopped before her and bowed. "I am here to assist."

Finn gestured around and demanded: "Could you always do this?"

"No. It's draining. It won't remain in place for long." Dead Bird walked around the table stacked with refreshments and surrounded by pretty revelers. He plucked a glass of blackberry wine from a girl in a scarlet gown and tucked an orchid behind Micah Govannon's ear. "Harahkte has already set his people among you. There are seven Unseelie here—one of them is already in the pool. And his Jacks and Jills . . . well, he's glamoured them invisible also." Dead Bird circled back to her. "I can help you see them. It won't last more than an hour. Don't move. Don't blink."

She flinched, steeled herself as Dead Bird raised a hand. All his nails were blunt but for a sharp, silver one on his forefinger.

He scratched her left eye.

As she staggered back, one hand over her wounded eye, the crowd rushed back into motion and noise. Dead Bird vanished into it. Jack caught her hand and spun her around. He looked ready to murder someone. "Did something weird happen just now?"

She let her hand drop from her eye and blinked rapidly. The pain and blurriness cleared. "The *Marbh ean* was here." She warily surveyed the room as the chandelier above vibrated with music. Beyond the masked revelers, she saw a tall man with white hair and ivory bull horns attached to his head. Dressed only in leather jeans and tattoos that reminded her of the labyrinthine patterns on Greek pottery, he looked around, his eyes mirror-bright. "There are Unseelie here, Jack."

Jack followed her gaze, but obviously didn't see the minotaur Fata. "Where?"

"Dead Bird stopped everything and scratched my eye and told me Harahkte and his people are invisible."

Outside, a girl screamed.

"The pool!" Finn headed toward it with Jack at her side. They ran past Micah, who took the orchid from behind his ear and frowned at it, then raced after them.

The pool was empty, but there was a stream of red on its surface. Claudette Tredescant, wearing a ruffled white bikini, was nursing an ankle as one of the male swimmers hovered protectively near her. Red smeared her hands. She said shakily, "Did someone dump barracudas in there?"

Micah sank beside Claudette and took her hand away to discreetly reveal a bite on her ankle. He met Jack's gaze.

Finn knelt beside the pool, drawing the silver dagger she'd sheathed in a fold of her gown. As Jack hunkered down beside her, surveying the pool, Finn looked up at Claudette. "Claudette, where is your iron and silver?"

Claudette lifted one wrist jingling with a bracelet of charms and raised her foot to reveal the silver toe rings she wore.

Jack grimly met Finn's gaze. "He's found a way to make his allies immune from silver and iron charms."

"And invisible," Finn reminded him.

Jack rose. "Micah, keep everyone away from the pool."

As Claudette shepherded the other swimmers away, Finn placed a hand over her right eye and peered into the pool.

"You see anything?" Jack kept his voice low.

In the deepest part of the pool, where the water was sapphire instead of tourmaline, a dark form glided. Finn's nascent heart thumped. She winced. "There—"

A young man swept up from the water. Svelte and silver-eyed, his hair so black it had streaks of blue in it, he wore blue swim trunks and a necklace of gray pearls. Finn watched as he climbed from the pool and prowled toward a girl in brown silk speaking with three other girls. No one seemed to notice him.

No one could see him.

Finn jumped up and wove toward the kelpie, who circled the girl and her companions. She stepped in front of the kelpie and met his startled, animal gaze. "Hello," she said brightly.

The kelpie scornfully addressed her: "You're the only one who can see me, braveheart."

Finn didn't look away from him. "Jack, there's a kelpie in front of me."

The kelpie froze as Jack moved up behind him and held an iron dagger directly against the kelpie's neck. The scent of the iron made Finn feel disoriented and sick. Even though the hilt was made of mahogany, not elder wood, Jack's hand shook slightly from the effort of holding the blade.

"He can't see me?" The kelpie didn't blink. He smiled. "The iron can't hurt me now. I'm one of the Nettle King's—"

"It's still an iron blade against your neck," Finn said gently. "I bet it'll kill you if it goes through you."

The kelpie was silent, which told Finn something. She continued, "What's Harahkte's plan?"

"If I tell you, you'll order your Jack to slice that blade into my precious skin."

"It doesn't matter, Finn." Jack met Finn's gaze. "Harahkte wouldn't have told them anything."

"He's using them as a distraction," Finn said. "What is he distracting us *from*?"

"Left or right?" Jack said, forcing her to make a decision she didn't want to.

She didn't drop her gaze from the kelpie as she whispered, "I'm sorry. Left."

The iron blade cut. With a cry, the kelpie vanished in a cascade of black water and delicate bits of bone.

IT WAS A NIGHT OF POSSIBILITIES, but Christie knew the possibilities had ended for Finn. There would be no returning to mortality for her. If the world didn't end tonight, Finn would walk into the dark forever.

Concentrate, Christie told himself as he moved through the partygoers in Sun-Stone's garden. The witch blood slithered through his veins. There was already a dark scrawl of poetry on his arms and hands.

In the garden strewn with girls with flowers wreathing their hair and guys in suits oblivious to the danger among them, music blared in a tribal combo of bass and fiddle. The DJ, his white hair spiky, turned his head. His eyes gleamed silver. He was one of theirs, a friend of the nymph Aurora Sae.

Christie inclined his head to one of the Dragonfly witches and smiled at Victoria Tudor, briefly admiring the curve of her throat. Then he thought of

Phouka, and a steely resolve to win this battle made him feel confident. He glanced around at the revelers and muttered, "Goddamn idiots."

As he was admiring a pair of girls in gossamer gowns, he walked into an invisible wall.

SYLVIE HEARD HER NAME CALLED and turned, one hand on the dagger strapped beneath the nearly backless gown of black silk wrapped around her body.

Sionnach Ri the fox knight, still an unnervingly sexy version of her best friend, swept her a bow. The constellation of lights in the garden reflected off the gypsy rings in his ears beneath his auburn curls. "Sylvie Whitethorn."

"Sionn—" He wound an arm around her and pulled her close. "Oh. Okay. I thought you weren't into girls?"

"Whatever gave you that idea? Do you see that Fata over there?" He jutted his chin.

Sylvie peered into a dark corner of the garden. "No."

"That's because they've been glamoured invisible."

Sylvie reached for her cell phone, tucked away in a tiny purse, but Sionnach gently caught her wrist. "Dead Bird will tell Jack and Finn that the Unseelie are here. Don't let the enemy suspect that you know."

"How can *you* see them?"

"I'm a fox. I can see through all tricks. You're beginning to smell like crow."

"I beg your pardon?"

"What do you think the Fatas did to the Black Scissors?" Sionnach wasn't smiling now. "They called a spirit of slaughter into him to use him against their enemies. He was an *experiment*. He became a killer before he found Zen or Buddhism or whatever. Now, he can scarcely keep himself together. He's doing the same to his tribe of *Taltu*."

"William wouldn't do that to us."

"Maybe he would," Sionnach said gently. "For the greater good."

Sylvie didn't believe it. "What do we do about the Fata I can't see over there?"

"I'll show you." As the music crested into a gorgeous combination of an Irish reel and a tango, Sionnach shoved Sylvie back, caught her, pulled her close, and spun with her. He pushed her away again, keeping hold of her right hand, before graciously spinning her back to him. "You've got a blade? Straight ahead. Behind me. Lunge one step."

"Okay," she said breathlessly, letting the elder wood knife slide into her hand.

Sionnach spun. He flung her outward, still gripping one of her hands. She pointed the knife and felt it strike something like flesh and bone. As she spun away, she saw a shadow streak across her corneas.

"Ah. You only wounded her. Well, she fled." Sionnach dragged Sylvie close and grinned. "There's two more Unseelie on their way. I think they're after you. Want to keep doing this?"

An insane euphoria overwhelmed Sylvie's common sense. She grinned back. "Yes. Have you brought a few friends?"

"Of course." The fox knight twirled her, instructing her on where she should strike. The Morrigan hummed inside her head. *I'm not you,* Sylvie lashed back at the divinity. *I'm me.*

As another shadow fled beneath Sylvie's blade, Sionnach Ri lost his grip on her hand and disappeared.

Sylvie swiveled around. They had come too close to the trees bordering the garden. Only a few guests drifted past as Sylvie peered into the darkness among the trees. "Sionnach?"

HIDDEN BY THE UNNATURAL SHADOWS that he'd been dragged into, Sionnach Ri stared down at the mistletoe blade embedded in his chest. He lifted a disbelieving gaze to the cold green eyes of his murderer.

Harahkte smiled. "Farewell, lover."

"Is that what you said . . . to the Dragonfly?" Sionnach collapsed, the light leaving his eyes. In a matter of seconds, all that was left of the fox knight was a scattering of fur and autumn leaves, swirling among the guests.

And a heart-shaped onyx stone, glistening in the grass.

WEAVING THROUGH THE MASQUERADE in her sapphire blue ball gown, Lily felt as if she was falling to pieces. She was worried about Kevin, locked away in Tirnagoth with a host of Unseelie. She was worried about the Black Scissors. She was worried about her dad, who would be arriving soon. And Finn . . .

She sank against a pillar. Finn was lost. Finn was a Jill. Finn would never be human again. *Little sister* . . .

Something spun like a column of flame, or blood, in Lily's peripheral vision. As the bass music pulsing from the speakers wound down to an eerie, tinkling chime—*Swan Lake* as if performed by dozens of amplified music boxes—Lily pushed up her half mask and moved toward the creature spinning alone in a hall near the stair.

Lily drew a silver blade.

The ballerina, in a red tutu and slippers, her white skin gleaming as if it was porcelain, wasn't a Grindylow. She whirled in a graceful fouetté and extended a hand toward Lily, who dropped her knife and clasped the ballerina's hand.

What am I doing? she thought.

By the time she saw the ghastly second face on the back of the ballerina's head, it was too late and she'd already begun to dance as she'd used to before the world of night and nothing had claimed her.

CHRISTIE STEPPED BACK from the puzzling, invisible obstacle at the border of the garden. He glanced back at the revelers as the electronic music was replaced by a live band. He glimpsed Professor Fairchild dancing with golden Aurora Sae, saw Lulu the witch speaking with Nicholas Tudor. Even in their masks, he could recognize his friends and allies.

He tentatively reached out and poked at the empty space before him, definitely felt stone. He continued to explore, moving around the barrier, hoping no one was watching. His fingertips brushed invisible foliage, glass . . .

As he began to whisper, he thought of what Phouka had told him: *Ever since air was first drawn through lungs and released as speech on the tongue, language has had power.* It had always had power for him, because he had worked so hard for it. The magic in his blood made his stomach grind as if he'd swallowed nettles. It was never easy. Driven by his voice and the words unpeeling from his skin and into the air, a torrent of blossoms and milkweed tufts swept around the invisible bulk of what seemed to be a large house . . .

Is that Sombrus? Terror shot through him. He had to warn Finn and Jack—

Giselle the Jill, in brown silk and a gilt deer mask, materialized out of the night and rammed a small, curved dagger into his chest. Christie staggered against the invisible wall, slid down, watched as she swung around and wove through the revelers.

Shock prevented him from moving for a minute. He felt blood trickle down his chest. With shaking hands, he undid his blazer and pulled Phouka's ivory book from the inner pocket. It had shielded his heart from the blade—driven through the book, only the dagger's tip had punctured his skin.

"Mr. Hart!" Professor Fairchild and Aurora Sae ran to him. Fairchild knelt and quickly examined the tear in Christie's shirt, the small cut.

"It's her heart." Christie's voice cracked as he thought of the girl with the auburn hair who had once been the queen of England. He stared down at the ivory book he gripped in both hands. "I stole Phouka's heart."

He jumped up. Fairchild and Aurora Sae rose with him, clearly bewildered by his behavior. Christie smacked a hand against the invisible wall. "Sombrus is *here*. It's invisible. We have to tell Finn and Jack."

Aurora Sae vanished into a tiny swarm of honey bees and spiraled away.

"She'll warn Finn and Jack." Edmund Fairchild set a hand on Christie's shoulder. "You've got an assignment out here and, I believe, a Jill to track down."

Still stunned by Aurora Sae's transformation, Christie glimpsed a silver dagger engraved with symbols strapped beneath the professor's blazer. "Help me find the Jill?" Christie asked.

"I'd be happy to."

"So." Christie tenderly slid Phouka's ivory book back into his blazer pocket. "What kind of Fata did you kill in your youth?"

"IT'S WRONG. The whole house is off center from the grounds. How could anyone not notice?" Finn stood with Jack in the center of SunStone's grand hall as revelers drifted around them. To the south was the ballroom, with the French doors leading into the garden and the pool. To the north was the entrance, the doors flung wide and manned by Mr. Wyatt.

"Who in their right mind would think an entire house would move?" Jack touched a pillar as if expecting it to give way beneath his fingers. He met Finn's gaze.

"It *is* Sombrus," she whispered.

Jack looked at her, grim, and marveling at the same time. "I didn't think Harahkte could do it. I didn't think he had that much power over Sombrus, to disguise it as SunStone. The real SunStone must be right next door, hidden in its proper place. You were right."

"We've got to get everyone *out*." Finn raised one hand. For now, she was glad she wasn't human.

Aubrey and Darling Ivy, who had been waiting for her signal, wove toward their respective assignments. Aubrey, elegant in Prada, jumped up onto the platform with the DJ. Shoving back his gilt half mask, he spoke into the mic, his voice reverberating. "Ladies and gentlemen, please join us in the garden for live music from some of your favorite local bands." One of those local bands included Jack's vagabonds, fronted by Farouche the ganconer and Darling Ivy the *ban sidhe*, an irresistible combination.

As music swept in from outside—the pulse of drums and the tricky fiddle accompanied by Darling Ivy's primitive howl—the crowd began moving into the garden. Professors Wyatt and Perangelo walked toward Finn and Jack. "Are you sure?" Wyatt said softly.

"Keep them safe." The alchemy of marigolds inside Finn rustled, an army of flowers. Harahkte had meant to hurt her by turning her into a Jill; he had only made her stronger. "And watch over Lily."

As Wyatt and Perangelo strode into the garden, Finn and Jack turned to face the entrance. The ballroom had emptied. Jack's hands were at his sides, prepared to reach for the blades he'd hidden in his clothes. Finn only had Eve Avaline's silver dagger. If things worked out as she hoped they would, that should be all she'd need.

She didn't reach for Jack's hand, nor he for hers. But she wanted him, and the sharp desire sent memories of his body and his lush kisses through her like an elixir. When he met her gaze, she saw that same desire reflected in his eyes. He was more than a lover. He was a friend. He was a comrade in arms. *And who thinks of her boyfriend that way?* she wondered.

A figure in a hooded jacket entered SunStone, the shadows that followed him becoming young men and women in sleek clothing, their faces painted with neon colors to resemble Day-of-the-Dead skulls. Their leader, the hilt of a familiar sword rising from the scabbard strapped over one shoulder, drew back his hood, revealing a skull mask of gold and ivory filigree.

Finn said calmly, "You don't need the mask, Harahkte. I know who you are."

SYLVIE PUSHED THROUGH THE DANCING CROWD. "Sionnach!" She cursed her short stature as she scanned the masked dancers for her martial partner. When she thought she saw a fox-knight-shaped silhouette, she stepped forward.

"Sylvie Whitethorn?"

She turned, an iron cross in one hand and the elder wood dagger in the other. A pale young man with ropy muscles, serpentine tattoos, and metal snakes twisted up into his black hair smiled at her. She met his silver-glinting gaze and saw the red line, like a crack in ice over fire, in his left eye. *Unseelie.*

"Heart widow." He bowed gracefully. "May I have this dance?"

"No thanks."

His ice and fire gaze drifted toward Victoria Tudor and a boy with red hair who was in Sylvie's drama course. "Perhaps I'll dance with one of *them.*"

Sylvie sheathed the dagger and tucked the iron cross into her bodice. She hoped the dark Fata didn't notice the tremor in her hands. "Okay. Let's dance."

Triumphant, the Unseelie closed his hands around hers. His silver nails pricked her wrists. As the music of Darling Ivy was replaced by a wilder band, the Unseelie twisted Sylvie around, violently. Those silver nails began to cut into her skin.

Sylvie jerked her knee up—when they were flesh and blood, a Fata's anatomy was the same as a human's. The Unseelie sank to the ground, choking. As Sylvie raised her dagger, he lifted something his hand had fallen on, a black, gleaming stone. He said, "*Fox heart?*"

Sylvie stepped back, astonished, as he crumbled into scales of flaky skin that drifted away in a web of shadow. Her heart rocketing, she reached down and picked up the obsidian stone that had destroyed the Unseelie.

She bowed her head when she recognized it as Sionnach Ri's heart, which she had once stolen.

FINN WATCHED AS HARAHKTE REMOVED THE SKULL MASK. The dancing lights cut across the severe angles of his face, the green eyes ghosted to razor silver.

"I didn't think," he said as his Jacks and Jills moved past him, toward the children in the garden, "it would take you long to figure out this was Sombrus. And don't think you can pin it with elder wood and send it into the void—I've fixed that design flaw."

"Look at you and your playmates." Jack spoke with that false, prowling lightness that meant he was sliding into his old, dangerous habits. "All tarted up like angels of the apocalypse."

"Apocalypse. That's the plan." Harahkte didn't take his gaze from Finn.

As Harahkte moved toward them, the glamour began to peel away from their surroundings, revealing decaying walls and broken glass, slashes of moonlight through the Gothic, lichen-stained windows of a mansion gone to seed. The marble pillars in the hall resembled trees. The stairway's balustrades were serpents carved from ebony. The stained-glass window at the top was an arch of fiery red and orange depicting a terrible and beautiful face with horns and writhing hair. They stood in the wreckage of Sombrus, the House of the Wolf and the Snake.

Caliban slid from the gloom to lay a curved knife against Finn's throat. "Aren't they pretty together?" Caliban set his chin on Finn's shoulder as he addressed Harahkte. "When we're done, you should stuff them and put them on display in your parlor."

Jack stood very still, his expression cold, merciless.

"*Crom cu.*" Harahkte didn't take his gaze from Finn. "Not her."

Caliban whirled and plunged the knife into Jack's heart. Jack fell to one knee, stunned.

Finn dove toward him. Harahkte caught her and pulled her back. "It's steel, not silver. He won't die yet."

Gently pushing Finn against a wall, Harahkte hunkered down before Jack. "I need you."

Jack wrapped one hand around the hilt of the dagger in his chest. He laughed, choked. Blood slid from the corner of his mouth. "I'm flattered, but you're not my type."

Harahkte gestured toward the dagger. "I need you to cut the key out of your skin, Jack. Only you can do it. If anyone else tries, it will fade."

Jack showed his teeth as he yanked the dagger out and pushed open his shirt to reveal the black key tattoo. He smiled despite his pain. "I figure, knowing

Reiko, this key is connected to the seven houses of the blessed. You get this, you get to open every Way in Fair Hollow—all seven of those abandoned mansions become open portals to the Ghostlands. No more restricted access. And it's Midsummer Eve, a perfect night for opening uncontrolled portals into the otherworld."

"Give me that key, Jack." Harahkte's voice was soft. When Jack didn't answer, Harahkte rose and turned toward Finn.

"You won't hurt her," Jack said with quiet conviction. "Because you don't want to be alone again."

A muscle moved in Harahkte's jaw, the merest hint of a flinch. Finn felt a tiny flicker of hope. Then Harahkte said, "I've got Lily Rose."

Finn stepped toward him and managed to keep her voice steady. "Leave Lily out of this."

"Your sister took her own life," Harahkte continued relentlessly. "She was a shade in the Wolf's house. Lot stole her as she was on the verge of death. She died when you took her out of the Ghostlands, and became a half thing, caught here. Jack took her place in Annwyn so that she might remain." Harahkte gently slid the knife of truth into her. "Now she is a gateway for the dead to enter the world."

Finn sank down against a pillar, folding her arms over her head. *Lily isn't dead. Lot made it look like she died. Lily didn't kill herself. She isn't dead. She isn't—*

"Harahkte." The quiet fury in Jack's voice made the name a snarl. "I'll give you your goddamn key."

Finn jerked her head up. Jack gripped Caliban's dagger. His face white and eyes ghosting, he began to cut around the tattoo on his chest.

Finn leaped up. Caliban knotted a hand in her hair and shoved her back. She fell against a pillar.

"I said not to hurt her, dog." Harahkte whipped a dagger at Caliban, who dodged it.

"*You, too?*" Caliban bared his teeth. "What *is* it with her? Has she got ganconer blood? She's making you *bleed*, Harahkte. She's making you *weak*. Instead of preserving her, you should cut her to pieces—"

A black key with art nouveau flourishes clanked against the floor and gleamed bloodily at Finn's feet. Finn and Harahkte looked down at it.

A buzzing noise made Finn glance up. A swarm of bees was spiraling downward. She stared at it and thought she heard Aurora Sae's voice: *Follow me.*

A shadow appeared behind Caliban and stabbed a dagger into the *crom cu's* neck. As Caliban fell, Finn met Jack Daw's gaze. Jack Daw, still holding the dagger, lunged at Harahkte. They collided. As they struggled, *her* Jack shouted, "Now, Finn!"

Harahkte slashed a knife across Jack Daw's throat and the doppelgänger came apart in shadowy tendrils. His dagger slid across the floor, to her Jack's hand. When Finn saw her Jack glide to his feet, she snatched up the key. She cried, "Harahkte!"

As Harahkte turned, Finn ran.

ANNA WEAVER DIDN'T FEEL SCARED. She sat in the backseat of Mr. Sullivan's SUV and watched as SunStone came into view. But it wasn't SunStone—Finn had told her that Harahkte would try to trick them. It was Sombrus.

As Sean Sullivan swerved the SUV onto the front lawn, he met Jane Emory's gaze, and they looked over their shoulders at Anna Weaver. Sean said, "I'd like to object to the plan once again."

"Sean," Jane gently reminded him, "Finn told you there isn't any other way."

"I need to do this alone," Anna said. She climbed out of the SUV, clutching the geisha compact that contained Absalom. She ran across the lawn.

A tall woman in a black gown appeared, her three-faced head slowly spinning. Anna halted like a deer in headlights and waited until the Unseelie creature had vanished around a corner of the house.

Then she dashed up the stairs. She knelt down before the doors and opened the compact, gazing at the flame in the mirror. "Rules keep you in shape. Remember? What's your first rule? Never harm the innocent. And your second one? Don't lose yourself."

She stood up. She dropped the compact mirror on the stone stairs and smashed it beneath one foot. Tiny flames unwound from the broken glass, lengthening, becoming streamers of radiance that spiraled upward in trails of colorful fire, becoming . . .

"Oh." Anna looked up in awe at Absalom's true form. "So *that's* what you are."

❖ ❖ ❖

SEAN SULLIVAN DUCKED OUT OF THE SUV and headed toward the party behind the house. Jane followed him. "Sean . . ."

"I'm going to find my daughters."

Fireworks burst up around SunStone. Sean and Jane stumbled back.

"Those aren't fireworks," Jane whispered.

CHRISTIE AND FAIRCHILD HALTED as multicolored lights in the fiery shape of something that looked unnervingly like a dragon swept up over SunStone and burst into tiny orbs. A sound like a gargantuan clockwork mechanism made the air shudder, followed by a humming vibration that could be felt in the bones. A drop of blood trickled from one of Christie's nostrils.

SunStone wavered.

"It's Sombrus." Christie's heart dropped into a pool of ice. "The *invisible* house was SunStone. *That's* Sombrus. The one they're in!"

He and Fairchild began to run.

AS LILY SPUN THROUGH THE GARDEN with the red ballerina, the glory of dancing was replaced by pain and panic. She felt as if her legs might shatter. She couldn't think of any heka with which to break the Unseelie's spell—the enchantment had hijacked her brain.

Another figure in red drifted up to them, shoved Lily aside, and grabbed the Fata ballerina's hand. Freed from the spell, Lily hit the ground, rolled up, and saw Devon Valentine, in his theatrical crimson, whirling with the two-faced ballerina.

Lily unsheathed the elder wood knife from behind her back, but couldn't get a clear stab at the Unseelie ballerina. As she watched, Devon Valentine and the ballerina began to unravel. Scarlet ribbons splashed the air with red.

Lily closed her eyes.

When she opened them, both Valentine and the Unseelie ballerina were gone. Red ribbons drifted, fading in the night.

Fireworks exploded over SunStone.

"*Finn* . . ." Lily began to run.

❖ ❖ ❖

WHEN SYLVIE SAW THE MONSTROUS, incandescent flames enveloping SunStone, she began running toward the house.

A girl in a deer mask stepped in her way. Sylvie recoiled.

Giselle the Jill removed the mask. She had crowned herself with daffodils. Her face was painted like a Day-of-the-Dead skull.

"I don't want to fight you," Sylvie said lamely.

"Oh, we're not going to fight." Giselle stalked toward her. Sylvie reached for the dagger sheathed beneath her gown. Giselle smiled adorably. "I've stabbed the boy witch in the heart."

"*What?*" Sylvie didn't believe it. *Christie . . .*

Giselle leaped. Sylvie inhaled a scream as the point of the Jill's dagger halted an inch away from her left eye.

Then Giselle's perfect skin fissured. Her mouth opened in a scream that she never voiced. Yellow petals drifted from her lips, the cracks in her skin. Shocked, Sylvie watched as Giselle crumbled, her flesh shattering, daffodils and vines squirming outward.

Sylvie slowly lifted her gaze to Aubrey, who dropped the elder wood blade with which he'd stabbed the Jill. Teeth gritted, he said, "Are you okay?"

Sylvie's eyes stung. "She got Christie."

"I just saw him running toward SunStone, so, no, she didn't."

Sylvie almost broke down, hearing that. "He's okay, then?"

"He was running, so . . . I've never killed anything before." Looking sick, Aubrey gazed down at the crumbled bits of Jill, then around at the deserted part of the garden in which they stood. The live music sounded distant.

Sylvie walked to him and gazed at him searchingly. "You haven't heard voices or seen war deities in your head, have you?"

"What are you *talking* about?"

"Never mind. Come on." She began moving toward the crowd and SunStone. The weird fireworks had stopped. "Something's going on."

"Hey." Aubrey strode beside her. "Since I kind of rescued you, can I get a thank-you kiss?"

"If we survive this," Sylvie promised, seeing Aubrey in a whole new light, "you'll get more than a kiss."

AS FINN RAN, following the bees that she hoped were Aurora Sae, she heard a massive clockwork sound throughout Sombrus. The walls bent inward. *It's happening.* She rounded a corner, dashed into the entrance hall—

—the doors slammed closed before her. The windows blackened.

Finn ran to the doors, attempted to yank them open.

The bees swept through the keyhole.

Harahkte came around the corner. "Give me the key," he said idly.

Finn turned, pressing back against the doors. "I don't have it. *Where is Jack?*"

He came closer, his eyes intensely green. "Jack is still alive. The key, Finn."

"So that you can let the Ghostlands flood the true world? No."

"Why not?" He came close, his gaze holding hers. "Why not, Finn? What do you love about this fucking world?"

"What do you *hate* about it?" As soon as she asked the question, she regretted it.

Harahkte gripped her wrists and dragged her in for a savage kiss. Realizing his true intentions, she fought—

But her brain was jolted by an image of a boy with a dirty face standing in the snow, watching a tribe of people in stitched animal skins leading reindeer away, abandoning him because he was cursed. She saw him running through a forest as men chased him, shouting. She saw him hanged in a plaza. She saw him clawing his way from ashes and charred logs. Rising from a river and ripping ropes weighted with stones from his wrists. Dragging himself across a marble floor, bullet wounds like holes in his skin . . . Dozens of lifetimes spent running and reassembling himself because he couldn't die—

He released her and she stumbled back and sank to the floor.

"You see why I want this?" He crouched before her. "This world tried to break me. It took away your mother. Your sister. So let's make a different one, one that your sister can live in without her needing to be destroyed. Do this, Finn." He gripped one of her hands. "For Lily."

And she did think about it. She saw the houses of the blessed become glowing ghost palaces that birthed the marvels and magic of the Ghostlands. And the horrors. She thought of a world creeping with Fata beauty, a place where death wasn't a certainty.

"You're not the same Harahkte," she said, keeping her voice steady. "You have his memories, that's all. And you *do* remember being Moth. Are you going to hurt me to get that key? You cut me open and filled me with evil flowers, remember? So, go ahead, hurt me to find that key. But I won't *give* it to you."

His angel-cold expression fractured a little then. A muscle in his jaw twitched as he rose. Then the ice returned and he said, "I don't have to touch you to hurt you. I only have to rip pieces off of Jack. We'll go back to him, shall we? And you'll tell me where that bloody key is."

Finn's heart wrenched and she realized, in the end, she'd tell him where the key was.

A mass of shadows gathered behind Harahkte and became hundreds of large, black moths that swept toward Finn. She flung her arms up over her face as the moths descended and Harahkte strode toward her.

The doors behind her opened. She fell back, out of Sombrus, into the arms of her sister and Aurora Sae. She saw a wall of moths before her.

When Harahkte surged from the moths in the doorway, Lily slashed at him with an elder wood blade. With a hard smile, he unsheathed the jackal-hilted sword.

He was yanked into Sombrus by Jack, who met Finn's gaze. Almost swooning with relief and joy, Finn pushed from her sister and gripped the door frame. "Jack!"

Jack, blocking the silver blade Harahkte cut toward him, looked at her and smiled.

"Finn!" Sylvie and Christie had arrived. As Lily attempted to break Finn's grip on the door frame, Sylvie and Christie tried to help pull Finn away.

"No!" Finn yelled. "Lily, tell Anna to stop Absalom! *Stop him!*"

"It's too late." Lily's voice was ragged. Finn saw Sombrus shimmer with otherworldly flames.

Jack smashed Harahkte into a pillar. As Harahkte staggered, Jack said, his words reaching Finn, "*I'll find you.*"

The doors slammed shut between them.

As Sombrus began to waver, Lily dragged Finn away. There was another massive clockwork sound. The net of flames settled over Sombrus's walls and the house began to fold in on itself.

Then it was gone. Pale ashes—the remains of the moths that had attacked Finn—drifted around her like strange snow.

AS THE DOORS TO SOMBRUS CLOSED, Jack spun on Harahkte and cut toward him with Jack Daw's dagger. Harahkte twisted out of range, lunged, cut upward with his sword. Jack stumbled, and Harahkte's blade slid beneath his arm. Jack staggered, felt blood stream from him as the blade withdrew.

Harahkte didn't smile.

Hundreds of scarlet and black butterflies burst from a nearby corridor and swarmed over Jack, forcing his silver-shocked body to come apart and ride the shadow with them.

CHRISTIE WATCHED SOMBRUS CRUMPLE like a toy house in a giant's fist and disappear in a whirlpool of blue, green, and white fire. A warm wind swept over the astonished revelers as the real SunStone Mansion, divested of its invisibility, emerged from the night.

Christie looked away from Finn to see Harahkte's Jacks and Jills beginning to slink away, their Day-Glo Day-of-the-Dead faces vanishing into the darkness.

Then he saw the shimmering wave sweeping toward them. *Magic*, he thought before he dropped.

SYLVIE WATCHED THE UNSEELIE, visible now, vanish into the shadows. A breeze drifted over her, fragrant with enchantment. She began a warning. "Finn—"

Then Sylvie crumpled to the lawn with everyone else.

SEAN SULLIVAN SAW THE HOUSE fold in on itself. When the spell began to emanate outward, striking down everyone in its wake, he heard Jane cry his name. He fought the sleep, forging onward, before he, too, succumbed.

A STORM OF GLOWING LIGHTS, vaguely serpentine, descended on the boarded-up Tirnagoth Hotel and kissed it awake, restoring its antique art nouveau glamour until it shone from within. The front doors fell open. A figure made of flames stepped out and cooled into the alabaster form of a fiery-haired youth.

"Well." Absalom's smile shone as he brushed debris from his clothes. "That was bracing. Those Unseelie put up quite a fight."

The Black Scissors and Murray, battered and alive, hauling Kevin Gilchriste between them, emerged from Tirnagoth. A host of grateful Fatas followed. As Phouka and the queen of the Blackhearts moved from the shadows, the Black Scissors glanced at Kevin Gilchriste's expensive watch, then met Phouka's gaze. "Half an hour until midnight."

"Not much time then." Fatigued, scarcely holding herself together, Phouka, with the Blackheart Queen, rode the shadows toward SunStone.

CHAPTER 26

We should be hidden from their eyes
Being but holy shows
And bodies broken like a thorn
Where on the black North wind blows.

—"His Memories," W. B. Yeats

The electrical charge in the air made Finn's hair crackle. As everyone dropped around her, Finn spun around to find that her sister had become a creature of briars and shadows. And she remembered what Harahkte had offered her, what she had refused. Her voice broke. "Lily. You're stronger than this."

The briars and shadows fell away from Lily, who glanced around uncertainly.

"Goddamn magic." Lily tilted her chin up. But her eyes were sad, and Finn turned to see what she was looking at.

Ankou was moving toward them through the sleeping revelers. Death's lieutenant had come as a young man, in tattooed skin, a top hat, and striped trousers. The walking stick he carried had a grip decorated with a small, crimson skull. He halted before them, his gaze alien and somber, and extended one hand toward Lily. Gently, like a lover, he said, "It is time, Lily Rose."

"No." Finn felt the world spinning apart around her. "You can't."

"If you do not come with me, Lily Rose," Ankou continued, "all that you love will decay around you. You are not meant to be here, in the realm of the living. If you remain, the dead will infect this world."

"Well." Lily turned to Finn with a brave, tear-bright smile. "At least we figured out how to save the world."

A dark determination swept through Finn. She kept her voice low. "Lily, we can—"

Lily gripped both of Finn's hands. "I took myself out of the world. *I* did it. Not the Fatas. Not Lot. I didn't want to be here anymore." Her voice was strong and proud. "I'm so, so sorry."

Finn felt as if claws were tearing her voice away. "We can run. We can go back to the Ghostlands. We can—"

"*Lily Rose.*" Ankou's disguise crumbled and he became a writhing darkness that breathed a glacial stillness and seemed to leech the world of color.

"No," Finn said. "*You will not take her.*"

The darkness drifted away. A beautiful woman with one gold streak in her black hair stood where Ankou had been. "You never did follow the rules, Serafina."

Finn felt everything around her tilt. She shouldn't have been able to shed tears because of what she was, but they swept down her face, tasting of salt and life. "*Mom?*"

Lily echoed her, her voice barely audible.

Daisy Sullivan, her gown the dark blue of a summer's night, stepped forward and folded her daughters against her. She was as warm and strong as she'd been when they'd been children. Her familiar ginger perfume caused an ache all through Finn. "Mom . . ."

"Serafina, honey." Daisy spoke gently into her hair. "It's time to let Lily go." She stepped back, her face serious. "You know that."

Finn's grip tightened even as she felt her sister's hands growing faint in her own. Their mother wouldn't be so cruel, wouldn't *take* Lily.

"Finn, it's okay." Lily glanced at Daisy Sullivan, who was watching them, one hand over her mouth, her eyes dark with anguish.

"Mom . . ." Finn looked pleadingly at their mother, whose gentle expression said everything that needn't be said. All that Finn had been through, all that she had *done* . . .

Even as her mother's lips brushed her forehead in a phantom kiss that made Finn's throat constrict, she couldn't let go.

Lily whispered, "Tell Dad I love him and I'm sorry. I'm so sorry, Finn. Please . . . let me go."

Finn felt her mother's fading hand caress her hair. Desperately, she said to Lily, "Pinkie swear I'll see you again."

Lily grinned, her eyes glimmering. She twined her pinkie with Finn's. "See you later, alligator."

Finn sobbed once. And let go.

FINN LAY IN THE GRASS with a starry sky above her. Tiny lights winked around her. A radiant girl with auburn hair and a crown of stars on her brow was plucking marigolds from within Finn's chest. Kneeling on her other side, a girl with the wise eyes of a serpent, the face of a young queen, and gentle hands drew the shadows from Finn's body. A third girl, an elegant white creature, her gown whispering like falling snow, was carefully setting Finn's heart back into its place.

FINN RETURNED TO THE WORLD to find her dad gazing anxiously down at her with red-rimmed eyes. Her heart was a startling racket after its absence. She inhaled, choked, felt pain and chill and utter loss. She was mortal again.

"Da . . ." She sobbed. "Mom . . . Lily . . ."

"I know." He gathered her into his arms. "I saw them just as I woke. I saw them."

DEATH HAD COME AND GONE. His spell shattered.

Sylvie scrambled up and stared around at the bewildered revelers, at the darkened, abandoned SunStone. Beside her, Christie groaned and staggered to his feet. He said, "Is it over? Where is Finn?"

Someone shouted, "Okay—who spiked the punch? Where's Askew?"

Sylvie saw Anna Weaver seated on the steps of SunStone, speaking with Professor Fairchild. Charlotte Perangelo was weaving through the crowds with Aubrey Drake and Darling Ivy. Micah stood near the remaining blessed, none of whom looked happy. *Are we all alive?* Sylvie wondered.

"Finn," Sylvie whispered just as Christie echoed the name and began running. Sylvie raced after him, toward the part of the garden where Sombrus had stood.

It was Sean Sullivan and Jane Emory who met them. Jane said quietly, "Finn needs a little time by herself."

Dread made Sylvie's hands icy. "Lily?"

Finn's dad sank down onto a stone bench. "Lily is gone." His voice was raw.

Christie looked devastated. "No . . ."

"What about Jack?" Sylvie asked, an ache in her throat. "He was in Sombrus with Harahkte and Caliban when Absalom sent it into the void."

"Jack's not here." Sean Sullivan put his head in his hands.

Sylvie looked past Jane and Sean, to where Finn stood gazing up at hundreds of orbs spiraling in the sky, the remnants, Sylvie realized, of all those shades trapped in Sombrus. Even from here, Sylvie could see that Finn was no longer a Jill, only a mortal girl.

CHAPTER 27

. . . And her eyes
They had not their own lustre, but the look
Which is not of the earth; she was become
The queen of a fantastic realm

—"The Dream," Lord Byron

Finn sat on the front steps of her house, watching Sunday morning progress on the street. She ached as if she'd been taken apart and put together again. She'd dreamed of Jack and Lily last night, the three of them sitting in a garden, the sun kissing their skin.

The screen door clattered. As her da settled on the step beside her, he handed her a bottle of root beer. There was a weary sorrow in his eyes. She laid her head on his shoulder and they sat in silence.

CHRISTIE AND SYLVIE CAME TO VISIT and found Finn on the swing set. Sylvie's eyes were bloodshot, as if she'd been crying. Christie was somber.

"I'm fine. Really." Finn couldn't talk about Lily. Or Jack.

Christie handed her a parchment envelope. Finn reluctantly drew out an ivory card that read in elegant gold script:

To the heroes. You're invited to the
After a Midsummer Night's Dream. Revel.

Sylvie, gripping the chains of the swing, told her, "We're going."

Finn returned the invitation to Christie. "I'm not."

THAT EVENING, Finn was carefully packing up Lily's room when she heard a sound from the open window.

When she saw who crouched on the sill, she wanted to shove him off it. "Absalom."

He sat there in jeans and a T-shirt with a surfboarding dragon on it. "Do you know what I was thinking about tonight?"

Finn angrily taped up a box. "How much everyone despises you?"

"Oh, that's not unusual." He shrugged. "I was trying to remember why we built Drake's Chapel. I mean, it was meant to catch the ultimate evil, but we've done away with three ultimate evils and never used it. So what's it for?"

"Moth wasn't an 'ultimate evil.' He was my friend."

"Yes. He was." Absalom tilted his head to one side. "Harahkte wasn't. When you first found the moth key, when you first found him, *Harahkte* could have awakened at that moment. But it was Moth who emerged from the Black Scissors's enchantment. *You* drew out Moth." He turned and gazed out into the night. "I wonder what's happening in Sombrus now?"

And he was gone, leaving Finn gazing at the stars and thinking about Jack trapped in Sombrus with Caliban and Harahkte.

SHE SELECTED HER PRETTIEST SUNDRESS of gossamer-gray silk, but chunky boots suitable for a hike. She drove Lily's car to the dirt road leading to Drake's Chapel and trudged up the trail with her electric lantern.

Drake's Chapel was as eerie as she remembered, its doorway a gaping hole beneath the dragon ship carving. As she stepped in, her lantern's light danced over the graffiti on the walls—stylized drawings of wolves and a serpent-bodied woman, of moths and butterflies and a black figure with a skull for a head. She whispered to the chapel, "Why *did* the Fatas have you built?"

She dropped to her knees on the floor and began sweeping away the debris of leaves, insect shells, and dirt. A spiral, an ouroboros, had been carved into the floor. When she touched it, it hummed beneath her hand.

It was a Way.

She rose and took from around her neck the pendant Jack had given her, the one with the lions clasping a heart. She'd once bound Jack to her with the ring that matched this pendant. He still wore that ring. She closed her eyes and whispered, "Thee to me. Thee to me. To this circle I call thee, by the ring with which I once bound thee."

Her lantern flickered out. The spiral in the floor lit up as if hundreds of fireflies had flown into the grooves beneath her feet. Power surged through the air. Finn went momentarily deaf.

When she opened her eyes, Harahkte stood before her, his face shadowed by the hood of his jacket. He wore the ring of lions-clasping-a-heart on his hand. Finn felt shattered when she saw that ring. She had hoped . . . she steeled herself and lifted her chin.

"Well." His mouth curled when he saw the silver dagger she held. "I'd say this is a surprise, but it isn't."

Finn's newly restored humanity curled in on itself when she met his ice-green gaze. "Where's Jack?"

"Drowned in his own blood."

Her heart twisted. "I don't believe you."

"You called on whoever wore this." He lifted his hand. Jack's ring gleamed. Harahkte's smile was white and cruel, and rage curled beneath his words. "Tell me where you hid that key in Sombrus."

"Somewhere *you'll* never find it."

He reached out and gripped her jaw so hard she thought it might break. "I've got nothing to lose, Finn."

"That's right. You've got nothing to lose, because you never *had* anything. You're immortal. You never lived a real life. You used people, and they left you or tried to kill you. And *you* want to end the world."

He leaned close to her, bent his head. "You made me *weak*. You made me *bleed*. And now we're alone."

"No, we're not." She felt as calm and still as a hunter. "There are *three* of us in this circle. Remember this?" She drew from her wrist Lily's charm bracelet. She caught his hand—scornful, he allowed it—and clasped the bracelet around his wrist. "It was the beginning." Then she stood on tiptoe and kissed him as if she were kissing Moth good-bye, sweetly and with a longing for something that would never be.

It caught him off guard.

She dropped the silver dagger. She stepped out of the circle.

Harahkte lunged. He struck an invisible barrier.

Finn continued, her voice cold with resolve, "A summoning circle, Jack told me, is controlled by the one who makes it. That would be me."

Harahkte bashed against the barrier again. The spiral beneath his feet turned a glimmering green.

"There are two of you in that circle now, Harahkte."

Harahkte laughed bitterly, his head down. "I should have killed you." He raised his head and his eyes, the green of toxic chemicals, shaded to summer emerald. The transformation was abrupt and achingly familiar.

"*Finn.*" Moth inhaled sharply, and she made a sound in her throat as if she'd been stabbed. He looked down, saw the silver dagger, and glanced back up at her. She didn't say anything. She watched him realize what she meant him to do. Agony twisted through her.

He bent down and picked up the silver dagger. "He can't die," Moth told her and there was strength in his voice. "But *I* can. With me, this body becomes breakable. I make it so."

"Moth . . ." Finn didn't move.

His head down, Moth pushed the silver blade into his heart. He dropped to his knees, his hair falling over his face. And then he burst into hundreds of white moths, the light that reflected from their gossamer wings mimicking the glimmer of tears on Finn's face. As the moths scattered, Sombrus's great hall, abandoned and crumbling, was superimposed over Drake's Chapel. Sombrus was caught, snared by the chapel that had been created by the Fatas hundreds of years ago, specifically for that purpose—to trap a dangerous magical house that was not a house.

Finn turned to follow one remaining moth down a Sombrus hallway overgrown with ivy and brambles. She *hoped* . . .

She found Jack, what remained of him, in the courtyard, his body discarded in a tangle of nettles. She sank beside him. She touched the hand missing the ring finger and her heart died. Harahkte had cut the ring from him.

She curled beside Jack's body.

IT SEEMED YEARS before Finn was able to rise and walk out of Sombrus, bereft of almost everything that had made her feel human. She left Lily's car because she couldn't drive in the state she was in. The walk to Tirnagoth was an hour of mindless despair that passed in a moment. Her throat ached. Her eyes stung. Her heart was ashes.

The sweet sounds and spinning lights of a revel led her up the broken road, past the tree with Jack and Eve Avaline's initials carved into it, past the creeper-veiled gates of Tirnagoth. As she moved toward the hotel, its art nouveau beauty struck her. She folded to her knees before it. Hating it.

"Finn."

She lifted her head. Phouka Banríon, in a dress of bronze silk and calf-high boots, was walking toward her, looking every bit the queen. Her auburn hair spilled over her shoulders from a tiny crown of stars.

She wore an almost human look of pity. "I felt Drake's Chapel awaken. Sombrus is held. You've lost him."

Finn whispered, "I tried to save Lily and Jack. I lost them both."

Phouka crouched before her. "Do you know why Absalom is so protective of Anna Weaver?"

Finn wanted to curl into a ball in the grass. "Why are you telling me—"

"Anna has been chosen to be a queen over the Fatas in this country."

Finn couldn't have heard correctly . . . "A queen. A *Fata* queen. No. You *can't* . . ."

"The Blackhearts insist on a monarch for our outlaw kind, here. Anna is a changeling." Phouka's ruthless tone softened. "She was meant for it. She is one of us."

"A changeling . . ." Finn rose. "What will happen to her?"

"She'll live until she's sixteen. Then she'll die and become one of us."

"*No.*"

"Memory to us is a curse and a blessing. Kings and queens keep those memories, those souls. Anna will keep the memories of Reiko's court, and rule them, and prevent the court from doing any more harm."

"Why? The Fatas didn't take *you* until—"

"I was human. I made a bargain with them. Anna is, technically, a Fata made flesh. Like the Dragonfly and Sionnach."

"You can't do that to her." Finn pictured Anna, cold and undead, doll-like on a throne, while teethy, clawed things knelt or bowed before her. "And 'made flesh'? Are any of you even blood, skin, and bone? Or just bundles of ectoplasm?"

"Some changelings," Phouka said quietly, "can become mortal if they love enough. Some of us once *were* mortal. Some never were. And others, the rare successes, have *become* mortal. A human chosen by us would have a choice. A human would be able to bargain with us." Phouka hesitated, then continued, "A mortal would live an entire life span until a natural death at a respectable age. Then we would come for her and make her a queen."

Finn felt everything settle into place, a numb serenity that was almost bliss. "I'll do it."

Phouka said gently, "A bargain made with us cannot be unmade."

"You think I can't rule them?" Finn was reckless with anguish. She could see that, in the life before her, she'd be content, even happy, before becoming a queen of shadows. And Anna would get to live the life she deserved, not knowing what she truly was.

"It's no easy thing you're agreeing to. You'll age, Finn. At the time of your death as an elderly mortal, we'll come for you and make you one of us. Then you'll serve until another queen or king arises. You'll be alone, immortal."

"But I'll always be who I am. Let Anna be mortal. Don't take that away from her. Please."

Phouka looked thoughtful. "When you bargained with the four elementals to enter Annwyn . . . did they ever give you anything in return?"

"No. They refused."

"Well then." Phouka smiled. "They owe you something."

JACK HAD LOST A LOT OF BLOOD while fighting Harahkte. As he staggered through Sombrus's corridors, he slid in and out of awareness. Without any infusions of Fata magic, his body was dying, the roses inside of him curling and blackening as they had not had time to do when he'd removed his own heart on Halloween night.

After he'd descended into shadows with the butterflies, he'd awakened on the floor of another chamber with Jack Daw gazing down at him. Naked and shivering with silver shock, Jack had laughed at his double. "Just because you're wearing my clothes and you've got my ring doesn't mean she'll love you."

"We'll see." And Jack Daw had left.

After a period of profanities and struggle, Jack had put on Jack Daw's sloughed clothing. Shoving the drapes from a window, he'd realized Sombrus wasn't in the void anymore. He saw familiar-looking woods and the lights of Fair Hollow in the distance.

JACK FOUND HIS DOPPELGÄNGER DEAD in a thicket of blood-red roses and thorns. Shaking with pain, he dropped to his knees beside the corpse of his past and experienced a surreal moment of mourning.

Then he saw the black key hanging on a chain around Jack Daw's neck. Finn had flung that false key away during her escape, and this cunning, desperate version of himself had found it—and Harahkte had found *him*.

Jack checked the wound he'd made in his own chest. It had healed before Harahkte had hurt him so badly. The tattoo of the key was back. It had all been sleight of hand . . . Jack pretending to gouge the key from his chest, dropping the false one, having Finn run with it while the real key remained within him, hidden by the bloody wound.

"Well, Jack." The familiar voice forced his head up.

A snow-haired girl crouched on Jack Daw's other side, the hem of her pale gown drifting around her bare feet. Jeweled rings decorated her toes. "Here we are."

"Norn." The name scraped out of his mouth. He laughed bitterly and coughed up rose petals. "You were the Snow Queen. You made Harahkte."

"And Finn Sullivan ended him."

Jack's failing heart soared. "That's my girl." He shut his eyes against a fresh agony.

"Do you know why I'm here, Jack?"

He was past the point of caring. The pain was gutting him now. He felt her winter hand touch his brow, and he opened his eyes. Four orbs of red, blue, green, and silver were spiraling toward him. The air had become a network of humming power. He gritted his teeth. "What—"

"To set right a wrong. Your murder."

The orbs swept down. Agony crested in his brain. He curled up, clawing at the grass. A convulsion slammed his skull back against the earth. A thousand volts of electricity shot through his bones. He inhaled fire. Water coursed through him. Air swept into his lungs, beneath his skin, into his heart. Earth molded him into bone and raw skin until he was sobbing, burrowing away from the nerve-blazing torture.

Then the Snow Queen, Norn, Death's bride, kissed mortality into him.

Life became a thousand thorns piercing him as she ripped the black key from his chest.

JACK OPENED HIS EYES. His body was as heavy as mud. He ached. He was thirsty and hungry. He could feel his organs working. Curled in the grass, he folded his arms around himself and shivered and began to laugh softly.

I'm alive. It wasn't the illusion with which the burning oak had graced him. The pain, the heaviness, the agony. It was *wonderful.*

He staggered to his feet as a mortal, wincing. He pushed through the tunnel of ivy and into Sombrus's ballroom. He saw the open doors.

When he heard a sound in the shadows behind him, as if something powerful and hungry and big was trying to keep itself quiet, he pivoted around.

The monstrous hyena emerged from the gloom, Caliban's sly eyes glinting in its ugly face. It spoke in a sly, twisted version of Caliban's voice: "I'll have that key, Jack."

Escape was behind Jack. But he couldn't let this thing return to the world. "Too bad. I don't have it."

His foot struck something that slid across the floor and glinted. His and Caliban's gazes followed the silver dagger's trajectory across the floor. They both raced for it.

Jack was closer. He snatched up the dagger.

As the *crom cu* lunged, howling, Jack whirled and leaped over the threshold, felt something slice across his back.

He spun and slammed the dagger into the *crom cu*'s chest.

As Caliban Ariel'Pan fell back into Sombrus, howling, the House of the Wolf and the Snake vanished.

Jack stood outside of Drake's Chapel.

TONIGHT, TIRNAGOTH HAD SHED all vestiges of ruin and returned to its former glorious self. The glow from its stained-glass windows painted Finn's skin as she wove among the Fatas, seeking Christie and Sylvie. She glimpsed what lay beneath the Fatas' skins, as if, by agreeing to become their queen, she'd been rewarded with the vision Dead Bird had lent her earlier. Bonfires and pixy lights illuminated moving tattoos, silver eyes like mirrors beneath masks of leaves or doll faces. The horns and gossamer wings might be false, but they were worldly representations of what the Fatas truly were.

Finn felt hollow and cold.

In the light-spangled courtyard, Farouche was playing the violin like a madman. Darling Ivy sat on the stone steps drinking from a bottle of elderberry wine with Ijio Valentine. Victoria Tudor was seated next to Wren's Knot, who had ivy wreathed into his braid and was gesturing with his doll-headed staff. James Wyatt was talking to one of Phouka's stern, black-suited inner circle. Nick Tudor and Claudette Tredescant were casually seated on animal-shaped motorcycles and speaking to a pair of fox knights. Professor Fairchild and Aurora Sae drifted past, hand in hand.

Finn didn't see the Black Scissors or any of his people.

As she searched for Sylvie and Christie, a host of black and red butterflies swept over her, their wings gently buffeting her. Alarmed, she turned and peered into the arch of red roses from which they'd emerged. Butterflies had been Jack Daw's tool. But they had been Lily's as well.

She walked toward the arch.

SYLVIE FOUND THE GAZEBO where she'd been told to wait. Adjusting her coiled-up hair and the expensive dress she'd halfheartedly bought for this second soiree, she paced beneath the Indian lanterns hung around the gazebo.

The strappy sandals were beginning to hurt her feet. She sat down. When a shadow came walking toward her, she sighed. "Oh. It's you."

Christie had also dressed nicely, in a gray suit and a red tie—for Phouka, Sylvie grimly surmised. "What are you doing here?" he demanded, and Sylvie scowled. "What are *you* doing here?"

He didn't meet her gaze. "Phouka told me to meet her here."

"Someone wanted to meet *me* here."

He narrowed his eyes. "It isn't the Black—"

"His name is William Harrow. He's Jack's ancestor."

"Oh. Of course." Christie moved slowly up the steps and leaned against the railing beside her. "How can we help Finn?"

"We can't." Sylvie hugged herself. "Lily really did die, Christie. And Jack isn't coming back."

WATCHING CHRISTIE AND SYLVIE speaking in the gazebo, Phouka stood unseen in the night she could weave around herself like a cloak.

The Black Scissors stepped from the dark, following her gaze to the boy and the girl. She didn't look at him as he spoke languidly, "When you've lived so long, it gets harder to let go. I bled when I cut myself shaving this morning."

Phouka glanced at him. He wore his dark coat and wide-brimmed hat, his traveling clothes. "You never told Jack who you were."

"He knows. I'm a shadow, Banríon." His voice was weary. "I shouldn't bleed. And this is cruel."

"To them? Or to us?"

"What do you think?"

"I think," she said softly, "I can't give up what I am for a mortal boy." She turned and walked away, sorrow trailing her like a ghost. William Harrow glanced back at Sylvie Whitethorn once. Then he let the shadows take him.

"I THINK WE'VE BEEN STOOD UP."

Sylvie gazed desperately, angrily, into the night. "Do you think being immortal makes you a jerk?"

"I think being a jerk is a *requirement* for being immortal." Christie began removing the rings from his hand, the ones the elementals had given him.

"What are you doing?"

"I'm choosing which world to live in."

AS SYLVIE AND CHRISTIE WALKED AWAY from the gazebo, Phouka's ivory book, her heart in disguise, fluttered, lay open beneath Christie's three elemental rings and the two daggers the Black Scissors had given to Sylvie.

FINN MOVED SLOWLY toward the arch of roses, cautious. She walked through it, into a smaller courtyard empty but for more of the unusual butterflies fluttering there. She tilted her head back as the creatures glided around her. They weren't butterflies after all; she felt the touch of tiny fingers in her hair, against the silk of her dress. She began to smile in wonder as she glimpsed miniature faces, heard their voices.

"Finn." Another voice, velvet and ashes, swept her disbelieving gaze down from the winged creatures, to the earth.

Jack stood only a few yards away. He was bruised and battered. His eyes, even in the moonlight, were dark with no silver reflection.

Finn didn't dare . . . didn't dare believe . . . after all the horror, after finding him . . . *He isn't real.*

As they walked slowly toward each other, she didn't dare believe he was anything other than a phantom. She placed a shaking hand carefully on his chest. His heart pulsed. He touched her face as if afraid she might break apart beneath his fingers. "Finn . . ."

Her fingers moved over his bruised skin, the cut on his lip, the gash above one eye. "I saw you *dead* in the courtyard."

"That was Jack Daw. He tried to trick Harahkte. He didn't make it."

She felt her own eyes widen as she gazed into his. Something had changed; the otherworldly glamour had fallen away from him—

"*Jack* . . ." she said in a raw, wondering voice. He was far more beautiful to her as an ordinary man.

"A chance in a million that four elementals would owe a certain braveheart a favor."

"Phouka," Finn breathed. She twined her arms around him, rested her head between his neck and shoulder. "I lost Lily."

He held her. "I'm sorry."

She sighed, a huge, shuddering breath. "I suppose you'll have to be careful now."

His thumbs were rough against her skin as he brushed the tears from beneath her eyes. She could see where the gray would touch his temples, and it made her smile.

"Don't step in front of any buses." She lifted her mouth to his.

"Or stick my finger in a light socket."

"Or eat bad shellfish."

"Or pet grizzly bears."

"Or swim in shark-infested waters."

They stopped talking, losing themselves in a kiss that set the elements in the air around them to glowing, as if the butterflies soaring through Finn had emerged in fiery swaths from her skin.

The kiss was no less epic because they were mortal.

HAND IN HAND, Finn and Jack walked up the path toward Tirnagoth. Its doors were flung wide to reveal the lobby with the red chandelier spattering light onto the chessboard floor.

Aubrey Drake and the other blessed came stalking out. They halted when they saw Finn and Jack, their eyes widening.

"What's wrong?" Finn demanded.

"Askew." Aubrey gritted his teeth. "He admitted to tricking Hester into the Ghostlands."

The shadows flickered in Jack's eyes. His fingers tightened around Finn's and she felt her mouth curl in a tiny snarl.

"Anna's in there." Victoria Tudor looked pale. "She heard it. It got ugly."

Finn and Jack hurried up the stairs, into the lobby, where Anna, wearing a dress of black-and-white plaid, stood before Absalom. Absalom's golden gaze, wary beneath strands of orange hair, flicked up to Finn and Jack. "You missed the excitement. She *hit* me."

"Phouka is leaving." Anna was a small fury. "And she's put *him* in charge."

"Oh hell," Jack said mildly.

Absalom met Finn's gaze, and she narrowed her own eyes as Absalom said, "Temporarily."

Anna turned her back on Absalom and walked to Finn and Jack. She hugged them each, before storming out of Tirnagoth.

"Females." Absalom sighed. "They're so irrational. That's why I stopped being one."

Finn, remembering how Hester had died in her arms, spoke softly. "Good night, Absalom. Let's go, Jack."

As they walked away, Absalom called after them, "So you're not going to speak to me anymore either?"

"I've got nothing to say to you, Askew." Jack exchanged a look with Finn. Finn glanced back over one shoulder and sweetly said, "You've got something on your mouth, Absalom."

AS FINN AND JACK WALKED THROUGH THE DOORS, smiling, Absalom lifted a hand to his mouth, where Anna's slap still stung. He tasted salt. A chill spiked through him. He slowly drew his hand from his mouth and raised it before his eyes. A newborn creature burst in his chest, pounding at his rib cage.

His hand began to shake as he stared at the blood—*his* blood—smearing his fingertips. "Well, *that's* never happened before."

FINN AND JACK HALTED IN THE GARDEN, where trellised roses arched around and above them. Finn wrapped her arms around his neck. Their bodies aligned as he kissed her and the seasons seemed to whirl around them . . . summer becoming autumn drifting with leaves, becoming the whispering snow of winter, fading into the pollen-glimmering spring, back into the heat of a summer dusted with insect wings.

Finn would never tell him about the bargain she'd made for his mortality, how she would continue on, immortal and unchanging, without him, long after he'd lived his mortal span.

They wouldn't have a Fata eternity together, but they'd have a mortal forever. And that was enough.

EPILOGUE

Anna watched Jack and Finn walking hand in hand down the rose-trellised garden path. Fireflies flickered around Finn's head like a tiny crown and the roses rustled like courtiers as Jack passed.

Glancing over her shoulder, Anna looked back at the Tirnagoth Hotel. Something fell away from her then, the *awareness* of Otherly things no longer nagging at her. A strange warmth curled through her. She pushed her bare toes into the earth and inhaled as if it were her first breath.

She felt as if she were waking up.

ACKNOWLEDGMENTS

I'd like to thank my tireless editor extraordinaire at Harper Voyager, Katherine Nintzel, who helped guide Finn and Jack's story through to its conclusion. I'd like to thank Thao Le of the Sandra Dijkstra Agency, for her wonderful advice. Without the assistance of either, this story wouldn't have happened.

Thank you to the team at Harper Voyager: Margaux Weisman, whose professionalism and prompt responses made things easy; David Pomerico, Harper Voyager's fearless leader; Jessie Edwards, hardworking and creative publicist; and copyeditor extraordinaire, Laurie McGee.

Thanks to my friends and family, for their support. And to the entire staff at the Sarasota, Florida, Barnes & Noble (including Sandy Gershman and Megan Sicks), for being unpaid promoters.

Thanks to the Qwillery, Melinda Harrison, Supernatural Snark, the Fantasy Book Critic, and Fresh Fiction, for allowing me to guest-blog early on. Thank you to Seanan McGuire and Ann Aguirre, for saying nice things about *Thorn Jack*. And thank you to all of the bloggers, tweeters, reviewers, and fans who loved Finn and Jack's journey. Without you, this book would *be* nothing.

And this acknowledgment would not be complete without thanking the small press magazine editors who gave me generous advice through the years, and to the ones who took a chance by believing in me.

IF YOU LIKED THE BOOK, HERE'S THE SOUND TRACK

"Dust to Dust" (The Civil Wars)

"Oró Sé Do Bheatha Bhaile" (Sinead O'Connor)

"Butterfly" (Bassnectar featuring Mimi Page)

"Nothing Has Been Broken" (Bassnectar featuring Tina Malia)

"Shadow on the Run" (Black Rebel Motorcycle Club)

"Far Too Young to Die and the End of All Things" (Panic at the Disco)

"Young Blood" (Birdy)

"Greensleeves" (Vanessa Carlton)

"Dancing Barefoot" (Patti Smith)

"White Teeth Teens" (Lorde)

"Violent Shiver" (Benjamin Booker)

"Young and Beautiful" (Lana Del Ray)

"Young Volcanoes" (Fallout Boy)

"Dust Hymn" (Purity Ring)

"You Don't Know Me at All" (Son Lux)

GLOSSARY

Annwyn (AHH winn)—land of the dead; the underworld

Ban Gorm (baan GORim)—Blue Lady

Banríon (baan nREEN)—queen

Buccan (BOO kan)—border patrol in the land of the dead

Cailleach Oidche (kah lee ahk ee YEE)—owl girl

croi baintreach (KREE banch rukh)—heart widow

crom cu (krom KOO)—crooked dog

Dubh Deamhais (doov DEE amayus)—Black Scissors

Fata (FAY dah)

faileas'leas (Fay LEE us LEE as)—the shadow trick

fear dorchadas (fahr doruk HUDus)—male witch

Gwynn Ap Nudd (Gwinn ah NOOD)—Death

Leannan (lah NAAN)—sweetheart

Marbh ean (maROO ae en)—Dead Bird

Phouka (FUU ah)

Reiko (RAY koh)

Taibhse na Tir (tahvs na TEER)—Ghostlands

Tamasgi'po (tamus GEE poh)—spirit in a kiss